PRAISE FOR OF MAGIC AND MEN

"Alluring and atmospheric, Of Magic and Men is a charming witchy book filled with secrets, lies, and Freyah who finds herself caught in the web between it all."

— **CASEY L. BOND**, AWARD-WINNING AUTHOR OF *WHERE OCEANS BURN*

"This is a fantastic fantasy debut novel for Meg Alivien! The world is so well-crafted and the writing is mature, thought-out, and beautiful."

— **V.B. LACEY**, AUTHOR OF *LONG LIVE*

"An enchanting tale full of strong female characters and delicious men, Alivien's fantasy debut will leave you spellbound."

— **OLIVIA WILDENSTEIN**, USA TODAY BESTSELLING AUTHOR OF *HOUSE OF BEATING WINGS*

"A fantastic romp of a novel from an incredibly talented author! Perfect for reading while cozied up by a fire on a crisp autumn night."

— **NATALIA MACIAS LUCIA**, AUTHOR OF *GIRLS OF SALT AND SEA*

OF MAGIC AND MEN

MEG ALIVIEN

Duke Books

Of Magic and Men

Meg Alivien

© 2023 Meg Alivien

Published by Duke Books

Developmental Edits by Beth Crowley

Copy/Line Edits by Amanda Chaperon

Map by Meg Alivien

Character Art by Madison Mills

Cover Design by Maria Spada

Print ISBN: 979-8-9878134-1-6

E-Book ISBN: 979-8-9878134-0-9

Printed in USA

TRIGGER WARNINGS

Graphic: Violence, Death, Blood

Moderate: Sexual content (with manipulated consent), Grief, Sexual assault, Pregnancy (side character), Medical trauma (complications with childbirth), Xenophobia (racism and prejudice towards demons), Death of parent, Chronic illness, Cursing, Emotional abuse (tactics of manipulation), Kidnapping

Minor: Homophobia

GHOMA
CASTLE LARAPUNA
BAY OF FIRE
SALDANNI FOREST
KNOX HILL
STUARTS DRAFT
LAKE NAGA
CITY OF BALANDRA
SOUTHERN SKY MOUNTAINS

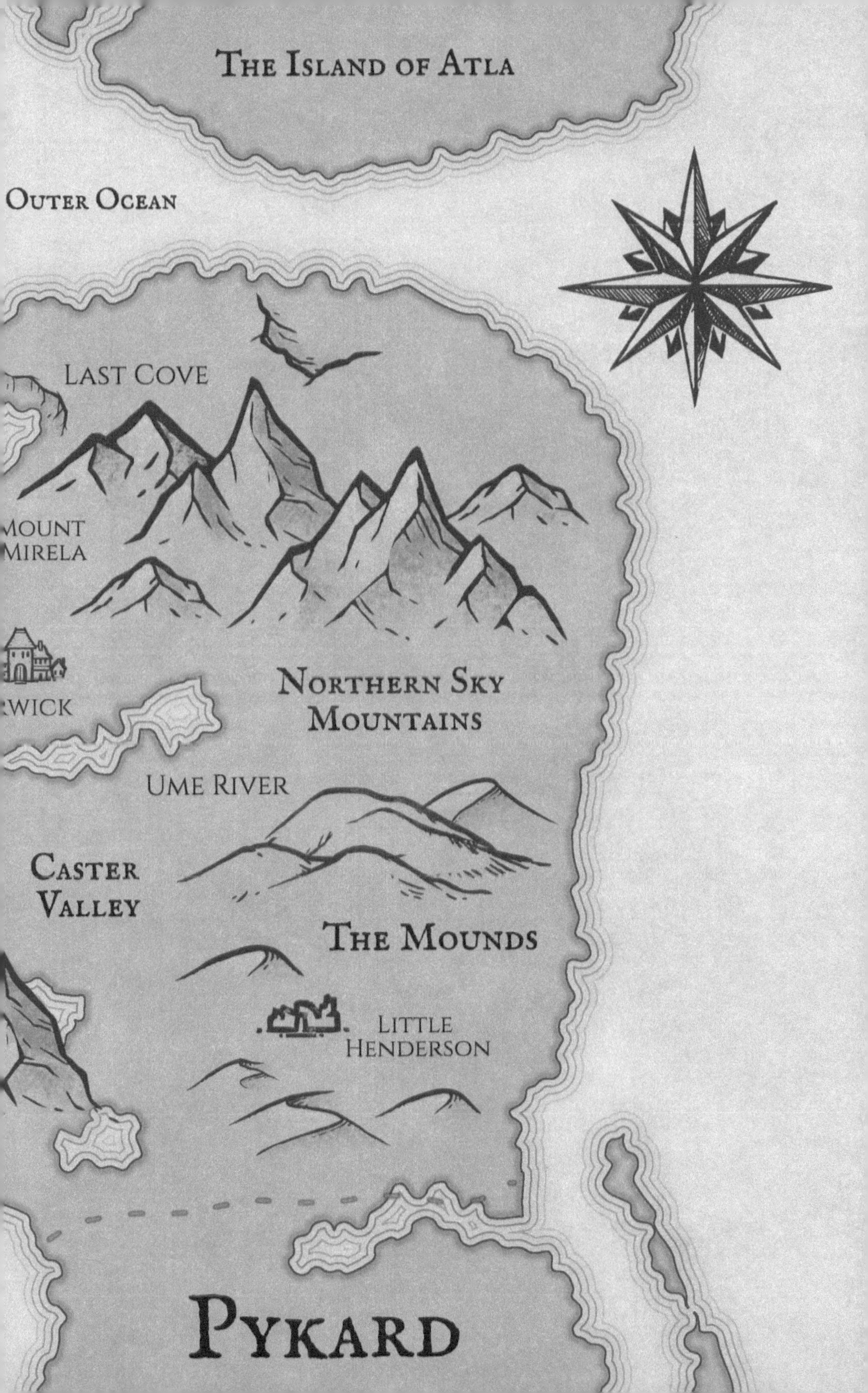

THE ISLAND OF ATLA
OUTER OCEAN
LAST COVE
MOUNT MIRELA
RWICK
NORTHERN SKY MOUNTAINS
UME RIVER
CASTER VALLEY
THE MOUNDS
LITTLE HENDERSON
PYKARD

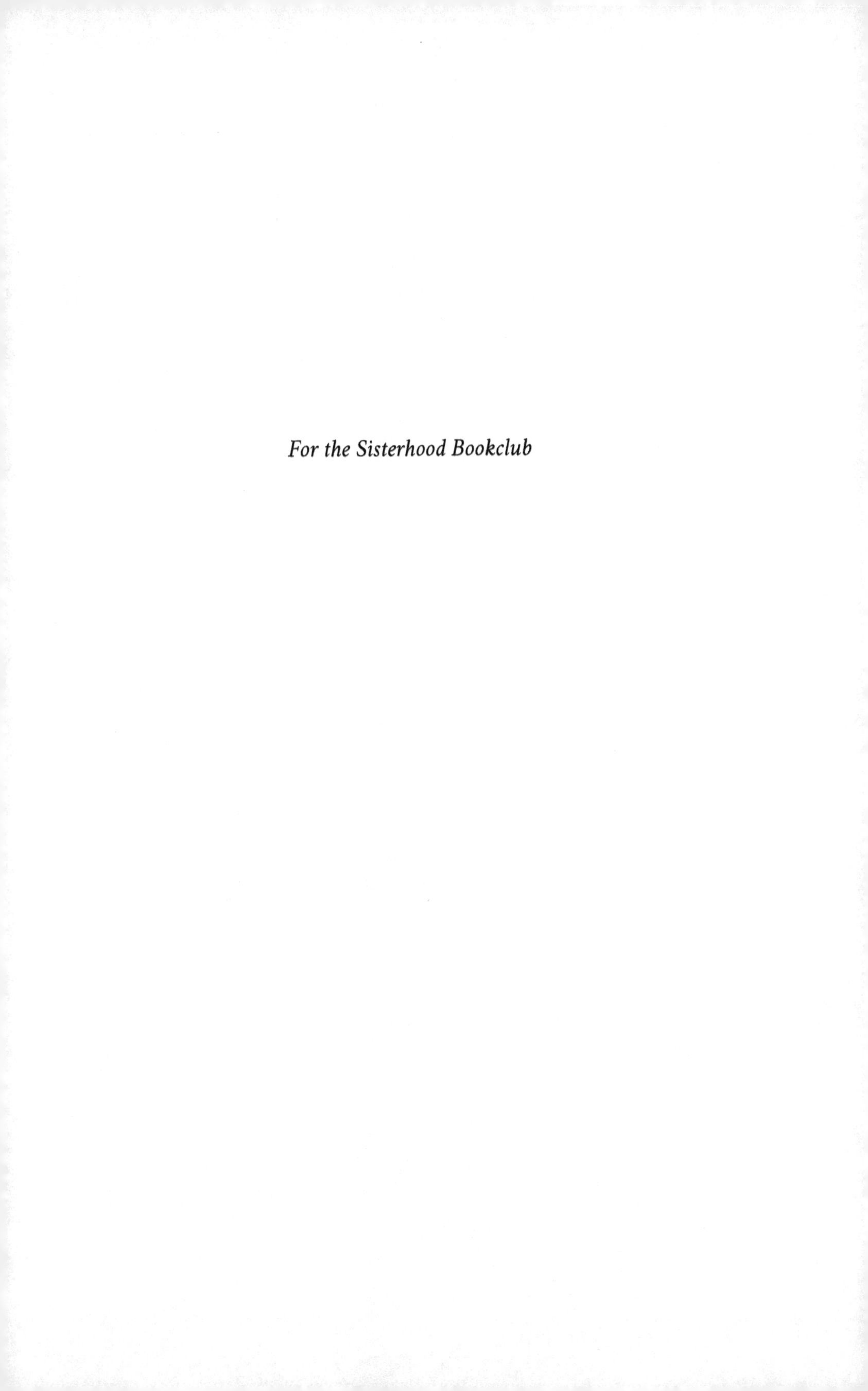

For the Sisterhood Bookclub

The Great War

On the first and coldest night of the winter season, Ruella Mansell entered the dining hall of Castle Larapuna and sat at a long, wooden table soaked with blood. It dripped slowly down the legs as Ruella took her place at the head, but she paid it no mind. The sticky substance had already ruined her finest leather cloak. What did letting it spread a bit more matter?

She was joined shortly after by her daughter, Adora, then Lorrill, her chosen advisor. Unlike Ruella, they entered the room with slight hesitancy; the evidence of what they'd done seemed to stimulate a wave of nausea within them both. Yet Ruella remained docile. She had remained oddly calm since the first sparks of magic were fired. No one had been prepared for the massacre that ensued, but witches were not cowards, so they finished what they had started.

They had thought their magic would be enough, and it was…for the most part. What they hadn't foreseen was the amount of blood that would be spilled. All that thick, crimson carnage. How had the witches overlooked the warlocks' greatest weapon? They were beasts, after all, and claws and teeth could do as much damage as magic.

Four others stood sentry at the far end of the table, but Ruella hadn't noticed them until one vomited in the corner of the room. The man clearly couldn't stomach the sight of all that blood, and it only solidified his weakness in Ruella's eyes. The newly self-appointed queen had never considered their kind—humans—to hold much importance. To her, they served no purpose other than filling an otherwise empty seat at the table.

They'd been invited to sit at said table by Lorrill, because they held high positions on the newly formed council. Ruella's advisor had suggested it was the best way to show good faith going forward. They were there to represent their people, but Ruella was not interested in what they or their people wanted. She had just defeated her greatest enemy. The warlocks were now all but extinct save the handful that survived the battle, and they would be dealt with soon enough. Unfortunately, at the present moment, there were other matters to discuss.

The politics Ruella would now be forced to deal with were merely a consequence of her victory—something she had to bite her tongue against and swallow without too much of a fuss. Lorrill was best at those matters. She was the witch most suited to make the day-to-day decisions, to delegate and sacrifice. It was why Ruella had chosen her to be her personal advisor.

Ruella didn't have the time or patience for such small things. She was above it, meant only to be the new figurehead for the country. Once Lorrill set the laws in motion, Ruella would enforce them, but for now it was essential that her own tongue speak them into existence. She was the new Queen of Ghoma, after all.

Ruella glanced subtly at Lorrill as they sat, and her advisor let a few words of encouragement slip into her mind.

"You won the throne; now it's your responsibility to rule over those that serve it."

Before speaking to the group, Ruella nodded, showing that she'd heard and understood Lorrill's silent message.

Ruella then coolly addressed the four humans at the opposite end of the table. "I'm glad you could join us. Please sit."

They did so quickly, possibly in fear that if not done fast enough, the queen would ask something much more terrible of them—as if sitting next to a pool of blood wasn't bad enough. The bodies had been removed since the battle, but the stale odor of death lingered in the air.

A man with tangled red hair and a matching beard sat with the most confidence, taking the chair closest to Adora on Ruella's right. Ruella recognized him as the Chancellor of Balandra, the capital city of Ghoma. She had seen the red-haired man known as Dante before the war and had used him to persuade most of the humans to stand down and leave the fighting to those with magical blood. Despite her lack of respect for the humans, it was never her intention to lose those she meant to rule over. There was no point in becoming a ruler if she had no citizens.

Opposite of Dante sat a brazen-looking older woman with stark black curls framing her narrow face. She took in her surroundings with slight discomfort but didn't appear completely repulsed. Ruella wasn't sure what her name was but was aware she represented those living in Little Henderson. Her people were the poorest in the country, their only source of income being the hunting and selling of game that roamed The Mounds. That far east, the land in Ghoma turned into a vast expanse of dry plains broken up by even dryer hills.

Seated furthest from Ruella on the left side of the table was Tobias Westonfall. She knew, thanks to Lorrill's briefing, that he was the current magistrate of Last Cove, a port town within Mount Mirela that served as the main center for trade in and out of the country. Few travelers explored the mountain ranges, but a great number of sea people to the north lived within the beacon of the mountain. It was rough terrain, even for a witch, but the humans that navigated it were seemingly carved from the mountain itself—all bones and calluses and rocky edges. For traders, the area was difficult to reach on land, but the town was easily accessible by water.

It was said that Tobias viewed the matters of his constituents with incredible importance—they were a proud people who leaned heavily on their independence—and it was clear he now blamed the witches for creating chaos in his typically peaceful and secluded mountain town.

But Ruella knew the true party responsible for creating the

fissures in her country. And as punishment, they were either dead or tied up in the next room.

"Are they all gone?" the dark haired female questioned.

Ruella glanced at her advisor for guidance. "Beryl Phyette," Lorrill introduced on the woman's behalf. "From the Mounds."

"I've heard rumblings," Beryl continued, glancing around the room as if the blood-covered walls had been the source. "But it can't be possible. Can it?"

Ruella nodded curtly. "It is. I promised you freedom, and that is what I've delivered."

"So now what?" Dante asked. "If all the warlocks are dead, who will sit on the throne?"

"That's why we're here," Ruella stated confidently. "As per the terms of our previous agreement, you and all of your people are no longer under the thumb of a tyrant. As thanks for my gift, I ask that you allow the witches—my family, to be specific—to rule over Ghoma."

Beryl, Dante, and Tobias nodded to one another in agreement, appearing to find this end of the bargain acceptable. But the fourth representative at the table, sitting so far from the edge that he cast himself in shadow, scoffed.

"You have an objection, Leonid?" Lorrill asked, squaring her shoulders in preparation to defend her newly appointed queen.

The man leaned forward slightly so the tip of his squashed nose caught the light from the hovering candelabras. Ruella had always thought the portly man resembled a pig, with his below average stature and round middle. He could very well pass as swine, if not for the lack of tail and an actual snout.

"Caster Valley has never wished to choose between the lesser of two evils," Leonid murmured. "Replacing one form of magic with another still leaves the humans without a say."

"And what is it that you wish to say, Mr. Gourmand?" Ruella asked, maintaining a calm and regal presence.

Leonid placed a nubby hand on the edge of the table, then pulled it back before accidentally making contact with any of the blood. He swallowed hard, then asked, "What will be different? What is it you can do better that the warlocks could not?"

Ruella let a wicked grin slip. "For hundreds of years, humans have had to live in fear from those that possess magic. You've been seen as lesser, merely because you do not possess the same gifts. I do not see you as such," she lied sweetly. "As your queen, I will not control you. I will protect you."

"Protect us from what, exactly?" Beryl asked.

"I have had a vision," Ruella explained. "In time—I am not sure how long—an entirely new sort of evil will be birthed into our realm. One that threatens both witches and humans alike. I do not know how or why, but something is changing, and I promise you, I will do my best to prepare for it."

Silence blanketed the room like a thick fog. Unease flittered amongst the humans that sat around the table. Future Sight was one of the ways in which magic set apart witches and warlocks. It was a unique talent only females possessed, and it was seen by the warlocks as their single bit of value. The warlocks had been exceedingly envious of it, constantly trying to harness it in ways that led to extreme violence against the witches, but no matter how hard the men tried to use the Sight for personal gain, it had been a vision that lost them the war.

"Now," Ruella started, effectively ending the conversation, "if you'll excuse me, I have something else that needs my immediate attention." The humans glanced around uneasily, but she stood with an unwavering finality. "My daughter will take it from here."

Adora looked wide-eyed at her mother, clearly not expecting to have been thrust into such a position. She was weaker than the others, and if she wanted to mark her place in the coven, she would have to learn.

But Adora's hesitance lasted too long. Instead, Lorrill got to her feet and proudly moved to stand at the head of the table in her queen's place. Even as she began to speak, all eyes remained on Ruella as she swept with determination from the room.

.　.　.

THEIR HANDS and feet had been tied together with barbed wire. They pleaded desperately with their eyes—the only weapons they had left—but Ruella wasn't going to fall for the defeated looks on their faces. There was one key thing to know of warlocks: they were Shifters. It was the opposing strength to the witches' use of Future Sight, and it had almost won them the advantage in the war, but Ruella had seen what needed to be done. Thanks to her Sight, she'd outplayed them through cleverness and cunning, and now it was time for them to pay.

As the designated leader of her coven, Ruella knew that an army was not truly vanquished until its leaders had fallen, and as much as she wanted to kill them all right then and there, it wasn't their bodies that needed to be destroyed. She was after their spirits—the source of magic within them. Extinguish the soul, and there would be nothing left of their magic to grow.

The high warlock, Killoren, was the only male still on his knees, while the other three sat with their backs slumped against the stone wall. Their arms were secured tightly in front of them and attached to their ankles to keep them immobilized. The barbed wiring that held their appendages in place had been laced with a suppressant serum, something Adora had cleverly suggested. Knowing the barbs would cut their skin, either they were forced to remain perfectly still, or the serum would hit their bloodstream and prevent them from shifting. Either way, they were stuck, and Ruella had them right where she wanted.

She approached Eliphas, the second in command, treading carefully over the legs of Zadimus and Dreven, which stretched out in front of them. They tried their best not to move. Their eyes sought out Killoren, perhaps hoping he'd hatched some sort of plan that was about to take action, but their leader remained silent.

Ruella crouched in front of Eliphas and sighed softly. "Do you remember what you said to me?" she asked, the question purring into the open chamber so softly it failed to echo.

The knot in his throat bobbed, but he dared not to speak. He was barely even breathing. Ruella leaned closer and cocked her head slightly. "You said you were going to kill me," she said. "But you lied."

"He meant it," Killoren spat, speaking on his fellow warlock's behalf. His tone was harsh, a combination of rage and physical pain. He'd been the only one to risk the attempt to phase, like she knew he would, and now the suppressant Adora concocted coursed through his veins like wildfire. Ruella could see his skin rippling, and she could only assume that the sensation was agony for him. What must it feel like to be so near the verge of exploding with no release?

She smiled maliciously at him over her shoulder. "Well it hasn't happened, so it mustn't have been true."

Killoren spat on the ground in front of him, and the substance bubbled black.

"*My, my*," Ruella sing-songed. "My daughter did some nasty work."

"None of you know what you're doing," he threatened. "What you've done will change everything."

"Yes," she agreed. "It will. But you seem to forget that we're the only ones that could possibly know that. I know exactly what I'm doing, and I know exactly what the consequences will be."

Without taking her eyes off Killoren, Ruella snapped Eliphas's neck. A strangled gasp broke from Zadimus's throat, and the others watched in silent horror as the witch guided the soul from inside Eliphas's body with deft fingers. It lifted from his throat like an insect crawling its way out of an endless pit, seeking out the ring of pure silver wrapped around the queen's middle finger. Like called to like, and in order to retain a soul in physical form, one had to have a conduit to tether it. Ruella plucked the spindly substance from the man's lips and crushed it in her fist. She'd killed his magic like she was squashing a bug.

Ruella stood and walked to the other side of the room, where a bowl sat atop a chipped stone table, waiting for her to deposit the substance. When she unclenched her fingers, what was once an airy substance had now turned into a thick black liquid. It dripped from her hand like the blood on the dining table in the council chambers, and Ruella watched, entranced with satisfaction. The other ingredients had already been prepared and, once combined with the new additive, simmered in the bowl. She waited until everything inside had settled, then she looked to her assistant.

An elder witch named Ava Leblanc had been hovering at the edge of the room, waiting for her cue. At Ruella's signal, the witch approached, holding three black stone goblets. Ava held onto the other two as Ruella took one and poured the new concoction into the goblet clutched between her fingers. She reveled in the sight as it hissed and smoked at the surface. After pouring the remains into the other two cups, she turned to face her victims.

"You can't make us drink that," Killoren insisted, bursting with even more anger now that another one of his own was dead.

Ruella laughed viciously. "Of course I can."

Ava was already retrieving a funnel from a glass cabinet that stood adjacent to the stone table. The funnel was long enough to shove down someone's throat, and Ruella did exactly that. She clutched Killoren's jaw in her grasp, relishing the defiance and fear in his eyes, and forced his mouth open. Ruella then plunged the long end of the funnel down his throat without giving the warlock time to anticipate it. Killoren choked and gagged as she poured the smoking liquid down the funnel. Smoke billowed from his nose as the last drops emptied from the goblet and trickled into his body. She removed the funnel and tossed the cup aside, then repeated the punishment with her other two living prisoners. After all three of the warlocks were blue-faced and writhing on the floor, she began to speak the words of her curse aloud.

"From this day forward, no man shall possess magic." Her voice lifted and filled the room. "May *Ghidorah* reduce you to your true form. As long as my lineage holds the throne, any man descended from witches will walk this world as a beast of his own making. A demon in the flesh—a disgrace, and a reminder that witches will never bow to *anyone, ever again.*"

1

FREYAH

Freyah Kenpaw had never known magic.

She knew it existed, but it lived on the periphery of her life. She was twenty years old, yet she'd never come across it within the Northern Sky Mountains that surrounded her and kept her safe. But the country of Ghoma was a lot larger than the fishing village of Last Cove. It held many secrets—ones that Freyah had an interest in uncovering.

She was on her way to The Hub after spending most of the morning at the bottom of the cliffs gathering limestone to sell at the Trade Center. She chose an unusual route through the col, wanting to take her time and enjoy the walk. Unfortunately, halfway to her destination, she got caught in the middle of a rainstorm. Despite how annoying getting drenched was, it wasn't nearly as bothersome as the thought of having to face her father, who had clearly warned her to take a cloak before she left.

Waves crashing against the rock face below broke in between explosions of thunder, creating an endless loop that rang in Freyah's ears. The rain was relentless. It seeped into her boots and soaked the skin beneath her clothes as she made the mile trek back up the mountain pass. The passage had been carved into the natural slope of the rock, but the incline was steep. Freyah had acclimated to it, having traveled nearly every inch of stone beneath her feet countless times since the moment she'd taken her first steps, but that didn't mean she was immune to the ache it brought to her tired muscles.

She struggled the last few feet, feeling the extra weight brought on by the water she now carried in the fabric of her trousers and tunic, but finally, she reached the brow. After taking shelter under the shelf that stretched out high above her, she paused to catch her breath and wring the excess water from her shirt. Then she continued through the cave mouth and into the mountain.

The main entrance to the center cavern was lit artfully by lanterns fueled by whale blubber. Being so close to the ocean, they had an abundance of the oily substance—so much that it was traded with others. Freyah didn't typically take this route, but it was the closest tunnel to avoid being further drenched from the sky's current tantrum.

When she reached the opposite end of the tunnel, she entered the massive center cavern of Mount Mirela referred to as The Hub – the epicenter for food, shops, and entertainment. Freyah relished the chaos of it. There was little room to walk when maneuvering the streets on a busy day. She constantly found herself dodging fish carts, swindlers, and even the occasional musical production being put on right in the middle of it all. Growing up in such a place was both familiar and full of surprises.

But her favorite part was the people.

Her mother had died giving birth to her, but Freyah had never felt as if a part of her was missing, because she'd been raised by an entire town. Her father, Brennan, was a very busy man, being Last Cove's sole blacksmith. His long hours meant Freyah spent a lot of time in the care of others, but she had never complained. Most nights, she slept over at her best friend Corianne's apartment. They would stay up late recounting folklore about the demons and witches that loomed in the shadows of Ghoma. Corianne's mother scribed and kept track of the town records, so she knew almost everything about

Ghoma's history, and the stories she told had riveted Freyah from a young age.

Her entire world view had been shaped by those stories. She dreamed of one day exploring the farmlands of Caster Valley, the desert land of The Mounds, and Castle Larapuna—the home of the witches. As she got older, Freyah realized just how small her mountain truly was. And though she craved knowledge and adventure, she was too scared to explore them on her own.

Last Cove was all she'd ever known. The mountain was her safe place, and the sound of the ocean was what calmed her when her mind wouldn't stop racing. As much as she wanted to learn about magic and uncover all the other secrets Ghoma had to offer, she wanted familiarity more.

She made her way through the Fabric District first, passing a handful of colorful displays. She spotted Mrs. Clarke closing the doors of her dress shop for lunch and Freyah waved.

The plump woman smiled broadly. "I've got your father's jacket, dear!" she called after her. "Tell him he's got 'til the end of the day to pick it up, or I'm selling it!"

"I'll grab it on the way back."

"Absolutely not. He needs to leave that smithy sometimes."

Freyah laughed, but the woman wasn't wrong. Her father rarely spent time outside of his shop, but she knew how much work it took to keep up with the high demand for steel. With help from his apprentice, he was able to provide everyone in the mountain with everything from weapons to tools to cookware, all handcrafted with precision. He even sold some of his work at various shops in The Hub to visitors passing through. On many occasions, he'd been asked to make weapons for the army—his work was well known for being the best of its kind—but he'd declined each time, his priority being his own people.

Eventually, Freyah reached the booth where Corianne sold jewelry and trinkets. Her best friend was really quite talented. She made necklaces and bracelets from the stones Freyah found buried within the mountain, and when they were able to trek to the summit during the summer months, she sold flower crowns. Freyah had many unique items in her own personal collection that Corianne had insisted were duds, but she didn't mind the tiny flaws.

Corianne was in the midst of haggling a deal with a short, elderly woman carrying so many sacks it was a wonder she didn't topple over. Freyah watched as Corianne managed to close the sale by throwing in a free jade crystal for luck. They exchanged goods for payment, and Corianne counted the coins twice.

"You're ruthless," Freyah said.

Corianne was slightly startled but immediately smiled at the sight of her friend. "That old bat wanted a black opal necklace for practically nothing," she fussed, brushing a strand of mousy brown hair out of her face. "You know how rare those stones are."

"You drive a hard bargain."

Corianne rubbed absentmindedly at the back of her neck and gave a sheepish grin. She was too modest when it came to recognizing her own best qualities, and it was something Freyah tried to shed light on whenever she found the chance. If given the opportunity, most people would walk all over Corianne for being too nice and too understanding. But even when Corianne made a point to stand up for herself, she felt bad about it afterward.

"Are you due for a break yet?" Freyah asked, changing the subject for her friend's benefit.

Corianne nodded. "Want to walk over and look at today's catch with me?"

Freyah assented and helped her place a large blanket over the booth to indicate it would be temporarily closed, then they walked arm in arm toward Fisherman's Row.

They took a shortcut through more booths and came out on the other side of the market. The not-so-subtle scent of fish wafted through the air as they got closer to the fishmongers. Despite the terrible smell, the displays in Fisherman's Row were quite stunning. Such vibrant colors from various sea life. Oranges, reds, and yellows. Some with stripes and some with spots. Small crustaceans and large rays. Skinny mackerel and fat carps. Their quaint little cove was good to its people, so there was always plenty to choose from when it came to having a sustaining meal.

Corianne promptly began sorting through a pile of crab legs, selecting only the ones with the most generous weight to them. Crustaceans were a rarity that only appeared when fishermen were able to sail far enough into the Outer Ocean to catch them. Because of this, they were expensive, so Freyah considered some fresh oysters being sold in a bunch for a decent price instead.

While she perused, she couldn't help but watch the people around her. Last Cove was secluded from the rest of the country due to the mountain range, but it was filled with many different types of people from different walks of life. It was a town that held on to its locals, but it also welcomed those that needed to escape. Those that had fled from city life, or simply wanted a change of scenery.

There were old men, worn and broken down by the sea, that had been brought to Last Cove for work and decided to stay. There were girls from wealthy families that didn't want to fall prey to their parents' plans to marry them off, so they'd escaped into the night and found themselves in a village within a mountain. There were even families lucky enough to have crawled their way out of The Mounds, only to choose a life of crawling up and down the mountain instead.

Then there were the demons.

Freyah didn't know much about their way of life, but she'd heard rumors of persecution in the capital city, and it made her thankful to call this place her home when it had become such a haven for others.

A disturbance in the crowd caught her eye, and Freyah turned to find people moving very quickly out of something's path.

"I'll be right back," she told Corianne, but the girl was too distracted by the shellfish in front of her to hear.

Freyah wiggled her way through some of the chaos until she was able to find the source of the disruption. Three soldiers dressed in all black fighting leathers were making their way down the street. They cleared the path in front of them simply by breathing, the symbol on their chests saying what they didn't need to. It was the mark of witches—an upside down triangle made from vines with a line struck through the bottom. The alchemical symbol for nature.

But what were they doing here?

The queen's soldiers never came as far as the mountains. There was never a reason. All of Last Cove's food shares were transported by sea, and other districts shipped their goods to the Trade Centers for pickup. There were soldiers known as Spyders that lingered in the shadows of each village, keeping an eye on the citizens from a distance and reporting back to the queen.

But the soldiers currently strutting about through The Hub were different. They weren't hiding, and their presence put everyone on edge.

Especially the demons.

Freyah's stomach turned when a bear-demon and his son scampered behind a stall as the soldiers approached. She knew very little about them, but that didn't prevent her from sympathizing.

According to Corianne's mother, witches had stolen all the magic from men and cursed their blood, isolating their gifts so they could only be passed on to females in their line. Witches who bore men birthed demons into the world—part man, part beast.

There were many demons living in Last Cove, but they kept to themselves. Most of the humans were open to their presence in the mountain, but some were not. Those people maintained a healthy distance. Freyah's father had always warned her to stay away from demons, and she'd never thought to question it.

The closest interaction Freyah ever had with a demon was with Jago, a lizard-demon who worked at The Book Shop in The Hub. He lived in the space above the store, having been taken in as a young child, and for Freyah, seeing him felt like being close to magic somehow.

Witches were the only beings that possessed magic, and their castle was located beyond the mountains on the other side of the country—an entire world away. Castle Larapuna sat at the edge of a cliff on the outskirts of a massive forest and overlooked the Bay of Fire. From the very top of Mount Mirela, Freyah could see the tips of the towers from across the water, but with the castle so far away, the presence of witches felt like folklore. Witches were despised by humans, but Freyah envied their magic like a fish envied a bird in flight.

When the soldiers finally approached, Freyah held herself confidently, shoulders back and head high as they passed. She did not want them to mistake her for a weak little girl. If one of them glanced her way, she would look them dead in the eye and hope she wasn't the first to blink.

They stopped at a vendor who sold trout by the pound, and the broadest and most rugged-looking soldier of the group began arguing with the elderly man behind the booth. He picked up a fish with his bare hands and tossed it to his comrade, but the other soldier hadn't been ready for the catch, so it slipped from his grip and plopped to the ground with a pathetic *squish*.

The elderly man behind the booth wrung his hands nervously. His lips parted and pressed back together in an attempt at a sort of protest, but he wasn't brave enough to speak.

Freyah knew there would be consequences, but she had to do something.

As she stepped forward, she swore she heard Corianne's faint warning blending with the noise of the crowd, but she ignored it and marched over to the soldiers. She couldn't stand by as they singled out an innocent man and his product. It wasn't only disrespectful, it was down right unsanitary.

Typically, Freyah would never insert herself into a situation that didn't concern her, but she could feel the embarrassment and shame wafting from the old man as he stood by helplessly while the soldier mocked him.

Secretly, Freyah related to her best friend in that she found it hard to be brave when it came to defending herself. But she wanted to be brave for others, to stand up for those that couldn't stand up for themselves.

Without giving herself time to second guess her decision, Freyah encroached all the way into the ringleader's personal space as he was about to pick up another fish and smacked it right out of his hand.

The soldier was stunned at first, and it took him several intense seconds to realize what had happened, but when he did, he straightened to his full height. He looked right into Freyah's now slightly wavering gaze and scowled.

To her own disappointment, she was the first to blink.

The soldier's scowl turned into an amused grin. He brushed a lock of unruly, dark brown hair away from his eyes and scoffed, as if she were a child that had meddled her way into adult affairs. He seemed enticed by her bravery, and somehow, without her intention, Freyah's protest had morphed into a game for him.

"I'm sorry," the soldier mocked her. "Are you the keeper of these fish?"

His tone was gravelly and deep, and he looked extremely rough. It was as if life had worn him down, chewed him up, and spit him back out. But somehow, he was also beautiful. His skin was tanned, and his medium-length, brown hair hung like a curtain around his face, casting threatening shadows across his grim features.

The soldier plucked another slippery carcass from the pile and held it up like a prize, then he placed two fingers on either side of the fish's mouth and pretended to make it talk.

Freyah was not amused. She was fuming.

Madam Lema's soldiers clearly had zero respect or concern for anyone but themselves. They didn't know kindness or community. They only knew one thing: following orders.

But what orders had brought them here to Last Cove?

Freyah never saw the queen's army travel this far east. It was known amongst citizens that Madam Lema had spies stationed around the country—it was what kept everyone on their toes and forced them to follow the rules—but Freyah had never seen a soldier in Last Cove before.

She looked up into the soldier's warm brown eyes as he waved the fish around like a limp trophy. Despite his current actions, they drew her in, giving her the confidence to make her next move.

Without thinking, she reached for the fish as it flew in front of her face and snatched it away, tossing it back onto the pile with satisfaction and leaving the soldier looking dumbfounded.

His scowl returned, this time more pronounced, and he resembled a kettle on the verge of steaming. Freyah swallowed the lump in her throat and straightened. She knew what she'd done was against the law—disrespecting anyone in the queen's service called for severe discipline—-but she wouldn't be afraid.

The soldier leaned forward, close enough that she could smell the stench of sweat radiating from his skin. But underneath, there was the subtle scent of tea tree oil. It clung to his dark, rugged beard and filled her nostrils.

He examined her with renewed interest, as if he was second-guessing whether or not to punish her.

His narrowed eyes relaxed, and he took a step back.

"You can have your fish," he sneered. "This time."

Then he stormed off, the other two soldiers close on his heels.

They disappeared into the throng of people along the street. When they were completely out of sight, she let out a long breath of relief.

Corianne had been hiding a few feet away behind a cart of fishing twine, but she reappeared by Freyah's side the moment the coast was clear.

"Do you have a death wish?" she hissed, grabbing her friend's arm in alarm. "I've never seen you do something like that. What if the Spyders saw you?"

Freyah hadn't taken the time to consider it. She'd only wanted to do something to help.

"I can't believe he just let you go," Corianne said.

"He's just gone to check if his balls are still there."

Freyah said it boldly, but her insides were roiling, and she tried her best to hold onto that feigned confidence despite her muscles trembling.

Corianne let out a nervous laugh. "You're a lot braver than me."

"I'm not," Freyah confessed, but Corianne grabbed her shaky hand and squeezed.

Together they went about making their selections in the market, an unspoken agreement hovering between them not to discuss what had just happened. Inside, Freyah was still reeling, but she focused on her task at hand. She chose a bright pink salmon of medium weight, knowing she and her father could easily split it. With some leftover lentils, they'd make a perfectly-portioned meal.

Freyah paid for the fish but found her mind wandering back to the soldier as the fishmonger gave her her change. The man went so far as to nudge the coins into her hand when she wasn't paying attention. She apologized, embarrassed by her own scattered thoughts, but still, she couldn't get the face of that soldier out of her mind.

Why had he given up and walked away?

As she made her way to her father's shop, Freyah worried that perhaps she'd gotten away with breaking the law a little too easily.

2

───────

FREYAH

*I*t was sweltering in her father's shop.

The forge in the center of the room flamed constantly, creating a pulsating atmosphere with wave after wave of dry heat and smoke. As Freyah entered the shop, her damp clothes and hair immediately began to steam. She felt sticky as she dropped off her bag and followed the sounds of clanging metal, finding her father hunched over a table in the back corner of the room, shaping what looked like a fresh set of knives. Her father was good at his craft, and there was something unique about everything he created. He loved his job, and Freyah loved watching him work.

He happened to look up in time to see her plop onto a stool in front of him, then he lifted his face shield and smiled. His long, dark hair was tied back with an old scrap of cloth, and he was wearing his worn leather apron.

"Find anything good today, little bloom?" he asked.

Freyah's previous confidence in The Hub dwindled even further at the nickname her father had given her. It had sprung from her fascination with the blue lilies that grew along the mountain trails. They had become her favorite flower, and every year in the spring, she waited eagerly to watch them bloom. Though the nickname was endearing, she was a woman now, and being referred to as 'little' made her slightly insecure.

Freyah's mouth pressed into a hard line, and she held up her nearly empty tote. He knew she helped collect materials for Corianne's business, but he also knew the part Freyah enjoyed most was adding to her personal collection.

She'd spent years studying the different types of crystals found within the Northern Sky Mountains, along with what magic they held when wielded by witches. When she was younger, she pretended she had her own magic and hoarded the natural stones like the chinchillas in the mountain hoarded bird eggs. She would fasten them to fallen branches with twine and wave them about, wishing she could change the weather or make herself fly. Truthfully, she had no clue what magic looked like, because the witches tended to keep the extent of their powers a secret. But from the stories Corianne's mother told, their magic stemmed from nature, and that had only sparked her imagination further.

"I wasn't able to make it far enough down the ridge before the storm," she said, answering her father's previous question. "But I sold some limestone."

"That's alright," he reassured her. "The storm will uncover something new for you tomorrow." He raised a knowing eyebrow, noticing her wet clothes. "Maybe next time you'll bring that cloak."

She rolled her eyes. "Yes. Tomorrow might very well be the day."

Her father laughed, understanding his daughter's sarcasm.

Freyah was her father's child, through and through, for he was sharp, witty, and overwhelmingly kind. Together they shared a bond closer than most fathers and daughters, but it saddened her to know that it was the result of her mother's absence.

He constantly reminded Freyah how much she resembled her mother, even more so now that she was older, and she knew it pained him to see her blonde hair and brilliant hazel eyes staring back at him.

She often felt out of place, looking so little like her father. Freyah's porcelain skin turned an angry red during the dead of summer, while his was tanned and damaged from the years he'd spent on the ocean as a young man. He'd been a deckhand before Freyah was born, and after leaving his sea legs behind, he'd picked up the skill of forging from Last Cove's previous blacksmith, eventually taking over the business.

Freyah got to her feet. "I'll get dinner started," she said, unloading the contents of her bag.

"Already?" he questioned.

"I got your favorite." She held out the small package of salmon wrapped in brown paper. "It'll take a couple of hours, but I thought we could smoke it with garlic and rosemary."

He responded with a pleased *hum* in the back of his throat. "That sounds delicious," he said. "Let me finish this piece, then we'll play chess while we wait."

AFTER FILLING THEIR BELLIES, Freyah washed their empty bowls while her father cleared the table. They easily fell into a quiet comfort while they worked. No need to fill the silence with words—simply being in one another's presence was enough.

So when her father initiated a conversation, Freyah was surprised.

"Mrs. Amone dropped off some laundry while you were out today," he said as he stacked their cups in the wash basin.

She let out a sigh. "I've told her she doesn't have to keep doing that. I'm old enough to do laundry now."

He chuckled. "Yes, you've been old enough for quite some time, but you know she enjoys doing it. She always has."

He was right. Corianne's mother had always been proud of helping others, especially Freyah, given her situation. Thanks to Mrs. Amone's constant doting, it was as if Freyah had had a mother all along—as well as a sister to keep her company. It was what she and Corianne truly were in spirit, if not by blood.

She gave her father a pointed look over her shoulder. "I appreciate her help. I'm just surprised she has the time. Ever since the council requested she transcribe all those old records, Corianne says she hardly leaves her study."

"I'm sure she knows her limits," he said. "Just be sure to thank her."

"You know I will."

A knock came at the door, and her father was quick to answer as she continued to clean up. Freyah didn't think much of it until an agitated voice carried to her through the open door.

"It's been two weeks, Brennan," the deep voice declared. "People are starting to get antsy."

Freyah's father hushed the man, so she stopped what she was doing. Putting down the wet rag she'd been holding, she walked across the room to peer around the corner, hoping to hear the conversation more clearly.

Her father stood halfway inside the doorway, the door blocking part of his face. But the stranger was completely hidden from view.

"I told you," her father stated in a hushed but calm manner. "We have to slow things down. Now that the pier's down, we have to be smart. The Spyders are watching."

Now that the pier's down?

About a month prior, the main shipping pier in the cove had collapsed due to some sort of structural damage. It was still being repaired and required a lot of hands to fix it. That meant exports bound for Larapuna had been delayed. Last Cove, like every other major trading town in Ghoma, was responsible for supplying fifty percent of their shares to the crown—something most did not agree with.

It only now occurred to her that this could explain the soldiers presence in The Hub. Maybe they'd come to collect.

The man let out a low groan. "We understand. We're all with you on this. It's just...seeing *them* in The Hub today got everyone all riled up."

Her father sighed, and Freyah watched as he moved to rest his hand on the doorframe. "Tomorrow night," he caved. "Spread the word that I'm calling a meeting."

The man's tone shifted positively. "I will. Thank you, Brennan."

Her father didn't audibly respond; he simply shut the door and wiped a hand down the length of his face.

Freyah couldn't imagine what sort of meeting her father would take part in, much less lead. Last Cove's small council held quarterly meetings to discuss trade and any issues that presented themselves amongst the people, but her father was not on the council. He was the town blacksmith. He made things out of iron and steel.

She hurried back to the kitchen and began putting away the clean bowls and cutlery as if she'd been occupied the entire time. Her father lumbered back into the room and sank heavily into a chair at the table. He peered down at the empty surface, as if forgetting that he'd already eaten. Freyah thought she saw unease on his face, but when he glanced up to meet her eyes, it had been wiped away.

Before she got the chance to ask, he informed her who the visitor was. "That was John Morrow," he stated casually. "I'm crafting a blade for him."

Freyah nodded, though she knew he was lying. Quite poorly at that.

"Where is it?"

He tilted his head. "Hmm?"

"The blade," she continued to pry. "Where is it?"

"Oh, yes." He cleared his throat and waved a hand flippantly in the air. "In the shop. It's not ready."

Freyah decided to let it go. She didn't want to call him out without knowing the full story. After all, it could be nothing. Maybe there was a complaint with his work, and he wanted to handle it with discretion. But what did Madam Lema's soldiers have to do with it? They *had* to have been who the man was referring to when he said "*them.*"

Their presence in The Hub had been uncomfortable, but Freyah had been the only one to truly get "riled up."

Had her actions been reported?

Was her father going to get in trouble for what she'd done?

Instead of outright questioning him, Freyah merely asked, "Is everything alright?"

He overexerted a smile. "Of course it is. Why wouldn't it be?"

Her palms began to sweat at the memory of how bold she'd been.

"I saw the queen's men in Fisherman's Row today," she confessed. "I might have…stepped out of line. Just a bit."

Her father's forced smile morphed into a disappointed frown. "Freyah, how many times have I told you to steer clear of strangers? Especially the soldiers. You can't test them. I've seen men punished just for looking at them wrong." He swallowed hard. "What did you do?"

"They were wasting that vendor's product," she said rapidly. "He was an old man, and he wasn't going to defend himself, so I stepped in. They didn't even do anything. They just walked away."

"That's it?" he questioned in disbelief.

She bit her bottom lip. "That's it."

Freyah could see him silently mulling over the situation, but the tension in the air was too much, so she pushed ahead.

"So…that wasn't because of me?" she asked, gesturing to the door.

He shook his head, his mouth pressed into a thin line. "No, Freyah. It was just John Morrow."

Once everything was cleaned up from dinner and Freyah had taken a moment to calm her nerves in front of the hearth, she made her nightly trip to the communal well.

Each family was allotted several large jugs to fill with water that would sustain them for a week at a time. Because of their size, Freyah had to wheel them in a cart through the long mountain corridors.

Inside Mount Mirela, tunnels and caverns split off in every direction. There were bath houses on each level of the mountain, as well as a council meeting room, kitchens and lavatories with sufficient plumbing, and enough apartment space for over two hundred families to live comfortably.

Freyah was busy wheeling back her full jugs when she came across someone in the tunnel. A small, hunched figure ambled toward her from the shadows, and as they shortened the space between them, Freyah recognized the figure to be Jago, the lizard-demon from the bookstore. As he ambled down the passageway, Freyah averted her eyes, keeping her head down until they'd passed one another.

She wondered what he was doing wandering the residential passages. Visiting someone? Or perhaps making a late night delivery? She'd never seen him anywhere other than the bookstore.

She kept her head down, not looking up until she turned the corner she knew would lead her home. When she did, several things happened very fast and all at once.

The lights along the corridor went black, and Freyah was cast into an impenetrable darkness. Out of that darkness, several hands descended and took hold of her shoulders and arms. When she turned her head to gather her bearings, she felt thick fabric sliding across her cheeks. There was something covering her face. The lanterns hadn't gone out—she'd been masked.

Freyah clawed at whatever she could get her hands on, trying to identify her attackers. They were tall and broad—most likely men, and her fingers found the smooth texture of what felt like leather armor with a raised emblem on the chest.

Bone-chilling realization hit her like an icy wind.

It was the queen's soldiers.

She screamed, hoping someone would hear her, and dug her fingers into the coarse stubble of a jaw and squeezed. One of them let out a deep growl and snatched her wrist, twisting it in an unnatural angle. Freyah was sure her bones would snap, so she weakened her efforts, but not before she was able to kick out and land a hit. She heard a satisfying grunt of pain followed by a body falling against her cart with a loud crash, sending water sloshing to the ground.

Taking the opportunity, she attempted to run, but she tripped on someone's foot in her path and fell hard on her knees, scraping the heels of her hands as she tried to feel her way around the rocky passage.

Then the soldiers' hands were back and, in seconds, her legs and arms were bound. She tried to scream again, but the sound was cut short.

Something hard hit her temple, and the rest of her senses faded away.

3

LYRA

Lyra Mansell was the complete opposite of her sister in almost every way.

The most obvious physical contrast was the color of their hair—Lema had dark-black locks, while Lyra's were the purest shade of white-blonde. But there were other, more complex things that set them apart as well. Lyra tried to be gentle and empathetic when faced with situations or people she did not understand. Her sister, Lema, did not. They might have shared the same emerald green eyes, but those eyes couldn't have been more different when it came to how they viewed the world around them.

Lema was the queen of Ghoma and more set in her ways than any of the witches that had lived decades longer in comparison. Lyra did not share her sister's temper, or her unyielding ability to hold a grudge. Lyra was forgiving, and she valued time. Her kind had plenty of it, so its meaning was lost amongst generations that spread across centuries. But it was not lost to her.

Lyra tried to take advantage of every moment, drinking them in like sunshine soaking into her porcelain skin. She allowed herself to feel things that other witches couldn't, do things they wouldn't, and more often than not, it was those lapses in the norm that landed her in the most unexpected of predicaments.

On a beautiful and cloudless late summer day, the Princess of Ghoma found herself in such a position. Lyra often ventured outside the castle on days such as these, either to explore the woods or travel into the closest village for a pint of crisp ale. She enjoyed nature, but being surrounded by others was her favorite pastime, especially those that weren't like her. It gave her perspective, something that the looming shadows of Castle Larapuna did not.

As of late, she'd been spending her time in the district of Caster Valley. It consisted of large expanses of open farmland, and its people were responsible for supplying most of the crops that sustained the country.

Lyra liked the aura that surrounded the area. The satisfaction of a hard day's work wafted from everyone she passed, and simply being there made her feel useful, even if she didn't participate.

On this particular day, she'd chosen to arrive in shadow by traveling through the trees. After selecting a secluded, younger-looking sapling tucked several yards within the forest, she placed an amethyst crystal to the bark. As nature accepted her request, a chasm opened within the trunk, and she stepped through it, coming out the other side of a tall birch. What would have taken multiple days only took a few seconds, and she was now on the outskirts of a small village called Knox Hill.

With a renewed sense of excitement fueling her steps, Lyra found herself succumbing to an urge to explore new parts of the town instead of wasting all of her time at the local pub.

As she walked the cobblestone streets, she passed a school, an apothecary, and even a temple. The only gods Lyra knew were Lillia and Ghidorah, the Mother and Father of Magic, but she found it incredibly fascinating that humans had a god of their own.

A witch's form of worship involved honoring nature and the seasons. Their magic came from the earth, drawing from its natural treasures like crystals, flowers, and rare metals. Such items were necessary for almost every spell, so it was important not to waste resources.

Though there was much to study within her own customs, Lyra was more interested in learning about humans. There were lots of things about them she found interesting, and it piqued her curiosity more and more each time she walked among them.

Unfortunately, she couldn't do that without hiding what she was.

Due to the ongoing acts of protest from the rebels, Lyra knew it would be dangerous to reveal herself proudly as a witch whenever she left the boundaries of Larapuna, so she disguised her features by muting the brilliance of her emerald eyes and dressing down in drab clothing.

It wasn't much, but they were little things that made a difference. All it had taken was a bit of dried chrysanthemum petals added to her tea earlier that morning and she was able to pass as merely human.

Witches drew attention because of their extended youth and unique beauty. They looked like dolls, compared to humans with their dirty nails and imperfections, but that beauty was wasted. They lived and died in the castle, with no true life experience other than what the elders passed down.

Lyra envied humans and their liveliness—their experience. She wanted to immerse herself in the world outside the castle and leave her perfection behind for a little while.

Other witches didn't bother with such nonsense. Whenever one did choose to venture outside the walls of their fortress, it was for the sake of procreating. A witch's sole duty was to extend the line of magic, and whenever they were in need of a man, they simply ventured out to find one.

It wasn't uncommon for a lonely man to fall prey to a beautiful witch, only for them to wake up the next morning with no memory and no knowledge of the child they'd helped to create. It was the only way to ensure the passing of magic from female to female, for if a witch were to birth a boy, the babe was immediately discarded in the woods and left to be raised by their wild demon kin.

As for the queen, well…Lema *never* left her castle.

Lyra's sister had become so estranged from the outside world that she'd created an entire branch of her army to serve in her place. They watched from the shadows of each village, making sure everyone fell in line, and reported back with whatever information she needed to maintain control. Lema didn't need to be there to instill fear in her people. Even from far away, everyone knew what the queen was capable of.

But Lyra knew there was more to Ghoma than lingering fear and scars from a previous war. There were beautiful things—small things—that made it worth stepping outside her comfort zone to explore.

When she found herself at the end of the street, she turned and continued along a dirt path that circled to the back of the temple and led to a small clearing filled with wildflowers. The sight took Lyra's breath away, so she wandered further, following the sweet floral aroma.

This was the type of moment she wished her sister could experience. This was nature—the root of their magic—and sometimes it was worth just basking in the beauty of it.

She reached down with two fingers and was about to pluck one of the buds by the stem when she was stopped by a voice from the other side of the field.

"What are you doing?"

The deep timbre made Lyra look up, and she found a man—no, a demon—standing a few feet away, watching her. Even from a distance, she could clearly see the outline of rounded ears protruding from within a head of dark curls and a tail twisting from behind his legs.

She delicately released the flower from between her fingers and smiled. "I'm sorry," she apologized. "They're so beautiful. I couldn't help myself."

She spoke gently, relying on the wind to carry her words, and he received them the way she intended: with grace and understanding.

"It's no problem," he assured, Lyra's power of persuasion working perfectly in her favor. She'd also added valerian root to that tea she'd drunk, in case she needed to talk her way out of something.

The demon began shuffling his feet anxiously. "You can take one, if you'd like."

"Thank you," she said, commending him on his kindness.

Lyra wasn't unaware of her effect on men. She tried, most of the time, to not let it get in the way of what could possibly be a genuine connection, but there were also plenty of times when she'd allowed her gift to steer the ship. It was one of the ways she was so often able to wiggle herself out of all those damn unexpected predicaments.

The only demon she'd ever interacted with before was Ryker, the general of the royal army, and being so close to another excited her.

She took a step forward, attempting to close the expansive gap between them. "What's your name?"

He hesitated, then placed both hands proudly on his hips. "Oram Foster, milady."

This intrigued her, for demons didn't typically have last names due to their parentage being so hard to trace.

Lyra removed the hood of her cloak, and her white-blond hair caught in a sudden gust of wind. It took on a life of its own, twisting and billowing out like wings on either side of where she stood, and Oram watched in awe. She was putting on a show without intention, but things tended to work out that way for her.

The princess bent her knee and addressed him by giving a polite curtsy. "It's nice to meet you, Oram Foster. You can call me Lyra."

Her attempt to do something different was wasted, because Lyra inevitably ended up in the small tavern of a local inn. Only this time, she had a drinking partner.

She and Oram sat in a corner booth for over an hour, talking and laughing over a pitcher of mulled wine. Lyra had taken the liberty of strengthening it up to her liking, and so far Oram hadn't seemed to notice.

"Did humans take you in?" she asked bluntly.

Oram blanched, slightly taken off guard, but nodded. "Yes. I was raised by humans. My mother…she made frequent visits to the castle, and there were several instances where she came across a demon child that had been abandoned in the forest. She took us in. I grew up with five brothers and sisters."

Lyra was stunned. She'd never thought about what happened to the male babies after they were cast out. She assumed they were taken in by the Wild Demon clans. It was possible that a few had ventured out on their own over as they got older, but knowing there were humans that were willing to put their lives on the line to save a demon child made Lyra's chest constrict with sympathy she hadn't known she could feel.

She didn't necessarily agree with the way things were done, but it wasn't something she could control. The decision to cast out demons at birth had been made before Lyra was born. It was just the way things were. Despite being the Princess of Ghoma, Lyra didn't have the power to question it.

"Do they still live here?" she asked, referring to the many siblings he'd mentioned.

"Only two," he told her. "My youngest sister, Yohannah, still lives with my parents. She's twelve. I live with my brother, Kirra." His shoulders slumped. "The others have moved on. I haven't spoken to them in years."

Lyra leaned across the table, clutching the sides of her mug with intrigue. "Is he like you?" Oram raised an eyebrow, so she clarified. "What *kind* of demon is your brother?"

Due to his small, rounded ears and thin tail, she'd deduced that Oram was most likely some sort of cat-demon. He also had a wide nose and brow, and his cheeks were fuller than normal.

"You know, it's not polite to ask demons what they are."

He was teasing her, but Lyra got the hint there was the slightest bit of genuine offense in his tone.

But Oram let the moment pass, and to her surprise, he began rolling up his sleeves. As the fabric was pulled away from his light brown skin, Lyra began to make out the markings that covered both arms. He pulled down the collar of his shirt, and she saw that they encroached as far as his neck. She'd assumed the black marks that protruded from under his shirt were tattoos, but no…

They were black tiger stripes.

"My brother is a second-generation fox-demon, so it's not as easy for him to blend in."

"Your features are so subtle," she said, voice trailing as she took him in. She reached to touch the skin on his wrist, and a shiver passed over him.

Demons were so incredibly fascinating. Lyra knew that General Ryker was the son of a warlock, so his demon features were extremely prominent, but she hadn't realized that they would diminish through the generations.

"How old are you?" she asked.

"Twenty-nine. Third-generation." He tugged his sleeve back down and fidgeted in his seat. "I can't hide my tail, but wearing long sleeves and a hat makes it easier for some people to interact with me."

"Is that why you were surprised to see me?"

Oram gave her a knowing look. "Yes. I don't typically see a lot of people when I'm working in the fields. It's a good place to hide."

"Well, you don't have to hide from me, Oram Foster." Lyra raised her mug. "I find you fascinating."

"Tell me something, since you've been the only one asking so many questions," he ventured. "Why are you so curious about me?"

She rested her chin in the palm of her hand and leaned heavily onto her elbow with a grin. "What's there not to be curious about?"

He ignored her sly response and continued with another question of his own. "Where are you from?"

"Around."

"Good answer."

Lyra beamed, unfazed by his attempt to turn the tables on her. "Does it matter? Can't I just be the mysterious and sultry stranger you had a nice chat with in a tavern?"

"*Had*?" he repeated, questioning her use of past tense. "Is our chat over?"

"It doesn't have to be." She was flirting openly with him now, and he was beginning to catch on. "Why don't we continue it upstairs?" she said suggestively, already making the first move and standing up from the table. She chugged what was left of the wine in her mug and slammed it definitively down on the surface.

Oram watched her with such bewilderment that Lyra wasn't sure he would actually take her up on the offer. But after about a second of deliberation, he stood and followed her to the stairs.

There was one other important trait that Lyra shared with her sister, something neither of them dared to admit to themselves or to one another. But when everything boiled down, the one true, raw thing that connected them was their selfish determination.

Their goals might have differed, but the ways in which they went about achieving them did not.

Both sisters were notorious for almost always getting their way.

LYRA HAD CHOSEN WELL.

Not only was Oram incredibly alluring because of his demon features, but underneath all that drab and dirty clothing from a day's work in the fields, he was stunningly handsome.

As he undressed, she studied his tapered jaw and full lips. The skin on his long face had been sun-damaged, and though his hands were weathered with calluses, his striped back and chest looked smooth as silk. She loved the way his small cat ears twitched at every sound, and his eyes, though full of mystery, made her want to melt into the warm amber of them.

Lyra waited patiently as Oram unbuttoned the top of his trousers. They hung low on his hips, enticing her with the sharp cut of a V that led down to a patch of coarse, dark hair. She didn't want to be too forward, so she waited for him to come to her as she lay on the bed, still dressed.

The room was small, meant for no more than sleeping and lovers meeting in the shadows. She'd never done something like this in a proper bed, with a man she'd had a proper conversation with. Typically, her needs were met in back alleys with quick transactions and no small talk whatsoever.

Oram was different.

He piqued every inch of her—curiosity, body, and mind.

Lyra wanted to learn everything about him: what haunted his dreams, the motivation behind working in the fields every day, and how he managed to keep in such delectable shape.

As he ambled toward her, pants undone and hard chest exposed, she could tell that he, too, was partaking in something out of the ordinary.

She reached up and grabbed the back of his neck, pulling him down to meet her mouth, and he opened for her in welcome, sliding his tongue along her bottom lip. A burst of butterflies took flight in her belly with the contact. As he lowered himself onto the bed and hovered over her trembling body, the tips of his fingers grazed the skin of her legs beneath her dress. The skirt had been hiked up to the tops of her thighs, and the lightness of his touch caused heat to throb in her core.

Nothing about this was normal.

Sex wasn't like this for Lyra. She quickly met her needs as they arose, and reported dutifully to her coven that she'd done her part in attempting to procreate each month, though without success.

But this, right here and now with Oram...they hadn't even removed their clothes and it was the most sensual experience she'd ever taken part in.

He actually wanted her.

Or did he?

Lyra couldn't help but wonder how much of her influence was still working on him. The valerian root would run out soon, and she had no way of knowing whether Oram would suddenly find himself in a shocking situation or one he'd willingly put himself into. So she held on as tight as she could to the lustful look in his eyes as he continued to push the fabric further up her legs.

She unbuttoned the leather bodice she wore over the dress and let it fall open, exposing her barely contained breasts. Momentarily distracted from his previous task, Oram hooked a finger into the thin collar of her neckline and pulled it down to take her peaked nipple into his mouth.

Lyra let out a sigh of satisfaction. He lavished the sensitive part of her breast with his tongue until her bones turned to liquid. She was merely a body of satiated blood and desire, and he was only getting started.

Oram parted her legs and fully removed his own trousers. Climbing back over her on the bed, he took a moment to fully examine her face. His hand cupped her cheek, and his thumb softly brushed a stray hair from her eyes.

"Are you sure?" he asked.

Lyra felt like she could cry.

The audacity of it—a man asking her permission—made her feel powerful and seductive. She'd always had control over the situation, more so than Oram even realized, but he was offering her an out. He was giving her a choice.

She made that choice easily by taking his length in her hand and guiding him to her. He entered her with slow precision, too slow for her personal taste, so she lifted her hips, causing him to fully sheath himself inside her. She was beyond the need for foreplay. They'd been building up to this moment throughout their entire conversation downstairs, and simply being in the room with him now was enough.

Oram let out a deep purr that started in the back of his throat and reverberated through the connection between them. He picked up the pace, and with every thrust, Lyra climbed higher and higher toward the peak of her pleasure.

Her fingers dug into the taut muscles of his back, feeling them ripple with every movement they made together.

"Gods above," Oram gasped. He was already nearing his climax, and her own grew in response. Lyra helped guide them both over the edge by taking the lobe of his left ear between her teeth. It was a sensitive spot for him, exactly as she'd hoped, and with that, they were both sent spiraling into an endless pit of euphoria.

As she lay there, coming down from her high, Lyra wondered for the first time if she'd actually managed to create something between them, either tangible or symbolic. It was possible that she'd finally completed her duty to continue the magical line of her family—how proud the elders would be.

She didn't necessarily despise the idea of having a child, but if there really was a small life form now taking shape in her womb, by Lillia's name, she didn't know what she was going to do with it.

4

FREYAH

*W*hen Freyah came to, the earth was shaking.

Beneath her, a rattling wooden floor pressed to her cheek. The room swayed, and she could hear the steady rhythm of wheels churning along crunching dirt.

She cursed herself aloud.

How had she allowed those strangers to take her so easily?

With Freyah being an only child—and a girl, specifically—her father wanted her prepared for the inevitable. It wasn't unheard of for girls to be taken advantage of, especially walking home alone in the evenings, right when the local pub was closing for the night. So she hadn't been completely helpless. She'd done everything her father told her to in a situation like that.

She'd fought back.

She'd screamed for help.

Yet, she was here.

Her hands and feet were no longer tied, so she managed to sit up despite the constant rocking of the wagon around her. It was mostly dark save for the tiny rays of light leaking through cracks in the splintering wood. It smelled damp and moldy, like something wet had been left to rot for weeks. There was also a strong scent of sealife. She was surrounded by several wooden crates, so she assumed they were filled with salted fish and other seafood from Last Cove, which meant she was currently stuck in a supply wagon.

Freyah crawled to the back of the wagon and peered through the crack between the doors, trying to glimpse her surroundings.

Ash trees climbed higher than the sun, nearly blotting out the sky, and beyond clouds of dust from the dirt road, Freyah could see the top of Mount Mirela peeking over the canopy.

They had reached the valley at the bottom of the Northern Sky Mountains.

She wasn't sure how long it would take to reach Castle Larapuna. Maybe six days at most. In that time, they would have to stop and camp, and so far they'd yet to take a break—unless she'd slept through it. She was uncertain how long she'd been knocked out, but the daylight peeking through the cracks was a dim orange, meaning the sun was now setting.

She'd been taken at night, so no more than a day had passed since they'd left Last Cove. She knew little about the journey they would be taking, only that they would eventually enter a long expanse of forest that surrounded the queen's castle.

Based on the stories Mrs. Amone had told, Freyah knew the stretch would be too vast to make it all the way through without stopping. That meant one of their camps would inevitably have to be inside the eerie wood. She feared being so exposed, but perhaps the soldiers would do the honorable thing and keep her safe.

It would seem she hadn't gotten away with disrespecting a soldier of the crown after all, and a gaping pit opened in her stomach at the thought of facing the queen.

The outlines of buildings began to take shape several yards from the trail once the wagon began to slow. As it turned and went over a large dip, she fell onto her back, and the ride became even shakier.

After a few more minutes, the tousling stopped, and Freyah let out a breath of relief. She braced herself, waiting for the doors to open.

Voices carried to her ears from outside—bickering and a few boisterous chuckles from multiple deep baritones.

"Avlon, get your lazy arse down here and help," one of the men demanded.

"Yeah, *lieutenant*," the other concurred in a mocking tone. "If you don't pitch yourself a tent, you'll be sleeping with the rats."

They were definitely making camp for the night.

But why stop on the outskirts of the village when they could just as easily book a room at an inn? Perhaps they didn't want any prying eyes taking a look at their captive. Or risk the chance of Freyah trying to escape.

"I'm going into town first," a third voice called. "You don't want to spend the evening without the proper provisions, do you?"

Freyah's heart skipped a beat. She recognized that deep, raspy drawl.

It belonged to the soldier she'd stood up to in The Hub.

One of the other men signaled his agreement. "Aye, good call. I won't be able to drown out those incessant beetles without whiskey."

"Why are they so loud anyway?" his companion complained.

"Must be mating season."

She must not have been paying enough attention before, but they were right. The air was filled with a consistent *clicking*. There weren't many insects that lived within the mountain, besides seaflies and the occasional gnat. The more Freyah listened, the more annoying the sound became.

She crept back to the doors and watched as two of the men began unrolling tarps and wooden stakes. The third, Avlon, strutted off behind them along the dirt road that led into the village. What little she knew of Ghoma's terrain was from the maps in her father's smithy, but seeing it in person was a completely new experience. The flat expanse of dirt rolling out in front of her was strange and unfamiliar.

Freyah had spent countless hours daydreaming about life outside of Last Cove, but this was not what she'd had in mind.

She waited and continued to watch as the men slowly erected the tents and gathered wood for a fire. She wondered which of the tents would be hers. Perhaps they would leave her in the back of the supply wagon all night. She doubted her comfort was on the top of their priority list.

It had taken them about an hour to complete the fire pit given all the joking around they were doing, and when one of the men began walking her way, Freyah stiffened, backing up from the doors until she was pressed flat against the opposite wall of the wagon. She tucked herself between the stacks of wooden crates and listened as the latch on the doors lifted and the hinges squeaked.

Freyah was greeted by a stocky and overly eager-looking soldier. He had several days worth of blond stubble on his cheeks, but the rest of him appeared clean and neatly pressed—the complete opposite of the burly, mountain of a man she'd made her stand against in Last Cove.

Where Avlon had been coarse and worn with obvious travel, this man looked like he'd just stepped out of a bathing chamber, fresh faced and full of energy. But the smile on his face wasn't exactly friendly.

No, it displayed pleasure for entirely selfish reasons.

Freyah knew better than to trust it.

"Time to stretch your legs, girl."

When she didn't move, he made to climb into the wagon after her, but she abruptly stood before he could, crouching slightly so as not to bump her head. He halted his efforts then placed his dirt-crusted boot back on the ground.

"Good girl," he mused.

Freyah's blood recoiled at the seduction lacing his tone, but she managed to keep her mouth shut this time around.

Without a single retort, she hopped down from the wagon and landed on a grassy field. She raised her hand to block the sun from blinding her. It lingered right in her line of sight and cast an orange glow over the village ahead.

"Do whatever business you need to over there," the soldier said, pointing to a cluster of willow trees behind the wagon. "But don't stray," he added with a wink. "I'll be watching."

Freyah figured now was as good a time as any to start asking questions.

"Why am I here?" she asked. "Are you taking me to the queen for penance?"

Both he and the other soldier by the fire let out obnoxious cackles.

"Don't worry, chickadee. It's not the queen you have to worry about."

Freyah stiffened. "What does that mean?"

"Oi, come on, Roman," the other soldier playfully chastised. "Don't scare the girl."

Roman turned around to face his friend by the fire and scowled. "You mind shuttin' your trap, *Nico*." He emphasized saying the other man's name aloud, as if Freyah knowing their names was a bad thing.

They were probably right. If they decided to try anything, at least she would know how to identify them later.

"Well, since we're all introducing ourselves," she interjected, sardonically, "my name is Freyah. It's been great getting to know you all, and this trip has been a real blast, but I should be getting back home."

She took a step toward the direction of the village, but Roman sidestepped and blocked her path. He placed a firm hand on her shoulder. "Not so fast."

His eagerness was back, and this time Freyah could clearly see exactly how slimy his intentions were. She shrugged him off and made to step away from him, but he continued creeping closer. Despite how orderly he appeared, Roman smelled like sweat and grime.

This was the first of several nights Freyah could be stuck with them, and she might only be able to fight off their uninvited advances for so long. Perhaps if she made things too difficult, they'd give up and let her be. They wouldn't want to draw attention to what they were doing, would they? Then again, there was a chance at least one of them liked a challenge. There were men back in Last Cove who enjoyed it when their women put up a little bit of a fight. It made things more exciting for them.

Roman inched even closer. She was running out of room to get away, and soon there would be no space left to put between them. Her back met the outside of the supply wagon, and a sharp edge of protruding wood dug uncomfortably into her spine. She tried to meet the eyes of the other soldier, but he was focused back on his work of building up the fire. It was now lit with small embers burning low to the ground trying to catch with the brush he tossed into the flames.

"You sure are a pretty thing," Roman muttered. He ran his tongue along his bottom lip, like he was preparing himself to taste her.

This was it. It was time to test her theory.

Once he tried something, she would push him away. Kick him in the balls, then knock out his teeth with her knee. If he still came at her after that sort of assault, she knew there would be little else to do.

Freyah steeled herself, lifting her chin. She took in a deep breath and clenched her fists at her sides. But before Roman could make his first move, a deep voice called out from the darkening horizon.

"What the fuck are you doing?"

The lieutenant had returned.

Avlon was now walking toward the camp with a burlap sack in one hand and a large brown bottle in the other.

Roman and Nico immediately stopped what they were doing, the latter taking an awkward stance as if he, too, was caught in the act of doing something foul.

As the lieutenant approached, Freyah wasn't sure if she should be more or less afraid. For all she knew, he was annoyed that the other men had attempted to claim her first. But as he placed his supplies on the ground beside the fire, Freyah could see the fury on his face. He was angry and seconds away from doing something about it.

"Step away from her," he demanded. "Now."

Roman took a step back, shriveling into himself under his superior now towering behind him. She'd forgotten how tall the other man was, all lean muscle and intimidating demeanor. His beard was short but full and matched the dark brown hair that fell in waves around his face.

Roman spun on his heel and backed into the wall of the wagon beside Freyah. As Lieutenant Avlon stood in front of his fellow soldier, hand poised on the hilt of the knife strapped onto his belt, she took the opportunity to move. She sidestepped away from the men and retreated to the safety of a low hanging willow tree that stood a few feet away from their camp, where Roman had instructed her to do her business.

Lieutenant Avlon stood his ground, waiting for Roman to say something or make another move. But that sleazy confidence that had once cloaked the soldier's attitude had completely diminished at the sight of his superior. As if the mere sight of the lieutenant made him want to wet himself.

It seemed it was all fun and games until Avlon decided not to play.

"You lay a finger on her, and you'll have one less to stick up your ass," the lieutenant threatened.

Freyah thought she heard Roman audibly gulp. Then he nodded in agreement. "Aye," he said, submitting with a shaky breath.

Roman waited until Lieutenant Avlon appeared satisfied with his response, then he walked sheepishly toward the fire pit.

If he had a tail, it would have been tucked between his legs.

Nico stood still by the fire, having witnessed the entire exchange with bated breath. Freyah was equally as stunned. She couldn't wrap her head around why the lieutenant would defend her in such a way.

Whatever the reason, Freyah wasn't willing to thank him quite yet.

She took a tentative step out from under the willow tree, trying to steady her heart and stop her hands from shaking. She kept a considerable distance between herself and the others, who were now gathering around the fire.

Lieutenant Avlon unpacked fresh fruit from the sack he'd been carrying and divided it between himself and the others. Then, from the pouch on his hip, he pulled out a small pack wrapped in parchment paper. When he unfolded the paper, Freyah immediately smelled the smoky scent of cured meat.

She hadn't realized how hungry she was until seeing the food displayed in front of her, and at the sight of Nico biting savagely into his piece of jerky, her mouth began salivating.

"Are you going to come get your share?" Avlon suddenly asked. "Or are you just going to stand there and watch?"

Freyah hadn't realized he was speaking directly to her, but when she met his eyes across the fire, her stomach dipped. Mostly from hunger, she assumed. But there was something about having the soldier's full attention on her that made her...unsettled.

Instead of cowering and continuing to look weak in front of him, she lifted her chin and walked purposefully toward the fire. She sat on one of the logs Nico had pulled from the outer brush, and the warmth of the flames licked her legs, soothing her nerves.

She glanced around the open expanse of the valley in the distance and debated whether or not to run. If she took a chance and tried, how far would she get before the soldiers caught her? And where would she go? She'd never left the mountain before, and she feared she wouldn't know the way back on her own.

Lieutenant Avlon held out a chunk of meat and gestured for her to take it. She debated whether or not to snatch it from him, similar to how she'd snatched the fish from his hand in defiance at The Hub.

He seemed to be remembering the same thing, because the look on his face was now something like...shame?

Freyah was too hungry to play games, so she took it willingly. Afterward, the lieutenant didn't give her a second glance, only returned his focus to the fire in front of him as if it were the most interesting thing in the world.

He wasn't being unfriendly, but he wasn't exactly welcoming.

Why would he be? He and his comrades had stolen her from her home without warning, knocked her out, and forced her into a smelly supply wagon against her will. She was surprised he'd done her the service of offering food, but she guessed having her wilt away from starvation wouldn't bode well for her intended punishment, whatever that might be.

Freyah sat quietly and chewed on the dried meat. It was tough and took a bit of force to tear off a small bite, but the taste was salty and gamey—a nice change for her, having mostly lived on a diet of fish.

She'd been so enamored by the taste that she hadn't noticed the lieutenant place some fruit next to her on the log. She looked down and found the juiciest-looking yellow apple she'd ever seen. She devoured it next, alternating between bites of meat and fruit, and her stomach grumbled with the satisfaction of her meal. Though it had been less than twenty-four hours since she'd had dinner with her father, she relished the sustenance.

The three men around the fire remained stoic as they too satiated their appetites, and Freyah felt awkwardly out of place.

This was no way to treat a prisoner, but she was glad for their misguided kindness.

As someone that needed planning and structure, she tried to prepare herself for what was to come when she inevitably reached the castle, but the uncomfortable silence they currently shared only confused her.

Was this how she'd be spending the next few days on the road to Larapuna? Either stuck in the back of a supply wagon or sitting in silence surrounded by intolerable men?

Freyah didn't think she'd last a week on the road in those conditions, but it wasn't in her nature to give up. She would keep herself together until they reached the castle, for that was where the next threat of danger truly lay.

Until then, thanks to Lieutenant Avlon, at least she knew she was somewhat safe.

As safe as she could be, anyway.

5

FREYAH

They headed out early the next morning.

Freyah had been instructed by the lieutenant to sleep inside the back of the supply wagon on the first night, and she'd taken to doing so every night since. Whether that was for her personal safety or not, she wasn't sure. But it didn't matter. She was happy to be away from the lot of them. The large, overbearing presence of all three men made Freyah feel significantly outnumbered. The smell of them alone made her want to get as far away as possible, so she'd found solace within the four walls of her makeshift sanctuary.

For three days, she followed the routine of eating, sleeping, occasionally relieving herself in a bush, and repeating the process. Every night, they made camp. After that first night outside the village she now knew was called Berwick, they crossed over the Ume River and camped outside of Knox Hill—another small village along their route that sat smack in the middle of the valley.

They'd passed another town along the way—what used to be a town, anyway—but given that the entire stretch of land was now underwater, there was nowhere to camp. Freyah wondered what had happened to cause such a severe natural disaster, but as the wagon rode by the eerie remnants of houses cresting the water's surface, an unwavering silence fell over the soldiers at the front. Their chatter had ceased the moment the water came into view and lasted until it became a speck in the distance.

The soldiers had chosen to take advantage of the stop in Knox Hill to stock up on stalks of corn, bushels of tomatoes, and various greens. Freyah recognized the labels on the crates as they stacked them into the back of the wagon being the same as ones received on the pier in Last Cove once a month.

That night, as they'd sat by the fire, Freyah heard loud crashes and chanting from what sounded like the center of town.

"Most likely rebels," the lieutenant had said. "Just a typical day for a bunch of angry people."

Roman hadn't stopped eyeing her since 'the incident,' and at her clear ignorance of the subject, he had given her a sly grin from across the fire. As if he was in on some sort of nasty joke.

Freyah hadn't realized the unrest was that bad.

She knew of talk within Last Cove about how the humans weren't happy with the current laws on food supply, and her town provided only a small fraction of what was sent to Larapuna on a monthly basis. The witches' castle was isolated from the rest of the country and surrounded by vast forest, so it made sense that outside assistance was required to provide them with all they needed to survive, but it seemed that the hard working men and women of Ghoma felt slighted by the demand.

Half of each district's shares went to the crown, which meant everyone had to work twice as hard only to reap half of what they'd sowed. The farmers in Caster Valley provided produce and grains, the fisherman of Last Cove gave up their fresh catches, and the merchants of the capital city created garment after garment for both themselves and the crown. No wonder the soldiers were so full of themselves— they didn't truly have to work for anything.

Freyah understood why that would make people upset, but she hadn't realized that people were starting to make a stand.

They were now approaching the part of the trip Freyah had been dreading the most. As they started their journey into the Saldanni

Forest, she watched and waited as the light faded through the cracks of the wagon around her.

Once the inside of the wagon was nearly dark, she knew they were within the cover of trees. She peered through the slats in the door. The trees were as large and dominating as she'd been told. The trunks of the redwood trees were as thick as three men with their arms spread wide. Roots drove up through the ground, creating small hills and valleys around them. They were so large that Freyah imagined she'd be unable to step over them, but there remained a clear path for the wagon to ride.

It was bumpy, but not nearly as rough as it could have been. They rode for hours, so long she was sure it was now nightfall, but she had no way to tell because of the constant cover from the trees above. They'd been shrouded in darkness the entire day, and the deeper they traveled, the darker it became inside the wagon.

Finally, they came to a stop. She waited for the sounds of wildlife as she sat perched against a large crate, but nothing came. It was eerily silent, so much so that the pressure from the lack of sound made her head feel like it was going to explode.

Then she heard rustling from the front of the wagon. After packing up outside of Knox Hill, she deduced that Roman and Nico were the ones who typically sat in the driver's compartment while Lieutenant Avlon mounted and led the extra horse.

A soft thump of boots hitting the ground replaced the silence, as well as a few creaks from the front of the wagon where the other two soldiers climbed down.

Like each time before, Freyah waited patiently for someone to open the doors and let her out. This time, however, when the doors eventually opened, it wasn't to let her out, but to let the others in.

Both Nico and Lieutenant Avlon stepped up into the back of the wagon, the former immediately making himself comfortable on a small patch of floor in the back corner while Avlon sat purposefully on a crate directly in front of Freyah. He was closest to the doors, and she watched him pull them shut and bang twice on the wood with a flat palm. From the outside, Roman slid the latch back into place, and she stiffened.

"What are you doing?"

Nico's grumbled response came from the back of the wagon. "Getting comfy, sweetheart. What does it look like?"

His face was hidden from view behind the crate next to the lieutenant, but she saw him stretch out his legs and cross them at the ankles, indeed appearing to make himself quite comfortable.

"I meant why are you doing that *here?*" She turned her attention to Avlon. "Aren't we making camp?"

The lieutenant made a gruff noise low in his throat. "Too dangerous."

Was there something in these woods that stood a threat to them?

"They're going to take turns keeping watch while we sleep," he said.

"Not you?"

"No. I'll be staying in here with you." He patted the outside of his leather vest, feeling around for something tucked underneath. When he found it, he pulled out a small block of partially carved wood and a switchblade.

Freyah scoffed. "Three of us are supposed to sleep in this?" She gestured to their cramped surroundings.

There was barely any space between the toes of her shoes and Avlon's boots, despite them sitting on opposite sides of the wagon. It was deeper than it was wide, but the extra space had been filled with additional crates.

Freyah didn't want to share anything with these soldiers. She'd hardly gotten any sleep as it was, attempting to keep one eye open through the nights to make sure one of them didn't try to make another move on her.

Lieutenant Avlon began whittling away absentmindedly at his carving, refusing to meet her gaze. "Unless you want to risk getting snatched up by one of the Wild Demon clans, then yes, we're going to have to deal."

Wild Demon clans?

Freyah swallowed hard. There was no way she was going to be able to relax enough to sleep. It was bad enough that she had to be in such close proximity to the men that had kidnapped her, but now she had to worry about being taken prisoner by a pack of wild demons, too?

She'd never longed for home so much in her life, and she feared she'd taken the safety of her mountain village for granted. She had no idea what to expect once they arrived at Castle Larapuna, but a large part of her now wanted that day to come faster—anything to get her out of this forest and behind safe walls.

"Think of it this way," Lieutenant Avlon muttered in his typical gravelly tone. "At least we'll keep each other warm."

SOMEHOW, Freyah managed to fall asleep, and she awoke some time later to the sound of obnoxious snoring. Lieutenant Avlon still sat on the crate across from her, fully alert, most of his attention on the nearly finished carving in his hand.

The legs sticking out from behind the other crate, now sprawled apart and shifted sideways, looked to still belong to Nico, so Freyah could only assume she hadn't been asleep that long if they hadn't changed shifts yet.

Lieutenant Avlon noticed her stir and looked up from what he was doing. Freyah pulled herself into a sitting position, folding her knees to her chest. The forest around them was eerily silent. No clicking beetles and no rustling from nighttime wildlife. She heard each intake of breath coming from the lieutenant's sturdy chest, following a steady rhythm in between the snoring of his comrade.

He eyed her pointedly. "Can't sleep?"

Freyah scowled. "How can I, with that bear sleeping next to us?"

Freyah swore the lieutenant actually smirked, but it was too dark and the expression too fleeting to know for sure.

"He only does that when he's comfortable," he said. "Must mean he likes you."

It was meant to be a tease, but the notion sent a chill down her spine. She didn't want to be liked by these men. She'd rather them despise her.

Still, she didn't let his comment linger. "I think not being exposed to the elements might have something to do with it."

"Of course," he agreed. "You're probably right."

There was an intriguing tension between them that Freyah couldn't put her finger on. She didn't trust him, but something made her want to bite back at his sarcasm, just like he seemed to enjoy hers. Maybe it was because he'd stepped in and prevented Roman from assaulting her, but Lieutenant Avlon had a different demeanor than the others. Not calming, but not quite alarming either.

Freyah leaned back against the crate behind her and stretched her legs. They came dangerously close to brushing against the lieutenant's, but she purposefully kept an inch of space between them.

He noticed and shifted backward in his seat.

"How much farther until we reach the castle?" she asked, trying to fill the silence.

He focused once again on his wooden carving. "Less than a day. If we leave at first light, we'll make it to Larapuna by late afternoon."

"Do you know what my punishment will be?"

He stilled but kept his eyes down. With his mouth illuminated by a small pocket of light, she saw his lip twitch. "Don't worry about it."

"*Don't worry about it?*" She sat straighter. "I was kidnapped from my home and am being dragged across the country with three men who immediately tried to assault me—I think I have the right to worry just a little bit."

"I never tried to assault you."

Freyah waited for him to address the rest of his crimes, but he remained quiet.

It seemed that the only accusation in that rant to disturb him was that he was a possible predator.

It was true—he hadn't tried to touch her. It was Roman who had been crude from the beginning, and though Nico hadn't approached her, he certainly hadn't made an effort to stop his friend.

Avlon had been…well, he was standoffish. Okay, and he was also very grumpy and a little bit rude. But he definitely hadn't tried to assault her.

"You're right," she admitted. "I didn't mean you." She looked over her right shoulder at the body still sleeping behind them. "Why do you work with them? If you know what they're like?"

"I didn't get to pick who I was assigned," he told her. "I'm just doing a job."

"And what job is that?"

He stiffened and stopped his work again. She clearly had a knack at asking him uncomfortable questions.

Good.

"That's none of your business," he finally answered.

Freyah scoffed. "Okay, clearly you don't understand the rules of respect." His eyes landed on her and narrowed. "Whatever you were instructed to do, you evidently went off script and decided to snatch me up along the way. So, you see, since that involves me directly, I get to know what the hell is going on. It's the *respectful* thing to do."

Lieutenant Avlon set the carving down purposefully on the crate beside him. He leaned forward and crouched on one knee directly in front of her, so close that if he lost his balance, he'd fall right into her lap.

"You're the one that made a scene and mouthed off to a soldier in the middle of The Hub," he growled. "Prisoners don't get respect."

A lump, too big to swallow, formed in Freyah's throat. Instead, she choked on it, leaving her skin clammy and hot.

He shifted back onto the crate. "You're an interesting one, I'll give you that."

The second time Freyah awoke, it was much later, and she was alone.

She sat up suddenly, wildly searching the wagon for another presence, but the lieutenant was gone, and there was no longer anyone sleeping behind the crates.

A surge of panic flooded her at what could have all of them needed outside, for Avlon had specifically said he would be staying inside the wagon with her.

She scrambled to her knees and crawled to the doors. Squinting between the slats, she immediately spotted the shape of a person standing just behind the supply wagon. She scanned the perimeter of the small space she could see. It was still extremely dark under the shadow of the forest canopy, but there were a handful of new soldiers surrounding the wagon, holding small lanterns, too far from their faces for Freyah to make out any features.

An unfamiliar voice spoke with a devilish undertone, sending goosebumps along Freyah's arms.

"You know the rules. We don't engage as long as you pass through quickly and quietly. But you've overstayed your welcome."

"Come on, Thax." That was the lieutenant. "You know we can't make it all the way through the forest in one trip. We had to rest the horses for the night."

He was the figure standing with his back to the wagon, blocking the other man from view.

"Technicalities, *soldier*," the stranger replied.

Avlon shifted subtly as his hand reached for the knife on his belt. It was small, and though it was hidden by shadows, she thought it looked similar to the blade he'd been using to carve his statue. She wondered why he wasn't reaching for the sword strapped to his back. Then again, something so small and easily concealed would definitely come as a surprise to an attacker.

It was a clever move, and Freyah appreciated it.

She watched and waited as the exchange continued.

"You never said we couldn't make camp," Avlon told the man.

"Ah, yes," the stranger sing-songed, "but you didn't make camp, did you? You parked your supply wagon in my territory and took a nap. Seems a bit lazy to me. Not to mention we found one of your horses a dozen yards away taking its fill from a stream." The man paused dramatically. "Don't worry. We took care of it."

What sort of ridiculous game was this prick trying to play? Had he killed one of their horses? And what made this part of the Saldanni Forest his territory?

Freyah had been expecting wild demons to be lurking in the trees, but not pompous assholes.

Avlon shifted his stance, and Freyah finally saw the stranger's face, now lit by the glow of one of the lanterns.

Her hand clamped to her mouth to stifle a scream.

What she saw looked like a thing of nightmares.

Standing before Lieutenant Avlon was a demon covered in dark, matted-brown fur. He had a long face, his wide nose curving downward to meet a set of leathery black lips. His eyes were black as night and set wide across his ferocious face. Two bone-white horns twisted away from his temples and encircled the sides of his head. He was a near-complete beast—few parts of his body even resembled the shape of a man, besides his torso and abnormally large hands. His chest was broad and his legs tapered off into thick haunches with two very solid-looking hooves digging into the dirt. He looked exactly like the massive and powerful oxen that roamed through the Northern Sky Mountains but, unlike them, he stood on two legs and spoke to Avlon like a human.

Freyah had to repress the urge to scamper to the other side of the wagon and hide. The ox-demon reminded her of Jago, given how animal-like his features were, but this demon was much more frightening to behold.

She tried to calm herself. Avlon and his soldiers obviously felt confident enough to stand toe-to-toe with the leader of a Wild Demon clan. Otherwise they'd have been hauling ass through the forest by now. She thought back to the small knife Avlon had reached for in his belt and cringed. What was a flimsy weapon like that going to do against a monster?

The ox-demon sneered and stood his ground. He was smugly set on his ridiculous semantics, probably assuming that Lieutenant Avlon and his men would back down. But what little she'd come to know about the lieutenant made Freyah think that wasn't going to happen.

Avlon remained as sure-footed as the threat before him, and

Freyah held her breath as she saw him once again twist his fingers around the handle of the small blade.

Again scanning their surroundings, she caught sight of Roman and Nico flanking Avlon. They were closer than she'd realized, and the two of them already had their weapons drawn—Nico with a thick wooden bow notched and aimed, and Roman holding a set of sharp-looking throwing knives. None of the other men looked to be armed, but did they really need weapons with such a powerful beast leading them?

Freyah glanced up to the canopy of trees and spotted the tiniest glint of sunlight leaking through the leaves.

Then something else drew her attention.

Movement.

It was subtle, but the tree limbs had shifted, even though the wind wasn't strong enough to cause it.

"Give us five minutes," Avlon suggested casually. "Then we'll be on our way." He flexed his fingers, curling and uncurling them beside the knife at his belt. It was the first sign of his unease.

The ox-demon smiled deviously, taking another strategic step toward Lieutenant Avlon, and Freyah caught the glint of an axe peeking over the demon's right shoulder. "Better yet, why don't we escort you?" he suggested. "If only to make sure you don't lose your way."

Freyah could tell by the way the demon's chin lifted and he casually rocked back on his heels that the gesture had not been made in good faith. He was boxing them into a corner and waiting to strike, like a game of cat and mouse. Predator and prey.

"Why the hostility, Thax?" Avlon asked, still trying to take control of the situation. "I thought you had agreed to a truce."

At this, the ox-demon's face turned from amused to stone cold. "That was before your queen sent those abominations into our woods."

Freyah had no clue what *abominations* the demon was referring to, and by the subtle shift of Avlon's head as he glanced at Nico to his left, it seemed neither did they.

Something about that mention, however, must have been enough to clue in the lieutenant that they weren't walking away, because it was then that Avlon finally seized the moment and yanked the knife from his belt.

In one quick swipe, Avlon sliced the blade across the ox-demon's throat just as he'd grabbed the axe. The movement was so quick, it took several seconds before blood began pouring from the opening.

The demon tried to speak, but only unintelligible gargles escaped his lips. Blood bubbled and oozed down his throat and seeped into the fur that matted his skin.

Freyah had missed it, but at the same time Avlon made his move, Nico had chosen to strike. Three men lay sprawled on the ground with small blades protruding from each of their necks. Their lanterns had smashed to the ground, but one remained alight, rolling across the soil to illuminate a face.

Another demon.

They were all demons. Some more animal-like than others, but all now dead.

Freyah saw more bodies a few yards away, having fallen from the trees above. Each struck with perfect shots to the heart or temple.

The ox-demon fell to his knees in front of Lieutenant Avlon. He dropped his axe and clawed frantically at his throat to stop the onslaught of blood pouring from his wound, but there would be no stopping it. The slice had been precise and deep. He would bleed out in seconds, but not before the lieutenant leaned down to whisper something into the ox-demon's ear.

Avlon claimed the axe for himself and, with a soft prod from his boot, pushed the demon onto his back to die.

There was no time for Freyah to take in the extent of what had happened before her three captors began scrambling, collecting weapons and spent arrows. She saw Nico make a run for the front of the wagon, and then heard the startled neighing of the horses. The wagon rocked as Roman climbed into the front compartment, then the doors opened.

Lieutenant Avlon slipped inside as swiftly as a bird. Before Freyah could get a better look at the carnage outside, he closed the doors, and they were both sealed away in familiar darkness.

He scampered past her to bang a bloodied fist on the front wall of the wagon, and immediately, it lurched forward. They were moving fast—faster than they probably should have been given the uneven terrain—but she didn't understand why they were in such a hurry. The demons were dead.

"What's happening?" she demanded, bracing herself between two crates in order to remain upright.

Avlon didn't dance around the question. "We need to get out of the forest before the others send scouts. If they find those bodies, we'll have an entire clan raining down on us before we get a strong enough head start."

The tension in his tone told Freyah it was a serious threat. There was no room for playful banter when their lives were potentially at risk.

"That demon. He looked like a…"

"Like a what?" Avlon snapped. His posture was rigid, still on high alert from what he'd just done.

Freyah wanted to say the demon had looked like a monster, but *animal* was perhaps putting it more politely. Either way, she got the feeling no matter which word she chose, it was going to piss off the lieutenant, so she pressed on with a different question. "Why did you kill him?"

"Did it look like I had another choice?"

He was right, of course. Even Freyah had been able to ascertain that the demon's offer to escort them through the rest of the forest had merely been a ruse. If they'd chosen to go along, she had no doubt it would have been Avlon's throat leaking all that crimson.

"I don't understand," Freyah pressed. "You mentioned safe passage."

"Apparently those terms have changed." He was cleaning the blade of his knife, wiping it along the thigh of his trousers. It was indeed the same switchblade he'd used before. When it was to his satisfaction, he flipped it closed, concealing the blade, and tucked it back into his belt. "That was my carving knife," he muttered crossly under his breath.

The muffled shout of one of the soldiers up front reached them. "Keep your eyes on the trees!"

"What's in the trees?" she dared to ask.

Avlon gave her a pitying glance. "That's where they hide," he explained. "They hunt, sleep, and live up there. Their houses are built into the trees."

She remembered the two demons falling from the branches above. "They live in *tree houses?*"

"Not as fun as you might think." He glared at her, watching Freyah's imagination run away from her. "It's not a fairytale. They do what they have to in order to survive."

Was she mistaken, or was the lieutenant sympathizing with the Wild Demons?

Instead of confronting it, she pointedly decided to ignore it. "How much farther until we're out of the forest?"

Avlon went to run a hand over his face but stopped when he noticed the still-drying blood. "We were halfway when we stopped, but the delay means we won't make it to the castle before nightfall."

Freyah nodded in understanding. Knowing they were more than halfway through the final leg of their journey was a comfort.

But then a more pressing reality crept in.

In a few hours, Freyah would be handed over to the queen.

Her chest tightened in anticipation. Her time with Lieutenant Avlon was coming to an end, and, to her surprise, she found herself a bit disappointed.

6

FREYAH

The rest of the ride was uncomfortable at best. They kept a steady pace for several hours before Lieutenant Avlon finally declared it safe enough to slow. After a long day of uneven terrain, the ground beneath the supply wagon eventually leveled, and Freyah knew that could only mean one thing: they were close. Only the queen's roads were maintained enough to allow for such a smooth ride.

Her nerves created waves of nausea in her stomach. It was finally time to face her punishment, but she had no idea what that punishment would be.

Disrespecting one of the queen's soldiers was an extreme offense, but still, she hadn't expected to have to serve time at the castle for it. Perhaps she'd work as a handmaid, or maybe scrub filth from the stone floors with a horsehair brush. After a week or two of servitude, when the queen was satisfied that Freyah had been rehabilitated, she would be allowed to return home.

It would be fine.

For the first time since her kidnapping, Freyah thought of her father. She feared his disappointment and wondered what he would do at home without her. Surely Mrs. Amone would make sure he was taken care of.

She then thought of Corianne. What would her best friend think of all this? Freyah knew Corianne would never judge her, but she would no doubt be concerned.

After finally reaching the outskirts of the Saldanni Forest, they stopped abruptly, and Freyah waited anxiously as one of the men exited the front cabin and began unloading their cache. She listened carefully, attempting to gauge the moment when they were ready to unload her, but when they seemed to be finished, the wagon shifted forward and began moving again.

It traveled a hundred or so yards before stopping again. She waited, preparing herself for the sound of footsteps, but there was nothing except the stifling press of silence against her ears.

Then, she heard the sound of the door hatch opening and was suddenly overwhelmed with the noise of the outside world, from the buzzing of insects to the rhythmic tweeting of birds. She realized that because she'd grown so used to the sounds of Last Cove—crashing waves against rock and the clanging of hammered metal from her father's workshop—the new noises were overly loud and intrusive. There was an unearthly stillness that lingered around her, a quiet she'd never experienced before.

She instinctively flinched as someone stepped up into the back of the supply wagon and pulled her to her feet, but when she realized it was Avlon's hulking form beside her, she relaxed. He helped her down, and she caught the subtle scent of tea tree oil clinging to his skin.

She followed that heady scent without hesitation.

Though she was scared of what awaited her inside the castle, Avlon had protected her, and her skin tingled where his rough hands touched her. It was soothing, and despite her better judgment, she trusted it.

Avlon escorted her down a sloping dirt path under the light of the moon, dust kicking up from their feet with each step. At the end of the path they stopped, waiting for a door to open, then resumed walking. She saw the soft, muted glow of lanterns ahead of her, similar to the tunnels in Mount Mirela, and the realization made her heart ache for home.

The further along they traveled, murmuring voices began to reach her ears, as did the screech of iron sliding across the floor. They passed through a sea of men jeering and yanking against bars of a cage, and it occurred to her that she was being escorted through the dungeon.

Lieutenant Avlon was going to toss her into a cage.

But when they turned the last corner, Freyah found herself in a small room with a door instead.

She blinked rapidly, trying to focus her eyes enough to make out the details of her surroundings more clearly. She spun on her heel, but before making a complete rotation, the door was shut, and she was alone.

OVER THE NEXT FEW HOURS, Freyah tried to keep herself occupied by pacing the length of the room. It was small—perhaps only twelve square feet—so when that failed, she took to making laps around the perimeter until she made herself dizzy.

She counted the stones in the walls that surrounded her and tried carving words into them with the edge of her nails, but it wasn't easy, and she only made her fingers bleed.

Was this her punishment? Spending hours in solitude instead of working off her infraction? She had no idea there were so many prisoners being kept in the queen's dungeons. She wondered what the others were being held for.

And why was she the only one without bars to see through?

To her dismay, that particular question was answered far too soon.

Right before Freyah reached the point of complete boredom, Roman visited her cell, and Freyah knew exactly why he'd come.

The door slammed behind him as he prowled into the small room. Swallowing hard, she was forced to back herself into a corner. She was stuck in a cage with a rabid animal that was fixated on its prey. He'd been denied his first meal, and he wasn't going to let it get away a second time.

"Finally," he said, voice hungry with lust. "I get you all to myself."

Freyah had never felt this helpless before. For most of her life, she'd prided herself on having a strong support system. People helped her when she needed it. She knew the basics of how to defend herself, and she had never backed down from a fight when she had her wit and a plethora of outlandish pride to shield herself against any argument. Those traits had helped her squeeze out of many uncomfortable situations, but they weren't going to help her now. In her panicked mind, there was nothing she could do.

The lieutenant wasn't here to save her this time.

She was completely alone.

Roman stalked toward her, the heavy stench of sweat and cigar smoke wafting from his clothes and his breath. Her heart pounded as she anticipated what was to come, and she hoped desperately that she could force her mind to go somewhere else. It would be the only way she'd survive it.

She fixated heavily on the tearing fabric as Roman ripped her shirt, as if the extra step of removing it was too trivial to him, too bothersome to be concerned with. It had merely been in the way of what he truly wanted.

It was a nice shirt—one of her favorites, due to the color resembling the shade of the blue lilies that grew along the mountain. She stared at the buttons that fell to the ground as Roman grabbed her by the waist and spun her to face the wall.

He pressed her body flat against the stone, and her cheek scraped against the rough surface. Here, there was nothing to focus on but the jagged rock and her now blurring vision. But she did not cry—Freyah would not give the man the satisfaction of seeing her fear—but it took everything in her to hold back the tears.

She clenched her jaw and braced for what would come next as he yanked at the waistband of her trousers, but she was startled by the sound of the door opening again.

Was someone else coming to join the assault? Or would they just stand by and watch as he stripped her clothes and her soul from her body?

Roman let out a low growl under his breath while working to undo his belt and addressed the new company with agitation. "You'll get your turn when I'm finished."

Freyah didn't know how much she could take. But the man didn't get the chance to touch her again. Instead, he was suddenly hauled off of her by the other person in the room.

She heard the sound of fist against flesh, and then her attacker was on the floor beside her. Freyah whipped around to find Lieutenant Avlon bent over, pummeling punch after punch into Roman's now bloodied face. She let out a shriek of surprise and horror, but it didn't mask the sound of raw physical violence playing out in front of her.

Avlon raised Roman up by the straps of his suspenders and slammed his skull into the stone wall. Roman fell like a rag doll and was out like a light.

Freyah sank into a crouch, scooting as far away from the now unconscious body as she could. She stared up at Avlon's raging expression and cowered, afraid of what he'd do next. But when he turned to face her, his fists unclenched at his sides, and his expression softened.

"Are you alright?"

As Freyah worked to pull her trousers back into place, Avlon proceeded to drag a severely beaten Roman out into the hall and prop him casually against the stone wall. He returned quickly and closed the door, but instead of coming to her, Avlon chose to sit. He inhaled a deep, calming breath and examined his knuckles, blood already crusting, the wounds already scabbing.

Freyah breathed heavily, unsure whether or not the threat had truly passed. She knew the lieutenant wouldn't touch her, but the way his face had hardened with rage…it had scared her.

She was uneasy being in the small space with him, completely unlike their time spent in the back of the supply wagon. She'd trusted him enough to fall asleep in his presence, but now? She was afraid to take her eyes off of him.

To his credit, he did appear calmer. The stress in his shoulders had relaxed, and his face was no longer contorted with explosive fury. She'd witnessed twice now that he was capable of violence, but only when the situation called for it.

He hid it well, given his casual demeanor, exactly like he hid the switchblade tucked away in his belt sheath. At a moment's notice, he could deploy his wrath like the flick of his blade, then disengage and fold it away for later use. The control was incredibly impressive, and Freyah was envious of his discipline.

They sat in silence for several minutes, not meeting each other's eyes but still keeping the other within their sights. Freyah shook silently from nerves and the adrenaline leaving her blood stream.

Then, as if this were any other day, Avlon pulled out his little wooden statue and began to carve. He whistled to himself as he worked, and it felt odd compared to his typical quiet nature while in her company.

Freyah wondered if the other men assumed he was having his way with her.

Avlon stopped what he was doing and met her gaze. She froze in place, thinking he might have read her mind somehow. Was this the moment when he would finally change his mind?

Maybe he'd had enough of playing nice, and he was bored.

Now he would finally do what he was supposed to.

"My name is Whit," he said, holding her stare with a determination that somehow made her calm rather than uncomfortable. "What should I call you?"

Despite how rough he was around the edges, Freyah didn't think him to be much older than her—in his late-twenties at most—but finally putting a name to his face...it made him younger somehow. More accessible.

Whit.

She rolled the name around in her head, testing the weight of it. She wondered what it was short for. Whittaker, probably.

Whittaker Avlon. What an interesting and unexpected man he was.

She cleared her throat and pulled her knees close to her chest. "Freyah," she told him quietly.

Whit's lips curved upward—he actually *smiled*—and he kept his focus on her. "Freyah," he repeated. "That's beautiful."

This was all so strange. The man in front of her was a new, wholly different person from the grumpy, standoffish lieutenant that had kidnapped her from her home. He was the man that had saved her from being assaulted twice. He was kind, and his rough features were beginning to look welcoming and intriguing rather than intimidating.

He wasn't conventionally handsome, at least not in the customary standard of beauty, but the harshness of his features drew Freyah in— his long nose and sharp jaw, and the scruff around his chin that bled down to his neck.

Before, she'd had no interest in getting to know Lieutenant Avlon, but now, sitting in the damp and dreary quiet of her cell, she found herself wanting to learn more about Whit—the man, not the soldier.

She opened her mouth, but he was already speaking.

"She took my sister," he said. Docile. Expressionless.

Freyah didn't respond—she didn't know if she should—but she bowed her head to show that she'd heard him. The "she" he referred to was Madam Lema: the queen that controlled everything.

The witch whose castle Freyah now resided in.

"She doesn't know you're here," Whit said. "I haven't reported to her yet. That's why Roman tried what he did." He sighed deeply, as if the words physically pained him. "Once she knows you're here, they won't be able to touch you."

Freyah hadn't thought about it before, but it had been Whit's decision to bring her to the castle. The queen didn't yet know that a crime had been committed, and if it were up to the other soldiers, it would stay that way. They wanted to keep Freyah a secret—to use as their personal plaything.

But the man sitting in front of her was not like the others.

Was Whit regretting his decision to bring her to the castle? If so, it was possible he could let her go and pretend none of this had ever happened.

Freyah picked at the calluses on her hands, formed by years of scavenging the mountain back home, and Whit shifted to place his carving knife on the stone floor. He seemed eager now, an emotion that made him appear softer.

As if he'd read her earlier thoughts, he said, "I can't let you go. Too many others know about you, so I have to tell her." He paused. "I have no way of knowing what she'll make you do—you could cook or clean, or be a handmaid, if she chooses that for you—but I would keep you safe."

The *if* of that sentence hung in the air like the stale smell of mold in the room, and Freyah mulled over it silently for several minutes. She'd broken the law; she had to serve her punishment. It was why she'd been dragged here in the first place.

So she agreed. "Alright."

Whit abruptly stood and made for the door. After a moment of hesitation, he turned back, taking two broad steps across the room to stand directly in front of her where she crouched in the corner.

He bent and placed his wooden carving on the floor beside her, before retreating back to the door and leaving.

Freyah examined the small statue for several seconds before deciding to pick it up. It was a bird, perched on a rock as if it were preparing to take flight. She'd never seen anything made with such detail before, like the tiny markings in the wood that represented its feathers, and the defined cut of the bird's beak opened wide in a silent cry.

She thought it was beautiful. So she tucked it away in her pocket as a gesture of good faith and waited for her unlikely ally to return.

7

WHIT

When Whit Avlon first set eyes on the girl, he'd considered her an inconvenience.

He'd been assigned to Last Cove to collect a shipment that had been delayed due to weather damaging their pier. The usual men from the village that delivered supplies to the queen had needed to stay and help repair the damage, so Whit and two Strike Team soldiers were forced to travel the long route across the country and retrieve the supplies themselves.

Whit was not a member of the tactical team. He was a guard, and had volunteered to go in Lieutenant Bernard Selmy's place. He'd wondered why it was necessary to send three tactical soldiers to retrieve a few crates of salted fish, but the curious thought didn't truly matter to him when all he'd wanted was an excuse to get out of the castle.

As a lieutenant of the Lower Guard, Whit rarely spent time above ground. His team guarded the dungeons, along with the south side of Castle Larapuna, and though he could delegate guard duty to those beneath him, he rarely found an opportunity to leave the keep. Whit greatly appreciated his new higher ranking, but the lack of stimulation was starting to get to him.

After leaving for the trek to Last Cove, however, he discovered that the two men assigned to go with him, Roman and Nico, weren't the best company. They were known for their obnoxious and fuck-all reputations, and the week's trip into the mountains had been long and way more stimulating than what Whit had signed up for. He was pretty sure there hadn't been a single moment of silence amongst the two men throughout the entire trip, and Whit's brain had begun the process of turning into sludge from listening to their constant mindless chatter.

So, naturally, by the time they'd made it to Last Cove to collect their bounty, Whit wasn't in the best of moods.

He could admit, he'd been short with the vendor about not having the correct amount of fish that was previously promised. But the girl...

She'd inserted herself into the matter like it was entirely her business, and it had rubbed him the wrong way. At the time, Whit was tired and annoyed and ready to leave behind the humid salt air that clung to his skin. Not to mention he was the slightest bit tipsy— Roman and Nico had insisted on grabbing a drink at The Ferry Stop after loading up supplies, but of course, one drink had turned into many.

But alcohol wasn't enough to excuse why he'd acted like such an idiot in front of the girl. Maybe there was a part of him that felt like he needed to impress the other soldiers somehow—despite the need to exert his authority over them, he still wanted to be liked—but he could acknowledge now that his actions had been disrespectful. The way she'd looked at him, like he was the most disgusting thing she'd ever set eyes on—that above all was what truly set him off.

So he'd decided to turn the inconvenience into something amusing, and at first, her misplaced anger seemed to be doing a good job at entertaining him, but she'd made him look stupid, and Whit did not like looking stupid. Especially in front of two subordinate soldiers.

But then he'd realized who she was.

Now that girl—Freyah—was curled into the corner of a stone block room, feet tucked beneath her to protect from whatever predator walked through the door next. She reminded him of an injured little bird, wings stowed away for later use. For when she was ready to fly.

She reminded him of Wendi.

Whit immediately pitied her. But there was a part of him that couldn't stand the sight of her. She looked too innocent to belong in this awful place.

The soldiers at Castle Larapuna had all but lost their sense of humanity. They no longer knew what it meant to love or be cared for. They claimed what wasn't theirs and spoke in vulgar tongues that only provoked a rise in one another for the sake of petty entertainment. And Whit had learned to play along.

Now he was officially one of them, and he hated being lumped into the same category as the man that had just tried to rape an innocent girl. She thought she was being punished for talking back to a royal guard, but there was so much that she didn't understand. So much that Whit was now wishing he could take back.

Not once had Whit considered laying a hand on her, though he should have expected that Roman would at least try. It wasn't as if the queen had never offered such things—she'd made it perfectly clear that common whores were available to them at a moment's notice— but this was different. To a soldier like Roman, the effort of hiding it and knowing that it was wrong was more exciting. He'd taken it upon himself to try and keep Freyah a secret, and Whit despised the man's lack of morality, but Roman had learned it from his queen.

Whit hadn't understood the depth of Madam Lema's cruelty until it was too late. He, along with his two younger sisters, Willow and Wendi, had left The Mounds with little food in their bellies and heavy packs on their backs. They never had much to begin with, so finding refuge in a magnificent castle had been very much like a fairytale.

It wasn't.

Whit and his sisters had been teenagers when they'd left the desert, knowing absolutely nothing about the world or how it worked, and they'd sought out Larapuna in the hopes that Whit would be recruited to the queen's army. It was the only option left that could support the three of them, and if they were lucky, the girls would find meaningful work as well.

They'd lost their mother to a terrible disease when they were very young—old enough to have experienced and formed critical memories, but still young enough to have missed out on so much more—so the three siblings had been raised by their maternal grandmother, Malka. Their father had been absent since leaving on a delivery trip, never to return, and the question of what happened to him, and why he'd never come home always lingered between the siblings.

When Whit was seventeen, Malka passed away, and it had been one of the hardest times of his life. But he'd had to stay strong for his sisters. That meant leaving The Mounds and searching for lucrative work.

The girls had refused at first, not wanting to leave the only home they'd ever known, but Whit had sworn to Malka that he would give Willow and Wendi a better life.

Upon arrival at Larapuna, the three siblings were taken behind the walls by several large guards seconds after stepping onto the fifty-foot perimeter, and despite protests from each of them, they were separated.

Whit still didn't know where the girls were taken that first day at the castle, because Willow still refused to talk about it. But that day was the first time Whit had set eyes on a witch in the flesh.

The next night, Whit had been allowed to stay with his sisters in a room with no windows. He trained to take his place among the soldiers, and the girls cried in his arms each night in fear that they'd made a mistake, but he reassured them they were safe. They were better off within Madam Lema's fortress than on the outside with no food, no shelter, and no way to protect themselves.

After a few weeks, Whit was chosen as a squire to Captain Filip Greve, and he spent his days serving the captain's meals and cleaning his leathers. Everything seemed to be working out, until Madam Lema claimed Wendi.

Whit's youngest sister was incredibly pretty and had caught the attention of many soldiers. The queen noticed this and forced Wendi to serve as a consort.

When Willow came back to their room that night with a black eye and soiled pants, Whit saw nothing but red.

After that, the girls planned an escape. And the three of them tried.

If there was one thing Whit would always be sure about, it was that they really and truly tried to get away.

But they failed.

Their plan had gone horribly wrong, and Wendi was claimed by the Wild Demons in the forest because of it. He and Willow lost their baby sister, a loss so crushing that they went back to the castle willingly.

After that, they kept their heads down. Willow complied with all of Madam Lema's future requests of her, even the terrible ones, and Whit sat back quietly, allowing it to happen.

He'd wanted so badly to fight for her, to try again, but he'd been too afraid to fail. So instead, he and Willow fell into the rhythm of their new life without protest.

Six years later, Whit was now a lieutenant over his own squad of guards, and Willow had been reassigned as a ward in the laundry room. He'd become somewhat tolerant of the new life they'd been forced into, but seeing the girl was a trigger.

Freyah.

She reminded him too much of why he'd decided to keep his head down in the first place.

At first, when he found the other soldiers laughing and congregating in one of the underground corridors, he thought nothing of it. He tried to avoid them and go about his business, but they pulled him in, telling him he wouldn't believe the prize Roman had brought back unless Whit saw it for himself.

They didn't realize Whit had been on that same trip.

They were planning to keep Freyah to themselves instead of handing her over to the queen.

What fools.

Whit had known what he was getting into when he opened that door to her cell, but he hadn't expected her to look so... well... he didn't know exactly.

The girl that had journeyed with him to Larapuna had been kind of scrappy and asked questions. But this version of her was broken.

She'd actually flinched when he closed the door. The sounds of the other men jeering and whistling crudely in the background were muffled, and after a few seconds, they faded away entirely. They'd walked away, giving him time to enjoy his turn with her. They thought he'd beaten his comrade to be selfish, claiming the prize for himself. Little did they know, he was protecting her from their games.

Whit didn't know what he was going to do to keep himself occupied, but he knew he couldn't touch her. Not only because it was wrong, or even because he still had a commitment to anyone else. No. He simply didn't want to.

She might have been momentarily damaged and beaten down, but a tiny light still glimmered in her spirit, and he was afraid that if his corrupted hands placed one finger on her, he would tarnish that glow forever.

For all he knew, this was the last straw for her in what must have been a very long, very degrading experience. He wouldn't be the reason she gave up. It wasn't in his nature to be so cruel.

He hadn't wanted to bring her here—hadn't wanted to arrest her for something so stupid—but he'd let Nico and Roman snatch her under the cover of night. He'd had no choice. He had to follow orders.

As he continued to hover for longer than necessary in the small cell, something told him not to leave her alone, so he decided to sit.

He picked a perfectly acceptable patch of floor on the far side of the room and pulled out a small wooden carving, along with the pocket knife that had once been his father's, according to Malka.

Whit had barely known his father, and what little memories he had were warped from the perspective of a four-year-old. The things he knew for certain were from stories passed on through his gran while she sat in her favorite chair, trying to fight off a new wave of aches and pains.

She'd had the same genetic disease as his mother, and Whit knew he had it, too. So far, the stiffness had only manifested in his hands, but he knew it would eventually spread. The disease had progressed a lot quicker in his mother, and only fate could tell if Whit would follow Malka's slow, debilitating path, or die swiftly like his mother.

He'd picked up the habit of carving small statues when he was a boy as a way to make toys for his sisters. As he got older, the task had proven practical in keeping his fingers limber. He'd brought a few of the carvings with him on the journey to Larapuna as a reminder of Malka, but he'd been forced to trade one of his better figures to a fishmonger he never ought to have trusted. The man had sweet-talked them into giving up their nicest woven blanket in exchange for a single day's rations. Whit had offered the carving along with it to ensure there was enough for all three of them. After that, he'd lost the motivation to create, and making something so insignificant felt pointless.

He'd been momentarily inspired to start carving again after losing Wendi, but with his new position as a lieutenant, he hadn't had the time to dedicate to the hobby. He'd started a new one on the road to Last Cove, and it was nearly finished. Somehow, it felt like the most personal of all his creations.

Freyah kept her eye on him from across the room, watching him carefully, but she remained quiet. If doing this gave her only an hour of peace, then that's what he was going to do.

So Whit began to carve.

He sat with her in silence, nothing besides the subtle scratching of wood filling the space between them, and eventually she made eye contact.

Whit didn't like that his thoughts were being crowded by this girl. She was getting in the way of his focus. He couldn't pretend that everything was fine with him and his sister when he realized how untrue that was for Freyah.

He'd promised Willow that they would keep their heads down and not draw attention to themselves. In order to put their colossal screwup behind them, they had to move forward and forget.

This was their life now, no matter how ugly it was.

But he couldn't stop thinking about Freyah.

Whit couldn't be sure how old she was, though he knew she'd been of age to work given that she'd been trading goods at The Hub back in Last Cove. He'd seen her pedaling valuable stones she must have found within the mountain. There were men whose job it was to collect such materials, for they were necessary for many of the spells and potions used by the witches in Larapuna, but those rare gems and metals were hard to find. It took skill—sometimes a lifetime's worth of it—and a massive amount of patience to find what one was looking for.

It meant the girl knew the mountain well. It meant she was smart and resourceful—traits he respected—but she was also beautiful. Her hair was as warm and bright as spun gold, and her eyes were a dazzling shade of hazel. Up close, they were the perfect mixture of brown and green, with a rim of amber around the edge.

But seeing her here in the dungeons took away that natural shine she'd emitted when standing up to him. Taking her out of an environment where she thrived had dulled her light to a point where she barely looked human. Her stubbornness and clever wit had been snuffed out. Now she was simply a frightened girl, stuck in a cage, unable to fly.

Whit wanted to free her. But at the same time, he wanted to keep her here in this tiny room, away from the horrors that awaited her from both the other soldiers and the queen. He'd yet to report that his group had arrived back at the castle, so Madam Lema didn't yet know Freyah was here.

Whit could go to the queen right now and tell her, fulfilling his duty. He was a guard, meant to seek out discipline for those that broke the law. But handing Freyah over meant putting her in the care of a witch he'd learned not to trust.

A witch he was now forced to obey.

He never should have brought her here.

Whit hadn't only been instructed to collect late supplies on his mission. There was something else. And that other thing—the thing that had been directly asked of him by Madam Lema herself—he was deeply, whole-heartedly regretting it now.

What was the worst that could happen? Madam Lema would more than likely assign Freyah to something demeaning, but would that be any worse than the punishment she was living now?

Whit couldn't be sure, but it seemed a waste not to try.

"WHY ARE you so concerned with this girl?" Willow asked. "She broke the law—end of story. You did your job, now move on."

Whit knew his sister would be upset, but it didn't feel right to not at least run his thoughts past her first. She'd come to collect his dirty uniform from that week and was stuffing it all into a woven basket to take to the washroom. She enjoyed her time there, knowing it was a simple job after what she'd previously endured, and Whit enjoyed the way she smelled after spending a long day amongst the suds. Fresh, with the tiniest hint of lemon. No longer like the men who had touched her.

The way she was forcing his tunic and breeches into the basket made her anger that much more apparent, so he tried to reason with her.

"I know it's none of my business— "

"That's right," she cut him off. "It's not. You shouldn't be getting involved."

"This is different," he said. "I don't want her to suffer what you and the other girls did. I want to give her a chance."

Willow turned on the spot and her eyes bore into him. They were dark and out for blood. "As if you know," she spat. She dropped the basket purposefully, and one of Whit's shirts fell out onto the floor. "*I've* suffered plenty. And everyone gets their fair share."

"Willow, how can you say that?"

He reached for her, but she recoiled. "Don't touch me."

The instinct had slipped out of him, for it had been so long since she'd allowed another's embrace, and sometimes he forgot.

"I'm sorry," he apologized. "Low, I'm sorry."

She absentmindedly fumbled with the ring on her left index finger, a simple gilded band. Just like his switchblade, it was gifted to her by Malka not long before she died—a token of their mother.

"Are you doing this for her, or for your conscience?" she asked him.

Whit shrugged honestly. "I don't know. It just feels like the right thing to do."

To his surprise, Willow let out a long, low sigh. She placed a hand gently to his face and gave her brother a defeated smile. "You did what you had to do," she said.

She quickly retracted her hand, but Whit didn't mind. That small touch was enough. He missed his sister. He missed spending time with her, laughing and sharing stories, and he even missed being there for her when she'd cried.

But he was thankful for the fragmented encounters they did share, despite how scarce they'd become. Because no matter what, it was something to hold on to. And sometimes, on days like today, it was everything.

Madam Lema wasn't angry that some of her soldiers had attempted to keep something from her. Surprisingly, she was very calm.

It was like watching a lion walk past an easy prey without a second thought. It wasn't natural, and it set Whit's teeth on edge waiting for the second she'd suddenly turn on everyone and bite.

The queen silently sat upon her throne of ivory, the sight of it lurching Whit's stomach. Madam Lema's slender fingers created a steeple that rested against her tapered chin, and her jet black hair framed her slender face in just the right way so it accented the stony set of her emerald eyes.

She thought to herself for several agonizing minutes while Whit and her personal guards stood on edge around her.

Waiting.

Then the queen got to her feet, causing all four of her guards to straighten their posture at once. She stepped down from her dais and walked stoically across the throne room, her guards at her tail. Left with little to no choice, Whit followed the procession close behind.

The witch-queen went to retrieve Freyah without a word.

Roman and Nico clung to the wall as she passed, shrinking into themselves with fear and extreme regret, but Madam Lema still said nothing. After entering the small cell, she took the girl by the hand and escorted her out of the dungeons without so much as a glance to any of her soldiers.

Except for Whit.

He was waiting at the end of the corridor, as he'd been previously instructed to do in times like this, and when Madam Lema approached, she handed Freyah off to him.

"Take her to my chambers," she instructed him calmly, no hint of inflection in her voice. "I'll be there shortly."

"But Madam." It was Roman who'd spoken up, his face still swollen and bruised from Whit's beating. "You said…"

The queen was on him in an instant, gripping his face tightly in her right hand, sharp talons pinching his bruising, purple skin. She did not look away from him as she repeated her order to Whit. "Take the girl to my chambers."

Whit did as he was told. He didn't look back over his shoulder to witness what he thought would likely happen next, but Freyah did, and the look on her face was enough confirmation for him.

Right before rounding the corner, Whit saw the vines that grew up between the cracks in the floor begin to quiver. He knew what they'd be used for, and he had no intention of sticking around to witness it.

8

FREYAH

reyah stood completely still as she waited patiently in the queen's chambers, not wanting to disturb the space around her with movement or even the sound of her own breathing. She had no idea what to expect now that Madam Lema was aware of her presence in the castle, but some small part of her thought that if she simply stood there, without moving, it would make things easier.

She didn't have to wait long, for not five minutes later, the queen burst through the doors, joined by another witch with short silver curls poking out in every direction; she was beautiful, her mahogany skin dewy and flawless.

The queen was like a corporeal shadow that dominated the space. Her hair was black as night, skin pale. And around her neck rested a silver necklace encrusted with shiny black jewels. Her eyes were an intense emerald green, more vivid than the average human, and her angular face was cut sharp with high cheekbones and lips painted a deep rust color.

She was perfect—so beautiful she was almost too much to look at.

Freyah kept her head down, trying not to stare, but the queen stepped closer and took Freyah's chin in the tips of her thin fingers.

"My men might have been foolish," she said, "but they were onto something."

The other witch sneered and let out a *humph*.

"You don't agree, Evanora?" Madam Lema questioned. "Is she not a stunning specimen?" She turned Freyah's face from side to side, examining her profile. "She could almost pass as one of us," she said, narrowing her eyes, then reiterated, "...almost."

Freyah focused straight ahead, keeping a blurry outline of the witch's face in her peripheral vision. She didn't want to look at her. Locking in on those brilliant green eyes made Freyah sick to her stomach.

Then Madam Lema released Freyah's face from her grip. She floated to the other side of the room on silent footsteps, where an oversized crimson armchair—the color of blood—sat in front of an open circular window.

She sat down gracefully while Evanora poured wine into a crystal goblet. "I imagine you're wondering what comes next?" Madam Lema presumed, but Freyah remained still. "Thanks to one of my soldier's better judgment, your situation has been rectified, but that doesn't undo the damage that's been done. I apologize for the turmoil you might have faced on Roman's behalf. He's been dealt with."

Freyah swallowed the lump forming in her throat. She'd seen the fear on Roman's face after the queen had led her from the dungeons. He'd known what was coming, and it seemed that Whit had, too. Freyah had barely managed to catch a glimpse of vines twisting up from the cracks in the stone floor before Whit ushered her up the stairs.

Madam Lema accepted the glass of wine from Evanora. "Since you're here," she began, "why don't we take advantage of our little situation?" To the other witch, she said, "What do you think?"

Evanora looked directly at Freyah. "I think that's an excellent idea."

They both waited in heavy silence for Freyah to say something, but she was confused. She'd committed a crime. Wasn't she supposed to atone for that?

"How will I be serving my punishment?" she asked hoarsely, then cleared her throat, hastily adding, "Your Grace."

At first, it was unclear whether or not the queen understood the question, but the moment passed, and her expression quickly morphed into that of intrigue. "Ah, yes. Lieutenant Avlon told me of your infraction. But I don't see any reason to lock you up and throw away the key. Especially after your...ordeal." Madam Lema watched carefully, her eyes scanning from Freyah's dusty boots to the tangled mess of hair falling from the braid over her shoulder. "I'm sure you didn't intend offense by calling the lieutenant out on his behavior. I'll place you with the laundry."

Freyah let out the breath she'd been holding. Laundry work would be easy. For a moment, Freyah had feared the queen was considering something much harsher, but she was relieved by the choice that had ultimately been made. Her time in the castle would hopefully pass swiftly and with ease.

But why was the queen letting her off so easily?

"This will be a beneficial arrangement for all of us," Madam Lema suggested.

Evanora cocked her head, reminiscent of a bird.

"I've been aware of the unrest amongst my people for a while now, but I've yet to take the time to sit down with any of them and hear what they have to say." She was pandering in a very specific direction, and before the next words were out of her mouth, Freyah knew exactly where the conversation was headed. "Perhaps you could provide some insight—help me to better understand the situation. Though my Spyders report to me regularly, it's not enough to know how the citizens of Ghoma truly feel. I hear their concerns, but I need someone that has lived among them to help me come up with a strategy. A compromise of sorts, to make sure the humans feel like their voices are being heard."

Despite the queen's courteous tone, Freyah could tell it was not a request, but a demand. She knew next to nothing about how to aid the queen with her predicament—she'd only just learned how far the rebellion was spreading, so what information could she possibly provide?

Freyah had only seen small acts of insurrection, but that didn't mean she knew how to stop it. And why would she want to, if it was the witch in front of her that had caused the unrest in the first place?

Despite that, there was only one right answer, so reluctantly, Freyah agreed.

"Of course," she said, forcing a lightness into her tone. She felt for the lump in her pocket that was Whit's wooden figure and held it tight —a lifeline in a moment of uncertainty. "I'll do what I can. Your kindness is greatly appreciated."

Madam Lema smiled broadly. "Perfect."

The first thing Madam Lema did after their conversation was give Freyah new clothes. The queen allowed her to bathe and wash her hair, then she showed her to a room within a high tower that was bigger and brighter than the holding cell she'd been in before. It had an actual bed, and there were bookshelves to display things, even though Freyah had practically nothing to fill them with.

Still, she placed the little wooden carving from Whit on the top shelf.

There was a bedside table with candles and a wash basin, and a loft space right above the bed with a ladder that fell next to the foot of the mattress. Though the width of the room was cramped and small, the ceiling looked high enough that she'd be able to stand upright in the loft. Freyah imagined it would be a good place to read, for within that elevated space was the only window that filtered light into the room.

Madam Lema had given her a brief overview of Castle Larapuna, emphasizing that there was plenty of work for everyone, and that they all had to do their part. Freyah would start her work in the laundry room in two days, but for now, she would be given time to settle in.

She didn't want time. She'd had too much of it already, alone in that dungeon, so keeping to herself didn't sound very pleasing. Part of her wanted to explore because, despite her fear of being somewhere new and strange, Freyah couldn't help but feel enchanted by the idea of staying in a castle. This was exactly the sort of adventure she'd always craved but had been too scared to reach for. She wanted to explore the grounds and find the library.

But then she remembered why she was there.

She wouldn't have the freedom to do such things while serving her penance. Although, so far, nothing about Freyah's situation had resembled a punishment.

Madam Lema hadn't mentioned how long Freyah's sentence would be, and it wasn't clear when she'd be free to go, but she'd ensured her safety by assigning her a personal guard to escort her through the castle.

After Madam Lema had left her room, Freyah tested the door to see if it was locked.

It wasn't.

She peered out into the hall, expecting there to be a guard waiting outside to make sure she didn't leave, but it was empty.

It was possible that she could slip out right then unnoticed, and she wondered if it could really be that simple.

Ultimately, she decided it wasn't.

Nothing ever was.

DESPITE HAVING a warm bed for the first time since leaving home, Freyah didn't sleep any more or less soundly than she had in that rickety supply wagon. Her thoughts spiraled like a spinning top, around and around in her mind. She couldn't accept the notion that she was safe. The change in her surroundings didn't mean her circumstances shifted with it. Freyah was still far from home.

And she was still alone.

Freyah had no support system in the castle. Back in Last Cove, she could depend on the strength and familiarity of her friends and the ones she'd learned to call family. She'd counted on them to help her whenever she needed it, but there was no one in Larapuna to help her now.

Except…maybe Whit.

No. The fact that he'd already helped her multiple times didn't mean she could trust him to help her again. The forced proximity of being on the road had probably caused him to take pity on her. Now that he was back at the castle, his days would go back to normal, and he'd forget all about her.

She stared up at the high ceiling of her room, desperately wanting to write to her father and give him some sort of sign that she was okay. She was alive—that was all he needed to know. Word had no doubt reached him that his only daughter was serving time for her stupid decision, but she hadn't been properly arrested, and no one had seen the soldiers take her.

That wasn't entirely true. The lizard-demon, Jago, had been roaming the corridors that night right before she'd been taken.

Had he witnessed what happened and told someone?

Freyah couldn't count on Jago to care about the wellbeing of a human girl. She was on her own, and it was up to her to remain strong and endure whatever she had to in order to go home.

That would be her goal—her purpose for waking up every day.

Freyah would serve her time, and perhaps find adventure along the way.

9

WHIT

Madam Lema summoned Whit to the Grand Hall.

Dinner had ended several hours before, so the Hall was vacant save for the queen's right-hand soldier, General Ryker.

Ryker was a second generation wolf-demon with long, shining white-gray hair and matching gray eyes. His teeth were cut so sharp that Whit was fairly certain the man could tear him limb from limb without raising a weapon. He was broad and solid—much stronger than Whit—with a bulky upper body that was covered in gray fur. His nose and mouth tapered into a long snout, and it gave him an imposing demeanor that assured everyone in the room that he was the one to fear.

Being the only demon working for Madam Lema, there was an unspoken agreement that he was protected. Despite the oddity of his presence in the royal army, he didn't walk a tightrope, afraid to step out of line. There was a confidence in him that reflected his certainty of never being cast out. It was reflected clearly in the way Ryker held himself amongst the other soldiers. He had no shame in his pointed ears or his billowing tail.

Whit approached the general carefully. Ryker gave him a look of sympathy and shook his head. They both knew that no matter how selfless Whit's actions may have been, Madam Lema would manage to spin the situation to her benefit.

But Whit was prepared for it—he'd known that bringing Freyah to Madam Lema would mean relinquishing her to the queen's manipulations. But knowing she was at least safe from the other soldiers made the situation a bit easier to swallow.

"Sit down, Lieutenant," a sultry voice instructed.

It was Madam Lema. She'd come in through the door behind the head table, so Whit hadn't been prepared for her entrance. He recovered quickly, pulling out a chair from one of the long wooden tables closest to him and lowering himself into the seat.

"I know you must think highly of yourself because of what you did," Madam Lema began, taking tantalizing steps toward him. "But I need you to understand why you aren't coming out of this unscathed."

She placed a hand on Whit's shoulder, her pointed black nails digging into his flesh, and she smiled down at him with sugar-coated disdain.

Whit remained poised and swallowed.

"I sent your team on a very specific mission, and each of you disobeyed a direct order, in one way or another. The others were greedy, and naïve. You, on the other hand, were just imprudent."

Madam Lema inhaled a centering breath, then continued. "You understand how things work around here, probably better than most, so that's why I'm choosing to be understanding about this. You saw that my soldiers were attempting to hide a secret under my own roof—something I would have given them willingly if only they had chosen to come forward from the beginning—so you turned them in. And I'm glad you did. But Lieutenant Avlon…you made a mistake by not coming to me the moment you arrived."

Whit opened his mouth to speak, but the witch-queen held up a slender hand to silence him. "I saw the carving you left for her," she said. "You waited almost an entire day before informing me that you'd returned. You hesitated to hand her over. Didn't you? You lied, just like the others."

Whit dropped his head.

"Now, whether or not you had your share of her is an entirely different story, and we're not going to worry about that. I'd rather move past this, so I can know that you've properly learned your lesson." She let out a sarcastic sigh. "I let the attempted runaway go as a first warning—you weren't fully acclimated yet, and you got skittish. But this was your second chance." She narrowed her eyes and focused them directly on Whit's. "And I don't give many."

Whit nodded fervently. "Yes, Madam."

"Good man." She tilted her head back and spoke to Ryker, who still lingered in the room. "General, let's get this over with, shall we? This mess has already taken up too much of my time."

Whit shifted his eyes to Ryker, who was retrieving a cast iron meat press from the fireplace. He hadn't noticed before, but it had been heating the entire time Madam Lema had been talking, giving the metal enough time to morph into the perfect implement of punishment. A clear message.

Whit fidgeted in his chair. His fingers clutched the seat beneath him and held on for dear life. The tiniest glimpse of remorse passed over Ryker's face as he approached. A silent moment of solidarity.

There was no way to prepare for this kind of torture, even though Whit had seen it done before. He'd watched another soldier get burned for hoarding a few supplies. Madam Lema did not tolerate thievery, much less secrets and lies, and she had a proclivity for fire.

"Next time I give you a direct order," the witch-queen added before leaving him alone with Ryker, "I suggest you don't question it."

Ryker held the flat side of the iron press against Whit's left cheek, and as the hot metal scorched his skin, he bit his bottom lip to hold back the scream he so desperately wanted to release.

He thought of Willow, and of Freyah.

He reminded himself that as long as he was the one receiving the punishment, they'd be safe. At least for the time being.

He bit down until he drew blood, and after inhaling the scent of his own flesh melting, he blacked out.

10

FREYAH

When Freyah saw Whit the next morning, half of his face was covered in bandages. It hid the skin around his left eye and the majority of his cheek, giving his rough features an entirely new and distorted image.

She tried not to stare, but it was hard to avoid. He'd managed to shave his beard despite the injury and, though he still looked rugged, the sharper look suited him. Even his hair was freshly washed, now cascading in soft waves to the base of his neck.

He was there to escort her to breakfast, apparently having been assigned by Madam Lema as her personal guard throughout her stay. If Freyah had to have a guard, she was relieved to know that it was someone she could somewhat trust, but the tension between them was still a bit awkward. She wasn't entirely sure how to act around him. He'd saved her life multiple times already, yet all she knew about him was his name.

When she'd first noticed his new injury, he'd shaken his head, silently urging her not to mention it. However, during the brief minute they were alone in the corridor, she chose to pry anyway.

"Is that because of me?" she asked.

Whit shook his head once and hummed low in his throat, but she knew it wasn't the truth.

"I'm sorry."

"Don't be," he insisted. Then he asked, "You're okay, right? Better than before?"

She couldn't tell him the truth—she couldn't admit that so far, despite the queen's curious hospitality, Freyah didn't feel any safer than she had before with Roman threatening to defile her body.

She was no longer in that room, but her mind was trapped there, and she couldn't find a way out.

Freyah decided it was best to lie. Whether Whit's injury had anything to do with her or not, she couldn't let his new scars be for nothing.

"Yes," she told him, forcing herself to swallow the lump in her throat. "Thank you."

He gave her a halfhearted smile then led her through a door at the bottom of the tower. They wound their way through several long hallways and down two sets of narrow stone stairs. It wasn't until they reached a set of larger steps that Freyah could tell where she was.

Ahead was a massive set of double doors enclosed within an iron gate that looked like the front entrance to the castle. They turned left, and Freyah was met with the sound of mingled conversations.

Before leading her into a dining hall, Whit stopped in front of her, forcing her to halt. He seemed to be contemplating something, and Freyah waited hesitantly for him to speak.

Finally, he cleared his throat and said, "I'm sorry for the way I acted in The Hub. It wasn't like me."

That was definitely not what she had expected, and the shock of it stunned her so much that all she could do was nod. Thankfully, her response appeared to be enough to satisfy him, because he smiled and nodded in return.

This soldier continued to surprise Freyah, but the kinder he was, the more confused he made her.

They continued on as he escorted her into what was the Grand Hall. Inside were several rows of long wooden tables lined with chairs, most of them occupied with soldiers and what looked like their families. They sat amongst one another with smiles on their faces while shoveling food into their bellies.

Freyah was taken aback by the casualness. She'd had no idea that an entire community of people lived within the castle.

Whit ushered her to the other end of the Hall. They stopped at two large tables that crowned the space. He pointed to a chair, and Freyah sat down with a cluster of young women who appeared to be around her age. Then Whit backed away and waited along the wall with a handful of other soldiers.

In front of her was another large table that sat vacant upon a raised dais. To her left, she counted six more tables like hers that sat twenty people each. The three closest to the front were filled with dozens of astonishingly beautiful women. Witches, no doubt.

She knew the exact moment when Madam Lema entered the room, because a wave of stillness passed over everyone.

All at once, each person in the Hall lowered their body to the floor in a kneeling position. Freyah didn't move, but a young woman to her right kicked her chair in warning, so she gave in and mimicked their actions.

She caught Whit's eye as he lifted his head, and his gaze quickly darted to the woman beside her. Freyah shifted her focus as well. Even with only a peripheral view, she could see a head full of thick reddish-brown hair braided across the woman's shoulders and freckles dotting the majority of her exposed skin.

Everyone got to their feet, and the redhead gave Whit a secret smile. He returned it, and it was much brighter than the one he'd given Freyah only minutes before. She felt an unexpected bitter pang of jealousy as she took in the woman's long nose and oval face. Then she realized who she was standing next to.

She took my sister.

Freyah mentally scolded herself.

This was Whit's sister.

Madam Lema took her place at the head table on its raised platform, and everyone in the Hall sat once again. Several other witches joined the queen, as well as a few of her higher ranking officers. Then she spoke, her voice carrying across the Hall.

"As you all know," the queen began, addressing the crowd, "There has been civil unrest in this country for far too long. I have provided what protection I can over the years, but the turmoil seems to spread every day like wildfire. I know all too well that many of you here have suffered losses due to the rebels, and I am forever regretful that I was unable to stop that."

The people in the Hall were completely focused on Madam Lema as she spoke, a clear sense of obedience reflected in each of their eyes.

"Ever since the reign of Queen Ruella," she continued, "we have fought to provide you with peace and protection from those that wish to cause chaos and destruction to the place you call home. My coven and I have tried for years to hold the radicals at bay, yet still…they persist." She paused, taking in the many eyes that watched and waited. "The group that refers to themselves as The First Men claim to have owned this land before any other. Their ignorance doesn't allow them to see that Ghoma has always known magic. Over the centuries, it's changed hands many times. It's been sought after, stolen, and used for both good and evil means, but it has never disappeared. Not completely."

Madam Lema touched her onyx necklace absentmindedly, as if she were reminiscing. "Magic is buried in the soil," she said. "It's in the air, and even in the furthest mountains. It can't be destroyed, but like all things, magic can change. It is up to me and the sisters of my coven, the last beings with the capability to wield it, to hold on to that power and use it for the greater good. For the good of Ghoma. That is why I have fought for you—why I continue to fight for you. It has been hard, but today," she said, "I bring you the first glimpse of real hope."

The audience took in a collective breath as shock rippled through the Hall. Freyah watched them all, sitting on the edge of their seats and holding hands with one another in anticipation. Then, her eyes landed back on Madam Lema, surprised to find the queen staring back.

Freyah's stomach dropped to her feet.

Madam Lema's eyes shone brightly as the candles hanging high above bounced light across her set stare. The queen then picked up a goblet and raised it to her people. "It seems we might finally have the key to stopping the threat of war."

The crowd began whispering amongst themselves, excitedly discussing the possibilities of what this news could mean, and as she took it all in, Freyah wondered what the queen could possibly have planned.

AFTER BREAKFAST, Whit appeared at Freyah's side, ready to escort her back to her room. Last night, trying to sleep in such a sparse space with nothing but empty shelves and vacant walls staring back at her, had been eerie. But after acquiring a few personal items from a pleasant handmaid, Freyah now had a handful of new clothes and whatever toiletries she might need.

She'd been given three dresses, one pair of leggings and a linen button-down shirt, along with a chemise for sleeping and several pairs of undergarments and stockings. There was also a pair of plain wool slippers and a brand new set of lace-up boots. They were the nicest pair of shoes Freyah had ever owned, but she couldn't bring herself to wear them. Instead, she chose to stick with her own worn-leather ankle boots that had trodden thousands of miles worth of mountain. They were reliable and would keep her grounded in this unfamiliar territory.

As she and Whit walked silently through the stone corridors, Freyah wondered what sort of rooms the soldiers were given. Were Whit's sleeping quarters as small as hers? Or did he have a larger chamber like the queen?

Freyah couldn't imagine him having that grand of a space, for it would be insulting to Madam Lema's importance, but perhaps he at least had a bigger window than Freyah. The circular hole in the loft was no bigger than her torso, and it provided a less than satisfactory view of the barracks.

When she couldn't sleep, she'd wandered up to the loft above her bed and found herself wondering which window was Whit's, imagining perhaps he was looking at hers, too.

Despite how little they'd spoken, Freyah was growing fond of the lieutenant. His presence beside her was soothing, yet something about him made her blood hum beneath her skin. She was grateful for the risk he'd taken in exposing his comrade, and it made Freyah sick to think there was nothing she could properly do to thank him, especially after finding out he'd been physically punished for it.

So she did the only thing she *could* do. She offered her friendship.

"How long have you lived here?" she asked, hoping to start a conversation.

Whit gave her a sidelong glance but continued walking. "Nine years."

Freyah's eyes widened in shock. He looked so young. "How old were you?"

"Seventeen," he said. "I spent the first few years as a squire, then I became part of the guard."

"And now you're a lieutenant."

He nodded.

"Do you like it?"

The corner of his lip turned up in a smirk, then he scoffed. "I don't think anyone's ever asked me that." His smirk turned serious. "It's kept us safe. Safer than we would've been."

"You and your sister, you mean?"

He nodded again. "Do you have siblings?"

"No," she said. "I've always wanted a brother or sister, but I'm an only child."

"Sometimes I think my life would've been easier that way."

Freyah couldn't believe Whit would admit something like that out loud, but she couldn't judge him too harshly. Other than the small truth he'd handed her while still in the dungeons, she didn't know his story.

She took my sister.

Those four words had haunted Freyah when he'd first spoken them to her. What did they imply? And did those same words now apply to her?

Freyah did not want to belong to Madam Lema.

"What's your sister's name?" she asked.

Whit's smile returned, this time full of genuine fondness. Seeing it made Freyah's stomach flutter. "Willow," he said. "She was the freckle-face sitting next to you at breakfast, actually."

So she'd been right. The young woman that had nudged her to bow—that auburn-haired beauty—was Whit's sister. *Willow.* Putting a name to the face made the woman's situation feel all the more real and slightly more sinister. What exactly had Willow endured in the nine years they'd lived in Larapuna?

"She works in the laundry room, too," he said. "You'll like her..." He trailed off but then added a subtle *"eventually"* under his breath.

They reached a bend in the hall that required them to turn left to continue on to Freyah's room in the west tower, but instead of turning, Whit continued straight.

He led Freyah down a long and winding hallway until they reached a wide set of iron doors, two massive marble statues standing sentry on either side. One was of a woman with a soft jaw and full cheeks, her long waves giving the illusion of movement despite being frozen, and she held a goblet in front of her as if she were raising it for a toast.

Her companion was a man with large, birdlike wings.

Whit caught Freyah staring and waited, allowing her to take them in. "Ghidorah," he told her, watching as her gaze lingered on the male statue.

"Was he the first demon?" she asked.

"A warlock," he corrected. "Before the curse, men could shift at will."

The frozen warlock had horns protruding from his temples, similar to the ox-demon they'd encountered in the forest, only these were much thinner. His cool stone face was contorted in permanent rage.

Freyah knew about the origins of the curse, but she'd never heard anyone talk about the warlocks before. She pointed to the other statue. "Who is she?"

He turned to face the stone woman. "Her name was Lillia. Together, they are the Mother and Father of magic."

It had only been a hundred years since demons lost their magic, but for Freyah, it was all she'd ever known. Suddenly, she was overtaken by an insurmountable amount of loss on their behalf. To know that something had been taken from them, something that had been rightfully theirs… Freyah couldn't imagine having to live with that knowledge every day.

She'd known why the demons were so angry, but she'd never truly understood it before. They'd once been like gods, free to shift at will and equally as powerful as the witches, if not more.

What had they possibly done to deserve such punishment?

"I brought you here to show you the library," Whit told her, tugging Freyah away from her now spiraling thoughts.

He pulled at a thick iron handle and opened one of the doors, stepping aside and allowing her to lead the way in.

The library was magnificent. That was the only word appropriate enough to describe this section of the castle. The ceilings were more than twenty feet high with a glass dome in the center that opened up to show the bright morning sky. Every wall was lined with bookcases made of aged wood, each containing at least ten shelves. A rolling ladder connected to a railing high above the bookcases sat covered in dust on the back wall. Past a set of stained glass double doors, the massive room connected to a greenhouse, foliage overtaking the glass-encased space outside.

"It's amazing." She spoke quietly, expecting her voice to echo, but it barely carried across the room. The immense amount of books and dust must have changed the acoustics.

Whit walked over to the closest bookcase and picked up a worn, leather-bound tome. "I thought reading could help you pass the time.

When you're stuck in your room, that is. I can bring you here when you're not working."

Freyah gave him a grateful smile, and she hoped he could read the hidden message behind it—the subtle note of thanks for providing her with something that could be her own in such a strange place.

"I used to spend a lot of time here," he said. "It's almost always empty. Makes a good place to think."

"I love it," she confessed. "But how did you know I like to read?"

Whit let out a low chuckle. "Don't all girls like books? Romance and all that?"

"I guess most do," she admitted. "But I could be illiterate for all you know."

The look on his face changed immediately to something close to shame. Then it faded into amusement, realizing her jest. "You're right. I guess I shouldn't assume." He opened the book he was holding and flipped to the first page. "If that's the case, I guess I'll just have to read to you."

He stood directly under a stream of sun that shone through the glass ceiling above as he read aloud. His dark, shaggy hair fell over his forehead as he bowed over the novel in his hands, and she couldn't avoid noticing how handsome he was.

The way he held himself, so determined and sure, made up for the bandage and his rough appearance. From that first moment in Last Cove, she'd only ever seen him in his uniform, but today, he'd neglected the leather armor with the emblazoned royal symbol and sported a long-sleeved white drawstring top and brown trousers instead. His pants were clearly worn, but he didn't seem to notice or care. It displayed a confidence that fit with his phlegmatic personality.

And yet his hair hid most of his face, as if he were hiding from something. It looked soft, and Freyah wanted to reach out and run her fingers through it.

Whit was droning on, reading an excerpt from *The Modern Laws of Herbal Magic*, completely unaware of how Freyah had been studying him. But when he glanced back up, his rich brown eyes meeting hers, she felt the need to recover.

"Thanks for the lesson," she teased awkwardly. "Not very romantic though."

He let out a dissatisfied *humph* and tossed the book onto a round wooden table, sending up a puff of dust as it landed. "You're right. This isn't what we want."

He began scouring the shelves for something to his liking. After three shelves containing nothing but apparent duds, he plucked a small purple book from the bottom.

"This looks promising," he declared.

He tossed it lightly to her, and she caught it against her chest.

Freyah looked down at the cover and read the title aloud. "*The Language of Love*." She hummed in interest and flipped it over. "Yes. Anything with love in the title should be romantic, right?"

"My thoughts exactly."

Whit strode closer, but stopped just before standing directly in front of her. Freyah could smell the musk on his skin, mixed with the subtle hint of pine and tea tree oil. He smelled like the forest, like nature itself.

"You'll have to let me know how it is," he murmured, voice low and possibly...suggestive?

Freyah allowed a full smile to bloom on her face this time. "I'll give you a detailed review."

LYRA

When Lyra returned to the castle after her long and invigorating day with Oram, it was past midnight, and the only souls wandering the halls of Larapuna were the soldiers on guard at the front gate.

Lyra easily slipped past them with a quick blending charm, taking a pinch of black tourmaline powder from a vial in her cloak pocket and blowing the substance into the air. It created a cloud of opaque smoke, and she stepped through it. At once, her body blended with the texture and colors of the castle, becoming one with her background and, as long as she tread lightly, she was completely invisible to the soldiers around her.

The only being that sensed her presence as she walked past the Grand Hall was the castle's resident gray cat slinking soundlessly through the corridors.

When she made it safely to her room, Lyra closed the door behind her and found Fatima standing completely befuddled at the end of the bed.

Her handmaid had most likely already been asleep, judging by the state of her dark brown hair and the imprint of a pillow on her cheek. Now, however, Fatima clutched a hairbrush like a weapon, and her caramel eyes darted back and forth over the surface area of the door in front of her.

"Miss Lyra?" she whispered. "Is that you?"

"Of course it's me," Lyra said. She removed her cloak, removing the blending charm along with it. Her body was her own again, and it was now the full focus of her handmaid's attention.

Fatima let out a frustrated groan and tossed the hair brush onto the bed. "Why do you insist on scaring me like that?" she fussed. "I swear, there's not a moment without magic in this place."

"You live with witches, Fatima," Lyra reminded her. "What did you expect?"

Fatima nodded curtly. "Yes, I suppose you're right."

Lyra adored her handmaid's naïveté about magic. It was fun to see the wonder in Fatima's eyes whenever Lyra performed even the simplest spells. Having a human handmaid had been custom for every witch in Lyra's family since her grandmother, Ruella, had ruled. They were meant to serve, but Lyra saw Fatima as more than a handmaid—she was her best friend.

From the first moment Fatima had arrived at Castle Larapuna as a young teen, Lyra saw something incredibly special in the girl. She had a kind and forgiving soul, and her sense of wonder almost matched the level of Lyra's. Fatima's family had sold her to the queen in order to afford the proper medicine for her sickly younger brother. Lyra had felt for the girl, so she immediately took her under her wing, preventing Lema from assigning her a job that was much more degrading.

Fatima was so grateful for what Lyra had done, she offered every bit of herself in servitude—so much so that Lyra had to insist she relax a little.

"Whenever it's just the two of us, you can be yourself completely," Lyra had told her. *"I'm not like my sister. I want you to have a life here."*

That sentiment had been the building blocks that formed the foundation of their friendship, and over a decade later, it was because of that bond that Lyra felt confident in sharing a secret with Fatima now.

Lyra began undressing. She removed the many layers to her outfit until she was down to her chemise and sat at her vanity, staring proudly at her reflection in the mirror.

"I met a man tonight," she said. "Actually…." She dragged the word out for dramatic effect. "He was a demon."

Fatima had retrieved the brush and began running it through the knots in Lyra's hair, but she stopped abruptly at the proclamation. "You really should be more careful when you go outside the castle." Her voice shook with concern. "Demons don't like witches. He could have attacked you."

"This demon was different," Lyra insisted. "Besides, he doesn't know what I am." She narrowed her eyes at Fatima's reflection in the mirror and added, "I'm also a lot more careful than you think."

Fatima dropped her head in embarrassment. "Sorry, miss. I just worry about you is all."

"I wish you wouldn't call me that."

It was a habit Fatima had yet to break, claiming that given all the princess had done for her, she owed Lyra the respect.

Fatima gave her a pointed look in the mirror, the same thought no doubt having crossed her mind.

She continued to stare at her own reflection. Her hair had been tousled every which way by the wind, as well as certain rambunctious activities. Lyra smiled at the thought and said, "He seemed to like me just fine when I invited him to bed."

Fatima let out a dramatic gasp. "You *didn't*! Did you?"

"Yes," she stated confidently. "I most certainly did. And it was well worth it." Fatima shifted her weight back and forth nervously, clearly on the verge of wanting to ask a follow-up question. "Go on," Lyra insisted. "What is it?"

"Well," Fatima began. "What sort of demon…what I mean to say is…did he have, you know?"

Lyra turned to fully face her handmaid. "Are you asking if he had a penis?" The golden skin of Fatima's cheeks flushed with splotches of red. "Of course he did. By Lillia's name, how on earth do you think demons mate, Fatima?"

Fatima looked mortified, squeezing the hairbrush so tightly that her knuckles turned white. Fatima sat down on the edge of the bed and tried to shrug off her embarrassment, but she was shy, so without Lyra to further steer the conversation, there was only silence.

"He's a tiger-demon," Lyra told her in a seductive tone. "He's got black markings all over his skin like tattoos."

Fatima looked up and met her eyes with intrigue. "Really?"

Lyra nodded. "He's quite beautiful," she mused. "More human-like than you'd expect. Apparently the younger ones are like that." She sighed dreamily. "I'll probably see him again."

"*What?!*"

"I'm telling you, Fatima...this demon was different. There's something special about him. I can feel it."

Fatima sighed and stood, returning to the task of brushing Lyra's hair. "If you really like him," she said, "I guess there's no reason the queen has to find out."

Lyra smiled in satisfaction. "My sentiments exactly."

The next morning, Lyra strutted into the private dining room she shared with her sister for breakfast, smug joy plastered across her face.

"What in Lillia's name has you so happy?" Lema demanded.

Her sister was sitting at the head of the long rectangular table and indulging in a plate of thick sausages. Her raven hair was pulled back into an intricately braided knot at the top of her head, and she was wearing one of her finest dresses.

"Why are you dressed so nicely?" Lyra jabbed back.

Lema scowled. "I have a small matter to attend to, then later today we have important guests coming to the castle. You should consider pulling out one of your better garments as well."

"I'll think about it." Lyra sat in the chair furthest from her sister and began slathering a slice of bread with butter and jam. "Who are these 'important guests'?" she asked. "Do I know them?"

"The chancellor of Balandra and his advisors are paying us a visit," Lema explained. "It's been brought to my attention that a group of radicals have been causing a disturbance in the capital. They are requesting military aid to better control the situation."

"What sort of radicals?" Lyra questioned. "What are they doing?"

She knew about the rebels, but only because she'd seen them for herself. Lema didn't know how much time Lyra spent exploring outside the castle, and she intended to keep it that way.

Lema rolled her eyes, as if the entire thing bored her immensely. "There have been multiple reports of vandalism, threatening messages. That sort of thing."

Lyra's demeanor shifted from lighthearted to somber. It seemed her sister was unfazed by the seriousness of the situation. "Are they threatening *you*?"

Lema laughed wickedly. "Who else would they be threatening, Lyra? I am the queen they all despise."

Lyra took an enormous bite of bread, and with her mouth full, mumbled, "Is it demons?"

The queen nodded curtly. "It would seem so."

An idea began to form in the back of Lyra's mind. As the two sat and ate the rest of their breakfast in silence, Lyra thought about the new resource she had at her disposal.

If there was a radical group of demons threatening to rise against the crown, it was possible Oram knew about it. News traveled fast in Ghoma, especially if the severity of the situation meant the chancellor of Balandra was at the point of needing the queen's assistance.

She'd already planned to make another trip to Caster Valley to see Oram again, and with Lema distracted by her important guests, today would be a perfect opportunity to slip away.

12

LYRA

The streets of Knox Hill bustled with excitement.

But it wasn't from the anticipation of a festival or the chaos of a busy shopping day. No, it was due to unrest and pent-up frustration.

Another act of rebellion had been spotted in the town square. Two farmers had stumbled upon a crude display in front of the remnants of the Trade Center that had burned down six months prior. Within the barren foundation of what was once the entrance, several crates of spoiled food were stacked higher than Lyra was tall. They surrounded a scarecrow tied to a wooden post, dressed in an emerald gown and black wig to resemble the queen.

The scarecrow held a sign that read *YOU CAN HAVE OUR SCRAPS.*

Lyra knew what it meant.

Whoever had done this was protesting the law that required all farmers and craftsmen to provide half of their shares to the crown each month. It was necessary for Larapuna to stockpile because they were so remote, and their only source of food came from Ghoma's own citizens. While that was true, Lyra knew damn well that they had enough food and supplies to last the better part of a year, and that was with everyone in the castle taking seconds at every meal. They didn't need the extra food when the common people were barely scraping by.

It was clear the rebels weren't slowing down, and if things were really this bad, Lyra had to say something to the queen.

She walked past the growing crowd as inconspicuous as possible, keeping the hood of her cloak pulled over her white-blond hair. Her intent was to pay another visit to Oram, but she wasn't entirely sure where he might be. She decided to check the tavern first, seeing as it was the last place they'd seen one another.

Upon entering the dim and dusty space, she scanned the room for any sight of him. There were many patrons scattered around the damaged tables and chairs, going about their conversations like it was any other day, and she wondered if they were aware of the commotion outside. If so, she imagined their hushed conversations were full of *"who do you think did it?"* and *"I bet that witch-bitch is gonna have something to say about it."*

Lyra sauntered past a pair of elderly gentlemen in the midst of a very intense game of chess and made her way to the bar.

The barkeep immediately spotted her and asked for her order.

"Cider please," she requested.

She stood watching as the man grabbed a round-bellied tin mug from a bucket and held it under a spout pouring amber liquid.

"Is that for me?"

A deep voice resonated from behind her, and Lyra turned abruptly to find Oram standing toe to toe with her at the bar.

She gave him a coy grin and thanked the barkeep as he placed her drink on the counter.

"I wasn't sure you would show," she told Oram.

He cocked his head and sucked his teeth. "Now, how could I miss the opportunity to see my new, beautiful friend? It's been so long."

"It's been a day," she corrected.

"Ah, well. Absence makes the heart grow fonder."

THEY SPENT VERY little time talking before continuing where they'd left off.

Lyra was fascinated by the marks on Oram's skin. She loved tracing her fingers lightly along every stripe, following the path where they curved around his torso and climbed all the way up his spine. She even found his ears intriguing—the way they moved at every subtle sound, like a cat. Despite his small animal-like qualities, Oram was very much a man, and she'd been able to attest to that multiple times, each more convincing than the last.

She wanted to drink him like wine, savoring every drop on her tongue, and lavish his hands on every inch of her skin. Lyra hadn't known such attentive sex before this. She'd had lovers, of course, but none as dedicated to guaranteeing her pleasure as Oram.

He might not know her very well, but he now knew her body. Anticipated her needs without her having to speak them aloud. That afternoon, he spent what felt like hours with his mouth between her thighs, sending wave after wave of pleasure through her until her muscles were left shaking and spent.

After wasting away another afternoon of passionate sex, Lyra realized she'd forgotten her plan. She'd been so distracted by Oram that she found herself questioning her initial decision to question him. It felt wrong, but there was still a need to see what he possibly knew about the rebel group of demons.

They'd lain comfortably in each other's arms for several minutes before Lyra finally gathered the courage to start asking questions.

"What are your parents' names?" she wondered aloud.

Oram hummed lightly as he stroked his fingers delicately through the white strands of Lyra's hair. "Galiana and Petra."

"Are you close with them?"

His chin was propped against the top of her head, and she felt him smile.

"I owe them everything," he answered in a wistful tone. "I do what I can to be there for them, like they were for me. And my siblings."

Lyra wondered what it would be like to have such a loving and largely diverse family. The idea seemed exciting, and much warmer than her own upbringing had been.

"What about you?" Oram asked, steering the conversation away from himself. "Why don't I get to ask about your life?"

Lyra *tsked*. "Because my life isn't as interesting as yours."

"Why don't you let me be the judge of that?" He turned his body to face her. "Come on. Tell me something shocking. I bet there's something special about you."

Lyra could feel herself giving in. It would be so easy to tell him the truth, to admit who she was and what it meant, but it would be equally as hard for him to reject her.

Their match wasn't a transaction. Though it had only been two days, it was something different to her now. More special. She was beginning to feel affection for the man next to her, and that was rare. Lyra hardly felt sentiment for her own sister, though she supposed there was a part of her that cared about Lema's well-being. Despite hiding her identity, Lyra felt as if Oram truly saw her.

He had connected to her soul just as much as her body.

Would it really be so awful? He knew by now she wasn't a threat, so surely learning of her faction wouldn't scare him away. She would still be the same woman he'd met in the fields.

Lyra hoped with all her heart that that would stand true.

So without overthinking, she sucked in a breath and spoke the words aloud. "I'm a witch," she told him, then waited for his full reaction.

She wasn't sure if he'd registered what she'd said. Lyra locked eyes with him and waited for the words to take shape in his mind.

She saw the moment that it clicked for him—the way the corner of his mouth changed his expression. He probably thought she'd been joking, but now...

Now he knew she was serious.

Oram pulled himself up into a sitting position. "I don't understand."

Lyra didn't respond. Only left him to his own deductions.

He wasn't looking at her anymore. Apparently his insistence for her to tell him something shocking had backfired. He hadn't been ready for it, and now Lyra feared she would have to take it back.

She could, if she really wanted to. She had ways of manipulating a person's memory so Oram would forget the entire conversation, but it required a lot of work, and Lyra would rather things be easy.

"You don't have to look so scared," she teased, attempting to keep her tone light. "If I wanted to hurt you, I wouldn't have slept with you."

Oram turned to face her with a look of disgust. "Why did you hide it?"

"Why do you wear long sleeves when you go out in public?" she countered.

Oram dropped his eyes again.

"Exactly," she said. "It's no different. If I were to walk through the streets as myself, I'd risk being killed."

"*You'd* risk it?" he retorted. "I'm a *demon*, Lyra. We're the ones constantly being persecuted. By *your* kind!"

Lyra had nothing to say to that. It was true, and there was no excuse she could give to change it. So instead she went a step further.

"I'm not just a witch," she admitted. "My sister is the queen. All of the anger out there, it's aimed directly at my family."

His look of disgust morphed into shock and rage. "Your family has caused a lot of damage to deserve that anger."

"I know. But I promise you..."

Lyra rose to her knees and placed both hands flat against his chest, her pale fingers stark against his richer skin tone, but he pulled away.

The act made her momentarily lose focus.

She blinked, then continued to speak. "I have no part in it. My sister is warped by centuries of prejudice. She can't see past the war that our grandmother started." Lyra hesitated. "Sometimes I think she wishes she had a war of her own."

"Why are you telling me this?" Oram asked, seeming desperate for something tangible in her confession.

"You told me to tell you something shocking," she said, only slightly teasing this time.

His seriousness didn't falter. "Let me ask a better question: when were you *planning* to tell me?"

Lyra dropped her hands. "I don't know."

He remained quiet, but his shoulders relaxed slightly. She could tell he appreciated her honesty, but he was still on edge.

"Are you afraid of me?" she asked, scared of the answer.

Oram paused almost a beat too long, but when he spoke, it was with confidence. "No," he said. "I'm just…processing."

He got up from the bed and began to pace. His lips were slightly parted, and he nodded slowly, as if trying to convince himself of something.

"Now that you know," she said hesitantly, "I need to ask you something."

He paused and furrowed his brow, but then gave her a slow, cloying grin. "My favorite color is green, if that helps."

Lyra grasped hold of his small hint of levity, feeling her emerald eyes shining. He truly was special, and the thought of ever having to leave this room made her heart ache.

She chose her next words carefully. "I don't know if you're already aware, but there's a rebel group causing some problems."

Oram became unnaturally still. "Yes. I'm aware."

"How much do you know about them?" she asked, pressing him.

He stiffened. "Why do I get the feeling you're about to accuse me of something?"

Lyra was taken aback. "What?"

"You think I'm involved? You were sent here to spy. Is that what this is?"

"No, Oram! No. Not at all." Lyra collected her panicking thoughts and took a deep breath. "I was just hoping you could help." She bit her lip and turned her face to hide from his gaze. "I know she's made a lot of people angry, but there has to be something I can do to make things better. I just don't know how."

Oram relaxed again. She felt awful for putting him through such an emotional ringer, but it felt good to purge her thoughts and fears onto another person.

He rubbed thoughtfully at his jawline and closed his eyes, probably debating with himself as she had done, choosing whether to tell the truth or feed her a lie.

She watched his toned chest rise and fall with each intake of breath, his brown skin pulling taut over the muscles there.

"It's not demons," he said, opening his eyes to her again.

"What do you mean?"

"The vandalism. The fires at the Trade Centers and threatening messages. It's not demons doing it. It's humans."

Lyra was glad he had more to say, because she found herself completely speechless.

"They want everyone to think it's us," he explained. "That way it keeps *your sister's* focus away from them. They want to fight back, but they can't risk having more food taken away from their families, so they blame it on the demons. Because who cares if an animal gets beaten in the street?"

Lyra shuddered, the words 'your sister' echoing loudly in her ears.

"We don't want a war," he told her. "We don't want to fight back. We just want to live a normal life. Just like everyone else."

Lyra finally understood.

All that clarity, yet Lyra still didn't know what she could do.

She had no influence over Lema. No one did. And for the first time, Lyra actually feared the world her grandmother had created.

13

ORAM

When Oram Foster planned to tell his brother, Kirra, about the mysterious witch he'd met, he wasn't sure how the fox-demon would react. He'd hoped for something similar to his own reaction—Oram thought he'd handled the shocking news with quite a level head—but, unfortunately, he knew his brother much better than that.

Kirra did not trust witches. He didn't trust humans that much either, besides the two responsible for raising them. Kirra was a very secluded and skeptical individual. Despite having a much better childhood than most of his fellow demons, he still felt a responsibility to share in their pain.

Oram did not hold that sentiment.

He recognized how incredibly lucky he and Kirra were to have been randomly chosen and plucked from the forest that day thirty-some years ago. He took advantage of the many opportunities he'd been given, knowing that he couldn't let them go to waste. Kirra thought their lifestyle was selfish and unfair to rub in other demons' faces, but Oram saw it as something not to take for granted. He lived his life to honor and respect those that couldn't.

The ones who never escaped the forest.

The ones who made it to Balandra but faced judgment and persecution every day from the humans among them.

He did everything for them.

For those that had not been so lucky.

What his brother would say already rolled around in the back of Oram's head as he walked the stretch of dirt leading to the small bungalow they shared. He was smart enough to know witches were the enemy, but he was also smart enough to see that Lyra was nothing like the others.

Oram opened the door and kicked off his boots, finding Kirra bustling about the kitchen as usual.

"You've been working later," his brother noted without turning to face him. "Are you troubled?"

Oram sighed, choosing to ignore Kirra's ill-mannered greeting, and began opening various cabinet doors in search of a clean glass. "Why do you assume I'm troubled?"

Kirra was mixing a pot of sauce that gave off the most delicious aroma. He was short, so in order to reach his work he had to stand on a generously-sized step stool, his bushy, cinnamon colored tail resting casually on the surface between his feet.

"You throw yourself into manual labor whenever you have something on your mind," Kirra told him matter-of-factly.

It was true. He knew Oram quite well.

"So?" Kirra insisted. "What is it?"

Oram gave up his search and sat at the small circular table in the center of the room. "I'm not troubled," he said.

Kirra's left ear twitched, a sign that Oram clearly wasn't going to keep getting away with giving such perfunctory answers.

Finally, he relented. "I, uh, met someone."

Kirra dropped the spoon he'd been using to stir, and it fell into the pot. "Shoot!" he screeched, trying to reach for the thing before it sank completely beneath the surface. He plucked it up just in time, and Oram watched wide-eyed as the utensil dripped globs of red sauce back into the pot.

Oram tossed his brother a rag. "It's not that surprising, is it?" he asked.

Kirra focused on cleaning the mess while silently stewing. His face held a look of judgment that Oram thought he'd been prepared for, but seeing it now made all the hope in his chest drop weightily to his stomach.

He hadn't even mentioned that the woman was a witch.

"You know how things have been, Kir. What did you expect me to do?"

"Perhaps give yourself a little more time to grieve your wife," Kirra jabbed.

The blow cut deep, deeper than his brother had probably intended, because before that moment, Oram had completely forgotten about Astra.

It was the first time in months that he'd gone more than five minutes without thoughts of his late wife swimming across his mind. They'd gotten married young—too young to truly understand the implications—and over time, their relationship had deteriorated because of it.

She was human, and she'd been blinded to the complications of marrying a demon by their whirlwind romance. It wasn't until after they'd signed the papers that Astra had finally realized her mistake. She couldn't handle the scrutiny from others. Couldn't face the looks at the market or the whispers behind her back.

They'd planned to end it, because even though Oram loved her, he didn't want to be the cause of her pain.

But they'd never gotten the chance.

Oram was never able to fix things, because the same day they had planned to sign the papers to dissolve their marriage contract, Astra was killed in a fire at the Trade Center where she worked.

The guilt and shame had eaten away at him for weeks afterward, and even now her absence gripped him tightly. Sure, their relationship had been falling apart from the moment it started, but that didn't mean he didn't miss her.

It had been six months, and somehow he'd moved past his grief without even realizing it by being drawn to someone new.

It was strange how the connection to Lyra had started, like his inhibitions had been diluted and filtered through the haze of lust and infatuation. He'd had his wits about him, but he'd made the decision to go to bed with Lyra quite rashly, and that wasn't like him. Even more so, he never thought he would move on so quickly.

Kirra could see how his comment was affecting Oram, so he did his best to reel it back. "How did it happen?" he asked, interrupting his brother's spiral.

"How do you think?" Oram chided.

"That depends. Was she drunk?"

"Are you insinuating that a woman would have to be drunk in order to find me interesting?"

"She'd have to have something clouding her brain to ignore that tail of yours."

Oram's eyes narrowed. "Look who's talking."

Kirra bristled and tucked his own tail between his legs.

Oram had shared a lot about himself and his family with Lyra, and he wondered exactly how much of that knowledge she would keep to herself. She didn't seem manipulative—she seemed lost. Like she was still trying to find her place in the world.

He tried to imagine what it must have been like for her growing up in a castle, being waited on by servants and never having to worry about security and protection. Most of the witches that resided in Larapuna never ventured past the keep. Why would they when they had everything they needed within those castle walls? And whatever they didn't could easily be delivered straight to them.

Perhaps that was why Lyra wanted to leave.

Instead of feeling safe, she felt stuck.

Living inside a cage was suffocating, no matter how fancy.

"I'm sorry," Kirra apologized, sitting down next to Oram at the table. "Tell me who she is." Oram gave him a knowing glare. "I want to know. Truly."

"Her name is Lyra. She's...well, she's the most beautiful woman I've ever seen."

Kirra's eyes widened in amusement. "So, *you* were drunk."

"Will you stop?"

"Fine, fine. Go on then."

Oram felt himself drifting into a pleasant cloud of nostalgia. He couldn't help but react physically when thoughts of Lyra came to mind. He'd been completely thrown off guard by her confession, but that didn't negate the time they'd already spent together.

"She's so curious. She's never really been out in the world to see things. She kept asking all about my life and what it's like being a demon."

"Where does this woman live?" Kirra spat. "Under a rock?"

Oram hesitated. "She's from Larapuna."

Kirra stood abruptly. "Oh no. No, no, no, no, no."

He began clamoring around for a lid to cover the pot and accidentally knocked over a container filled with ladles and spatulas in his wake.

"Oram, if she works for the queen, you definitely need to steer clear," he said. "You can't trust someone that surrounds themself with witches."

He reached for an empty mug next to the wash basin, filling it with water from a ceramic jug, and drank desperately, like he was trying to cleanse Oram's admission from his head completely.

Oram swallowed and spoke his next words slowly. "What if...she *is* a witch?"

Kirra spat a spray of water from his mouth and began coughing hysterically.

"Kirra, hear me out."

"Absolutely not." Kirra's short arms flailed about. "I knew you would end up doing something like this to us. You trust too easily, Oram. You've always been this way." He placed his hands on either side of his own head, as if to hold his brain in place, or to prevent it from oozing out of his fur-covered ears.

Then, he steadied himself. Kirra released his hands from his skull and let them fall to his sides. "This is it," he stated melodramatically. "You told her about mum, didn't you?"

"Umm...yes."

"You know she's going to tell the queen," Kirra said. "Everything they've done for us will have been for nothing."

"What does it matter? The witches know by now that humans take us in. There are demons everywhere. Balandra is full of them. And how can it be for nothing?" Oram gestured to the house around them. "We're standing here, Kirra. That's something. We wouldn't be in this house, living in this village, or supporting ourselves without our parents' efforts. The queen can't take that away, no matter what she does."

"It matters," Kirra spoke carefully, "because our mother didn't just take in *a* demon. She took in *six*. Drawing that kind of attention is never good."

Oram crossed his arms defiantly, refusing to admit that he'd made such a careless mistake.

"Did you even think about Yohannah?" Kirra asked.

He hadn't.

It was like a second punch to the gut having his little sister's name thrown at him in such a way, but Kirra was right. Yohannah was only twelve. If the queen gave the order to have Galiana arrested, what would become of her?

"We would take care of her," Oram said, answering his own question. "You know that."

Kirra stood very still, except for his tail, which methodically swished from side to side like a calculating pendulum. A pause lingered between them for several beats, then, instead of continuing to defend himself, Oram chose to leave the conversation at that.

"What's done is done," Oram said, lowering his chin, his voice steady but thick with defeat. "I'm leaving at the end of the week to take this month's delivery to Larapuna."

It was because of the fire that they'd been unable to use the Trade Center, and for the last six months, Oram had been forced to hand-deliver supplies to the castle himself.

Each month, it was a constant reminder of what happened to Astra, but this time, he wouldn't be consumed by what he'd lost. He had something new to focus on—something he'd found.

Kirra clasped his hands together and stared at his brother with a painful, watery gaze. "Oram, just be careful. That's all I ask."

14

MADAM LEMA

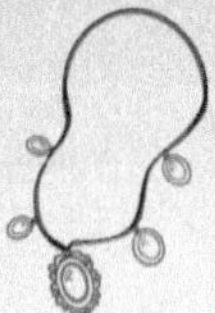

*L*ema Mansell was very much like her grandmother.

Specifically, she'd inherited the trait of carelessness when it came to the complexities of ruling a kingdom. There were always jobs for her to oversee and decisions to make—it was the part of being queen she revered on a daily basis—but like Ruella, Lema dumped whatever else she could in her advisor's lap.

Unfortunately, there were certain things that Evanora did not have the authority to approve, so Lema was forced to make an appearance.

She made her way down the stone hall with long strides, the heels of her shoes clicking across the surface and alerting those around of her impending presence. She basked in every scared look or dutiful bow she received.

Even the men in her army feared her. They knew the depths of her magic, and they'd witnessed firsthand the retribution she dolled out for falling out of line, so they remained loyal.

When Madam Lema entered the meeting chamber adjacent to the Grand Hall, each of her high-ranking officers stood to greet her.

Ryker, the major general, stood directly to the right of the queen's chair at the far end of the table. By the other chairs were his two colonels, Corvus Nyadahma and Arek Vanko, and the tactical captains, Filip Greve and Victor Stanton.

Madam Lema sat in her seat, and the others followed, save for Ryker who remained standing. She turned her attention to the head of her special forces branch, Colonel Nyadahma.

"Report on the rebels," she commanded. "Now."

The colonel returned to his feet. Half of his ochre hair cascaded in thick, coarse locs over his shoulders, the other half secured neatly in a knot at the crown of his head. He had dark stubble on his cheeks and a full goatee, a thick scar running through his right eyebrow, and his rich brown skin was illustrated with runes.

He addressed his queen in a professional manner. "Madam, there has been no news to report on the demon rebellion for several weeks."

It went by almost unnoticed, but Madam Lema caught the small glance the colonel sent in Ryker's direction, the only demon in the room.

"My Spyders have heard no whispers, no rumors." He cleared his throat. "The riots in Balandra have diminished significantly due to our military presence, and it is my belief that, with a bit of patience, they will come to an end entirely."

Madam Lema let out an impatient breath. "*Patience*," she repeated. "The Mother seems to be asking it of us all these days." She pursed her lips and narrowed her eyes at him. "I don't have time for patience. Tell me, do you consider your men capable of basic intelligence?"

Nyadahma straightened with pride, completely missing the queen's subtle jab. "Every soldier working for me is highly skilled, Madam," he stated confidently. "I do not take anyone under my command that is anything less than excellent at what they do."

"Yes, Colonel, your reputation precedes you. But that is not what I asked." Madam Lema leaned precariously into the colonel's space. "Are they intelligent?" she asked again.

The colonel stuttered. "I-I don't understand."

Madam Lema shook her head in frustration. "They must not be, because their intel is wrong," she explained in a falsely-disinterested tone. "You see, I've been told of a recent protest in Caster Valley. It would seem that the unrest in the capital city has not subsided, but in fact... has *SPREAD!*"

With that last word, Madam Lema's voice reached a register that caused everyone in the room to flinch. Everyone except for Ryker. The wolf-demon had obviously come to expect his queen's sudden outbursts and had become somewhat numb to it.

Madam Lema paused long enough to draw in a steadying breath. She closed her eyes and tried to focus on getting through the rest of the meeting. They'd only discussed the first topic, and she couldn't reach her limit when there were still several more items on the docket that needed her attention.

Where is Evanora when I need her? she thought.

"I want more Spyders in the villages," she told the colonel, having calmed herself. "They can deal with this matter directly."

A stiff silence swept over the room. The other officers watched and waited for the colonel's response. Then, after shaking off the shock, he complied.

"Yes. Of course," he assented. Then, he hesitantly asked, "Forgive me, Madam, but do you believe the situation truly warrants it? If we're able to contain the protests, then perhaps–"

Lema stood abruptly, causing Colonel Nyadahma to collapse into his chair mid-sentence.

She glowered down at him, resisting the urge to rip out his tongue and nail it to the table. "Are you questioning my judgment?"

The colonel shook his head vigorously. "No, Madam."

"Good." She sat back down and the others seemed to relax. "You will send three additional Spyders to every village," she ordered. "First thing."

Nyadahma nodded curtly, and they continued on with the rest of the meeting.

After some further discussion on the state of the country, Madam Lema dismissed the men. They all exited the room save for Filip

Greve, the defensive captain of her tactical branch. His hair was closely cropped and russet brown, with a thick mustache long enough to curl at the ends.

"This month's shipments have arrived, Madam," he informed her.

She stared at him blankly. "And?"

"Your approval is required for some *particular* items."

Madam Lema's lips formed a tight smile.

She got up and allowed Captain Greve to escort her from the room.

In the entrance hall, the queen watched as merchants from across Ghoma scrambled about before her like ants in the dirt. She couldn't care less about the food or supplies they were bringing into the castle.

Madam Lema was there for something she'd specially requested, something that would help her gain a deeper insight into the future of her reign.

She'd kept it to herself, but her Future Sight was growing weaker with every passing year. She was getting older, and despite witches living longer lives, the more they aged, the more their powers waned.

Unlike her predecessors, she'd been unable to see any resolution past her obstacles for some time. Her grandmother, Ruella, had used the Sight to foresee her successes and even her own death. It was how she'd managed to win The Great War and hold on to the throne. There were no rebellions, no questions about her leadership. But not long after, her daughter took her place on the ivory throne, and all the work Ruella had put in to ensure that power never rested in the control of men was being diminished by lax laws and giving demons too much freedom.

The queendom was weakening, and fear and confidence in the Mansell dynasty was losing momentum. That hesitancy was then passed on to Lema after Adora's untimely death, and it had then become her job to batten down the hatches and tighten the loose ends.

Lema made sure the people of Ghoma knew who was in charge, and that the demons never forgot their place.

But she hadn't seen the rebellion coming.

Typically, she would have been given a sign about things such as this, allowing her to snuff out the problem before it caught fire. But her Sight had failed her. The people were protesting against the crown, and their cries of outrage were gaining momentum. Madam Lema was slowly losing her influence over the country, but she was not ready to give it up.

After consulting with a few of the elder witches on many occasions, Madam Lema had sent scouts to obtain a rare stone known as Hematite found exclusively in the Northern Sky Mountains. Contact with the rare element would not only elucidate but expand visions for witches with the Sight.

She needed clarity, and she needed as much of it as she could get her hands on if she wanted to put a stop to this impending insurgence.

General Ryker approached from across the entrance hall, followed closely by two men clearly worse for wear. Their faces were gaunt, their skin sallow and pale. They'd been gone for weeks, but even so, their arrival had been sooner than expected.

Ryker tilted his head and gestured for the queen to follow them to another location. Captain Greve took a step in their direction, but Lema halted him in place.

"Thank you, Captain," she said. "That will be all."

He nodded obediently and went on his way.

The less to know about her problem, the better, and so far Madam Lema had managed to keep it mostly under wraps.

Only Lyra and Ryker knew how dire her situation truly was.

Madam Lema joined the three men as they entered a passage connected to the back of the entrance hall and descended a narrow set of stairs. This path was not often used, but if followed the entire length, it provided a direct route to the dungeons below the throne room. Before that, however, it split left and curved back around to the front of the castle.

After turning the corner, they all stopped in front of an ancient wooden door. The men knew better than to try and open it, because despite its dilapidated appearance, it had been sealed by ancient blood magic put in place by Queen Ruella, and only a witch in her bloodline could unlock it.

Madam Lema further approached, and they all stepped aside for her. She nicked the palm of her hand with a sharp pinky nail then placed it flat on the surface of the door. She was rewarded with the sound of locks clicking in and out of place and the door swung open.

The room was small, filled from floor to ceiling with shelves of potions and various ingredients. There were varying sizes of bottles with different colored liquids, vials of powder, small stones, and animal teeth. A scrying bowl sat alone on a table in the middle of the room, and directly opposite the door sat a very old, very weathered-looking chest.

One by one, they filed into the room. Once they were all inside, Ryker closed the door behind them.

Madam Lema watched as one of the men reached into his pack and pulled out a canvas drawstring bag. He held it out and dropped it into the queen's outstretched hand.

She hid her enthusiasm—it was best not to let anyone else know just how important this find was to her. Showing no emotion, she opened the bag and reached inside. There was no need to pull the crystals out and examine them. She knew the men had been successful just by feeling their smooth surface and the surge of energy they gave off as she touched them.

Quickly, she cinched the bag closed and handed it to Ryker, who stuffed it into his jacket for safekeeping.

"I trust you'll be expecting your payment," she stated to the men.

They looked up eagerly, nodding their heads.

Madam Lema gave them a wicked grin. "Very well."

She struck faster than a snake, slicing both their necks with the tip of the sharpened nail of her index finger, and they fell to the floor in a heap, bleeding out almost immediately due to the poison she'd mixed into her nail polish.

They'd received a quick death as payment, and she was satisfied with the exchange.

"Clean this up," she ordered Ryker as she flicked the blood from beneath her nail. She then wiped it casually on one of the men's shirts before leaving the room.

15

ORAM

Oram had just finished dropping off two dozen crates of fresh crops when he spotted Lyra descending a set of massive stone steps to the left of the hall.

She was absolutely radiant—even among the other witches, she stood out as if a ray of sunshine lit her path.

He didn't want to make it obvious that he was trying to attract her attention, so he purposely bumped into a soldier as he placed the last crate on the pallet.

The soldier spun on him with a nasty expression, like he'd just eaten sour fruit. "Watch where you're going!"

The confrontation had turned many heads, but the only face Oram was interested in seeing was Lyra's. She glanced over at the scene, and her eyes immediately went wide. Then she hurried into the dining hall behind them.

Oram's stomach dropped as he walked out the front entrance, hoping she would follow.

He made it all the way back to his cart without turning around, when he heard her soft voice in his head.

"It's good to see you."

Oram whirled around to face the castle, expecting Lyra to be standing right behind him, but she was standing at the doors, too far away to have spoken to him that clearly, but he'd heard her perfectly.

His expression must have given away his surprise, because he saw her place a hand over her mouth and suppress a laugh.

"I didn't mean to scare you," her voice echoed again, lips unmoving. *" It's too risky to speak in front of everyone."*

He wasn't sure if he could communicate back to her, but he forced his mind to think the words anyway, hoping she would hear. *"It's okay. I've missed you."*

It had been a week since their last encounter, and he had wondered how soon he'd get to see her again. Every afternoon after their second meeting, he stopped by the tavern after working in the fields, but she hadn't shown up again.

"I thought you'd be mad at me," the voice in his mind spoke carefully.

"I'm not," he thought. *"I just needed time to figure things out."*

He saw her smile from across the front lawn. Then her words traveled to him again. *"I'll come see you as soon as I can. Things are hectic right now, and it's best I stay close."*

Oram nodded to show he'd heard her. But as his eyes left hers, they fell directly on someone else standing not too far behind Lyra, just inside the doors.

He recognized the wolf-demon as General Ryker, the head of the queen's army.

The general gave Oram a curious expression, as if he suspected something odd, and the blood drained from Oram's face as he turned back to his cart and climbed up into the driver's seat.

He didn't risk looking back.

He held his breath the entire ride to the outer gates and prayed to whatever god was listening that he hadn't just risked Lyra's life.

Oram didn't know what the consequences would be for her, but he was smart enough to know that witches and demons fraternizing would be looked down upon.

When he finally reached the main road, Oram released all the air from his lungs, but he kept his eyes solely on the path in front of him.

There was a chance—it was a very small and unlikely chance, but a chance nonetheless—that the general hadn't put two and two together.

Perhaps, it was nothing.

But perhaps, he had just made a terrible, heinous mistake.

16

FREYAH

$\mathcal{A}$ week had passed since leaving the mountain, and Freyah missed Last Cove fiercely. She craved the salty air and the security of home. Her heart ached for her father, and she wondered how he was coping with her absence.

For the first two days, she'd mostly been secluded in her room, and she tried to pass the time by reading the book she borrowed from the library the day before, but she'd finished it in only a few hours and was ready to exchange it for another.

Whit had offered to take her to the library whenever she liked, but he had already bid her goodnight after dinner, and she didn't expect to see him again until morning.

She decided it was time to start testing the waters and find out exactly how much freedom she had. So, Freyah waited until the sun set behind the barracks outside her window, then with small, quiet steps, she exited her unlocked room and ventured down the tower steps.

It was her third night at Larapuna, and she'd yet to grasp the layout of the endless stone corridors, but she remembered the library wasn't far from her room. Even if she got lost, Freyah wanted to see what secrets the castle had to offer. She wanted to see the people that lived here: where they slept, or how they felt about sharing a roof with the witches.

Most of all, Freyah needed to find out what Madam Lema wanted from her.

Was she truly the key the queen had been referring to at breakfast yesterday morning?

She found her way to a long hallway full of closed doors. Each had a sconce hanging to the right of the frame and a number etched into the wood. She assumed these were the apartments in which the soldiers' families lived while they trained and worked in the barracks. Each door was no more than five feet apart, so she couldn't imagine them having much living space inside. Freyah's room was located in a turret of the smallest western tower, and even that felt more accommodating than the looks of this.

Freyah meandered further through Larapuna's twists and turns, finding only more locked doors and a few empty rooms. Though she knew there were hundreds of people living within, the castle felt barren. Like an empty structure of bones with no soul, completely opposite of her bustling mountain home that was full of life.

After almost an hour of wandering, she passed under a stone archway into a new hallway lined with statues dressed in old-fashioned armor. A single door at the end sat slightly ajar. She approached it and stopped at the edge of the frame to peer through the crack.

Freyah saw empty amphitheater seating, but there was a muffled voice drifting out into the hall from within the room.

"What is it exactly you hope to gain by using the girl?"

The words came from an old, exhausted voice—an elderly woman by the sound of it—and something told Freyah they were referring to her.

She leaned in as close as she could while still hiding herself in the shadows.

"Do you realize how stressful it's been trying to keep this country in line? No one wants to listen to us anymore. We're losing our influence. I can't use my Sight as easily as Grandmother could. I can only imagine how difficult it will be for the next generation."

Freyah's attention snapped back, and she recoiled into a hesitant crouch. The other person in the room was Madam Lema. Though Freyah's intent had been to find out more about the queen's motives, she hadn't planned on eavesdropping quite so plainly.

"I'm glad you brought that up," the elder said. "The clock is ticking with every day that passes, my dear. You're well into your seventieth year, and you've yet to continue the bloodline. It won't be long before that door of opportunity slams shut."

"I have more important things to worry about than filling my womb with a child," Madam Lema spat. "We've been using Future Sight to keep the peace for centuries. How will I know what to do if I can't see it? Do you not realize how critical this is? I could have stopped the rebellion before it even started if I'd been able to see it coming. This worthless thing isn't working."

Freyah leaned further into the threshold and caught sight of the queen standing barely within her line of sight. She couldn't see what "thing" Madam Lema had been referring to, but she didn't want to move any closer and give herself away.

A chair scraped across the floor.

"You have lost sight of what's most important, dear. You think I don't know what you've been tampering with? I can smell the blood on you." The elder released a heavy sigh. "Whatever it is you think you can get that girl to do isn't going to help your Future Sight. You found the resource to fix it, and it didn't work. Take that as a sign from Lillia that there are things you need not see."

Madam Lema pressed a hand to her throat and brushed a thumb over the necklace there. "I don't need her to help me see the future—she's going to help me control it."

The queen then took a step toward the door, and Freyah's heart leapt into her throat. She darted as quickly as she could to the end of the hall without making a sound and ducked behind a bronze statue of a soldier. As she did, she accidentally brushed against the metal armor, shifting it just enough to cause a small *ting* to ring out in the silence.

Freyah held her breath.

She didn't dare peek her head out to see if Madam Lema had heard, but she waited for several seconds, listening to the witch's footsteps as they retreated down the other end of the hall.

A minute later, another more fatigued and unsteady set of steps followed. The elder witch took off in the opposite direction, heading straight to where Freyah stood.

Freyah squeezed herself into the tight space and hoped the old woman had poor eyesight and would pass right by without a second glance.

It seemed as if the woman was doing just that, but Freyah's eyes widened when her steps suddenly hesitated.

The small bit of freedom she'd been allowed was being forcibly stripped away as she imagined the witches locking her inside the tower without a key. She'd never see her father or Corianne again.

But just like that, the moment passed, and the old woman continued down the corridor, one meager step at a time.

Freyah released the breath she'd been holding and wiped a bead of sweat from her brow. The mission had proven to be fruitful—she'd never in her wildest dreams expected to gather that much information so easily—but it had come at a risk.

Sneaking around without Whit as her protective shield was going to be dangerous. She would be better off having him by her side, which meant she would have to confide in him about her trepidations.

He'd helped her before.

Hopefully he would help her again

She made it back to her room without being spotted, but just before opening her door, she caught sight of movement in her peripheral vision. Her heart thumped wildly and she froze.

As she focused her eyes in the dimly lit stairwell, she saw the outline of a long, wispy tail and four legs. It was a cat—an actual cat, not a demon—and the surprise was almost as shocking as if she'd been caught by one of Madam Lema's soldiers.

Freyah hadn't expected there to be pets roaming about the halls of

Larapuna and wondered to whom the feline belonged. Perhaps it was merely a stray seeking food and shelter from the elements.

As her heartbeat slowed back to its normal rhythm, she bent low and held out her hand. She *tisked* softly with her tongue in an attempt to coax the cat closer, thinking there was no harm in showing it some affection.

The cat was a smoky gray color with short, fluffy fur and bright yellow eyes. It eyed Freyah suspiciously from the shadows, but after deducing she wasn't a threat, it crept carefully closer. It sniffed her hand, testing her scent and possibly looking for a treat. Then, to her surprise, it brushed affectionately against her leg and purred.

"You're easy to please," she said in a hushed tone.

The cat circled her where she squatted and released a small, high-pitched *meow.* It was more of a squeak, and Freyah found it incredibly endearing. She inspected its hind quarters and gathered that it was a boy.

"I don't have any food for you, but I know where to get you some," she told him. "Come back tomorrow morning, and I'll take you to breakfast."

He squeaked again and sauntered off, as if truly understanding her offer.

She smiled to herself.

Perhaps she'd made a friend after all.

THE CAT DID NOT RETURN the next day, but after breakfast, Madam Lema invited Freyah to join her in the royal gardens later that afternoon.

She immediately thought the worst, assuming the queen had discovered her traipse through the castle the night before. She tried to formulate whatever excuse sounded the most believable as to why she'd been lurking around the castle unattended, but she decided it was probably best to keep her mouth shut altogether. Freyah wouldn't say anything incriminating unless directly confronted about it.

Whit appeared at her door to escort her as the sun was at its highest peak in the sky. When he took in her outfit, he gave her a soft smile.

"You don't like the dresses," he assumed.

Freyah had been wearing the same linen button down and black leggings for three days. Madam Lema had presented her with dresses after obtaining her new room, but Freyah hadn't touched them. After what happened with Roman, the thought of wearing them made her feel exposed. She was much more comfortable in pants, especially while still being surrounded by so many soldiers every day.

But she didn't want to tell Whit that. Instead, she said, "I'm used to wearing pants at home on the mountain. It's safer."

It was true, but what mountain did she have to climb in Larapuna?

Whit could probably tell it was a poor excuse, but he didn't question it. Instead, he led her to the library, this time taking her out onto the veranda and into the lush garden.

Freyah hadn't been outside the castle walls since the day she arrived, and she was immediately elated by the light breeze that swept across her cheeks upon stepping out into the freshly manicured garden.

There were a variety of plants lining the stone pathway in front of them, along with an iron barricade tangled in vines. She didn't recognize many of the flowers, for most of them looked completely foreign and a little bit mysterious, but she saw her favorite blue bud blooming behind a row of small, yellow leafless stems.

Whit stopped and allowed her the time to admire them. Freyah had fallen dutifully into the new routine of spending her days rereading the book she'd borrowed quietly in her room, but she hadn't realized how much she craved the feeling of nature around her. Throughout her life, her days were filled by climbing the mountain and breathing salted air. Nature was in her blood, and she'd needed the reminder that the world was still out there.

For now, just this small venture into the gardens was enough to scratch that itch, like a soft caress against her longing to be free again.

It was as if Whit knew this was what she needed.

As he watched her soak in the sun's rays and bask in the beauty of the flowers, Freyah felt incredibly grateful for his kindness. Though most of their time together was spent walking to and from her room in the tower, at night, when she was tucked away in her bed, Freyah realized she actually enjoyed his company.

"Have you been enjoying the book?" Whit asked, pulling her attention away from the foliage.

His bandage was gone, and the mutilated skin around the outside of his left eye was angry and red. The damage stretched down to the top of his cheekbone, and though she hated it for him, Freyah thought the new addition actually suited him. Whit was the type of man that was expected to have scars, both on his flesh and his heart. Now it was easier for others to see them.

She rested against the iron fence and continued breathing in the fresh air around her. "I finished it actually. I think I might take you up on your offer to escort me to the library. I'd like to find another one, and it would be good to get out of my room when I can."

Whit nodded and dropped his gaze to the path at their feet. "I hope it was enough," he said quietly. "Telling her about him."

Freyah found a concerned expression on the lieutenant's face. He was referring to Roman and what the man had attempted. She couldn't be sure, but it seemed as if the memory pained him nearly as much as it haunted her.

Was he trying to make up for it somehow?

Over the days that followed Whit's decision to officially hand her over to the queen, Freyah had come to understand what he'd actually done for her and appreciate it fully. A stranger, someone that had every reason to dismiss her, risked pain to himself in order to take it from her. It was a sacrifice she would never be able to repay, but she wanted him to know how much it meant to her.

"It was everything," she told him. "You saved me, Whit. And I don't know how to thank you."

It was the first time she'd spoken his name out loud, and the sound of it brought a smile to his face. He even slackened his stance just the slightest.

Maybe that was all she could do.

It would be enough to bring him peace of mind.

They continued walking until the stone path met with a wide gazebo adorned with gilded spires. Beneath the structure stood Madam Lema and the witch Freyah recognized from the queen's chambers, Evanora. It looked as if they'd been arguing, but their conversation was cut off quickly by Freyah and Whit's arrival.

Before they were close enough for the witches to hear him, Whit placed a hand on Freyah's lower back and said, "It wasn't my decision to bring you here. I want you to know that."

Freyah didn't know how to respond.

She was still trying to take in his words and what they meant when Whit addressed the queen and bowed nobly. "Madam."

His hand left the place on Freyah's back, and she found herself wishing it had stayed.

Madam Lema barely acknowledged his gesture. She waved her hand, telling both Whit and Evanora they were dismissed. Freyah didn't want to be alone with the queen, but she had no real choice in the matter, so she planted her feet and waited for further instructions as Whit and Evanora walked back up the stone path.

Freyah gave a final fleeting glance to him as he disappeared, and she was happy to see that he too had turned back for one last look.

Madam Lema stepped off the landing of the gazebo and took hold of Freyah's arm in a casual, yet slightly forceful manner. "Walk with me."

It was clearly a command and not an invitation.

"I want to tell you just how happy I am that we were able to come to this little arrangement," she said. "Working together in times like this is so incredibly important."

Freyah cocked her head. "Arrangement?"

"Yes," Madam Lema concurred enthusiastically. "I helped you, and now you're going to help me."

The queen hadn't actually helped Freyah with anything, but she didn't correct her.

Madam Lema had spoken about how Freyah's insight could help with the current conflicts within the country, but it still wasn't entirely clear what *insight* she could provide. Freyah only knew what everyone else did, and she didn't imagine Madam Lema was completely oblivious to the opinions of her own people. It was as if she thought Freyah was sitting on some privileged information. But there was nothing to sit on. No special knowledge from behind enemy lines or secret plans from the rebels. Freyah had never even seen an actual member of The First Men in person. Their identities were purposefully kept hidden, and no participant would ever admit to being involved.

"I'll try my best," Freyah said, "but I'm not sure how much help I'll actually be."

Madam Lema's expression remained poised. "I have no doubt you'll be able to give me exactly what I need."

The two stopped when they reached an elaborately designed iron bench sitting in front of a patch of white flowers. They looked like enormous balls of cotton, small fragments blowing lightly in the wind and landing on the surface of the bench. Freyah touched one, surprised to find the surface waxy between her fingers.

She watched Madam Lema take a seat, and Freyah felt assured enough to do the same. "Will I be starting my job in the laundry room tomorrow?" she asked, breaking the silence.

"Ah, yes," the queen confirmed, as if she'd forgotten. "You will be starting tomorrow afternoon. For now, I'd like to talk."

Freyah tried to swallow the lump lodged in her throat. The sensation felt like a warning, but she waited patiently for whatever the queen had to say.

Madam Lema turned and plucked a white bud from one of the many stems behind them. "This is Eriocyper," she said. "It helps with memory. When you consume it, it unlocks echoes of moments your mind may have forgotten. Things you might have seen or heard but didn't seem important at the time."

The queen handed the bud to Freyah expectantly, so she took it. She held and examined the flower carefully but didn't know what else to do with it.

"I'm still not sure how I can help you," Freyah told her, unsure what the strange flower had to do with anything. "I know very little about the rebels. Only that they're called The First Men."

"What have you seen of them in Last Cove?"

There were rumors that the pier collapse hadn't truly been a consequence of bad storms, but Freyah didn't believe it. "Nothing really," she said. "I've just heard rumors. Nothing helpful."

Obviously sensing Freyah's hesitancy, Madam Lema nodded to the flower in encouragement. "With that, you'll be able to help more than you know."

With Madam Lema watching her so expectantly, Freyah was forced to consume the foreign flower.

It tasted as waxen as it felt, but it dissolved quickly on her tongue. She swallowed, expecting to immediately start hallucinating visions from her past, but nothing happened. She felt completely normal.

Except for the wave of exhaustion sweeping over her.

Freyah abruptly became very, very tired. She fought to hold her eyes open, but it was too tempting to close them. She felt warm and wholly relaxed. Her mouth tried to form words, to tell the queen that she needed to go lie down, but she couldn't make herself speak.

She was already drifting off into the open embrace of slumber.

AS SHE SLEPT, she dreamed.

Small scenes played out in front of her as if she were part of them, but she was not. She was watching, remembering, from another part of her mind entirely.

She saw herself as a young girl sitting on her bed reading a book about Ghomarian folklore. She saw her father in the next room, filling several small casings with powder and then dropping them each into different bottles filled with liquid. Even in the dream, she could smell the scent of something like garlic in the air. Her current subconscious mind tried to pull herself closer to the scene, but the door in front of her shut, and Freyah fell into another memory.

She saw her father standing solemnly in front of a grave marker, and an extremely young Freyah placed a blue lily in the dirt.

A stranger approached her father and said, *"We scraped as much from the rocks as we could."*

Her father replied, *"Not today."*

"But sir, it might not be enough."

Her father turned sharply to face the man, his back to his daughter now a few feet away. *"I said, not today."*

A loud ringing pierced Freyah's ears, and she was thrown into the memory of a building exploding into flames. She saw thick clouds of dust and heard the screams of people inside. Below the scene, she saw the arms of a father closing around his daughter, followed by a whisper. *"They won't hurt you, Freyah. You will always be protected by The First Men."*

Freyah felt the sting of tears in her eyes. Her vision blurred. And when she blinked, she saw the moment her father answered the door —the same night she had been taken.

"Tomorrow night," he spoke quietly. *"Spread the word that I'm calling a meeting."*

Then, Freyah's eyes flew open.

She was back in her room in the western tower of the castle, and realization struck her like lightning.

Madam Lema had been right about the Eriocyper.

All the small memories she'd forgotten about her father over the years were now front and center in Freyah's mind, as if they'd only happened yesterday.

She now knew two things: she really had been sitting on privileged information, and it was because her father was a member of The First Men.

17

FREYAH

After sleeping the entire afternoon and night away, Freyah awoke the next morning with a pounding headache. The effects of the Eriocyper had worn off, but the lingering symptoms were nearly as mind-altering as the magic itself. The dull throbbing in her temples made her want to crawl back under the covers and hide from the light, but today was the first day of her job in the laundry room.

She placed two bare feet on the floor and stood.

Her experience with the strange flower made it clear that something much bigger was happening than she originally thought, and it had been right under her nose.

How had she missed something so huge?

She'd always thought she shared an open and honest relationship with her father, so how was it possible that he had hidden this part of himself so well?

The memories that appeared to her in her dream were buried so deep she'd never thought to question them, but now they couldn't be ignored. Her father had not only been involved with the rebellion for years, but he was responsible for actual harm.

The Eriocyper was supposed to help clear her memory, but it had only made her all the more confused. She needed a solid ally—someone she could bounce all the ideas floating in her head off of—and it was time she put some official trust in Whit.

She decided she was going to tell him everything, and she hoped to the gods that he had some insight on how to help.

Freyah searched the shelves for something clean to wear. She'd need to do some washing of her own soon, or else she'd have no choice but to wear the dresses Madam Lema had given her. Crouching down, she was surprised to find a new pile of folded clothes she didn't recognize. She thumbed through the fabrics and found four new pairs of leggings, as well as several tunics that came with leather bodices.

Had someone delivered them while she'd been sleeping?

She dressed quickly, feeling more comfortable than she had in a while. The leather bodice gave her the perfect place to stash a weapon if need be, and it secured her breasts more than the bralettes did on their own.

Because she felt so confident in her outfit, she decided to wear the new boots instead of her old ones.

When she exited her room, Whit was nowhere to be seen. Typically he was there before she woke, waiting patiently outside the door for her to get ready. But today, the hall was vacant.

Not a moment later, however, she was greeted by the sight of Whit jogging hurriedly up the tower steps. His hair was damp, and he was in his casual uniform. Freyah couldn't help herself as she took in the broadness of his shoulders and the way his white tunic stretched tightly across his chest.

"Sorry I'm late," he apologized with a heavy breath. "Early training session this morning. Ran a bit over."

"What are you training for?" she asked.

Freyah fell in step beside him as he turned and began walking back down the steps, leading her to breakfast. It was a silly question. The muscles in his biceps that strained against the thin material of his shirt were enough to tell her that he spent plenty of time working on his figure. But she wasn't sure how much of that time was spent on combat. She knew he was a soldier that had been assigned as her personal guard, but Freyah didn't know what all his actual job entailed. Most of his time was spent escorting her to and from her room, and she hoped he wasn't too bored of her company.

"We have team defense training once a month," he answered, "but I like to put in the extra effort."

"Like what?"

"I run the perimeter of the castle every morning, and I do stretches every night before bed."

The image of a shirtless Whit doing extensive stretching immediately clouded her vision, and her cheeks flushed. "W-why the stretches?" she stammered.

"There's a disease in my family that affects the joints. I lost my mom and grandmother because of it. By the end, Gran could barely move. So far it hasn't affected Willow, but I've felt the early signs of it. I'm trying to ward it off as long as possible."

Freyah's flustered nerves immediately dissipated. Whit had lost his mother, too. It was something she'd never shared in common with anyone before.

"I'm so sorry." Her condolences felt hollow, so she decided to confide in him by sharing her own painful loss. "I, um...I lost my mother, too. I actually never knew her."

With those last few words, she reached out to grab his hand, lacing her fingers through his and squeezing.

Whit's steps slowed as he turned his head to face her. Gazing at their clasped hands, he gave a small nod of appreciation, a smile tugging on his lips, but he didn't stop walking.

Freyah now knew that kind of pain also—that no matter how hard things got, it was always better to keep going. Because if you stopped, the world might come crashing down and bury you.

As his gaze traveled back up to her face, he took in the new clothes she was wearing. This brought a true smile to his face, showing off a dimple in his chin.

"You look nice," he said, slipping his hand from hers and returning to a soldier's stance as they continued walking.

Freyah blushed and straightened the bodice. "Thanks."

A thought registered at the mention of her clothes. Whit had been the only one to note her choice to wear the same thing every day, and she'd specifically told him the reason she didn't wear the dresses.

"Did you get them for me?" she asked hesitantly, not wanting to overstep and assume something.

Whit kept his face stoic, trying to remain the ever perfect guard and not the friend she was coming to know. But the way he pushed his hair away from his face answered her question. The way his shoulders slightly relaxed when he was with her.

Whit nodded curtly, but didn't acknowledge it any further.

It was enough to stir a kaleidoscope of butterflies in her belly.

AT BREAKFAST, Freyah indulged in thinly-sliced ham and eggs. To her surprise, Whit chose to sit next to her at one of the servants' tables instead of with his fellow soldiers across the room. He was the only man at the table, but he didn't seem to mind. His focus was entirely set on her, and her hands became clammy because of it.

She was nervous around him now for entirely different reasons than before. She was no longer scared or concerned about being with a stranger. Freyah's comfort around Whit had grown into something she couldn't quite put her finger on, but it was becoming increasingly difficult not to notice that dimple in his chin, or that he actually pushed the hair away from his face when he was around her, like he didn't want to hide from her. And there was something in the way he spoke to her, as if her opinion truly mattered.

She watched as he stuffed large chunks of fruit into his mouth before swallowing the previous bite. Juice dripped lazily down his chin, and she had to fight the urge to lean over and taste it herself.

She had to get a grip.

There were more important things to deal with, and Whit wasn't meant to be a distraction from them. She needed his help—she simply needed to pluck up the courage and ask him.

"Listen, I've been meaning to ask you something." Freyah leveled her tone so she sounded more assured. In her head, however, she was still trying to brush the inappropriate thoughts away.

Whit finally swallowed and wiped his chin with his sleeve. He took a sip from his water goblet, his elbows resting confidently on the table, then he met her eyes. "Yes?"

She still wasn't used to that rough gravel in his voice. At first, it had made him seem intimidating, but now, it sent tingles down her spine.

"I might have overheard something the other day, and it has me wondering…what is it Madam Lema wants from me exactly?"

Whit opened and closed his mouth multiple times without speaking. His brows pulled together, as if he were trying to formulate an answer that would please her.

"Do you know something?" Freyah asked more directly.

At this, Whit sat straighter. He took another swig from his goblet then sat it down. His fingers tapped nervously against the table.

"Not here," he told her under his breath.

He glanced suspiciously around the room, but everyone else was tucking into their breakfast, paying no mind to anyone outside their own conversations.

Whit took her by the arm and pulled her away from the table.

He led her to the place that had somehow become theirs: the library, a place of seclusion and intimacy. It wasn't just that he had been the one to take her there, it was the way the room was filled with so many layers of knowledge. Underneath piles of dust were novels that held pages written from history and memory. And within those pages were hundreds of stories and secrets.

Freyah now saw Whit the same way. He might have been scarred and tough on the outside, but he simply needed to be dusted off and listened to in order to shine once again.

The room was empty, as it had been the first day he brought her here. The sun was high in the early morning sky, and its light filled the space with a warm glow through the domed glass ceiling.

Whit took a quick scan of the room to make sure there were no hidden guests, then he rested his hip against the edge of one of the tables and crossed his arms over his broad chest.

"So, what did you hear?" he asked, getting straight to the point.

Freyah cleared her throat and leaned against the table across from him. "I was exploring the castle..." she began, but he immediately interrupted her.

"Alone? Without a guard?"

"Yes, without a guard. It was late, and I wanted a new book. Besides, how else am I going to see what Madam Lema is really hiding?"

He gave her a slow, disbelieving head shake. "You could have asked me." Then he added, "You can trust me."

She felt guilty for not confiding in him sooner—after all, he'd been the one to rescue her on multiple occasions—but there was nothing she could do to change her past decisions. What mattered was that she was talking to him now.

"I do trust you," she told him. "I just needed to see for myself." She placed both hands on the table behind her and leaned back. "I overheard Madam Lema talking to an older woman. She mentioned something called Future Sight and how it was getting weaker with every generation. She talked about using someone for something, and I'm pretty sure she meant me."

Whit's eyes narrowed on her. His fists clenched. "Use you how?"

"I don't know," she admitted. "I hoped you would."

Whit thought on it, then uncrossed his arms. "Future Sight is how witches see visions of the future. It's been used since demons were created, and long before that." He stepped closer and casually brushed the hair that draped down her chest over her shoulder. His fingers grazed her collarbone, and the sensation made her shiver. "But I don't see how that's connected to you."

Freyah tried to maintain her composure, but his closeness sent her cheeks flushing with heat. It was the second time he'd purposefully touched her in such a way—the first being his light hand on the small of her back, when he'd told her it hadn't been his decision to bring her to Larapuna.

Both touches were intentional, meant to command all of her senses and attention, but this one was slightly different. It held an invitation—one she desperately wanted to respond to.

Freyah had never been forward when it came to showing her interest in others. In the past, Freyah allowed them to steer the ship and initiate every move. It was clear Whit was doing that now, but there was something about him that made her want to be bold and initiate something of her own.

He drew out her impulsive nature.

Whit was looking at her expectantly, and she'd all but forgotten they were in the middle of a conversation.

"If she can see the future," she said, mind still hazy, "how come she hasn't been able to stop the rebels?"

"You said it yourself," he recounted. "She's getting weaker. And that's valuable knowledge to have, since she wouldn't dare let anyone else know that."

Neither of them had moved. Whit didn't inch any closer, and Freyah didn't shift away. Together, they hovered there with nothing but an arm's reach between their bodies, caught in the gravitational pull of one another.

"There's something else," Freyah continued. "Yesterday, when you showed me to the gardens, she gave me something—a flower called Eriocyper. She said it would help me remember things, and that's how I would help her." She gathered her next words close to her chest before releasing them, for she didn't want Whit to judge her, or her father, too harshly. "It worked. I remembered all these odd things about my father." She paused. "I think he's involved with The First Men."

The revelation didn't shock Whit. If anything, it made him more curious. He took another step forward, appearing eager to learn more. Or maybe it was simply to be closer to her.

"You think, or you know?" he asked.

"I'm not sure. But it makes sense. The pier in our shipping port had structural damage, but I'm starting to think it wasn't the weather that brought it down. And I remembered a fire." She faltered slightly, remembering the screams. The panic of people running and the dust settling over crumpled bodies. "If he did that..." She shook her head. "I just can't believe he would be capable of something like that."

It was the thing that bothered her most.

The knowledge was shocking, but the betrayal was a stab to the back. Freyah would have understood if her father had trusted her enough to confide his ideology. Even so, it was hard to rationalize the acts that had caused injury and harm with the intentions behind them, no matter how pure. She needed to know why, but she wouldn't get the answer until she talked to her father.

"A man came to him the night I was captured," she confessed, still hesitant. The subject was a bit of a sore spot between them. "He looked to my father for instructions," she said. "Like he was a leader."

Whit opened his mouth to speak but his attention was suddenly pulled to the doors behind him. His head snapped back, neck craned as if listening for something.

"Did you hear something?" Freyah whispered, now on alert.

He listened for a few more seconds, then relaxed.

"No. It's nothing," he said, giving the doors another sidelong glance before fully facing her again. "It's possible your father oversaw a small branch of the rebellion. They're scattered everywhere now, and every district has someone in command that reports to the top."

"Who's at the top?"

"No one knows," he said. "It makes sense that Madam Lema would want to gain some sort of leverage over one of the smaller leaders."

"That leverage being me," Freyah concluded.

"The unrest has only grown over the years, and pretty soon it's going to reach its peak. Ghoma can't handle another war. We lost too many men the first time."

Freyah understood. Another war would be devastating.

Was Madam Lema using her as a threat against her father, to warn him to back off? If so, it would seem that Freyah wasn't only here to serve penance for her crime. Was she a bargaining chip?

She scowled. "If the queen wants to use me for leverage, then it's just a coincidence that I ended up in her castle?"

Whit's eyes were pleading. He looked like he desperately wanted to say something—she could see it bubbling under his skin—but of course, he decided against it. "Maybe."

There was most definitely more to the story. She'd thought that having Whit on her team would be helpful, but so far it was only providing her with more questions than answers. He clearly knew something, but he wasn't going to be the one to tell her.

"What about the Future Sight?" she diverted. "What could that possibly have to do with me?"

He stroked his chin and gazed with intense focus at the shelf of books to his right. There weren't going to be any answers for them in there, at least she didn't think so.

"Maybe I can do some digging," he suggested. "I'll ask Raven. She's a witch that's helped me in the past. She might know something."

The knowledge of Whit being friends with a witch sat uncomfortably in Freyah's gut. Exactly how intimate was this friendship?

More importantly, why did it bother her so much?

"Okay," she agreed, refusing to show her sudden jealousy. "But Whit…" She held her tongue, debating whether or not to speak her worry aloud, but she said it anyway. "I trust you. That means you can't tell anyone about my father."

She had to know that he wouldn't betray her confidence.

The space between them was now no more than a hair's breadth, and he was staring at her assuredly without blinking.

"I would never jeopardize you or your father's safety," he said. "I swear it, Freyah."

He was close enough that she could feel his breath on her cheek. Heat flushed her face again, but this time she couldn't hide it. She wanted to touch him—to place a hand on his chest and inhale the scent of him, tea tree and pine—but she was still too afraid to make the first move.

He leaned forward so that his forehead pressed firmly against hers and closed his eyes. "I've wanted to kiss you ever since you slapped that fish out of my hands," he whispered. Though his words were funny, they felt like a soft caress. "But after what that bastard did, I didn't want you to think I was anything like him."

"I don't," she told him breathily.

"I promise you," he said, now using his thumb to draw small circles against her hip. "You are always in control with me."

He pulled away with longing and the slightest bit of satisfaction written on his face, then he squeezed her hip gently and turned to walk away. "Let's get you back in there before someone notices you're gone."

Freyah's entire body was flushed with heat, building between her thighs, and her muscles clenched in response. Something had just changed between them, and she desperately wanted to explore it.

Did Whit know what sort of reaction he'd elicited in her?

Of course he did.

"You can't do that," she protested, her voice slightly higher than normal.

He stopped and faced her again. "Do what?"

She scoffed and threw her hands in the air. "Don't play coy. You know what you just did."

Whit smirked and raised an eyebrow. "And what was that?"

"You started something," she said. "And now you need to finish it."

He lifted his eyes to the ceiling as if gazing directly upon the gods. "Thank fuck," he growled, and then he was on her.

In three long strides, his lips crashed against hers. His hands were in her hair and on her back as he pressed his entire body flush to hers. But the feeling of his firm chest and thighs moving against her wasn't enough. She needed more contact. More pressure. Her skin was on fire, yet there wasn't enough friction between them to set her ablaze the way she craved.

Whit seemed to sense her ferocity, because suddenly both of his hands were on her hips, lifting and setting her on the table.

Freyah gasped into his mouth, and Whit's tongue claimed hers.

Warmth built in her belly, and the sensation of it was unlike anything she'd ever felt before.

There were people back home in Last Cove she'd found attractive —some even beautiful enough that she'd shared their beds—but Whit triggered something stronger from her. Something primal and wild.

Freyah had never been this bold when it came to her sexual desires. She felt shy when it came to physical pleasure. Yet she couldn't stop herself from slipping a hand around the back of Whit's neck and digging her fingers in his hair. The long strands felt like silk sliding through her grasp. She felt daring, so she pulled slightly, testing his reaction, and when a deep groan escaped the back of his throat, she knew he approved.

She loved the way his stubble grazed against her chin, leaving her skin raw and used. He was marking her in more ways than one, and the sensation only spurred on her eagerness to be close to him.

Freyah's thumb slid across his temple and down to the place his ear should be, but there was nothing there. It was odd, but her desires were too strong to consider it.

But then her fingers brushed what felt like the soft texture of a bird's down along his cheek.

She jerked back.

Whit's eyes were no longer the warm shade of brown she'd come to know so well. His pupils had dilated into massive black orbs, and what should have been white was now a bright saffron with the instincts of a predator.

Freyah clamored backward on the table, and upon seeing her reaction, Whit stopped to examine himself.

His fingers were now tipped with sharp talons. Together they watched as the skin on the backs of his hands morphed into a leathery-looking texture.

Freyah's heart pounded uncontrollably in her chest. The excitement she'd previously felt had turned to sheer and utter fear unlike anything she'd felt toward Whit before.

Layers of thin tawny feathers had sprouted from around the

contours of his face. They spread over his cheeks and up into his hairline.

"You're... you're a *demon*?" she cried.

Instead of answering her, Whit made a run for it.

Only this time, instead of running toward her, he was running away.

18

WHIT

Whit didn't think. He just ran.

His legs guided him through the lower corridors, boots pounding against the stone floor. He didn't care how much attention he might be drawing—it was early, and most of Larapuna's residents would still be eating breakfast—but he kept up his pace nonetheless.

He had to get to Raven before anyone saw him.

He couldn't let anyone get a good look at his face.

Godsdamnit, those stupid feathers—that was what he hated most. He could feel the tell-tale itch crawling along his scalp as they spread to his hairline, and the joints of his hands ached from where they'd hooked into claws.

He had to hurry.

As an ignorant teenager, Whit hadn't known that Madam Lema didn't employ demons in her army. Living so far from the castle meant he'd had the luxury of safety. Demons didn't hide in The Mounds—they walked freely, knowing they were an entire country away from their biggest threat—so Whit had always assumed there was nothing to fear.

It had been his decision to trek across Ghoma and seek work

under the queen. And by the time he and his sisters reached the castle, it was too late to hide.

Besides Ryker, Madam Lema would never accept a demon into her army.

Because to her, they were no more than animals.

Perhaps it had been fate that sent Raven to evaluate him before being presented to the queen and offering his service. One look at his scared yet defiant face and she'd known exactly what he needed to survive.

When she offered him a way in, Whit had taken it eagerly, unaware of the strings that would come along with it.

He always hated being a demon. Having little to no memory of his father was hard enough, but to grow up learning that the man who made him wasn't human? That was devastating.

Whether his father left willingly or had gotten himself killed, he abandoned a child who he'd cursed to live a life of judgment and hardship. Because of this, Whit never wanted kids of his own. He refused to pass on his cursed genes.

He couldn't blame his mother—given her sickly state, he knew she'd had to depend on others. She probably accepted help and companionship from the first man to come along and set eyes on her.

But he wasn't there for her when she needed it most.

The only thing he gave her was three children, exacerbating her symptoms to the point that it killed her, and then he'd bid his farewell.

Beyond the need to hide, *that* was the true reason Whit had taken the elixir from Raven—he didn't want to see another trace of similarity to his father. He wanted to shed the connection like the skin of a snake, to be reborn and start anew.

Raven had warned him that he would be playing a lifelong role—a ruse that would cost him his life, and possibly hers, if discovered.

It was that warning that swirled around in his head as he climbed up a winding wooden staircase and up to the northern tower.

He approached Raven's chambers and announced his presence by banging forcefully on the door. After waiting several seconds for someone to answer, he banged again.

Finally, the door flung upon.

"What in Lillia's name!" Raven barked.

Her dark hair was tied into two intricate braids that fell down her back. Her narrow umber eyes were heavy and red with lack of sleep, and there was a shawl draped around her slender shoulders.

When she saw him—demon features and all—her bloodshot eyes went wide, and she yanked him inside by the collar of his shirt.

"What happened?" she demanded, immediately walking over to her work station to begin preparing his elixir. "I gave you enough for the week."

Whit sat in a leatherback chair and held his head in his hands, letting out an exasperated sigh. "I know," he groaned. "I forgot to take it this morning."

Raven whipped her head around to face him, her pale cheeks now flushed with anger. "You *forgot?*"

He gave her a condescending stare. "Yes, I *forgot.* I was running late to escort Freyah and I just..."

"You got distracted is what happened," she interjected. "And what did I tell you about distractions?"

"You and Willow both need to get off my back, alright? I can't be on my toes one hundred percent of the time. Mistakes happen."

Raven stopped working and leveled on him with a cold stare. "You knew the risk. And you agreed. *Mistakes* cannot *happen* when it comes to this." She held up the glass vial, half full with a grainy, pale blue liquid. "Or it'll be both our heads. Do you understand?"

Whit met her eyes. "Yes," he growled.

"Good." She added a sprinkle here and there of various ingredients Whit had no clue how to identify, then she corked the top of the vial with her thumb and shook it. "This one is stronger," she instructed, "so don't take your next dose until tomorrow night."

When the contents were mixed to her liking, Whit watched as the color of the liquid changed to a deep royal blue. Raven handed him the vial that smelled of tea tree oil and he shot it back quickly. Whit barely had time to register the bitter taste on his tongue before his claws began retracting.

Relief washed over him like a warm blanket and he immediately relaxed. "What about the next one?" he asked.

"You'll have to start taking it at night now. You've messed up your schedule."

"Is that going to change anything?"

"No..." she dragged. "Just don't take it too early or it won't last throughout the next day. Wait until the last minute when you're going to sleep."

He nodded. "Thank you, Raven. I'm sorry this happened."

"You should be," she chided, her tone slightly less harsh.

The two of them had spent many nights together thanks to the secret they shared, and Whit had come to know her as one of the slightly less awful witches in the coven. But that didn't mean she was to be underestimated. Raven could be wrathful when she wanted to be, and he knew very well if this mistake were to happen again, she would not be as forgiving.

Whit stood to leave, giving her a nod to show his thanks once again, but she stopped him.

"You only come to visit me when you need refills," she purred. "This new girl you're guarding must have really piqued your interest."

There was no way to respond to her accusation without giving away his true feelings for Freyah, and an admission like that was dangerous leverage to give to a witch.

Instead, he gave her a somewhat flirtatious smile to soothe her ego.

"I'll see you next week, Raven."

19

FREYAH

*L*ater that afternoon, Freyah was assigned her first shift with Willow in the laundry room. Having an actual job meant she'd have less time to spend reading, but Freyah had a feeling the queen would want to keep her as occupied as possible now that her memories were sharpened.

Madam Lema hadn't asked to meet again, so Freyah hadn't yet been forced to share the new information she'd acquired concerning her father. She was glad to stay away from the witch-queen for as long as possible, for Freyah now feared Madam Lema's ability to read her mind. She'd learned that witches could see the future, but Freyah was still unsure of the total stretch of their abilities.

Her time in the laundry room with Willow ticked by slowly. Whit's sister wasn't much of a talker. The girl kept to herself, concentrating solely on the job in front of her. There were a handful of other girls that worked alongside them, but Willow steered clear of their chatter and petty gossip.

Freyah stuck closely to Willow seeing as she was meant to be her guide in learning the systems of washing and collecting each different type of garment. There were the uniforms for the soldiers, dresses for the handmaids and other wards, and the more intricate, fancy attire that belonged to the witches. Each had to be handled with specialized care, all the way down to the type of conditioning oil used on the soldiers' fighting leathers.

Freyah had barely taken in Willow's instructions. She was too distracted by the bombshell that had been dropped on her that morning.

Her revelation about Whit had been earth-shattering. All this time, he'd been pretending to be human. But how?

She didn't think it was possible for demons to hide their features like that. But with access to a castle full of witches and their magic, she guessed anything was possible.

Freyah was utterly conflicted. She'd just begun opening up to Whit, and she felt she could trust him with the secrets about her father. But now, after learning that he'd hidden such a significant part of himself from her, was it even possible to hold on to that newly found trust anymore?

It was a massive secret, and keeping it from the entire army *and* the queen must have been incredibly difficult for him.

Freyah's head spun as she attempted to gather clean trousers from the wash basin. She knew she was moving slowly, but her work productivity was hindered by the swirl of thoughts in her head. She had to focus on something else, or she'd drive herself mad. So she attempted to eavesdrop for any interesting information that might slip out in conversation amongst the other girls.

The exchanges were fairly dull. Mostly the women shared stories about soldiers, debating which ones were considered attractive and which could be easily manipulated into providing particular perks for them. By the time Freyah hung all the wet trousers on the line by the window to dry, she was beginning to lose interest.

Her ears perked up, however, when someone mentioned a witch.

Freyah listened closely as a petite woman with a short black bob and almond skin mentioned that her once-reliable soldier friend was no longer bringing her chamomile from the garden to help her sleep. A boisterous blonde replied to this, explaining that all the other girl had to do was ask Raven to make her a sleeping draft.

That name brought about a collective sigh amongst the other girls, but it struck a bitter chord inside Freyah's chest.

Was this the Raven that Whit had mentioned?

He said she'd helped him, but what did that mean? Was she responsible for the magic that disguised his demon features?

"I wish there were more witches like Raven," a quieter, younger-looking girl with vivid red hair spoke. "She helped me so much the first month I was here."

The others agreed unanimously.

The dark haired woman then said, "I hardly see her around anymore. The queen's kept her so busy that she rarely leaves that tower of hers."

"Figures," the blonde noted.

Freyah looked to Willow as the others continued talking, and Willow's eyes quickly darted away from hers.

"I sometimes see her in the gardens gathering ingredients," the redhead offered softly. "Maybe you can catch her next time."

The first woman gave a satisfied nod and returned to her work.

Freyah looked to Willow again, but she was now focused back on folding a stack of soldiers' uniform shirts. Freyah wanted to ask her what she knew about the witch named Raven, but she started with a vague question—something else that had been plaguing her mind.

Freyah walked back to where Willow stood. "It seems that most of the workers here have lived in Larapuna for a long time," she started. Willow gave her a side glance, but continued folding. "Do you know anyone that's left? You know, gone back home?"

Willow straightened and narrowed her eyes. "Why are you asking?"

Her deep auburn hair was tied back with a lace ribbon, and there were dozens of flyaways framing her flustered face. It was hot in the laundry room from all the steam, and it reminded Freyah of her father's smithy, causing a pang of homesickness to flare in her chest.

"Just curious," Freyah lied. "I still don't fully understand how everything works. Do people come to work at the castle because it pays more? Or are some people working as discipline like me?"

Willow's expression scrunched into annoyance. "Why don't you worry about your own situation?" she snapped, completely dismissing Freyah's question. "You wouldn't want to get caught up in someone else's mess."

The warning took Freyah by surprise. Willow clearly had zero intention of getting involved with Freyah's supposed mess, but she didn't have to be so rude about it.

"What's your problem with me exactly?" Freyah dared.

"I don't have a problem with you," she said. "I have a problem with what my brother has done for you."

Freyah sat defeated on the edge of the wash basin. She hadn't thought about the risk Whit might be taking in choosing to help her, and now that she knew his secret, it made his choice all the more dangerous.

"She took my sister."

It was as if the siblings had seen the risk of sticking their necks out first hand. And then it occurred to her…maybe they had.

"You tried to escape, didn't you?" Freyah whispered faintly.

Willow's jaw set, then she whirled on her, coming so close that her long auburn hair whipped across Freyah's cheek and stung.

"Whatever you're thinking," Willow told her, "don't. You think it's bad now? It can always get worse. It's best to remember that."

She stormed off, leaving an upturned bucket of soapy water in her wake.

Freyah was left stunned.

Part of her felt sorry for the girl. And despite her current trepidations against Whit, she felt sorry for him, too. They had obviously been through something terrible, and Whit's recent actions had triggered his sister to fear a repeat consequence.

Freyah understood Willow's fear, but she wasn't going to let it control her own decisions. Her father was now possibly at risk, and she wasn't about to let the queen use her as a pawn in some fucked up game of war.

Freyah now knew she had to escape and make it home to Last

Cove. She had to warn her father about Madam Lema and the possibility that she knew who he was and what he had done.

Screw paying her penance.

Freyah didn't care about the risk—all she knew was getting away from Larapuna was the most important thing.

At the end of her shift, Freyah made a point to hang back, ensuring she was the last to leave the room. Near the drying rack were several pairs of scissors for cutting fabric. Without thinking, she grabbed one of the larger sets and stuffed them into her leather bodice.

It was somewhat impractical, but she needed a weapon.

Just in case.

Because she was going home.

FREYAH WAS startled awake by the sudden inability to breathe.

There were hands over her mouth, and she desperately tried to suck in air through her nose, but her panic made it harder to draw air into her lungs.

She could barely make out the silhouette of Madam Lema hovering over her in the darkness of her room, but it was the long nails pinching Freyah's cheeks and the intense smell of wine wafting from the witch-queen's breath that truly gave her away. Freyah tried to force her eyes to focus, but she still couldn't breathe, and the lack of oxygen was making them water.

"I knew that innocent facade of yours would wear off," Madam Lema said, her voice slick with sinful delight and laced with unspoken threats.

Freyah tried to scream, but the queen shushed her.

Madam Lema reached under Freyah's pillow and retrieved the pair of scissors she'd hidden away before going to sleep.

The amount of calm emanating from the queen made it that much harder for Freyah to muster any for herself. It was as if she was stealing it from the room and hoarding the emotion, leaving Freyah with nothing but panic.

Madam Lema was wrong—Freyah hadn't been playing innocent. But she was past being naïve. It was the queen that had finally let her mask slip.

But how had she known what Freyah planned to do?

Madam Lema whistled for someone, and heavy footsteps responded. A demon she didn't recognize who wore a soldier's uniform entered the room. Illuminated by the light outside her door, Freyah could make out the silhouette of a wolf, and he held what looked like a small bucket.

The demon soldier approached the bed and waited obediently as Madam Lema held the scissors tightly in the fingers of her free hand and dipped them into the bucket. She then let them hover next to Freyah's face.

Heat radiated from the metal, and a wave of fresh fear crawled up her spine. Was she about to be burned by magic somehow?

A vision of Whit's face flashed in the forefront of her mind.

Thinking quickly, Freyah bit down on one of Madam Lema's fingers. The queen yanked back her hand and reflexively slapped her. The sting on Freyah's face stunned her enough that Madam Lema was able to pin her down. She was now stuck underneath the witch's full body weight, and her arms were no longer free.

Freyah didn't take the queen as the type to do her own dirty work, but something about this felt personal.

She felt the tiniest prick from the tip of the sharp scissors, and she watched with wild eyes as the queen placed a drop of Freyah's blood on her tongue.

Madam Lema moaned with exaggerated pleasure, as if the iron taste was the sweetest nectar.

The demon soldier was still standing there, watching as Freyah cringed and braced herself for the scalding hot scissors to make contact with her cheek, but that was not the queen's plan.

"It would be a waste to scar that pretty little face of yours," Madam Lema patronized her.

Freyah stopped squirming and tried desperately to calm her shaking muscles, but the queen was ripping open her shirt. Freyah froze with panic. Before her mind could register what was happening, the scalding surface of the scissors seared her flesh. They'd been turned into branding irons by whatever substance was in that bucket.

Madam Lema pressed the scissors down firmly into Freyah's left breast, and Freyah screamed madly into the witch-queen's hand.

It was unbearable. Torture.

And the queen was going to make certain it left a permanent mark.

Freyah was certain she could feel her skin melting and dripping down her chest. She could smell it. A stench like charcoal and sulfur filled her nostrils.

When the scissors finally lifted away, Freyah nearly vomited at the tearing sensation. Bits of her flesh clung to them like wax.

Her head spun wildly, trying to fight against the scorching feeling of fire on her skin, and her entire body flushed with heat. For a moment, she felt herself drifting into the escape of oblivion. She was losing consciousness from the pain, and she welcomed it. But before she was gone, the demon soldier approached with another bucket and poured cold water over the burn.

There was a single millisecond of relief, and then the pain rushed back.

Madam Lema stood and tossed the scissors into the now empty bucket.

"Now you and your guard will have matching scars," she sneered. Then the queen and her soldier left without another word.

Freyah remained stiff with her hands at her sides. She couldn't move, for she feared it would hurt even worse. All she could do was lie helplessly on her back and cry.

To her horror, the door opened again, and she feared the worst: that Madam Lema had come back for more. But it was a different presence that entered the room.

Willow sat on the edge of the bed and lit the lamp. Freyah squeezed her eyes shut, forcing out the light and her tears. Willow took her hand.

"You have to come with me," she instructed her. "I need to tend to it."

Freyah shook her head, but even as she did, Willow was pulling the covers away from her legs. She helped Freyah sit up, and another rush of pain hit her hard and fast. Freyah gasped and sobbed, but Willow held tight to her hand.

She led her carefully down the tower steps and to the closest washroom. Freyah had never utilized the castle's facilities, having only used the personal wash basin in her room to clean herself each evening. The showers were similar to those inside the mountain, but she couldn't fully appreciate them while she was in so much pain.

Willow turned the faucet under one of the showers and made sure it was a tolerable temperature before helping Freyah under the stream. She lowered her to the floor and Freyah winced. The water was shocking at first, but after a few seconds the coolness was enough to numb the burn. It felt better than the icy water that had been dumped on her.

Willow clearly knew the proper procedure for situations like this.

Had she tended to Whit's burn as well?

Freyah's body shivered, but Willow kept the water running for several minutes. Then, after determining it had been long enough, she closed the valve.

Freyah remained where she was on the floor.

She saw a basket of first aid supplies sitting next to Willow, ready and waiting. It was apparent that Madam Lema was allowing this to happen. Willow was part of her plan—the aftermath, anyway. After the dirty work was complete, it was Willow's job to clean up the mess. Freyah wondered if there were others, besides Whit, that Willow had been instructed to nurse injuries for. She wondered if Willow ever had to do this for herself.

"I thought I could just leave," Freyah muttered, her soft words reverberating against the shower walls.

"And that was stupid," Willow chastised her.

Freyah could hear the echo of *I told you so* in her tone. Willow hadn't been subtle in her refusal to help Freyah, and because of that, Freyah was certain her being here was not a coincidence.

"You told the queen," Freyah stated flatly. Willow wouldn't meet her eyes. "This is because of you."

"You needed to know," she hissed, not denying Freyah's accusation. "You needed to understand. Nothing you do will ever make a difference. This is your life now."

"So you just let her mutilate my body?" Freyah cried. "You knew I was going to try to leave, and you went straight to *her?*"

Willow carefully patted Freyah's chest with a moist towel, causing her to wince. "You're better off scarred than dead," she said. She then squeezed out a thick ointment onto her fingers and began methodically rubbing it into the burn.

Freyah hissed and attempted to distract herself from the pain.

"I hope she did this to you," she cursed.

It was harsh, but she meant it.

Willow pressed her lips together in a tight line. "There are worse means of punishment."

What else could Madam Lema do?

The possibilities were endless; she knew it was true, but Freyah tried not to count the ways in which the witch-queen could make her life a living hell.

She didn't care about Willow's warnings. She needed to escape. This incident, along with everything else she'd learned, only proved that Freyah could not stay in this castle any longer.

Madam Lema had finally shown her true intentions, and Freyah could no longer trust Whit to help her through it. It was up to her to fight through this alone.

Freyah had always depended on those around her for support and guidance, never having had the courage to brave the outside world and step outside her comfort zone. But being brought to Larapuna had forced her out of it without a choice, and there was no one here to hold her hand or show her the way.

She was alone.

She wanted desperately to fight back like her father, but after this failed attempt, Freyah wasn't sure she could find the inner strength to try again.

But she knew it was there, buried deep within her. She would force it to the surface and do what was necessary to find a way out, for she couldn't rely on others to help her this time around.

She would have to do this on her own.

And she would not fail.

SEVERAL HOURS PASSED as Freyah lay motionless in the darkness of her room. She'd been assisted back onto the bed by Willow after she thoroughly wrapped her wound and layered it with a special salve.

It hurt too much to move, so she remained on her back, staring up at the blank ceiling for what felt like an eternity of stillness.

She tried to use the time to plan—to think up some sort of new escape—but the pain took precedence in her mind. She could concentrate on nothing but the burning sensation creeping across her chest, pinching and pulling at every layer of skin as it devoured her flesh.

Freyah closed her eyes, and she felt herself drifting into the memory of her father. His eyes appeared first, bright and golden. They glistened and gleamed against the black, calling to her to be lifted from the darkness.

She followed the light they emitted and was greeted with hands and arms. They reached for her and the familiarity pulled her in.

The embrace felt balmy.

Not a burn, but a soft and comfortable warmth.

Something whispered into her ear using her father's voice.

"They won't hurt you, Freyah. You will always be protected by The First Men."

LYRA

nother week passed before Lyra was able to venture beyond the walls of Castle Larapuna. Lema had tasked her with creating a wearable amulet that would hold the shiny new stone she'd claimed, and it had occupied Lyra's time, day and night.

Her sister had been in a tizzy about having the amulet completed as soon as possible, so like the loyal younger sister she was, Lyra spent day after day in one of the largest drawing rooms, painstakingly peering through a magnifier and clamping tweezers.

This area of the castle gave her space and a considerable amount of light to work, but it was drafty and too empty for her liking. She craved the constant flow of people in and out of the Grand Hall, or the busyness of the cramped streets in Knox Hill. Instead, she was stuck in an empty room all by herself and forced to make something she didn't really understand.

It was well known amongst the coven that Lyra was a skilled crafter. She could wield and manipulate various materials to her liking, having created many talismans—both ornamental and practical —for other witches, her most common request being jewelry.

Lema had requested a necklace made from a rare element called Hematite. Lyra knew the stone could enhance their Future Sight, so she could only assume her sister wished to see something a bit more clearly. But to create something wearable for everyday use? Having a constant tether to magic was dangerous.

There was meant to be a natural flow to it, a give and take between each witch and the piece of nature she wielded. Magic was never meant to be hoarded, and by using the necklace as a constant talisman to the future, Lema risked unraveling more than what Lillia wanted her to see.

Future Sight was a gift not to be taken for granted. If abused, the Sight had the possibility of leading Lema down a very dangerous path. But, yet again, Lyra found that it was not her place to question Lema's motives.

It had taken many hours of intricate labor, but Lyra had finally managed to bend the Hematite to her will and create one of the most stunning pieces she'd ever attempted. She was impressed, almost wishing she could keep the necklace for herself, but a part of her was also proud to give something so beautiful to someone else.

It was hard to love Lema, but Lyra did nonetheless. Her older sister was determined and stubborn, but so was she. As much as Lyra wanted to judge Lema on her passion-driven decisions and impertinent nature, she couldn't deny that those same traits simmered within herself as well.

On the outside, they appeared as two very different flowers—one with soft white petals, and the other with vivid leaves and spiky thorns—but the roots were the same. Both sisters were derived from the same soil and carried the same poisonous traits. Once consumed, Lema's venom acted immediately, while Lyra's took time for the effects to take place.

The stress of the rebellion weighed on them all. Lyra hadn't told the queen, but secretly she'd tried to access her Future Sight, just to look for any possible solution to their problems. Unfortunately, the Sight didn't work like that.

It could not be controlled, only harnessed when presented to you.

It was why she needed to tell Lema that the necklace should not be worn at all times. But she already knew that Lema wouldn't listen.

Ever since learning that the rebellion had spread to Caster Valley, the queen had become desperate for more power. Greater access to magic.

Lyra wished there was a way to force everyone to stop drawing lines in the dirt. No more humans against witches against demons.

Oram had told her it wasn't demons causing the fires and vandalizing shops, and she'd since learned that it was actually a group of humans who fancied calling themselves "The First Men" who were responsible. Apparently, they were adamant on having someone without magic to sit on the throne.

Lyra had informed Lema about all of this, though she hadn't given up where she'd received her intel. But Lema refused to believe who was behind it. Her deep-seated prejudice caused her to see everything through the eyes of their grandmother, and that meant placing all the blame on the demons.

Despite demons being personally affected by what the witches had done over the years, it was the humans of Ghoma that were the most frustrated with Madam Lema's rule, and Lyra could easily understand why.

There was no one currently in power that had their best interests in mind. No one to represent them and understand their daily struggles. The witches didn't know what it was like beyond the castle walls, and the only reason Lyra did was because of how many times she'd snuck out over the years and spent time with humans. She'd visited their shops, sat at tables with them in pubs, and watched children laboring in their parents' fields only to give more than half of their crops to the crown while they starved.

It was unfair, but Lyra couldn't stop it. She was the younger sister —the princess, not the queen. She didn't make the decisions, and she didn't wage the wars. She was merely meant to sit back and watch it all crumble.

As Lyra made her way to Lema's chambers, she passed several storage rooms packed with rice, flour, and dried meat. She tried to imagine the difference it would make if Larapuna demanded a little less supply every month and instead gave back to its people. Lyra had never quite understood why the queen insisted on stock piling so many goods. Being less greedy would solve so many of the problems they currently faced, but Lema would rather have her storage rooms full to bursting than appease the cries of the rebels at her gates.

Lyra continued down the corridor, past the dining hall and through groups of soldiers swapping posts during shift change. She climbed the wide stone steps that spiraled up to the queen's tower—the tallest one just above the southern gates, facing the west—and when she finally stood outside her sister's door, Lyra found herself stalling.

She clutched the necklace in her hand and admired her craftsmanship one last time. The orange light from the fire in the sconces reflected subtly off the deep onyx stone. It still held its original shine, but it had been manipulated into a perfect oval and was now encased in a round, silver setting attached to a delicate chain.

Lyra rolled the stone between her fingers, letting the chain slip through her grip and dangle in the dim light of the hall.

Something told her she was making a mistake.

But before Lyra could change her mind, the door to Lema's chambers opened, and she was standing face to face with Raven, the queen's personal herbalist.

Raven had been born with very little magical ability, so her place within the coven had initially been questioned. It wasn't until Lyra's own mother, Adora, recognized Raven's talent for potions and recommended she'd be of use to the crown that the elders finally allowed her to stay.

Lyra had pitied the young witch, but she was relieved to know she'd proven her worth. She was glad to see that her sister kept her around even after their mother's sudden passing. After all, being born without magic in Larapuna wasn't just a disappointment: to Lema, it was a crime.

Raven gasped in surprise. "Princess," she doted. "You startled me."

"I should have knocked," Lyra confessed, sidestepping the witch still in a formal position and entering her sister's quarters. "Please, forgive me."

Raven nodded and straightened. She slipped quietly through the door and closed it behind her, leaving Lyra seemingly alone.

She heard Lema bustling in the next room. Several thuds and what sounded like papers rustling floated through the apartment. Lyra followed the noise until she found the Queen of Ghoma kneeling on the floor of her study with a glass of wine in one hand and a leather bound book in the other.

"What are you doing?" Lyra asked gently, not wanting to spook the restless creature before her.

Lema swallowed a large gulp from her glass and, without looking at who'd walked through the door, asked, "Have you any idea where the rest of our records are kept?"

"Records of what?" Lyra asked. They kept records of births and deaths, of magical abilities and when they manifested, but she wasn't sure what Lema was asking for specifically.

"Old magic," Lema clarified. She finally looked up after tossing aside the book and flipping through another stack of parchment. "I need to reference a vision."

Lyra rolled her eyes. "Who's vision?"

Lema answered tautly but vaguely. "No one important. There's just something I need to see."

"Have you not consulted the elders? They would know where those records are kept."

Lema heaved a heavy sigh and fell back onto her ankles. "You know I'm not on good terms with them at the moment. I've asked too many questions."

"About what?"

"About everything!" Lema barked.

Lyra tensed and took a seat on a plush velvet chair.

It wasn't only the relationship between the queen and her people that was fraying. The tension between the queen and the Council of Elders was growing with every passing day, and apparently Lema couldn't leave well enough alone.

"What is it you need to see?" Lyra asked, then she reconsidered.

Lema's only response was the irritated flare of her nostrils and a curled lip. Refusing to answer, Lema focused on the page in front of her.

Lyra was still clutching the necklace in her hand, but she'd kept it carefully hidden between the folds of her skirt. This would be the opportune time to present Lema with what she'd requested. It would help her see whatever it was that needed seeing. But Lyra still hesitated.

It wasn't like handing over a gift.

It felt more like handing over a weapon.

Lema looked up and stared openly at her. "Did you need something?"

Lyra cleared her throat, as well as her mind, and held out the necklace.

It spun as it hung from her grasp, and Lema's eyes went suddenly wide at the sight of it.

"You've done it!" she exclaimed, jumping expectantly to her feet. "By Lillia, it's perfect!"

Lyra watched as Lema examined the piece of jewelry carefully. She turned it over and over in her palm and then closed her fist around it, pressing it firmly against her chest.

"I can feel it," she said in a hushed tone. "This is what I've needed all along." Then, she gazed directly into Lyra's eyes and offered a genuine, "Thank you."

Lyra felt uncomfortable by Lema's gratitude—she'd never witnessed it before—but she smiled anyway. "Of course."

Not wanting to linger, Lyra got up and walked back through the sitting area of Lema's chambers, heading for the door.

Before she left, she sent a secret prayer to Lillia, hoping that whatever vision came to her sister, it wouldn't cause irrevocable harm.

THERE WAS something else Lyra had planned on telling Lema during her visit, but instead, she'd kept it to herself.

She'd felt odd for the past couple of days. Waves of nausea would crash over her in the middle of breakfast, and she found herself becoming increasingly tired as the day pressed on. By mid-afternoon, Lyra tended to feel an overwhelming need to take a nap. She thought perhaps it was due to all the hours she'd dedicated to making the necklace—she'd overworked herself somehow—but it was Fatima who'd suggested it might be sickness and went on a hunt for some elderberry syrup.

When her handmaid returned, however, she was joined by a healer named Astrid, and at the sight of them together, Lyra sat abruptly upright in her bed.

Fatima had retrieved some extra blankets as well as the elderberry, and after setting down the bottle, she began unfolding and fluffing them around Lyra's legs. Astrid stood back and watched with knowing eyes.

The witch was certainly a sight for sore eyes. Though she was well into her ninetieth year of life, her beauty shone bright like the cerulean sparkle in her eyes. As the oldest and most experienced healer, she held a seat on the Council of Elders. Her gray hair was long and settled around her hips. She had dark skin with rune markings etched under her left eye, and she wore chunky blue earrings made from crystals and wrapped with twine.

Astrid continued to watch Lyra carefully as Fatima fussed over her comfort, and finally, after Lyra insisted she was fine, Fatima stepped away and began preparing a tea.

Astrid took the opportunity to step forward and speak. "Your handmaiden says you are not well."

Lyra settled back against the pillows. "It's just a bit of seasonal irritation. I'll be alright after some rest and warm tea."

Astrid did not look convinced. Instead of asking any further questions, she leaned over Lyra, intimately close, and placed a cold hand on her silk-covered stomach. Lyra was wearing only a nightgown, and the gesture felt extremely invasive. She froze under the witch's touch, but then she felt a pulsating sensation.

Something settled inside her, nestling in and waiting.

"What did you do?" Lyra asked.

Astrid closed her eyes. In her other hand, she clutched a crystal Lyra recognized as spirit quartz. It looked as if she was listening for something, but no sound came. At least, nothing that Lyra could hear. Something must have spoken to her though, because Astrid then gave a curt nod and pulled her hand sharply back to her side.

"I sense two heartbeats," she stated matter-of-factly.

Fatima nearly dropped the porcelain teacup she was holding. It shook in her notably steady hand, and Lyra focused entirely too hard on it. She wasn't processing the words that Astrid had spoken. The only thing that made sense was that there was a small chip in the porcelain pink cup. Lyra had never noticed any broken china before, and she wondered if Lema knew about it.

If she did, she would probably demand it be thrown out.

"Does that mean...?" Fatima was as shocked as Lyra felt, only she was able to voice it with words. "Miss Lyra, you're pregnant!" She was trying to coax her friend back into the conversation with the exciting news, but Lyra's brain was fuzzy.

"She will need an excess amount of care over the next few weeks," Astrid explained. "The gestational period is short for us, so we must take every step to ensure we do what is best for the pregnancy right from this moment until it's time for her to deliver."

The elder witch was speaking directly to Fatima, but Lyra finally started to listen.

"She will require a special diet," Astrid continued, "and we must monitor the progress. I suspect she's about nine days along. That leaves us less than a month to brew the proper potions."

Fatima nodded her head vigorously, but Lyra doubted her hand-maid was absorbing the information any better than she had.

Astrid clasped her fingers together in front of her. "I'll be back later this evening."

And with that, she was gone.

Once the door closed behind Astrid, Fatima let out a deafening squeal. "By the Mother! This is wonderful news!" She hesitated, backtracking her expression after seeing the uncertainty on Lyra's face. "This is good, isn't it?"

Lyra sunk down and buried her face under the pillows. "I'm not sure *what* this is yet, Fatima," she mumbled, her voice muffled.

Fatima let out a murmur of understanding. "Is it...?" She broke off before finishing the thought.

Lyra tossed the pillow to the foot of her bed and met her friend's gaze. "Is it what?"

"You know," Fatima suggested, then lowered her voice. "*The demon?*"

Lyra couldn't answer out loud. Instead, she simply nodded.

Fatima's face grew taut, her eyebrows pulling together in worry. "But what does that mean? What if it's a boy?"

"Then it won't have magic," Lyra stated blankly. "You know how it happens by now, Fatima."

"Yes, but," she paused. "It'll be a demon. They'll cast him out."

"I know that," Lyra said.

Fatima allowed a small reassuring smile to escape the corner of her mouth. "I hope it's a girl then," she said. "It's been a while since we've had a new witch around here."

Lyra closed her eyes and pictured a small girl with pale hair and emerald eyes, and she didn't stop herself when thoughts of a little boy with catlike ears crept into the background.

What in Lillia's name was she going to do?

Better yet...how was she going to tell Oram?

21

LYRA

The problem with keeping secrets was that they lived beneath the skin, itching and begging to be let out, until one day they broke free. Lyra was good at keeping secrets, but this particular one would be tough to hide.

Telling Oram would be scary, but she had to do it.

She needed some sort of guarantee that someone would protect her child. For if it were to be a boy, there would be nothing she could do to stop Lema's demand to either kill it or abandon the infant in the forest, and Lyra wouldn't let that happen.

Oram would understand. He had to.

She would be showing soon, and there would be no way to hide it from her lover the next time she saw him. She had to tell him sooner rather than later.

The castle buzzed with the excitement of a new child. Passing down magic was critical for the coven, as well as growing their numbers. And this child would not only usher in a new generation of witch; it would also be an heir to the throne.

Lema had taken the news surprisingly nonchalantly. Lyra hadn't necessarily expected her sister to be outright happy about it, but she had at least thought it warranted some sort of reaction. They'd both been pressed by the elders for years to produce offspring, and the ability to procreate got slimmer the older they got, but neither sister had made the matter a priority. It certainly wasn't part of Lyra's plan. Not when she'd been so blindsided by her new feelings for Oram.

It would be a true testament to the sturdiness of their budding new romance, and Lyra prayed to the Mother that it wouldn't wilt.

The affair was nothing to be ashamed of—the only crime had been that he was a demon and she was a witch. Such relationships simply didn't happen. Partly because of the heavy biases that lingered in the air of each town like smog clouding people's vision. It had been ingrained into their very being that demons were less-than, and those that lived beside them—the ones that raised them and kept them safe —were shunned.

Lyra tried to imagine what it had been like for Oram's parents, raising so many demon children despite the world giving them every reason not to.

Caster Valley was full of working class citizens, people of the land. They always had a layer of dirt that clung to their skin, proof that they worked hard for what they had, and didn't mind doing a little extra for others. Galiana and Petra had to be incredibly selfless people in order to do what they'd done. They'd put the wellbeing of the inno-cent before their own, and Lyra was incredibly jealous of that. She could never be that selfless, for she was too caught up in her own selfish desires to ever stop and think about anyone else's.

But Oram had been different. He'd actually taken the time to get to know her, and she wanted to know as much as she could about his world and his passions. She wanted to understand what made him tick, and each conversation they'd shared made her feel a little more connected to him.

He was a good listener. A good male. And Lyra hoped those traits would take the brunt of what she was about to confess to him.

She'd received a letter from Oram a few days ago inviting her to the home he shared with his brother, Kirra. It had been delivered discreetly by messenger owl, and the creature had tapped precariously at her bedroom window early in the morning. There were many species of fowl capable of sharing messages, but Lyra always preferred the owls. They seemed the most dedicated to the job, like they took pride in it somehow.

At the sight of the tawny bird clutching a small, tattered piece of parchment, her heart had leapt with both excitement and fear. She'd never seen where Oram lived, and she was looking forward to learning even more about his family.

As she made the quick journey to their village, she reminded herself over and over that she wasn't there to deliver bad news. It wasn't a death sentence.

At least, not for them.

"ARE YOU SURE?"

Oram sat very still on the ledge of the stone fireplace, a cup of steaming tea clutched tightly in his hands.

Lyra stared at her stomach and how the small bulge made the hem of her dress ride up higher than it should. "Yes," she said.

Oram took several sips then placed the cup down beside him. "This is definitely surprising," he admitted. He noticed Lyra's uneasy demeanor and moved to kneel in front of her. "Did you think I would be upset?"

Lyra wasn't sure how to answer. The things that had transpired between them weren't enough to call what they had a relationship, but it wasn't casual either. There was a bit of romance sprinkled into the lust and the adventure—it was what she enjoyed most about it—but this was bigger than that. Bringing a child into the equation meant permanence. There was no chance of backing out and changing their minds if things didn't work out the way they planned.

And what if it changed the way they saw each other?

Would he even desire her after something like this?

"I don't know," she confessed. "But it's not really about that."

Oram's brow furrowed. "What is it about then?"

"You know how males are treated, Oram. If I give birth to a child without magic…a child like you…"

"He'll be abandoned to the forest," he said, finishing her sentence.

"Maybe," she conceded. "But I don't doubt my sister will do something worse simply because he is mine. I won't be able to raise him." Lyra looked him directly in the eye, needing to make her next words very clear. "That's why I need you to promise that no matter what happens, you'll look after him."

He looked surprised. At her words, perhaps, but more likely at her lack of faith in him. "Of course I will. I would never abandon my own child. My own *son*," he emphasized.

Lyra nodded, taking comfort in his declaration. But he wasn't finished.

"There's another side to this, too," he said. "What if it's a girl?"

"She'll be fine. That's not what we have to worry about."

"For you, maybe," he countered. "But how involved would I be? Would I ever see her?"

She hadn't thought about that. Lyra had been focused solely on the threat of giving birth to a boy. But a girl?

Her life would be spared. She'd be fine. But would she have a father?

"I would make sure that you do," she told him.

But did Lyra truly believe she was capable of making such a promise? Nevermind *keeping* it?

She would certainly try, but that meant standing against her sister —standing against the queen. Something she'd never done before.

So instead, she rephrased. "I would find a way."

22

ORAM

Oram hadn't expected such life changing news first thing in the morning.

It was hard to listen to Lyra speak in such a fearful manner, as if she were waiting for him to yell or curse or issue threats.

But he hadn't done any of those things.

That wasn't who he was—such hostility wasn't in Oram's nature. He might not love Lyra just yet, but he loved what they had. And he didn't want to lose it.

He wasn't the only one processing the news, however.

Unbeknownst to Lyra, Kirra had been in the next room, doing his best to eavesdrop against Oram's wishes. He'd already sworn to Oram that he wouldn't get involved—according to his brother, Oram had made his bed, and Kirra only hoped that he was comfortable in it.

But Kirra had been waiting for the other shoe to drop since the moment Oram first mentioned the witch, and now it finally had.

Oram waited patiently for Kirra to say "I told you so," but it never came.

At least, not at first.

The fox-demon might have been hermit-like and incredibly shy, but he typically had no problem expressing how he truly felt and speaking his mind.

For the rest of the morning, after Lyra left to return to the castle, the brothers sat in uncomfortable silence, Oram stoking the fire while Kirra kept himself busy with balancing the finances of their crop shares. The nights were getting colder, and it took a constant fire to keep the house warm. Soon the crops would stop growing, meaning they would have to live off the nonperishables they'd stockpiled for the next six months.

After withstanding all the quiet he could, Oram turned to his older brother and demanded a reaction. "Just say it," he insisted.

Kirra stopped what he was doing and removed the thin wire glasses from his face with a sigh. "Say what?" he asked, feigning ignorance.

"You know what. You told me from the beginning that getting tangled up with a witch would bring nothing but trouble."

"And?" Kirra drawled.

Oram grimaced. "And here we are. Trouble."

"It seemed to me that you were quite pleased with the news."

"I wasn't *pleased*," Oram corrected. "I just didn't want her to be afraid to tell me."

Kirra hopped down from his wooden chair, causing a few papers to flutter off the table, then walked somberly to the kitchen. "You don't have to involve yourself at all. You do know that, right?"

Oram couldn't believe what he was hearing. "Of course I do. Why would you even suggest that? After what happened to you? To *us*?"

"It's not the same," Kirra opposed. He climbed onto his wooden stool to refill the kettle and spoke openly to his brother as he pumped from the well and proceeded to place the copper kettle over the hearth. "A girl born in that castle would be raised in luxury. But a boy would have to suffer in a corrupt world. Why take the risk?"

"You mean end the pregnancy? The witches would never risk losing one of their own."

Oram had no more words after that.

They had been abandoned from infancy, taken in and raised by the kindness of human strangers. Because of his own personal experience, Oram would never let history repeat itself. Especially not with his own child.

Kirra was supposed to understand that.

It should have been the end of the conversation—the end of Kirra's doubt and the beginning of their agreement to help Lyra in whatever way they could.

Instead, they were at a stalemate.

"I'm going to help her," Oram said, letting out the words slowly. "I thought you'd feel the same, but I guess I was wrong."

FREYAH

*I*t hurt to breathe.

Every tiny movement of Freyah's chest felt like razors clawing at her flesh—like it was still being ripped away, whatever was left of it.

Whit brought breakfast and a stack of new books to her room a few days later, which was the first time he'd shown his face since letting his true self slip.

The effort was most likely meant to be a sort of peace offering, but Freyah knew it would take a lot more than some food and a good romance book to move past what had happened between them in the library.

It wasn't much—a slice of toast and some soft fruit—but still, it was more than what Freyah could stomach at the moment. She nibbled at the buttery crust of the bread and watched Whit as he observed the books on her shelf.

"I brought something new for you to read," he said. "Since I wasn't able to take you back to the library."

He was attempting casual conversation, and she hated it.

"Thanks," she said begrudgingly.

She didn't know how to act around him now.

He was back to looking human. No more leathery skin or ears out of place. His eyes were back to their familiar warm shade of brown, and claws no longer protruded from the tips of his fingers.

He sat at the end of the bed and placed his forearms on his knees.

Freyah eyed him pointedly.

Speaking was a chore. She was so utterly exhausted that she found it difficult to form her own thoughts, let alone speak them out loud. So they sat in heavy silence. She didn't want to ask him to leave, but she also didn't want to make small talk and pretend that what happened wasn't a big deal.

She'd been mulling over the idea in her head for days while her body tried its best to heal, attempting to reason with herself that Whit being a demon didn't change anything, when in reality, she knew that it did.

They'd been building a bridge, and his secret had cut the ropes. There was nothing to hold on to as they crossed and attempted to meet in the middle. It would now require an act of balance, and they both needed practice at mastering that.

Freyah had also been thinking up possible ways out of the castle that wouldn't draw too much attention. She tossed around dozens of different possibilities of escape, such as wearing a disguise, holding someone hostage, and even the daring idea of simply jumping from one of the large library windows. But no matter how good the idea seemed, she managed to come up with a better reason not to do it.

Mostly, she was too scared to do it alone.

She didn't want to talk about the demon thing, so instead, she decided to use Whit's company for something else.

"The other day," she started, "Willow all but confirmed that you two tried to escape." She set aside her plate and waited for his reaction. "Is it true?"

Whit looked at her apologetically. He didn't appear caught off guard, so he must have been prepared to have this conversation at some point, but he was definitely hesitant to answer.

"Think about what you're asking."

"I don't care," she dismissed. "Willow has already tried to dissuade me, and it's not going to work. Just tell me."

There was a small flicker of anger in Whit's eyes, but he blinked it away and focused on the stack of books he'd set on her bedside table.

Freyah could tell he wanted to ask what Willow had done, but he was clearly deciding against it. Not that Freyah would have confided in him about it anyway. She didn't want to force him to pick a side. And besides, she knew it wouldn't be hers he chose.

Whit stood up and paced the length of the room. "We left while everyone was away," he said. "It seemed like a good idea…at the time."

"What happened?"

The uneasy tension between them pulled taut to the point of breaking. It expanded and lingered in the room like a tall redwood, taking up space and threatening to derail the conversation.

But Freyah ignored it. She needed to hear this.

"I had two sisters," he began. "Willow was assigned as a consort the day we arrived, but Wendi…She was too young, so she became a handmaid. They were both too young, but we just tried to accept it. At first, Willow said she was fine—she would suck it up and do what needed to be done—but things got worse for her, and I couldn't stand by and watch those bastards defile her any longer.

"There was a major meeting happening that week. All of the elders were there and most of her higher ranking officers. Given so many important people were all in one room, it meant the guards would be focused on the meeting. So we waited for the right moment, and once it started, we left through the dungeons and ran for the forest."

Having to recount the memory was already taking its toll on him. Freyah heard each sentence grow thicker in his throat, making it harder to get out. She saw the pain surface in the way his posture stiffened and his voice dropped an octave, settling into a deep grumble. She strained to listen to the last of his words, not wanting to miss a single detail.

"Wendi never made it back," he murmured. Then, with a little more vibrato, he continued. "She'd been caught by the Spyders. I hadn't known Madam Lema had a few stationed at the edge of the forest, and once they saw us, there was nothing I could do to stop them."

His voice broke on the last few words, and it took him a moment to compose himself. "They paralyzed her with venom-laced arrows and dragged her into the brush," he said. "I remember one of them had this awful smile on his face, like he knew there was nothing I could do. I never saw her again."

Freyah's heart was barely beating. Her pulse had slowed to a near deadly rate, and she couldn't remember if she was still breathing. She drew in a purposeful breath but remained silent. She didn't know how to respond. What words were there to possibly say after learning about something so horrendous and cruel?

Thankfully, Whit broke the silence for her.

"Willow was so heartbroken, she no longer saw the point in trying," he explained. "She felt it was her fault, because we had chosen to leave for her."

Whit crossed the room and sat back down at the end of Freyah's bed. "I know you've probably already considered it, but Freyah…it's not possible. Even with a distraction like that—it was mostly luck and good timing, but still—it didn't work."

Freyah *hadn't* considered it.

She didn't realize such an opportunity could present itself. But if she found the right time—waited for the right event to take place—it was possible.

But the forest.

That was something that had escaped her mind entirely. She had completely forgotten about the Saldanni Forest. There were Wild Demon clans living in those trees, and there was no way she'd get past them on her own.

Whit reached out his hand and brushed her arm lightly with his thumb. "I'm so sorry, Freyah," he said. "I never meant to lie to you."

Her previous attempt at ignoring the topic shattered with his touch. It made her skin blaze, and not only the part that had been burned.

Though a part of her wanted to be close to him, the other part knew she no longer could.

"You *did* mean to," she corrected him. "You've been lying to every-one. Does *anyone* know about you?"

He nodded slowly. "Two of the guards on my team. They're my best friends. And…" He paused and removed his hand from her arm. "And Raven."

Whit having a secret witch friend didn't bother her anymore. At least, she told herself it didn't. Freyah was now more concerned with the logistics behind his cover-up.

"How does it work?" she asked, genuinely curious. "I don't under-stand how you've hidden it all this time. Is it magic?"

"It's an elixir." He placed both hands in his lap. The hair on his forehead was back to falling over his eyes, and he didn't bother pushing it away.

He was hiding again.

"Raven makes it once a week," he explained. "And I have to take a measured dose every night before bed. I used to take it in the morn-ings, but that day I forgot. Training ran over, and I was late coming to escort you, so I missed my dose. That's why it happened. That and… well…because I was experiencing a strong surge of emotion."

Whit watched her carefully. He looked as if he wanted to say more —to try and explain further—but he'd told her the truth. She knew it was all he could do. But she still needed to know why.

"I think I understand," Freyah told him. "But why did you hide it? I saw a demon soldier the night she burned me."

She shifted forward slightly, risking moving closer to him, but it was too painful.

Whit saw her attempt and met her halfway. He touched the edge of the bandage across her chest as gently as if he were handling a baby bird, then he pushed the hair away from her face and tucked it behind her ear.

Freyah's instincts were still to let him reach out to her, so she didn't pull away but turned her cheek into his touch.

"Ryker is different," Whit explained. "No one knows why. But he's been in the queen's service for a long time. As for the rest of us, I didn't realize how hard it was to be a demon until I left home. We were isolated in The Mounds. But here, and in the capital, we're stared at and ridiculed, and there's always a risk of violence against us. That's why I had to hide it—to protect myself. But also to protect Willow and Wendi."

Whit's hand dropped from her face but remained close, resting comfortingly on her thigh over the blanket.

It was hard, but Freyah let his explanation wash over her.

She soaked it in and really listened.

"I didn't know either," she confessed. "It's different in Last Cove, too. Being so far from the witches makes them feel safer, I guess."

The 'them' in her sentence felt sour on her tongue.

Because it wasn't about *them* anymore.

It was just Whit.

His knee was now pressed against her hip, and the added contact sent her pulse racing.

"Freyah."

He whispered her name like a prayer, and the sound of it raised goosebumps on her arms. Without overthinking it, she let him slowly lean in and brush his lips lightly against hers.

Though her frustration and fear surrounding Whit's demon nature had taken up a huge chunk of her mind, her heart still craved his touch. The feeling of safety he gave her was too strong. Too alluring.

And right now, the most important thing to her was the taste of his tongue and his fingers along her skin.

Not Madam Lema's motives. Not even her father.

Nothing.

Just Whit.

Whit and his strong arms and firm chest. The softness of his hair and the stubble on his chin. And his scar—the maimed flesh that would forever haunt the left side of his face. It all caused a flutter to erupt in her belly. It begged her to cling to him. To feel the calluses on his hands scraping and clawing at her hips.

She wanted to feel the weight of him on top of her. She wanted to admire every inch of him, for he was a work of art, and she wanted to study him with precision.

Unfortunately, Freyah was still injured, and despite the slow pace and care behind the kiss, their desperation and passion was too much. Physically, she wasn't ready for this, and it disappointed her to no end. But in reality, if she was honest, she wasn't mentally prepared either.

She winced as he pulled her closer, and he immediately stopped.

"Did I hurt you?" he asked, a look of concern crossing his features. "I'm so sorry. What do you need?"

"I'm fine," she lied.

He refused her claim and helped her back onto the pillow. He kissed her forehead, letting his mouth linger for longer than necessary, then pulled back to look into her eyes. "I won't let her hurt you again."

Freyah took his promise with a grain of salt. She knew it was more complicated than that, and if she truly planned to try and escape, Whit couldn't be involved. After knowing the full story, she wouldn't put him or Willow in jeopardy.

They'd already suffered enough.

Abruptly, his mouth pressed into a hard line, and his eyes clouded with a realization that he had something else to say.

He took her hand in his.

"I didn't just come here to apologize," he admitted. He waited for a beat then spoke somberly. "You should know something."

"What?" she asked, unsure if she actually *wanted* to know.

He sighed and dragged a rueful hand down his face. "Madam Lema is sending soldiers to Last Cove. They're going to arrest your father for conspiring against the queen."

Freyah's throat closed. Thick saliva coated her tongue, but she couldn't swallow it. It nearly choked her.

"*How?* How did the queen find out? I haven't told her anything since having those dreams."

"I think it was Willow." His words were bitter, and he was obviously disappointed in his sister's betrayal, but not enough to be truly angry. His voice was still too calm for Freyah's liking. "I think she followed us to the library that day. I'm not saying what she did was right, but I suppose she thought she was protecting you. She doesn't want anyone else to try what we did."

"So instead she tosses *my father* under the cart? How is that protecting me, Whit? And why are you making excuses for her? She's the one that caused this!" Freyah yanked down the neckline of her chemise to show off her burn, and the action created the desired effect.

Whit's eyes darkened as they zeroed in on the injury. His features had hardened into a look of fierce rage, but they quickly faded into something else.

"It's complicated," he said, but the words were clipped. "You don't know what she's been through. I might not understand her intentions, but I know they're good."

The excuse was a hasty attempt to de-villainize his sister, but Freyah wouldn't hear any of it.

"When?" she demanded, pushing past him to get up from the bed. The stretching of her skin made her want to crumple to the floor into the fetal position and cry, but she fought against it. "The soldiers—when are they leaving?"

Whit didn't try to stop her. Instead he focused solely on the gray-stone floor between them. "Two days," he said. "I'm so sorry."

This time Freyah did choke.

She gasped and coughed, but the movement made everything hurt more.

She was suddenly struck with the image of her father being blindsided in his shop—of being taken away in front of everyone, humiliated and scared. Not knowing what would come next. Freyah understood that fear all too well, and she could not bear the thought of her father sharing that same uncertainty.

She began to hyperventilate. The walls of her small room felt like they were closing in. It was all her fault. She'd agreed to go along with Madam Lema's ridiculous suggestion to "work together," knowing that something had been off about it.

If only she'd figured it out sooner. Freyah had handed over

damning information without even realizing it. She should have known the queen had ulterior motives.

She should have fought harder, been braver.

She should have protected her father better.

"Calm down," Whit urged her. He stood and placed a hand on either side of Freyah's face, but she pulled away from him, a new wave of pain tightening along her burnt chest.

She could see that her repulsion was breaking him, but she didn't care.

"He's just being arrested," he tried to explain. "Madam Lema hasn't said anything about discipline yet."

He reached for the glass of water on Freyah's bedside table and handed it to her. She drank desperately, as if the water was the answer to all her problems, but it only made her choke more.

Whit took the glass and sat it back down. The look of concern on his face made Freyah's imagination continue to run wild, and she couldn't get her words out fast enough.

"He'll be sentenced to death, Whit! What if he was involved in the fires? His actions have killed people! She'll have his head for treason!"

Whit touched her face again lightly then pulled her against his chest. "It's okay," he said, still trying to soothe her. "I won't let anything happen to him, or to you. I promise."

Freyah wanted to fight him off, but she could only cry. She allowed him to hold her, ignoring the sharp pain in her chest as it pressed flush against his.

She was furious—at Willow and the queen, and maybe still a little at Whit—but she needed to feel another soul supporting hers. She couldn't hold herself up anymore. That tiny bit of inner strength she'd found was dwindling, and the appeal of letting herself melt into him was too enticing.

Whit would hold her up.

Whit would be her strength.

But she couldn't give up. Not completely. There was still time, still a chance to stop this, but she wouldn't be able to do it alone. Despite her hesitance to trust him again, Freyah needed Whit's help.

They separated and their eyes met.

Freyah didn't have to ask. She knew from the look on his face that he would do whatever she asked, and she felt the smallest pang of guilt at dragging him into something that might cause him more pain—more loss—but she let the feeling pass.

He was going to help her, and that meant she wasn't alone.

MADAM LEMA

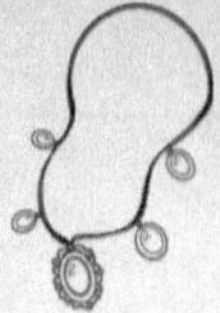

"*T*hat will be all, Rhea."

The queen rose from her silken bedsheets and strode across the room to retrieve her robe.

"But you've only climaxed once, Madam. Surely I can please you more. Allow me to use my mouth this time."

"I said, that is all," Lema barked. Her consort was satisfactory in every area of her job, except knowing when to leave.

At least the female didn't need telling more than twice. Rhea crawled off the bed and gathered her garments from the floor, dressing quickly, then exited in haste.

Lema donned her silken robe and made her way to the formal sitting chamber of her apartments. It was twilight. The deep purple and blue horizon outside the glass windows made the sky look bruised, filling the space with a subtle melancholy. While she'd been tending to her physical needs, she'd missed the sunset, and as she sat in the shadowed corner of her bedroom, staring longingly through the glass, she tried to remember the last time she might have seen one.

It made her feel inferior, not having witnessed a sunset in so long, for something about it felt necessary to living. But what did she know about living, really? She was nearing the end of her first century of life, and she'd barely set foot outside her own castle. Lema knew next to nothing about the country she ruled over, only having seen a small percentage of it in her youth. But living was for those that didn't have responsibility, and she had far too much of that.

According to witch custom, it was high time she'd delivered offspring, and she was almost two decades overdue. It gnawed at her brain most days when she wasn't consumed with harnessing her Future Sight or pleasing the Council of Elders. It didn't help that the highest elder, Ada Leblanc, was constantly reminding her of her duty to the coven.

When Lema heard the news that Lyra was carrying her first child, it should have pleased her—at least one of them was doing their part —but who was she fooling? Lema was jealous. Jealous of something she would probably never have.

She was jealous, yes. But she was also disgusted.

It was Astrid that had told her the news. She'd personally attended to Lyra and felt the sign of life within her womb.

Lema hadn't realized her sister had been leaving the castle. It was one of Nyadahma's Spyders that had spotted the princess in the town of Knox Hill and reported back, but given how consumed Lema had been with the rebellion and her diminished Future Sight, she hadn't thought much of it.

It was the news of the pregnancy that made Lema start to question it.

She didn't know why, but she needed to know who the man was that had finally been deemed worthy enough to coax into Lyra's bed. So the queen had instructed the Spyder to keep a close watch on the princess.

And what he discovered was far more shocking than what Lema had expected.

Her younger sister had ventured to the district of Caster Valley and visited a small bungalow on a farm in Knox Hill. The house belonged to two demon brothers, and Lyra had stayed inside with the occupants for over an hour.

Lema thought it was strange in and of itself that Lyra had any acquaintances in the valley, but it was what the Spyder had seen as Lyra was leaving that truly made the queen boil with fury.

According to the soldier, Lyra was standing just past the threshold of the house, nearly closing the door behind her, when a tiger-demon stepped out and coaxed her back. He'd grabbed her arm in a gentle manner and pulled her into an embrace. His fingers had tangled in her hair and his mouth had lovingly found hers.

By the Spyder's judgment, this wasn't a casual interaction. This was proof of a relationship—one that had been happening for a while.

It was the ultimate betrayal.

Lyra was fraternizing with the enemy. The devil in the flesh.

Demons were the scum of the earth, and Lyra had chosen to climb into one's bed. She now had its devilish offspring growing inside her, and she would answer for that crime.

Under no circumstance would Madam Lema allow her sister to give birth to such an abomination.

As the image of Lyra embracing the demon flashed across her mind again, Lema shuddered, trying to temper her rage.

She heard the door to the antechamber open quietly. It was Ryker, no doubt notifying her that Lyra had finally returned to the castle. She couldn't wait to see the look on her sister's face when Lyra realized her little secret was out of the bag.

Ryker bowed as he entered her chamber. "Madam."

His greeting felt too formal, especially coming from him.

The queen and her general had shared a unique relationship over the years, and their closeness tended to be questioned by those that witnessed it. Whispers always seemed to follow the wolf-demon wherever he went, wondering how he'd been accepted into Madam Lema's army and rise to the rank of general.

It wasn't because of who he was, but what he'd done for her that allowed him to hold such a position. Though it went against everything in her nature to place such trust in a demon, she knew he would never betray her. If he did, there would be no room in her heart for trust ever again.

"Is she back?" Lema asked. She pulled the ties of her robe tighter around her waist, making sure most of her porcelain skin was covered from view.

Ryker averted his eyes, and she knew his canine senses had probably smelt the sex that lingered on her body.

"She just entered the castle grounds," he said. "Do you want my men to fetch her?"

"You go," Lema suggested. "So she understands how serious this is." Ryker nodded but did not move to leave. "Is there something else?" she asked.

He hesitated, an act unlike his typical demeanor. Lema might have had more personal reasons for appointing him as general, but she wasn't blind to his menacing appearance and how it struck fear in those that answered to him. This unsure, cowardly version of him was unsettling to watch.

"Well spit it out," she demanded. "What is it?"

Ryker cleared his throat. "Colonel Nyadahma received a letter this morning informing him that Jorah was injured."

Jorah was one of the Spyders that had been sent to Caster Valley. Along with a small team of soldiers, his presence was meant to put a stop to the protests that had begun popping up in some of the smaller villages. They'd originally been sent to Knox Hill, the very same village Lyra had been caught visiting, and it now made sense how the princess had known about the protest that happened there. But the last Lema had heard, Jorah and his men had been moved to Berwick, a much smaller village on the other side of the Ume River.

"We don't know the extent," Ryker stated. "But the letter mentioned a fire."

Lema immediately understood the implications of that statement. And it only enraged her further. Having to deal with Lyra's disgraceful actions against the coven was stressful enough, but now Lema was once again being reminded how much the country hated her. The fire was most likely another political stunt meant to rally people against the crown.

"Where?" she asked. Ryker looked at her blank-faced, so she elaborated. "*Where* was the fire?"

The general blanched slightly. "The Trade Center," he confirmed.

It was clear now what the rebels were trying to accomplish. So far almost every protest had involved the destruction of the Trade Center located in each district. There were two locations in Caster Valley—one on either side of the river—and now they'd both been destroyed.

The rebels were smart. They knew cutting off supplies didn't hurt anyone except those living in Larapuna.

Lema's patience was running thinner by the day, and if one more person threatened her authority, she was going to snap.

She clenched her fingers into the fabric of her robe and tried to remain calm, but the attempt was near impossible.

"Send more men," she instructed. "I want every nook and cranny of this gods-forsaken country occupied by my soldiers."

"But Lema–"

There it was—that familiarity that connected them. He took a step forward, finally deciding to enter her chamber fully. His gray eyes glinted in the sunlight that lit the edge of the room, but then they dropped to her hands as they clutched the fabric of her robe tightly around herself.

In her haste to dismiss Rhea from her chambers, Lema hadn't thought about fully dressing, nor covering her hands.

Ever since she'd started wearing the Hematite necklace full time, she'd found herself turning to Blood Magic more often to solve her problems. As such, the tips of her fingers had slowly begun turning an inky black. The color spread over the pale pigment of her skin like spilled ink, blossoming and pooling into the crevices of her skin.

It had alarmed her at first, but then she'd remembered the black stain that blighted her grandmother's fingers before she died. Others had accused Ruella of using Blood Magic, but she'd never let anyone see the evidence of it. Lema's grandmother had learned to cover her hands in public, and no one outside the Mansell bloodline knew the truth of what she'd been willing to risk for the coven.

Instead of drawing further attention to her stained fingers, Lema tucked her hands under her arms and coaxed Ryker to continue.

"But what?" she asked.

For a brief moment, Lema thought he would be bold enough to question her, but he followed her lead and moved on to what he'd wanted to say originally.

"We don't have enough soldiers to spare sending them to every village. But more importantly, sending soldiers to constantly patrol the streets will cause people to panic," he told her. "The country is already on edge because of the rebels, and if you send more soldiers, it will only make them more angry. People died in those fires. They're scared."

"Let them be," she said. "They should all be afraid of what I decide to do the day I've finally had enough."

Ryker didn't argue. He knew better than to question her in such a state. He bowed his head in defeat and said, "Very well. I'll go fetch the princess."

Then he left to follow his orders.

Lema found a more presentable dressing gown to throw on before heading for the meeting chamber downstairs, her nerves on the verge of fraying.

Nyadahma's elite Spyders weren't proving to be enough to deter people from rebelling, but if she wanted to send the rest of her soldiers, who would be left to defend the castle?

An idea struck her.

It was possible she could remedy that problem. but she would need the right witch to help her do it. And the elders weren't going to like it.

Lema smiled to herself. *Good,* she thought. *Let them try and stop me.*

LYRA

Lyra knew something was wrong the moment she stepped through the giant double doors at the front entrance of Larapuna. Even without being greeted immediately by General Ryker, Lyra had sensed the unease in the air around her. The taut anticipation of something terrible to come, like the feeling right before stepping off the edge of a cliff.

As she was escorted to the meeting chamber at the back of the Grand Hall, Lyra continued her attempt at sweeping her unease under the rug. Part of her knew what was coming—she'd been waiting for a delayed reaction since Lema had first heard the news of her pregnancy. Lyra expected the dramatics from her sister, but leading her to a private chamber escorted by the general of the army? That communicated something much more sinister.

Lema's hair was unbound, dark strands falling into the space of her cleavage and over her shoulders. Lyra rarely saw her sister in such casual attire. Lema was dressed in a simple but presentable dressing gown that fell to the floor and a pair of satin gloves that came up to the wrist, and she appeared unsettled.

The queen paced back and forth along the length of the table, the thin maroon fabric of her gown billowing behind her dramatically. It accented the intense hue of her eyes, showing exactly how rattled she was.

"You may leave us," Lema ordered Ryker.

He hesitated, but after seeing the set of Lema's jaw, he obeyed.

"I thought you'd be happy," Lyra suggested, taking a seat at the head of the meeting table.

Lema scoffed. "Happy? Oh yes. I'm so happy that my own blood has betrayed me with such blatant cruelty." Her voice lacked fervor. In her current state, she was unable to achieve sarcasm properly.

If Lyra didn't know better, she would think Lema actually sounded hurt.

"I don't understand," Lyra said. "I'm having a baby. I'm fulfilling my duty as a member of this coven. I'm passing on my magic."

"You are creating an abomination!"

Lema's yell echoed through the high ceiling and cascaded down the narrow set of stairs behind her. Lyra only knew they were there because she'd snuck behind the tapestry that hid them on several occasions. It was one of the best routes out of the castle, cutting through the dungeons and coming out behind the soldiers' barracks. Lyra wondered if the prisoners down there now could hear the queen's anger.

But that thought only lasted a second, because the thought that proceeded was much more dire. There was only one reason why Lema would refer to her unborn child as an abomination.

She knew about the father.

"You had me followed?" Lyra accused.

Lema barked out a hollow laugh, her sarcasm coming across properly this time. "That's all you have to say?" She swooped down upon Lyra like a hawk and latched her talons tightly to either side of the chair's armrests. "You dare breed filth into our family, and yet you're concerned about your privacy?"

Lyra bristled, but remained collected. "How long?" she asked. "How long have you known about him?"

Lema straightened but remained in front of her. "I've had my suspicions about you for a while, always sneaking off without a word, but I only just confirmed it." Then she took a step back and recoiled. "You went to see the creature."

Lyra cringed at the word. *Creature.*

Would Lema dare use such derogatory language in front of Ryker? Thank the Mother he was no longer in the room.

"Then you should know that Oram has agreed to raise the child if it's a boy," Lyra said, feigning nonchalance. "You don't have to worry. It will be dealt with."

"That it will," Lema agreed snidely. "I won't allow you to besmirch our grandmother's legacy. That child will not be born, no matter what it turns out to be."

The statement hit Lyra like a crashing tidal wave. "You can't mean that," she cried, getting to her feet.

Their faces were inches apart. She could see the lines that marred her sister's mouth and eyes, the stress that was wearing on her. She was starting to look her age.

"You wouldn't kill a witch," Lyra muttered in disbelief.

Lema smiled. "Anything with demon blood is cursed to be a monster. I would never take that chance."

"I won't let you!"

"Try and stop me!"

Lema's hand shot towards Lyra's abdomen, but Lyra was equally as fast. She'd grabbed Lema's wrist seconds before she was able to make contact.

And in that moment, everything stopped.

AT FIRST, *there was nothing.*

An all-consuming whiteness that blurred at the periphery. A haze, thicker than clouds but not opaque. For there was something on the other side to be seen. A figure in the distance, standing tall and proud.

It was hard to decipher the full body of the figure, because the curtain of white moved to and fro in front of it. Between swings like a pendulum, there were fragments being exposed. A leg and a shoulder. A narrow torso.

But yes. There it was. The top of a head, and flowing down like a cascade of foamy water was hair the purest shade of white. It blew in the wind, though there was none to be felt.

No sooner than the figure was fully revealed, it transformed.

Legs shortened and began to crouch. A back elongated and thickened, revealing powerful muscles beneath. A jaw distended and unhinged, bearing sharp fangs. Eyes the color of jade crystals pierced through the whiteness. And then there were stripes. Jagged black lines cutting through the endless nothingness and revealing a creature with fur the purest shade of white, like freshly fallen snow.

A beautiful, majestic beast in its truest form.

It was surrounded by others now. Kneeling. Heads and hands pressed to the earth in respect and fear. They worshiped and praised the thing standing before them.

But then there was blood.

Deep crimson leaked between the creature's paws and pooled at its feet. It came from a nonexistent place. Somewhere others could not reach, but they could feel the pain nonetheless. It tore from their lungs in violent screams. Cries of desperation.

Stop! Please! Help us!

But no. The blood would not stop. It poured in from nothingness.

Elsewhere. The birthplace of magic, and the end of it.

The creature bowed its head then lifted it again to the emptiness above.

Every cry was snuffed out by a thunderous, ROAR!

AFTER THE CONNECTION BROKE, Lyra fell back into the chair she'd been sitting in. She let out an exasperated exhale, feeling the pain of the collision in her lower back.

Lema was no longer standing either. She'd been thrown back and tossed on the floor. Her robe was tangled between her legs, trapping her within the silken fabric that bunched beneath her.

As reality set back in, Lyra tried to grasp at all the mental puzzle pieces now swimming in her mind. What she'd seen didn't make sense. Or at least, not yet. They'd shared a vision—something she'd never known to happen between two witches before. Future Sight typically came to a witch individually, but their connection had triggered something, and Lema's face now looked haunted.

Had she seen the same thing?

Lyra bent at the waist and rubbed her back, awkwardly trying to massage the soreness away, then she felt for the life in her stomach. A small pulse beneath her hand told her the child was alright.

She knew her next priority should be to see if Lema was alright. Losing her balance slightly, she stumbled over to where her sister lay on the floor. Lema was alert and casting wild eyes around the space, searching for something. As if she was trying to grasp for what she'd just seen and bring it back.

Heavy footfalls thudded into the room, and Lyra looked at the door to find Ryker standing battle ready, sword drawn and senses on high alert. Lyra softened and settled back onto her heels.

"Lema, are you alright?" she asked, gently shaking her sister's shoulder.

But it wasn't her sister that responded.

It was the queen.

With a voice darker than the deepest ocean, Lema Mansell raised her head and spoke directly to her general. "Take her."

FREYAH

The next time Madam Lema sent for her, Freyah was prepared.

Before leaving her room, she'd mined the deepest recesses of her inner strength to find courage and dredge it to the surface. She was prepared to receive either another punishment or to prevent her mind from being sifted through like garbage. Though Freyah couldn't imagine what else Madam Lema could possibly want to know after learning the truth about her father, she was ready for whatever might come.

She walked in strained silence with Whit through the shadowed halls, her chest aching as it rubbed against the fabric of her shirt. Her wound was still wrapped with a thick layer of bandages, but every movement felt like tiny pinpricks along her skin. The salve Willow had provided was helping to ease the pain, but it required a new application every few hours, and Freyah was past due.

After entering the queen's chambers, Freyah watched as Whit turned and prepared to leave. It was harder watching him walk away this time. She didn't want to be left alone with the witch that meant to punish her father—to possibly punish her for his crimes.

"You can stay, Lieutenant," Madam Lema said from her chair by the hearth. "This won't take long."

Whit's fingers stilled as he gripped the brass handle of the door, then he let go and turned on the spot to face the queen.

Madam Lema gestured to the plush velvet chair opposite her own and looked to Freyah. "Please sit."

Together, they sat in front of a large wrought iron grate while Whit stood sentry by the door. The queen kept her hands laced together in her lap, and Freyah noticed for the first time that the tips of her fingers were stained a deep crimson. As if she'd dipped them into an inkpot the color of blood, so dark it was almost black. The strange effect must have been new, because Freyah hadn't noticed it the last time they'd spoken. Whit seemed to notice it, too, because he was looking at the queen's hands with wide eyes.

"Do you know how demons were created?" Madam Lema asked, breaking the silence.

The question was so far from what Freyah had expected that she actually had to shake her head to clear the confusion. But she knew the answer. "They used to be warlocks," she said. "Until witches cursed them and stole their magic." She could practically feel the awkward tension radiating from Whit across the room.

"We didn't steal anything," the queen corrected. "We shared our magic willingly, until they decided to take advantage of our generosity. You see, women with magic have always had a special gift that men covet. The warlocks could shift into an animal at will, but witches…we can access Future Sight."

A flash of the statues Whit had shown her outside the library—the Mother and Father of magic—briefly crossed her mind.

"They needed us for our visions," the queen continued. "But instead of asking nicely, they started forcing witches to do their bidding. We foresaw any and all conflict and helped them rise to power. We saw their collapse as well," she smiled crookedly. "Only we kept that to ourselves."

"So you tricked them," Freyah stated bluntly.

Madam Lema scoffed. "We used their own greed against them. It was my grandmother that performed the curse. She took back our power and put them in their rightful place."

Freyah thought of Whit, forever stuck in a half state between man and beast, all because of something that had happened a hundred years ago. Something that was completely out of his control. "You're punishing generations of men for their ancestor's sins," Freyah said with disgust.

Madam Lema's eyes narrowed. The tone in her voice sharpened. "And you believe it won't happen again? Men are selfish and cruel. They use us for our gifts and our bodies. Things they wish they had. Even now, humans and demons alike are threatening to rise against us."

"Demons only want what was taken from them!"

Freyah fully understood that now. She felt Whit's pain. She saw his body tense from the corner of her eye. She could sense that he desperately wanted to stand up for himself and his kind, but he couldn't. So, Freyah did it for him.

He was the first demon she'd come to know on a personal level, and it was only because she hadn't known the full truth that she'd even given him a chance.

It made her sick that she'd never given anyone else that same opportunity. She thought of Jago at home in Last Cove, and she silently made a promise to herself that when she finally made it back home, she'd make a point to befriend him.

Madam Lema stood and strode to a large mahogany desk. Freyah could see various pieces of torn parchment scattered across a marble surface.

"It doesn't matter what they want," she stated firmly. "It cannot be undone."

Freyah felt the continued urge to protest. She could sense a flaw in the queen's logic. Something didn't fit. "If that's true," she objected, white-knuckling the arms of her chair, "why are you so afraid of them?"

The queen's face darkened. Freyah thought she could see literal shadows crawling beneath her skin. "I do not fear them, girl," she spat.

"They annoy me. I wish to squash their rebellion under my heel and be rid of them." Then her expression softened, and the shadows dissipated. "That's why I need you. You are the key to ending The First Men."

Freyah felt her stomach drop.

It was then that Whit finally chose to speak up. "Demons have nothing to do with The First Men. You know that."

"Well it would seem that you are misinformed, Mr. Avlon."

Whit shook his head, but Freyah spoke before he could argue with the queen further. "I don't understand. How am I the key?"

Madam Lema scoffed in incredulity. "Don't play daft. It doesn't suit you. Your mind has been cleared and I've seen it all. I tasted what you saw in your dreams. The burn was just for fun."

The blood.

Freyah remembered the sound that had come from Madam Lema when she'd tasted it. But what sort of dark magic had allowed her to see into Freyah's mind?

Madam Lema stroked a lock of her raven hair, twirling it around her index finger. It looked like a snake coiling around its victim. "It's Blood Magic, dear."

Maybe the witch really could read her mind.

"I had my suspicions about who your father was—the role he played—but I had to be sure. I needed *you*. You see, I thought by bringing you here, your father would come for you."

It was all clicking into place. It truly was no coincidence that Freyah had ended up at Castle Larapuna. Madam Lema had known the moment Freyah stepped foot in the dungeons, because it was all part of her plan.

"You knew about me?" Freyah asked, cheeks flaming with fury. She risked a quick glance to her guard, but Whit was stone-faced. She centered her attention back on Lema. "Even before he brought me here?"

"Of course I did," Madam Lema boasted. "Who do you think sent him to get you?" She lifted a slender finger to point directly at Whit, her long nails catching a glint of light from the fire.

It was the final part of the puzzle she hadn't wanted to admit existed.

Lieutenant Avlon had not merely been sent to Last Cove to collect a delayed supply drop. He'd been ordered to retrieve Freyah Kenpaw and bring her to the witch-queen.

The look of fear on Whit's face was soul-crushing. She could see the guilt and regret painted as clearly as the smug pride on Madam Lema's. He hadn't wanted her to know. It was yet another thing he had chosen to keep from her.

But this...

This was so much worse.

The truth of it sat on Freyah's chest like an anchor sinking heavily to the bottom of the sea. It crushed her lungs, causing the room around her to feel small and suffocating.

She couldn't face it. Not now. Not with Whit staring at her like that. Like a man that had just realized he'd made the biggest mistake of his life. If she looked at his face for too long, she would fall prey to his guilt and feel sorry for him.

And that was the worst possible thing to feel right now.

Instead, she focused on Madam Lema. "You let me sit in that dungeon," Freyah spoke quietly, processing the realization. "You were going to let your soldiers rape me."

"That was an unexpected snag. Lucky for you, Lieutenant Avlon has a moral compass."

The words were so casual, so easily dropped into the conversation like pebbles spilling from her pockets onto the stone floor. And in front of Whit no less. Freyah gathered the words and felt their weight. "You're despicable. You're a *monster*."

"No, my dear," Madam Lema quickly clarified. "*Men* are the monsters. They always have been. But no more. Not as long as I'm the queen."

Freyah couldn't understand such cruelty. What had the warlocks possibly done to deserve having their magic stripped away from them in such a callous and spiteful manner? There had to be more to the story, but Madam Lema wasn't going to be the one to tell her. No, the witch-queen had other priorities. More important matters to attend to.

"I've summoned you here to inform you that I'm sending a group of soldiers to arrest your father. He will be brought to Larapuna and tried for conspiracy against the crown."

Freyah already knew this, thanks to Whit, but hearing the queen confirm it only turned her fear into a raging, nasty monster in her chest. It fought with the weight of Whit's betrayal, and together the two emotions clashed like tidal waves. They clawed at her skin, trying to escape.

"I will spare his life," Madam Lema continued, "if he agrees to put a stop to his treasonous acts, call off his men, and form an alliance with the crown."

It was apparent that her father had some sort of leadership role back in Last Cove based on the interactions Freyah had witnessed between him and others, but how far did that authority reach? Surely he didn't have enough influence to sway an entire rebellion.

"What makes you think he has that much power?"

Madam Lema cocked her head quizzically, her perfectly-arched eyebrows pulling together. "I thought you were smarter than this, Freyah." She paced the length of the room. Each time she came close to Whit, he recoiled into himself. Freyah saw a lock of hair fall protectively in front of his face. "When you want to destroy a pyramid, you don't just remove the top. You create ripples—small but significant changes to fracture the foundation. With enough ripples, the entire thing comes crumbling down."

Freyah was done with the conversation. Madam Lema's explanations meant nothing to her, and it was pointless listening to any of it. Freyah didn't care why the queen did what she did. It didn't matter how she planned to take down the rebellion. The matter of most importance was warning her father and getting to him before it was too late—before Madam Lema's soldiers did.

Freyah got to her feet abruptly, and Madam Lema stopped her pacing.

"You're quite right, we're done here." Then the queen addressed

Whit. "Lieutenant Avlon, please escort Miss Kenpaw back to her rooms. She'll have no need to roam the castle. The other guards will make sure of that."

THE AIR in the halls was stifling. Freyah walked briskly, the echoing footsteps from Whit's boots close behind her.

"Freyah, wait. *Please.*"

She wasn't slowing down. Like with Madam Lema, she had no interest in hearing Whit's explanation. It made no difference now. The faith she'd placed in him was irrevocably broken beyond repair, and Freyah couldn't imagine ever finding the will to trust him again.

She wasn't even upset about him hiding that he was a demon anymore. She knew how hard it must have been for him, and she understood the risk he was taking by choosing to hide it from the queen. She knew he didn't truly have a choice when it came to keeping the truth from Freyah when he did. They hadn't known each other well enough for him to place such an important piece of himself in her hands.

But what about after, when things had shifted between them?

Freyah wanted to believe that Whit would have told her eventually. In time, he would've opened up completely and laid himself bare. But a simple mistake had beaten him to the punch and confessed everything for him. A minor slip-up, and now everything was different.

But that wasn't the knife that was currently twisting in her heart. It wasn't the part that stung so deep Freyah felt like she would never catch a full breath again.

Whit had been responsible for her abduction. It was a direct order from the queen, and he'd followed it to the letter. How could she ever know what parts of him were genuine after this? And what parts had been an act simply to get her here easily, without fuss?

He caught up to her, the tug of his hand on her arm gentle but insistent. "Freyah, please listen to me."

"I don't want to!" she cried. "Don't you understand? I can't even look at you right now without wanting to fall apart. And I can't fall apart. I have to get to my father. I have to stop this!"

"I know," he assured her. "I understand that, and I can help. But Freyah, I swear, the soldier that brought you here is not the same soldier standing in front of you now."

"Things changed, right? After getting to know me, you changed your mind? Felt bad about it?"

Whit stared at her, awestruck. "Yes."

"It. Doesn't. Matter," she enunciated with venom. "I might not trust you anymore, but I still need your help. So you're going to help me. You're going to do whatever you can to stop those soldiers from hurting my father. Send a carrier pigeon, get your friend Raven to enchant it so it can fly at top speed. Warn him. Because if you don't help me—if you don't do everything in your power to make this right —I will do everything in *my* power to make sure you regret it."

WHIT

*W*hit had not left things with Freyah in a comfortable place.

Although they'd seemed to come to a sort of understanding, there was still a thick layer of distrust now caked onto the relationship they'd built. He could have told her the truth about everything from the start, but would she have looked at him the same after knowing? Would they have shared that kiss in the library? Or would she have avoided his gaze, not daring to get too close to an untrustworthy demon?

It wasn't only his life he was making easier with the choice he'd made—it was Willow's as well. Merely being related to a demon would label her an outcast, and they'd had too much stacked against them already.

But Whit had piled on one more thing: the need to protect Freyah. And he worried his choices would soon come crumbling down upon them.

Freyah no longer trusted him, but she still needed his help. Just because she'd drawn a line between them didn't mean he was going to give up. He cared too deeply now. There was no way to erase the feelings of tenderness that filled his belly when he saw her.

He'd made a lot of mistakes in his life, but one of the biggest had been bringing Freyah to the castle in the first place. He hadn't expected to fall for her—hadn't planned to care about the girl he'd snatched from Last Cove—but here he was, standing in the middle of the training yard staring blankly at the sky and trying to keep his heart from shattering in his chest.

Having Freyah upset with him didn't sit well in his gut. He needed to make it right, to do whatever it took to gain back her trust and prove his loyalty.

Freyah now knew that he'd been the one ordered to bring her to Castle Larapuna. She'd assumed she was being disciplined for disrespecting a soldier, and Whit had let her believe it. Because it was easier.

If she didn't hate him before because of his blood, she would now because of his actions. But he'd made her a promise: he was going to protect her and her father. Nothing bad would happen to them as long as he was standing, and he prayed to Ghidorah that nothing would knock him down.

He'd been holding a set of jumping ropes for twenty minutes, the frayed fibers dangling limply from his fingers. His training was important to him—it was something he did to hold off the degeneration of his joints. It couldn't be avoided forever, but by constantly pushing his body to stay moving and strong, he could postpone the inevitable, even if it only gave him one more day.

His best friends, Perry and Oliver, joined him most days, but they had trouble keeping up with Whit's rigorous schedule. And now that his emotions were in knots, he'd needed a major distraction. He was pushing himself twice as hard as usual, but he'd lost himself in thought, the guilt finding a way in despite boarding up all of his doors. His friends were taking advantage of the break, but after half an hour, Perry finally broke the silence and cleared his throat.

His friend was sweating profusely, beads of moisture dripping from his temples and down the sides of his stubble-lined face. His natural poufy curls stuck out in every direction, and he was breathing heavily, still trying to catch his breath after a long rest.

"You good, man?" Perry asked, clapping a large hand on Whit's shoulder.

Whit reeled in his focus and turned his head to face him. "Yeah. Sorry. Just a lot on my mind."

"Do you really need to go on this trip?" Perry insisted. "Traveling all the way to Last Cove twice in one month is a lot for anyone. Even you."

Oliver ambled over to chime in. "Yeah, why *are* you wanting to go again?" His typically well-kept blond hair was matted to his forehead, also slick with sweat.

A different pang of guilt stabbed at Whit's gut, this time for forcing his friends to push too hard. He hated that they felt they had to keep up with him, but he knew them well enough now that they were just trying to be there for him, despite not knowing why. That was the thing about Perry and Oliver: Whit could comfortably sit in silence and brood without saying a word about what was wrong, and they both would sit beside him. Apparently the silence had gone on too long, however, and this time they were asking questions.

Whit released the ropes from his grip and let them fall to the muddy ground. It had been raining earlier that morning, and the soil beneath them was still soaked with moisture. "I have to make things right," he told them.

He'd already confided in them about everything concerning Freyah, but they didn't know about the latest wrench that had been thrown into the mix.

"I'm the one that brought her here," Whit said. "It's my fault she's in this mess, and now her father is in danger. I have to do what I can."

"And you think volunteering to go retrieve him is going to make things right?" Perry challenged. "What exactly do you think you can do?"

"I don't know!" Whit was already frustrated because he didn't have a plan, but he didn't want to have to explain that to his friends. "I can warn him," he suggested. "Make sure they don't hurt him. You know how the others can be."

Perry nodded curtly. He did know. Being a publicly named criminal of the crown would give Madam Lema's soldiers all the permission they needed to treat Brennan like absolute dog shit. They'd make his journey to Larapuna as torturous as possible, and they'd enjoy every second of his misery.

"She's never going to let you on that team," Perry stated matter-of-factly, referring to the queen. "Especially now that she knows how close you are to the situation."

"I know," Whit sighed. "But there's got to be another way. Freyah knows everything now."

That statement caught Oliver's attention. "Wait, you mean she knows about the order?" he questioned with disbelief. "She knows you were sent to find her?"

Whit closed his eyes and inhaled deeply. It was confirmation enough for all of them, but that wasn't all. "There's something else," Whit continued. "She knows what I am. She saw."

Both Perry and Oliver's eyes went wide.

Perry shook his head, trying to understand. "You mean...?"

"She knows I'm a demon," Whit said in a hushed tone.

Both of his friends released the same question at once. "*How?*"

"I forgot to take my dose that morning. I was running late, and I didn't think. I was too concerned about leaving her without an escort —I just...I got distracted."

Oliver sat on a pile of thickly-chopped logs next to Whit's previously abandoned shirt that was draped casually over the wood. He dragged a hand over his face, his fingers catching on the piercings on either side of his bottom lip. "This is bad, isn't it?" he asked.

Then Perry added, "Did anyone else see you?"

Whit knew how seriously his friends were taking the news. Besides his sister and Raven, Perry and Oliver were the only ones that knew the truth about Whit's identity. They respected their friend's decision and would never risk his secret getting out.

Whit assured Perry that he hadn't been spotted. Or at least he was ninety percent sure, but he wasn't going to tell him that. Even the slightest chance would send Perry into a spiral of concern, and Whit knew how damaging that could be. Oliver would never hear the end of it, and Whit had no intention of putting that extra strain on their relationship.

Perry lowered his head, the sun casting shadows over the dark, freckled markings under his eyes. Though he stood taller than Whit, at the moment he appeared very small. Whit had never wanted to drag his friends into his own mess, but he knew better than to push them away. They would be there to offer help whether he liked it or not, so it was best that he suck it up and accept it.

Other soldiers were now watching the three of them huddled together, curious about their conversation and what could possibly be so important to interrupt Whit's routine workout.

"Need something, shitface?" Oliver jeered at the two soldiers lingering nearby.

Whit recognized Nico among the group. He'd seen very little of the soldier since arriving back from their two week trek to Last Cove and back, and Whit wondered if he'd been assigned to the team retrieving Brennan.

"Just wondering what you girls are gossiping about over there," the other soldier taunted. He wore a length of green cloth tied around his head, thick red hair flowing from underneath the material. He smirked, and Whit could see the glint of a gold tooth.

"Wouldn't you like to know," Oliver threatened, rising to his feet, but his partner was already there to place a protective hand on his arm.

Perry then stepped in front of Oliver and spoke calmly. "Move along, Conrath."

Whit knew Oliver's tendencies to jump to aggression, and he really didn't feel like dealing with a brawl right now. Luckily, Perry knew him, too—well enough to know when to step in and stop a fight before it started.

Thankfully the two soldiers decided to concede and walk away, but not before Whit heard Conrath mutter a curse under his breath. "Pussies."

Oliver lunged but Perry was right there to stop him in his tracks. He held him back with a powerful arm across his partner's chest, and Oliver struggled against the weight of it. But he eventually gave in. Conrath and Nico guffawed all the way to the top of the hill, where the rest of the soldiers were training.

Whit was tired. He didn't have the energy for this when there were so many other things nipping at his conscience. He needed to make sure he was on the team going to Last Cove, but he had no clue how to accomplish that without the queen's approval. If he somehow managed to sneak out with the others, they'd most likely notice him tagging along and start asking questions. He'd considered leaving ahead of them and warning Brennan before they arrived, but he couldn't risk the man running off. The queen would know someone had warned him, and the blame would no doubt fall on Whit.

Time was running out. There would be a group of four men leaving first thing tomorrow morning, and Whit needed to be one of them.

"I need you to find out who's been assigned to Last Cove," Whit instructed Perry. He was still talking Oliver off the ledge, but they both looked significantly calmer. "Can you ask around? I can't because it'll stir too much attention."

"Of course," Perry agreed. "Whatever you need." He let go of Oliver and placed both hands on his own hips. "But even if I do, how are you going to get yourself onto the team? You'd have to take someone's place."

Whit retrieved his tunic from the logs and pulled it forcefully over his head. "Just leave that up to me."

PERRY REPORTED BACK LATER that evening with four names: Fallon, Cleetus, Paul, and Micah. The former three selections made sense to Whit because they were all members of the alpha strike team who worked directly under his peer, Lieutenant Selmy. The latter choice did not. Micah Wighthall was a Spyder—part of the queen's special forces branch.

The Spyders were typically stationed in the villages to act as spies on Madam Lema's behalf. They were highly trained in combat and rarely seen. Micah, however, was one of the few stationed at the forest border to keep the peace with the Wild Demon clans and make sure no one overstepped their boundaries on either side.

Whit had an innate dislike for the Spyders. They were too unpredictable for his taste, but more importantly, it had been a Spyder that killed Wendi.

He would not let that happen to anyone else he cared about.

Whit completed his nightly rituals per usual. He checked the locks on each door of the dungeon. The task proved to be quick because there were only a handful of prisoners being kept behind bars, and most of them were completely docile because of the amount of time they'd been there. He checked in with Oliver, who was stationed at the entrance and ready to start his evening shift, then he walked to the barracks under a sky full of glistening stars and watched as the lights in the castle extinguished one by one.

Men were washing themselves in the outdoor shower stalls, and Whit tried to keep his eyes averted as he passed. As soldiers, they weren't given much privacy, but he'd grown used to it over the years. Whit typically showered first thing in the morning, when the sun was but a sliver of orange at the edge of the horizon and all the other men were enjoying their last few minutes of sleep.

But tonight would be different. Whit knew that the Spyders stationed in the forest typically used the showers in the middle of the night because they were on opposite schedules from the rest of the army. This gave Whit a greater chance of getting Micah alone. He would wait for the opportune moment, and then he'd make his move.

Micah was the one to worry about. He absolutely could not be on that team by morning. Whit didn't necessarily have a plan—if he was honest, he never did—but he knew if he could incapacitate Micah long enough to take his place on the team, they'd be gone before anyone else noticed, and there would be little the queen could do about it.

Whit waited until everyone had settled into their bunks, then after enough time had passed to guarantee they were all asleep, he crept past his fellow men and ventured out into the night. He kept close to the building, allowing the shadows to cover him, then found a small alcove tucked between two storage sheds that stood opposite the bathing stations. It was there that he slipped inside to wait.

Completely covered with darkness, Whit crouched low to the ground and watched for any sign of movement. Over an hour passed, and his legs began to cramp from holding his position. He was about to stand and stretch when he heard rustling from across the lawn and a handful of murmuring voices. He sat back on his heels and listened carefully, as three men came into view, appearing like phantoms from the trees behind the barracks. They made their way to the showers, all three of them shirtless and with towels draped over their shoulders.

At this distance he couldn't make out which of them was Micah, but Whit remained where he was, knowing that he wouldn't be able to make a move as long as it was three against one.

The Spyders were definitely intimidating. Each of them had their own cryptic markings tattooed across their skin, covering their chests and backs, but only one had alchemy runes inked completely down his arms.

Whit zeroed in on the tallest of the three. A singular lantern hung from a post and dangled above the showers, giving the men enough light to see what they were doing. The illumination gave Whit a clearer view of his target's dirty blond hair, and as the men took their time washing every inch of their bodies under the streams, he never took his eyes off of the back of Micah's head.

Ten minutes later, the other two men redressed and wrung the water from their previously braided hair. Micah had left his woven locks intact, and the thick braid rested heavily on his broad shoulder, weighted with moisture.

The others were already leaving, but Micah remained where he was. He took his time turning off the water and toweling dry, whistling to himself in the dark.

When the other Spyders had disappeared into the tree line, Whit stood and began moving toward his target. He took one precious step at a time, not wanting to signal his approach before getting close enough to inflict lethal damage. He'd brought his carving knife, the hilt still stained with the blood of the ox-demon he'd killed in the forest on the way to Larapuna.

He watched as Micah slipped back into a pair of trousers. Gripping the handle tighter, Whit waited until he was within ten feet of his target, then he raised the switchblade at an angle perfect for piercing the Spyder's throat.

Whit didn't hear the other weapon as it was unsheathed, nor did he notice the blade until it was already swiping through the air. It sliced through the muscle of Whit's right forearm and blood gushed down the crook of his elbow.

Micah had heard him. And he'd struck first.

The Spyder had hung back on purpose, waiting for his attacker to make a move. And Whit had fallen right into the Spyder's trap.

Whit grabbed at his arm with his free hand and pressed firmly against the wound, the switchblade still gripped tightly in the other. He barely had time to register what was happening before Micah was swiping at him again. This time he went for the inside of Whit's thigh, but Whit was barely able to sidestep out of the way before the blade could make contact with his femoral artery.

He'd made a mistake.

Whit had seriously underestimated the Spyder's skill, thinking that the element of surprise would be enough to best a trained spy. But he was in too deep, and there was now no other choice but to fight his way out of it.

"You dare sneak up on me and attempt to shove a knife in my back?" Micah growled as he took a new stance.

Whit was only a guard. What little training he'd had in combat wasn't nearly enough to compete with this Spyder's skill with a blade. But Whit was smart. He could figure this out. He had vengeance for his sister fueling every strike. He simply needed to outsmart his opponent.

One wrong move was all it would take to gain the upper hand.

Micah sneered, water still dripping down his hulking muscles and drawing attention to the runes on his skin. "Always a quiet one, you were. I didn't expect you to have the balls for something like this." He cocked his head. "A bit much, don't you think?"

Whit ignored the man's attempt to antagonize him, but the words still lingered in the back of his mind. How did this Spyder know who Whit was?

They continued to circle one another in the tight space, each waiting for the other to make a move. Whit couldn't look too eager. He needed to wait for the ideal moment before striking. Too much bloodshed would be time consuming and messy, so he needed to aim for a simple killing blow.

"It took you long enough to make your move," Micah said vehemently.

Though Whit tried to fight it, the statement struck a nerve. He narrowed his eyes in confusion. "What are you talking about?"

The Spyder merely laughed, his lips drawing into a sneer.

Whit's confusion quickly morphed into anger, and he felt the vein in his neck pulse as he clenched his jaw. The Spyder was only fucking with him.

Micah stepped back and took a long pause before saying half-heartedly, "She never even fought back. Did you know that?"

Whit's entire world stopped. His head spun violently, and he felt his body sway with disbelief. It wasn't true. There was no fucking way the man standing in front of him had been the one to kill Wendi.

But the smug grin on Micah's face was enough to confirm it.

Whit tried to place memory to the Spyder's features, but he hadn't had a good look back then. The Spyder had been in uniform, face smeared with warpaint, so there was no way Whit could have known who he was at the time.

But it was obvious now. And Whit cursed himself for not seeing it before.

It was the smile that gave Micah away.

Whit lunged, but the Spyder was quick to follow. Micah's hits were powerful, each landing perfectly where they'd inflict the most damage. He used his fists and forearm to land precise blows to Whit's kidneys, lungs, and gut. They knocked the wind from Whit's chest, but he stayed on his feet.

Whit continued to struggle, and then by pure luck, he managed to slice Micah's thigh with his blade.

It was enough to make Micah pause. Both men looked down to see deep crimson blooming through the fabric of the Spyder's trousers. But then something happened that Whit did not expect. As Micah's eyes peered up into his, Whit watched in awe as his pupils turned into vicious slits. An actual growl erupted from Micah's throat, and suddenly his body began to morph into something Whit had never seen before.

The Spyder rose onto the balls of his feet as his legs elongated and broke free from the fabric of his pants. His chest rippled, and Whit saw the muscles shift and stretch as Micah grew several feet in height. His jaw unhinged and became a muzzle full of sharp teeth. Then, to Whit's horror, Micah's back hunched and contracted as several long claws ripped through the skin of his fingers. Parts of the Spyder looked similar to Ryker—a wolf in nature—but this version had been manipulated into something much more sinister.

So many questions ran through Whit's mind as he tried to decide what to do next. He had barely stood a chance against a skilled Spyder before, but now? He was no match for this beast. Had Micah been another demon in hiding? No wonder he chose to keep his true nature a secret—the creature standing before Whit was absolutely terrifying.

Whit could no longer map Micah's footwork or punches, because there was no semblance of a man left in the creature he now had to fight. The Spyder was all beast—no strategy or calculated moves. Simply instinct and animal nature.

Micah swiped furiously with his oversized claws, nearly catching him in the face, but Whit managed to step out of reach. He dodged each snap of Micah's jaw with nothing but the small knife in the hand of his injured arm, and he wished more than anything in that moment that he had a better weapon. As a guard, Whit was only allowed to arm himself while on duty. It would take a much larger blade to strike a killing blow now.

Or would it?

Whit had managed to take down the ox-demon by surprise with nothing but his simple carving knife. If he timed it right, it was possible that the switchblade would be enough for this.

Micah landed on all fours and howled a warning to the moon above. The beast was about to strike, and Whit had one chance to stop it.

The mutated wolf-demon made one large leap toward Whit with his jaw open wide for the kill, and as he landed atop his prey, a high-pitched whine filled the air. Whit's switchblade was buried deep into the side of Micah's neck. He felt the blade cut through muscle and artery and lodge itself there as he was brought down by the weight of Micah's demon body collapsing on top of him. Whit's boots slipped in the water beneath him, and he landed hard on his back.

The Spyder jerked wildly atop him as blood spurted around the weapon now protruding from his jugular and filled his mouth. It sprayed across Whit's face and pooled in the water, creating rings of crimson.

He shifted out from under the massive weight and took a deep breath. As he looked down at the slain beast before him, only one thought came to mind.

"That was for my sister," he murmured.

Dark blood seeped from Micah's throat and swirled in thick ribbons across the stones beneath him. Whit held his right wrist and tested the movement—the angle at which he'd held the blade as Micah's weight fell on top of him had injured the joint. Now not only was his forearm bleeding profusely, but his wrist was beginning to swell and stiffen.

He wanted to bask in his victory, but there was now a gigantic mess to clean up and a body to get rid of. He waited until all movement ceased, then he grabbed the demon by his legs and began hauling the body from the showers.

The task proved to be incredibly difficult due to Micah's weight as a demon, and with Whit's injuries, there was no way he was going to be able to finish the job on his own.

The last thing he wanted to do was involve anyone else in his mess, but he needed help if he wanted to bury a body before dawn.

WHIT

"By Ghidorah's name," Perry gasped as his eyes fell on the slain creature before him. "I've never seen a demon like this before."

"Neither have I," Whit agreed. "But that's not what's important right now. I need to get rid of it."

Perry looked as if he had a million questions—even more than Whit—but he was smart enough not to ask them. Instead, he rolled up his sleeves and took a deep breath. "Alright. Let's do it."

It took a few hours, but together they were able to bury Micah under the latrine, knowing that the waste would hide the smell. Afterward, they hurried back to the bathing stations to wash away whatever blood and dirt they could, and after a significant amount of water had been spent, the final streams of red dissipated into the grass and soaked into the earth. The stones beneath the showers were now stained a rusted brown, but there was nothing else to be done. Whit hoped the other soldiers would pass it off as clay.

Now there was the matter of ridding himself of any evidence. Whit stripped away his sleep shirt that was soaked with both his and Micah's blood and tossed it into a fire pit at the front of the barracks.

There were a few spare tunics hanging from the clothing line, so he grabbed one to change into later.

He hadn't anticipated getting hurt, which was incredibly stupid and poor preparation on his part, but he needed to stitch up the deep gash in his arm so he could cover it. His long-sleeved uniform would hide the wound from suspecting eyes, but he didn't want to leave it untreated and risk infection. For this, he needed supplies.

"Do you have any first aid supplies in your bunk?" Whit asked as Perry stripped out of his own soiled clothing.

He shook his head. "I'm sorry, mate. I don't."

It was possible that Willow would have such supplies, but after her blatant tattling on Freyah, Whit wasn't entirely sure he could trust his sister to keep her mouth shut. Unfortunately, that meant his next best option was Raven.

Asking her for a favor twice in one week would cost him. What that cost would be, he didn't know, but he couldn't worry about that now. He now had less than two hours to clean up and make his way to the courtyard to meet the team before they took off for Last Cove.

Perry clearly knew where Whit's mind had led him, because he was already shaking his head solemnly in defeat. "If you go to her, you need to ask about him." He gestured to the area of freshly dug dirt they had created behind the barracks.

His friend was right. Whit needed someone to explain what the fuck he'd just witnessed, and there was only one person that would be able to.

Raven wasn't typically one to ask questions, but he'd never gone to her for help with anything like this. Providing the elixir to hide his features was an unspoken exchange that happened once a week. It had become expected, and there was no need for inquiries after Whit had ingested the concoction hundreds of times. But this was different. Tending to his wounds was an intimate gesture. One that required payment in return.

He knew he would have to give her what she'd been asking for—what he'd been denying her ever since bringing Freyah to the castle.

Perry must have known it, too, because the look on his face was now one of sympathy. "Do what you have to do," he said. "Just don't let her fuck with your head."

Whit nodded regretfully and parted ways with his friend. He thought of nothing but Freyah as he made the long trek to Raven's tower. Despite trying to do the right thing, somehow he'd managed to add something new to his long list of regrets.

Just like before, it took several knocks at the door before Raven finally appeared at the threshold. She was not amused in the slightest.

"What have you done this time?" she asked, the light of the moon casting a backlit glow around her slender frame.

In the blackness of her room, she appeared ethereal. Her hair fell loosely over her shoulders and down to her waist, and she was wearing a lavender silk robe that clung to her like water.

Raven noted the blood dripping steadily onto the stone floor, then she lifted her eyes and marked him with a hooded glare. "Why are you bleeding on my doorstep?"

"Please," he begged her. He was cradling his wounded right arm with his left, but the attempt to staunch the blood had failed. Whit knew there would be a small trail leading to Raven's chambers, but before he could think about remedying that mistake, Raven was already rubbing an oil onto her palms that smelled like grape seed. She waved her hand and the splatters of blood dissipated, each drop evaporating one after another along the trail like dominoes in a row. Whit couldn't see past the curve in the descending stairs, but he had no doubt that Raven's cleansing spell would clear it all.

Raven then stepped aside, allowing Whit room to enter. Her expression was stone-like, mouth pressed into a firm line and her dark brows narrowed.

"Sit," she instructed with a hostile tone. He did as he was told, knowing it would do him no favors trying to explain the situation. "At least your feathers aren't showing this time."

Though the comment was sly, he could tell it was a poor attempt at a jest. Raven was infuriated that he'd brought trouble to her door once again. He could see it in the tense set of her shoulders as she pulled out a roll of bandages and antiseptic liquid from her work desk. Her jaw was locked, no doubt fighting against all the words she wanted to spew at him, but she held her tongue when he showed her the injury.

Raven worked meticulously. She poured the antiseptic over the gash in his skin, and Whit watched as it bubbled. After several seconds, she wiped it with a cloth and began applying a thick gel directly into the wound. He winced at the intense cooling sensation, but it soon dissipated and was replaced with numbness.

"Do you want me to stitch it?" she asked tartly.

He gave her a quizzical look, assuming she'd heal it with magic.

"I'm out of yarrow root," she explained. "I have a gel that will help bind it, but it will open again. I suggest you let me stitch it. Especially if you have things to attend to, as it would seem you do."

Her knowing gaze caused a lump to form in the back of his throat, but he swallowed it down. "Just make it quick."

Raven's needlework was indeed swift, and Whit hardly felt the sting of the thread pulling through his skin thanks to the numbing gel. When she was finished, she knotted the thread and bit the end with her teeth, then she wrapped her work with a cloth bandage several times before tucking the end into the fold. She wrapped his wrist as well, without him having to ask.

Whit had cleaned a lot of blood from his skin in the bathing stalls, but there were new rivers now drying along the inside of his forearm and crusting in the crook of his elbow. Raven took care to wipe away all that she could see, then she stood and walked to the other side of the room. She disposed of the soiled rag and replaced her tinctures on the shelf.

Now that he was clean, he slipped the new shirt over his head.

"Are you going to tell me who you quarreled with?" Raven pried, her hip now leaning casually against the work table.

"Funny you should ask."

Her only response was the uptick of an eyebrow.

"It was a demon," he began, purposefully holding back. He needed to see what information she was willing to give up on her own.

But Raven's face remained unfazed. "And? Did he steal your toast at breakfast?"

Whit scowled. "It was Micah."

This caught her attention.

"Are there others taking the elixir like me?" he asked.

"Of course. Did you think you were that special, to be the only one?"

"This was different," he said. "He didn't shift on accident like what happened to me. It was like he…*chose* to."

Raven's mask of indifference slipped back into place. "And how do you suppose he managed to do that?"

"You tell me."

Raven let out a dramatic sigh and straightened. "I suggest you don't start asking questions about things that don't concern you."

"How does it not concern me? Are you saying there are still demons out there that can shift at will?"

"I'm not saying *anything*," she hissed.

"He wasn't natural, Raven." Whit was sick of her constantly giving him the runaround. It had been her choice to drag him into her shady business in the first place, yet she still kept him in the dark. "His demon form looked like an actual monster," he said. "Just like the thing they make us out to be."

She still wasn't budging. Her face showed nothing but cool apathy. Only the tiniest twitch of her jaw gave away that his questions had struck a nerve.

"Stay away from the Spyders," she told him. "And take this." She handed him a bottle of the blue elixir he hadn't even thought to ask for, and he gazed at her in question. "You know, you really do have exceptionally poor planning skills," she said. "Were you really going to travel all the way to Last Cove again without any extra elixir?"

"How did you—?"

"You're not as mysterious as you think."

Whit smirked and got to his feet. "I'm sorry for burdening you with this."

"You know," Raven started, "the first mistake was understandable.

In all the years you've held your secret, you were bound to forget a dose once or twice. You managed a very long time without slipping, and it was easy to forgive you for that first mistake. But this..." She crooked her head with the intimation of a predator.

She'd ensnared him the moment he stepped into the room, and now she was reeling him in.

Whit had been right; he was not going to receive another favor for free. He saw it clearly in the clever glint of her eyes in the moonlight.

"You know that this is different, don't you?" she coaxed him.

Whit sat back down, waiting for her inevitable request.

"Not only have you asked for my help twice now," she continued, "but you've left me high and dry with no one to warm my bed. We had a good thing going, Lieutenant. And this new behavior is very unlike you. You must be extremely captivated with that girl if you're willing to risk your life to protect her father. Tell me, does she please you as I do?"

His throat constricted.

The request was to be expected, but bringing Freyah into the conversation was not. Still, he refused to give the witch the satisfaction of showing his reaction. Whit made no comment to confirm or deny her question about Freyah. Instead, he held his posture and steadied his breath.

"What would you like me to do?" he asked calmly.

Raven's lip curved upward. She took a teasing step toward him and spread the opening of her robe to show off the sheer nightdress underneath. He could see the peak of her hardened nipples through her dark locks of hair that fell to her navel and the rosestone-colored flesh that led down to her center.

She did not speak, only mounted his lap and hooked her fingers around the back of his neck, tugging so that his chin jutted up force-fully towards hers. Raven bit her lip and began to move against him. His cock was hard, already betraying him despite his mind and his heart protesting against it. He couldn't resist his body's natural reaction to a beautiful woman he already knew the touch of.

She whispered seductively into his ear, but Whit could hear the undertone of contrived manipulation that laced her words. "You don't mind, do you?"

He shook his head and let her undo the buttons of his trousers. Her deft hand slipped him from the protection of cloth that shielded him from her demands and then gripped him assertively. Claiming him. She was already exposed, and as she lifted the trim of her night dress, the feel of her slick folds sliding down to encase his cock sent an unpleasant shiver down his spine.

He hated that he could already feel the beginnings of his arousal morphing into an unwanted orgasm. His muscles remained stiff as she sank down onto him again and again, and all the while he kept his eyes on the skin at her neck. The vein there, pulsating.

She rode him slower than he liked, drawing out the build up for longer than necessary. She was clearly demonstrating her control. When he finally felt her clenching around him, seconds away from reaching her peak, Whit tried his best to hold back his own climax. He didn't know how it was possible, but somehow he managed to stop himself from spilling into her.

Thank the gods.

When she was done, Raven lifted herself from his lap and straightened the fabric of her slip. She tied her robe securely around her waist and walked purposefully to the door, the scowl on her face deeper and more refined than he'd ever seen. Though he was soiled and completely unnerved by her actions, she merely left him with two spiteful words.

"You're dismissed."

2 9

BRENNAN

*A*s the last autumn leaves of the season began to turn in the mountains of Last Cove, Brennan Kenpaw found himself aching for his daughter.

It wasn't a new feeling. He'd been consumed by the same depthless pain for two weeks, ever since the morning he'd woken to find his only daughter's bed empty and no trace of her presence in the house.

That first week, The Hub was in a frenzy. Brennan had used what little authority he had to call on his brothers of the rebellion and form a search party.

Initially, Brennan had feared that Freyah had taken a tumble on the mountain. Perhaps she'd ventured the trails that night due to insomnia and lost her footing. But it seemed unlikely. Freyah knew Mount Mirela like the back of her own hand.

When she failed to turn up, Brennan became more and more concerned. He couldn't understand how something so unthinkable had happened. No one in town had seen her after she'd left The Hub that afternoon. He'd spoken with Freyah's best friend, Corianne, but the girl had confirmed the same story he'd heard from others in the Trade District. According to witnesses, Freyah had had a small confrontation with one of the queen's soldiers, then she'd purchased a fresh salmon from the fish market and gone straight home.

The rest of the night they'd spent together, playing chess and enjoying a home-cooked meal. After that? Nothing. No hint or whisper of where she went or what might have happened to her.

Brennan remembered Freyah telling him about her run-in with the soldiers, for she'd initially thought that the visit from John Morrow had been concerning her outburst. Despite the small scuffle in The Hub, the incident hadn't seemed to draw much attention. This in itself was odd, for Brennan knew that it was the sort of gossip his town loved to devour like fine wine. What was even more strange was that no one had come to him—not a single person had taken the time to question him about the encounter—and that above all was what drove Brennan to start asking questions of his own.

First, he paid a visit to The Ferry Stop, where John Morrow and Fisher Mack spent their evenings.

The cavern bar sat tucked away in the depths of the mountain, past the communal bath house and several large gathering chambers. Brennan could hear the sound of strings plucking a calming tune as their echoes bounced along the stone walls. He had no business drinking tonight, but he knew he'd have to down at least one glass if he wanted either of his friends to talk. Despite being loyal to the cause, they were finicky when it came to trusting his leadership.

Brennan had never asked to lead a faction of the human rebellion. Involving himself with The First Men had been his late wife Lanora's suggestion. Her own hatred for the witches had stemmed from years of personal torment under Madam Lema's reign. As a young girl, she'd been a handmaid for the witch-queen and spent years tending to her every need. Hours were spent making sure the witch was pampered and served the finest delicacies. She helped bathe her, clothe her, and had even been instructed to personally entertain her on many occasions. That entertainment varied from night to night, but more often than not it led to being asked to occupy the queen's bed. It wasn't until Madam Lema deemed Lanora no longer satisfying that she was finally allowed to leave.

Lanora and Brennan had found one another years later, but that time spent within the walls of Larapuna had been burned into her psyche. There was no escaping the torment of feeling worthless and empty. Those feelings trickled down through the years, and they found a way to grow and thrive. But it was a sadness that never truly went away. Lanora held a hatred in her heart for the queen. It had lived there since the moment she and Brennan met, and it remained until her last breath.

The First Men was a means to an end.

The rebellion might have started long before them, in the very beginning of Madam Lema's reign, but Brennan had been the one to help it seep into the mountain of Last Cove. Every move he'd approved for the rebellion had been meant to make things complicated for the crown. From the outside, the witch-queen's crimes weren't always clear, but Brennan knew the truth of what happened behind those castle walls. It was why he now feared the worst for Freyah. If she'd somehow found herself in the clutches of those soldiers, there would be next to nothing he could do to get her back. The last thing he wanted was for his only daughter to face the same fate Lanora had, and the possibility of it frightened and enraged him to no end.

As he entered the bar, he found John Morrow sitting alone at the counter, talking quietly with the barkeep and sipping on a short glass of amber liquid. Brennan took his time ciphering through the white noise of chatter all around him, hoping to pick up on something useful. Most of the patrons were consumed by their own lives, talking of long days in the mine and the upcoming hurricane season bringing hoards of new sea-life to the shores. He, too, was hoping for a fruitful storm season in the coming fall, but his business did not depend on it like others. John was a boat captain, and most of his time was spent traveling the rough waters of the Outer Ocean. Because of this, the man was a connoisseur of information. He was the one Brennan depended on to bring news from Pykard, Ghoma's neighboring southern country, for if there was something to know, John knew it.

Pykard was a free nation, no longer under the thumb of magic, and it was their governing model that Brennan hoped to one day replicate. There were now First Men representatives in every district of Ghoma that took action with this goal in mind. With every protest and each act of rebellion, they grew closer and closer to swaying the people of Ghoma to follow their lead. Humans deserved to be represented fairly, and The First Men knew that the only way to accomplish that was to be rid of the witches.

Brennan took a seat on the empty stool next to John and waved at the barkeep to bring him a glass of the same light whiskey.

John lifted his and nodded in greeting, then chugged the last shot from the bottom of the glass. "I'll take another," he said.

Brennan relaxed his shoulders and made himself as comfortable as possible on the hard wood of the stool. It was possible that John knew nothing of Freyah's whereabouts, but it was equally as plausible that he knew something and wouldn't be willing to share without proper coaxing. After all, the information he brought from Pykard didn't come free—it was exchanged for repairs and replacements on all his fishing spears or boat parts. It took a certain amount of investigative skill to gather intel on how Pykard ran their government. They were a very secretive nation that kept their liberties close to the belt, but with the right contacts and a proper eye, it was possible to learn enough. If Brennan truly expected the people of Ghoma to accept his proposal, he had to deliver. Ghoma had been a monarchy for hundreds of years, and it would take an educated influence to change that.

Brennan squared his shoulders. "I need your help, John."

The barman, Lest, placed a fresh glass in front of both men. "Are you asking about your girl?" he asked as he filled them a third of the way with liquor.

Brennan looked up excitedly. "What have you heard?"

John took a sip and then swirled the remaining liquid thoughtfully, answering on Lest's behalf. "Rumor is that lizard-demon saw those royal suits snatch her in the night," he said. "Right outside your door, and didn't do a damn thing about it."

Lest placed both hands on the bar counter and sighed. "It's true,

Brennan. I heard the same thing this morning. They have him. Gonna question him for details."

Brennan clasped his fingers tightly around his glass and squeezed.

There were only a few dozen demons living in Last Cove, but Jago was first generation, so his appearance set him apart from the others. Though most people in the mountain paid demons no mind, there were still a few, like John, who despised them—especially Jago.

But Brennan always made it a point to leave Jago be—what was it to him if he let some demon live his own damn life? It didn't affect him in the slightest, and he'd never personally held any ill will against the male. But this—the thought of a demon standing back and watching carelessly as Freyah was kidnapped under the cover of darkness—lit a fire under Brennan's skin.

"Where?" he demanded. "And why am I just now hearing about this?" He raised his glass to take a swig but halted at John's next words.

"I only just found out," John answered matter-of-factly. "Turns out the little shit came forward and told Matthias everything earlier today."

Matthias Anders was the town magistrate and Brennan's sworn personal enemy. Also a secret member of The First Men, Matthias always took issue with the rebellion's effectiveness. The man constantly questioned Brennan's passion for the cause, claiming their actions weren't enough, that they didn't send a strong enough message. It had been Matthias's grand plan to blow the shipping port to smithereens, knowing good and well that a bomb had been what killed so many people twenty years before. But that didn't excuse Brennan's involvement. It had been his knowledge and expertise that helped create the explosives that were planted beneath the weakened joints of the pier.

He never wished for violence. He aimed for their protests to be simple and safe, definitely nothing that would ever put his friends and loved ones in danger.

But things were different now.

Everything changed after what happened to Lanora.

Matthias had convinced him that a little collateral damage was sometimes necessary to get the point across, but Brennan had regretted his change of heart ever since.

Now Matthias had claimed Jago, and Brennan knew that son of bitch would drag his feet with this just to piss him off. For pure spite. And that wouldn't stand.

"Where do they have him?" Brennan asked, slamming down his glass on the counter. He'd yet to take a sip, but now he didn't think he could stomach it.

John scoffed. "Where do you think? Right where that creature should've been the entire time: behind bars."

BRENNAN RUSHED to the jail sector without a second thought. He needed to find the first moment alone with Jago he could and grab it before Matthias and the rest of his police could get their claws into the demon and influence the story. It would be hard—much harder than Brennan had anticipated getting the truth from John would be, as he hadn't expected the man to be so forthcoming with information—but he couldn't afford to waste any more time. Freyah had already been missing for two weeks, and every moment not spent looking for her was a moment squandered.

Panting and out of breath, he came upon three patrol officers standing outside the sector entrance. They were yammering about the big news, openly discussing the possibility of the town's first hanging in The Hub.

"Perfect," Brennan huffed sarcastically to himself.

Things were already escalating out of his reach.

"Serves him right," one of the officers stated proudly. "He's never contributed before, and just when the time comes for him to step up, he chooses to let a girl get snatched."

"Despicable," another chimed in.

"I certainly wouldn't trust him around my daughter," the former added.

Brennan approached cautiously. He might as well have been waving a white flag given how meticulously he took each step, hands resting unobtrusively in his pockets and head bent low.

When he raised his head again, Brennan saw that the somewhat reserved and silent third patrolman was the one to notice him first. He'd merely been nodding his head in concurrence with the absurdities his fellow officers were spouting, but at the sight of Brennan, the man immediately straightened and spoke with conviction. "Aye, what're you doing down here?"

Brennan removed his right hand from his pocket, painfully slow, and raised it in a friendly greeting. "I want to speak with the prisoner," he told them with as much authority as he could muster. All three officers trained their eyes on him and waited for further explanation, so he added, "I've heard this concerns my daughter."

"Come on, Brennan," the first man baited. "You know we can't do that."

His cohort attempted, "But he's..."

"I don't care who he is. Matthias's orders. You heard him."

Brennan bit his bottom lip and sighed. He'd been afraid of this. It would seem that talking to Jago wasn't going to be the hardest part. It would be getting past this merry band of knuckleheads.

"May I speak to Matthias then?" he suggested, lowering his hand.

All three men exchanged a glance with one another. This was apparently an even more absurd request than the previous one. Still tucked safely away in his left pocket, Brennan tapped the fingers of his left hand impatiently against his thigh.

"I guess if you wanted to see him, you could check in his office," the first patrolman answered vaguely. "He might be there. But if he's not, we can't help you."

Brennan nodded once and turned on his heels back the way he'd come. Matthias's apartment was located along the same passage as the bath house, separated from all others that lived on the opposite side of the cavern. It consisted of three individual living spaces, an office, and a private bathing chamber. The office had its own entrance, and when Brennan approached, he could make out the shadows of someone's feet pacing back and forth along the floor on the other side.

Brennan didn't bother knocking on the door; he simply pushed the latch and stepped inside. He was greeted with a look of shock from the magistrate that quickly morphed to an irritated leer.

"Brennan," Matthias welcomed sourly. "To what do I owe the pleasure?"

Brennan wasted no time with pleasantries. Matthias knew exactly why he was here. "I want to speak with the demon," he demanded. "I need to know what he saw."

"There's no need. We've already questioned him and are conducting a thorough investigation into the matter."

"Why was I not informed?"

Matthias stroked his chin thoughtfully, completely unperturbed by the sudden outburst in his office. "Mr. Kenpaw, my officers were just on their way to update you on the matter. It seems they must have missed you, given your impatience."

The subtle patronizing tone in Matthias's voice made Brennan's temper boil. He'd come toe to toe with this bastard before and had come to expect the belittling remarks, but this situation called for more restraint. This was his daughter's life being politically moved around like chess pieces on a board. Brennan would not tolerate passive aggressive statements and misleading truths.

"Let me see him, Matthias."

The magistrate remained eerily composed in the presence of Brennan's growing frustration. His fingers were now steepled and resting against his chin, elbows tucked in as if he were ready to pray. But he was merely preparing his statement—something that would no doubt shift Brennan's annoyance level a little higher. He noticed for the first time that there were wisps of gray growing around the man's temples. They were both getting older, and the responsibilities of day-to-day life were becoming more taxing. Brennan had managed to stave off the graying of his own hair for the time being, but he very nearly expected to see the sprouts of some any day now given his current state of stress.

"I understand that you are very close to this situation," Matthias said. "Perhaps a bit too close to see things clearly."

Brennan was right, the comment had definitely triggered further irritation.

"You need to keep in mind that these things are handled in a delicate manner," the magistrate continued. "We mustn't overstep when it comes to the creature's willingness to cooperate with us. He needs to trust us enough to be completely forthcoming with whatever information he has. And I must say, having the father of the girl he witnessed the capture of storming into his cell and demanding answers? Well...I fear that might deter him from speaking freely."

Nonsense. It was all utter nonsense, but still the perfect excuse to keep Brennan away. And to his dismay, the magistrate had only just begun.

"Your insistence on derailing our efforts brings to question what else you might be unable to oversee without bias." Matthias placed a steady hand on the corner of his desk and smiled solemnly. "Perhaps it's in your best interest that I temporarily remove you from your duties as district leader of The First Men. At least until the current situation is resolved. I fear, given the circumstances, you might act irrationally, and we must stay the course."

Brennan openly scoffed. "You're kidding."

"Oh, no. I most definitely am not," Matthias rebuked. "The others have already agreed. Until further notice, you are now relieved of your duties to the rebellion."

It was as if Freyah's kidnapping had been the perfect opportunity for Matthias to swoop in and take control. The plan practically laid itself open at Brennan's feet. He could see it clearly, and there was absolutely nothing he could do to stop it, for it was already done.

When it came to retrieving his only daughter, it seemed that he would be on his own. But before he could properly respond, the door to Matthias's office burst open again. This time it was one of the patrolmen that had been standing guard outside the jail sector. If he was here to warn the magistrate of Brennan's arrival, he was a bit too late.

"Sir, royal soldiers are here," he said frantically, panting and dropping forward to grip at his knees and gasp for air.

"Here?" Matthias questioned. "Why?"

The patrolman managed to draw in enough air to sustain him for the moment, so he stood straight, delivering the last words Brennan wanted to hear.

"They've come to arrest a member of the rebellion." He then turned to Brennan with equal parts regret and apathy. "They've come for you."

WHIT

Another week had passed, and the journey to Last Cove had been much more perilous this time around. It was as if the elements themselves were fighting against their arrival. The wind had whipped ferociously through the valley with a determination to slow them down. By the time they'd made it to the base of Mount Mirela, Whit's cheeks were red and raw from exposure to the elements.

It was only the beginning of autumn, the leaves on the trees of the Saldanni Forest having turned and cascaded to the ground in waves of gold and crimson, but the sheer force of the wind blowing toward them from the Outer Ocean made the temperature feel twice as cold as it actually was.

Also in contrast to his previous journey, his companions had remained mostly quiet and to themselves. Whit had managed to convince the others that Micah had been called to a last-minute mission by the queen that took higher precedent.

Fallon was a fairly meek soldier, following whatever order was put in place by the closest man in charge. Whit didn't have to worry about ruffling the man's feathers, for the unexpected change in leadership hadn't seemed to bother him. Fallon had merely kept his large, acquiescent eyes on the road ahead, only stopping every dozen or so miles to question when the next bathroom break would be.

Cleetus and Paul, on the other hand, were seemingly more interested in the matter of Whit's sudden and unexpected appearance on their team. They kept their eyes speculatively glued to his every move, despite having quietly nodded their heads in understanding after being told of Micah's new mission. What hadn't quite sat right with Whit was the reason for Micah Wighthall being on the team in the first place. It seemed to Whit that his fears of Brennan being severely punished were more tangible than he'd imagined. If a Spyder was responsible for retrieving a criminal, that meant his treason was of the highest severity, and Madam Lema meant to torture the man for information, even before he stepped foot in her domain.

Whit knew this journey was a necessary evil—he had to protect Freyah's father at all costs—but it felt wrong. Simply being a part of this mission made his stomach twist and turn inside of him. Taking Micah's place meant delivering yet another victim to the queen, and the knowledge that this would be the second person Whit handed over in such a short period of time felt like a betrayal to his own conscience.

Brennan Kenpaw had committed a crime, that much was true, but Whit knew that whatever Madam Lema had in store for him would be much worse than anything he deserved. Whit had to do what he could to stop the impending sentence. It could mean the difference between life and death for Freyah's father, and if the latter came to pass, there would be no coming back from that. This was the last chance Whit had to earn back Freyah's trust, and if he failed, he'd never forgive himself.

Whit trudged up the stone pathway that led to Last Cove's land entrance, and he noticed that there were only a handful of men stationed along the ridge to stand guard. He knew that Last Cove was a settlement full of outsiders, but once welcomed into the mountain, those outsiders became part of a tribe. The residents of Mount Mirela took care of their own, and they very rarely involved themselves in matters outside their territory. The fact that the rebellion had bled into the rocky terrain of this seaside village meant that the unrest in Ghoma was truly taking root, deeper and more firmly planted than the queen was willing to acknowledge.

Until now.

Madam Lema's previous search for the source of the insurgence had borne fruitless results, and Whit knew that was because The First Men were not careless with their creed. Though sometimes loud and meant to stir commotion, their movements were calculated and their mission simple. They strived to create doubt among the citizens of Ghoma, especially with those who'd remained on the sidelines of the debate. No one batted an eye when it came to demons being treated unfairly, but the minute humans started crying for justice, everyone took notice. The First Men knew how to rock the boat, and the tides of peace were becoming more unsteady by the passing day.

Whit knew Lema had messengers on her side within every district of the country. He hadn't been able to identify her confidant in Last Cove in the past, but he knew it had been that informer's tipoff that had led her to Brennan in the first place. It was how she'd come to know about Freyah—why she'd commanded Whit to retrieve her. Now that same informant was ready to hand over her father on a silver platter. Whit couldn't imagine what a man like that had to gain by working with the witches, but it wasn't his job to understand. Whit's sole job was to warn Brennan. Other than that, Whit could only hope for the best.

They entered The Hub of Last Cove, leaving behind an overcast night sky. It was the same weather that always seemed to linger over the Northern Sky Mountains, constantly providing showers of melancholy and expected gloom. At the moment, however, the clouds had yet to break, and the four soldiers were able to march along the passage in dry gear, making their approach less brash. Whit tightened the strap of his fighting leathers. He didn't know what to expect when they announced their intention to arrest Brennan, but he was prepared for a fight nonetheless.

Having never interacted directly with The First Men, he wasn't familiar with their ways of dealing with confrontation. All he'd witnessed were their vulgar displays of protest in a handful of town-ships throughout his travels—the most blatant one had been on a visit to Balandra four years prior. Whit still couldn't get the image of that burning temple out of his head. The way the flames had licked at the walls, charring the stone and completely disintegrating everything on the inside. The building had stood as a monument to Lillia, and it was common for school children to visit and pay their respects once a year. There had been seventeen still inside when it caught fire.

There were certainly some things Whit understood about The First Men, but their cruelty was not one of them.

He hoped to the gods that Brennan was not that type of leader. The acts of rebellion in Last Cove had been small. Nothing too noticeable to anyone from the outside. A pier collapse here, a purposeful delay of supplies there. He'd heard about an explosion that occurred before his time, but other than that, their acts were mild. Still, Madam Lema had been fishing for whatever evidence she could gather, and she'd managed to snatch one of the smaller members right from his local pond. Sentencing Brennan wouldn't put a stop to the rebellion, but it would send a clear message to the leaders higher up the chain.

As Whit and his men reached the slope of the ramps that led to the higher levels of the cavern, they were abruptly stopped before entering The Hub.

An older man with silvery hair and a receding hairline halted their steps by placing a palm out in front of them. "State your business, soldier."

Whit stood a bit straighter and retrieved an official scroll of parch-ment from the inside of his vest pocket. Being the highest-ranking officer in the group, the other soldiers had handed it over willingly. "I'm Lieutenant Avlon, sir," he said, introducing himself, his tone professional and steady. "I'm here to deliver a summons."

Whit handed the scroll to the man in a perfunctory manner and the gentleman took it, eyeing the paper suspiciously. After unfurling it and reading the words carefully, Whit watched the man's eyes grow wide with fear. He looked down to study the paper again, but his attention was suddenly captured by something over Whit's shoulder. Behind them, Whit turned to see a young man walking casually up the slope.

"Why aren't you watching the prisoner?" the silver-haired man barked.

The young guard casually shrugged a shoulder as he approached. "Shift change."

The older man shifted his gaze back to Whit and smiled nervously. "A moment, if you don't mind."

Whit nodded and watched as the two men whispered agitatedly a few yards away, then the guard took off at a sprint back down the slopes. He blew past Whit and his team, absentmindedly knocking Fallon in the shoulder as he passed. The guy was no doubt running off to warn someone of their arrival.

The older man returned to stand in front of Whit. "I'll escort you to the meeting chambers, Lieutenant. Let's conduct this business away from prying eyes."

Reluctantly, Whit and the rest of the team followed their escort. They walked steadily up the incline that led to the second level of the cavern, and when they approached a meeting chamber, the old man unlocked the door and opened it for them to enter.

"The name's Earl, by the way," the man said offhandedly. "If you'll just take a seat, the magistrate will be right with you."

Whit and the others stepped into the space and found seats at a small oval table large enough to fit six. Whit made sure to place himself in the one closest to the door. Though Last Cove relied on its magistrate to conduct official business and pass judgment on crime, they still held a formal council, as was tradition in every district of Ghoma. Even the queen sought advice from the Council of Elders. It was the country's way of following an order that had been put in place since its founding. The first witch-queen Ruella even put forth an effort to create a council of human representatives from each territory that convened bi-monthly at the castle. However, that precedent had been one of the first things Madam Lema dismantled at the beginning of her reign.

Whit watched as Cleetus bounced his leg impatiently while they waited in silence for their charge to show himself. Whit also wanted this matter resolved as quickly as possible. All of the unnecessary hoops were merely dragging out the inevitable. One way or another, Brennan Kenpaw was leaving with them tonight.

Despite the rest of the team's protests, Whit had decided against staying the night. The quicker they got back on the road, the less time he spent away from Freyah.

He hated the idea of her being left alone in that castle with nothing but her current negative thoughts to stew on. What if his time away drove them further apart than his actions already had?

Freyah had been the first glimpse of true happiness Whit had felt in such a long time, he'd nearly forgotten what the emotion felt like. The last time he'd felt it was before the death of Wendi—before dragging his sisters from their home and forcing them to live in a waking nightmare full of deception and loss.

Whit had caused the people in his life so much pain, he couldn't think of a single thing that made him worthy of love. But he'd felt the possibility with Freyah. And yet now, even that brief suggestion of hope had been ripped away.

Fallon was the only one that remained standing in the room. He moseyed around the space, taking in the stalactites that dripped naturally from the ceiling. Whit watched him reach out and touch his fingers to the textured stone wall.

"Strange," Fallon murmured, mostly to himself. Then, to the others he said, "I can't imagine living in a place like this."

"Yeah," Paul agreed. "Being down here is making me claustrophobic."

Cleetus had nothing to say on the matter, but his eyes couldn't resist trailing upward to the spikes dangling above his head.

Whit thought he might like living in a place like this.

He'd always preferred small spaces and the idea of being safe and secure. The less emptiness around him, the less he had to watch his back. He was comforted by the notion of four walls and a low ceiling. It reminded him of being in the dungeons, and perhaps that was why he'd been able to manage working down there all those years without losing his mind. At least the residents of Last Cove had the open sea to look out upon when things felt too closeted. All Whit had was the grounds of Larapuna, and a threatening forest filled with nothing but bad memories.

Ten minutes passed before the door opened. In stepped Matthias Anders, followed by Earl and the man of the hour, Brennan Kenpaw.

He looked nothing like Whit had pictured, mostly because he looked nothing like Freyah. His hair and eyes were dark and his skin was tanned, the complete opposite of Freyah's pale complexion and sunlit locks. Whit could only assume she had received those traits from her mother.

Fallon finally took a seat and the other men followed suit. Earl, however, stood sentry by the door. He folded his hands properly in front of his waist, his feet set wide, and waited for further instruction. Whit wondered what the man's position was and why he was allowed to attend this meeting.

The magistrate cleared his throat and addressed Whit directly. "I've been informed of the queen's summons," he began. "But I must ask on what grounds she has made this request. What evidence does she have proving that Mr. Kenpaw is involved in such treasonous acts?"

Brennan shifted to the edge of his chair. He looked as if he had something to say, but he remained silent.

"As you are most likely aware by now, the queen of Ghoma has Freyah Kenpaw in custody," Whit said. "She was brought to Larapuna for disrespecting a member of the queen's army."

He neglected to mention that he had been the soldier in question.

"However after some questioning," he continued, "she has produced sufficient evidence against her father proving that he has been leading Last Cove's hidden chapter of the rebellion known as The First Men."

The statement couldn't have sounded more scripted if Whit had prepared it himself, but it was Madam Lema's words that spilled mechanically from his lips.

"She was kidnapped," Brennan interjected hastily. "Whatever questioning you've subjected her to was no doubt under duress."

Whit's chest constricted, and he had to fight the urge to agree. He knew very well what had been done to Brennan's daughter, but he could not break character. Not here, and definitely not right now.

"Unfortunately, that is not up for debate," Whit spoke authoritatively. "I am merely here to carry out the demands of my queen." The statement tasted like bitter fruit on his tongue.

"What information did Miss Kenpaw provide, if I may ask?" Matthias questioned.

He was clearly prying in order to understand how much the queen knew. Was Matthias the informant from which Madam Lema had learned of the Kenpaws? If so, he was most likely playing double agent.

Whit knew he had to give them something, so he licked his lips thoughtfully and provided what small bit of truth he could. "The queen has seen memories, Magistrate. Firsthand accounts of incriminating acts that Freyah had witnessed over the years."

"There!" Brennan barked. "You see? That witch has used magic on my little girl. We can't trust what this stranger is claiming." He then forced his full attention to Matthias.

The magistrate was attempting to maintain his composure and failing. He could either give up one of his men, thus admitting to The First Men having a foothold in his town, or disobey an order from the queen. Either way he would be losing something important.

If Whit was right about his assumption, he knew exactly which option Matthias would choose.

Matthias then faced Brennan with a look of restrained sympathy. "It is not my place to question the queen," he said. "I'm sorry, Brennan, but I have no choice but to comply." Then the magistrate's eyes shifted back to Whit, and his expression changed to that of guile. "I have reason to believe that this man was responsible for the trade pier collapsing in our port." He was posturing, but there wasn't a damn thing Brennan could do to defend himself.

"You manipulative son of a bitch!"

Brennan's burst of outrage could be felt deep within Whit's own chest. He could feel the treachery flowing between the two men, and though Whit now had no doubt that Matthias was Madam Lema's informant, he would be forced to officially arrest Brennan. Matthias could have denied everything and protected Brennan. But he hadn't. He'd served him up on a silver platter. That meant the magistrate had nothing to fear from the queen.

Whit stood as Brennan rose to his feet. He placed a hand against the man's chest to stop him from jumping over the table and clawing out the magistrate's throat. Whit could clearly see the look of unfiltered rage behind his eyes. He looked like he'd been thrown under the cart for something he hadn't done, but Whit couldn't be sure how deep this betrayal went. There was the smallest hint of satisfaction emanating from Matthias. Whit saw it in the subtle lift of the corner of his mouth and how the tension in his shoulders had suddenly relaxed. It was that shift that made it even harder for Whit to follow through with his next move.

Whit took hold of Brennan's arms and brought them around to his back. Cleetus appeared beside them with a set of metal cuffs on a chain, prepared to bind his hands.

"By order of the Queen, Madam Lema Mansell, ruling sovereign of Ghoma, you are under arrest for treason in the first order." Whit spoke the words with condemnation and disdain, not for Brennan, but for the witch-queen. "As a citizen and provider of goods and services in this country, this is a direct violation of your sworn commitment to the crown. You will be brought to Larapuna to face punishment for your crimes. Do you understand?"

"I want to know what you've done with my daughter!" Brennan demanded.

After securing his wrists, Cleetus steered Brennan to the door that was already being held open by Earl. Matthias merely watched with a vacant expression.

So much for these men putting up a fight, Whit thought to himself.

They were giving up one of their own way too easily.

Brennan continued to protest as he went back through the tunnels and out into The Hub, but Whit lingered back with the other men. He waited for Matthias to exit the chamber and approached him with the intention of sending a clear message, but as he got close enough to spot each of the silver buttons sewn onto the magistrate's jacket, Whit knew there was nothing he could say to unsettle the man that had just handed over one of his own citizens.

Nothing perhaps, but one thing.

Matthias noticed Whit hovering and straightened his jacket, yanking on the collar and brushing invisible lint from the fabric. "Is there anything else I can assist you with, Lieutenant?" he asked.

Whit stood extremely close and basked in the man's unease. He purposefully crowded his space, taking Matthias's jacket in both hands and straightening out the lapels as a belittling gesture. "If I find out that you're hiding something," Whit threatened, "I will personally come back here and punish you myself. Are we clear?"

Matthias swallowed harshly and nodded. He took a wide step out of Whit's reach and hurried up the slope behind the others. If there was even the slightest chance that Matthias had set Brennan up, Whit would make sure to bring it to light. For a slight against Brennan was a slight against his daughter, and Whit was determined not to break his promise to protect them both. Even if that meant breaking a few of the magistrate's bones.

31

FREYAH

It had been eight days since Whit left with a small team of soldiers for Last Cove. Freyah had spent the majority of that time either staring out the tiny window in the loft of her room or drifting into a thought spiral while she completed her laundry duties. She waited for each sunset and dreaded every sunrise. The days were long and lonely, and they forced her to dwell on the things that haunted her mind.

When Freyah had finally felt like she was getting a grip on her current predicaments, things had spiraled catastrophically out of control. She'd been slammed with one terrible betrayal after another—the worst of which being that Whit had lied to her all this time. Not only had he hidden the fact that he was a demon, but he'd kept a key piece of information about Freyah's capture to himself.

It hadn't been an unfortunate accident or untimely coincidence that she'd been kidnapped and brought to Larapuna against her will; it had been part of the plan from the very beginning, and Whit had been the one to see that plan through.

All this time, Freyah had merely been bait for her father. Leverage to gain information about The First Men, and a tool for Madam Lema to use however she saw fit.

Not once had Whit offered to tell Freyah the truth of why she was here. Not once had he confessed his deception. And for that, Freyah wasn't sure how to ever forgive him.

Unfortunately, she still needed his help.

She needed Whit to ensure her father's safety on the way to Larapuna. He'd warned her of the other soldiers and their tendency to take punishment into their own hands, and she couldn't bear the thought of what they'd do to her father. Not to mention the hardship of the trip itself. Her own journey from Last Cove to the castle had taken almost a week, and that had been before hurricane season. Storms would be brewing all along the coast of Ghoma now that the weather was changing, and depending on how rough their trek was, it could take twice as long for all the men to make it to the mountains and back safely.

Until then, Freyah was stuck waiting anxiously for their return. She worked four days a week with Willow and the other girls in the laundry room, and though it wasn't the most rewarding or satisfying use of her time, she had to admit that the monotony of folding and hanging clothes helped the lonely days pass more quickly.

While she worked, she thought about what she would do once her father was in the castle with her. She wished there was a way for Whit to help him evade capture altogether, but Freyah didn't think he'd be willing to risk his position in the guard for something so boldly treasonous. Especially not for her.

Everything had changed between them. Things would be different once Whit returned, and Freyah wasn't sure they would ever be able to get back to where they were before. Or if she even wanted to.

Their flirtations had only just begun, and now it seemed they would never get a chance at exploring a true connection. How could she forget or forgive what he'd done? Everything Freyah had suffered at the hands of the queen had been dealt by Whit's hand. Only a week ago, she'd wanted those hands to touch her in ways that brought her immense pleasure, to tangle in her hair and caress her body. But now, the thought brought bile to the back of her throat and tears to her eyes.

At the moment, Freyah was taking her time making sure the creases in the soldiers' pants were crisp and perfectly aligned. She let the clean smell of soap and floral incense cloud her mind so that her troubles didn't consume her. But as much as she didn't want to think about it, she had to formulate a plan.

She had to be ready when her father arrived, but she still had no idea how they were going to sneak out of the castle. She'd already failed her first attempt thanks to Willow, so at least she knew to be a bit more discreet this time around. But things would be even more difficult now that Madam Lema had her eye on Freyah. She was outmatched by a queen that seemed to anticipate her every move. Because of that, Freyah came to the conclusion that if she wanted a real chance at escape, she'd have to have magic on her side.

Too bad I haven't managed to befriend any witches since I've been here, she thought. *Unlike Whit and his special friend Raven.*

It was then that a new idea crossed her mind.

She remembered hearing some of the other girls mention that they'd received tonics from Raven to help them sleep. Apparently the witch was fairly kind to those that worked at Larapuna, even going so far as to help a demon hide in plain sight. Though the idea of confiding in a witch she'd never met and asking for help felt incredibly daunting, Freyah would have to try. This was a golden opportunity, and it would be foolish not to take it.

She could be brave.

She *would* be brave.

For her father.

Willow was currently occupied with teaching a younger girl how to repair tears in the men's fighting leathers. While her attention was elsewhere, Freyah sought out the closest girl to her right that had been scrubbing at the same mysterious stain for over half an hour.

Freyah moved closer under the pretense of adding her freshly creased uniform pants to the finished pile. She couldn't remember the girl's name, but she recognized her golden-blonde hair. It was quite similar to her own, and it made Freyah wonder where she was from.

More specifically, she'd been the one to mention the sleeping draft, so it made sense to ask her about Raven.

The girl was humming contently to herself without a care as to how loud she was being, so much so that Freyah had to clear her throat multiple times to get her attention.

The girl greeted her with an unnatural amount of cheer. "Oh hi there! Did you need something?"

Freyah collected herself and tried to speak as casually as possible. "I heard you talking about a witch that gave you a sleeping potion," she started, "and I was wondering how I might be able to get that."

"Oh yes, of course! You just need to ask Raven. She's helped a bunch of the girls with various needs. Insomnia. Anxiety. Food poisoning." The girl ticked each ailment off enthusiastically on her fingers one by one. "One time she even gave Sanora a balm for her skin because she kept breaking out in hives every time she worked with the laundry. Turns out she was allergic to the soap. Can you imagine?" She then laughed as if this were the funniest thing in the world.

"Yeah, that's something," Freyah deadpanned. It was clear she'd have to steer the conversation to keep it on track. "But how do I find Raven? Where are her chambers?"

The cheery girl beamed and tilted her head like Freyah was asking a question that had an obvious answer. "Well you can just follow the cat, of course."

"The cat?"

Freyah hadn't thought about the cat since their singular encounter outside her room. She'd yet to come across the creature again, though she had to admit, she'd wanted to see him. Having an animal companion would certainly help her feel less lonely.

"You mean that fluffy gray one that squeaks like a mouse?" she asked.

"That's Zadimus," the girl confirmed. "Just ask him to take you to her and he'll lead you there."

It felt too simple, and also a little bit strange, but Freyah accepted it. "Thanks, umm..." She drew out the sentence, feeling embarrassed. "I'm sorry, I forgot your name."

The girl introduced herself properly by extending a hand. "No apology necessary. I'm Jessa. Typically I would be the one to show you the ropes, but it seemed that you were in good hands with Willow, so I didn't want to bombard you. It's nice to see a new face around here."

"Yes, well… I won't be here much longer."

Jessa seemed to frown at that, but it was only noticeable by the slight tilt of her lower lip. She recovered quickly and replaced her confusion with a boisterous laugh. "You're a hoot. Find me at dinner tonight and I'll be sure to introduce you to the other girls."

Freyah nodded weakly and gave Jessa the best imitation of a genuine smile that she could muster. She had no intention of attending dinner.

Tonight, she had to follow a cat.

THE TASK TURNED out to be way harder than Freyah anticipated.

She'd only seen the cat once, and Larapuna was a very large castle. It had many winding staircases that led to endless corridors and rooms that fed off of one another like an endless labyrinth. The layout reminded her an awful lot of her mountain home, and if Freyah could navigate the caverns of Mount Mirela with confidence, she could certainly find her way through this ridiculous maze of stone.

When the new soldier that stood outside her room knocked on the door to escort her to dinner, Freyah had feigned sickness so that she'd be excused from attending. She'd waited for the sound of his footsteps retreating down the tower, then she had slipped casually from the tower and down the stairs, holding her breath with every echoing step. To her own dismay, however, she was now beginning to regret the decision to skip dinner.

Not only was she hungry, but now she was lost.

Her original plan had been to follow the same route that had led her to the meeting room where she'd eavesdropped on Madam Lema, seeing as that was when she'd last seen the cat. But her memory wasn't as good as she'd thought, and she'd found herself at the end of two different corridors that both led to dead ends.

She was circling back to where she'd started for the third time when she finally caught a glimpse of hope. There was a small-statured man lingering outside the doors to the library, and at first glance, it appeared that he was simply another guard. But with a closer look, Freyah noticed that he wasn't in uniform.

The man was wearing simple clothing stained with dirt and grass, most likely from working outside, and right now he seemed to be waiting for someone.

She fell back to hug the corner of the wall behind her and stood by to see who would appear. Her curiosity always seemed to get the better of her, even when the timing didn't call for it, and though she needed to focus on finding the cat, something told her that the answer was right in front of her.

Then, like a divine sign from the gods, a small shadow shaped by the iron sconces on the opposite wall made its way down the hall. It grew larger as it approached, revealing the outline of a thick, fluffy tail swishing back and forth. Freyah peered around the corner and looked down to find mister Zad himself strolling purposefully toward the man awaiting him.

The man squatted down to the cat's level and held out a small leather pouch cinched together with string and bulging with weight.

"Tell her I need extra this time," the man instructed in a hushed tone, speaking directly to the cat. "I'm going to the capital."

To Freyah's surprise, the cat opened his mouth and took hold of the pouch between his teeth. With a quick swish of his tail, Zad padded back down the corridor. The man wasted no time walking off in the opposite direction, and Freyah had to shrink back behind the corner to avoid being seen.

When the coast was clear, she jogged after the cat. He was now leaping across the stone floor with the grace of a gazelle, so Freyah had a hard time keeping up, but she tried her best to match his pace.

They didn't run into anyone else lingering in the hall, so she guessed that the cat had only one meeting tonight.

What an odd thing, she thought.

Did this cat belong to Raven?

If so, it looked as if he was conducting business on her behalf.

They were now heading further into the depths of the castle than Freyah had ever ventured before, so far that the stone beneath her feet was becoming more and more worn, clearly older and in worse shape than the rest of the castle. The walls began to curve in on themselves, and eventually she found herself inside a tower much like the one she slept in. A staircase appeared before her, but unlike the stone steps that led to her room, these were made of rickety, rotten wood.

The cat easily leapt two steps at a time all the way to the top, but Freyah hesitated as she placed a booted foot on the pliant board in front of her. It creaked and bowed beneath her weight, but it didn't break. One step at a time, she ascended to the top of the spiral staircase and arrived at a warped wooden door. As she reached the landing, she was just able to catch sight of the flap of a small, round opening at the bottom left corner falling back into place.

Freyah listened quietly for any sign of life behind the door, and she was rewarded by the subtle clinking of glass. Raven was in there.

Suddenly, the palms of her hands clammed up with sweat.

Who was she to ask a witch she'd never met for a favor like this? Sure, she could say that the other girls had sent her, but it didn't mean that Raven would automatically say yes. And what was it exactly that Freyah wanted anyway? A potion to make her invisible? A flower that would disguise her and Brennan as guards? Anything that could help them get out of the castle unseen.

But did those things even exist?

She was debating on turning back when the subtle creak of the door opening startled her into stillness.

The witch that Freyah had imagined in her head was nowhere near as breathtaking as the one standing before her. She had long, inky black hair similar to that of Madam Lema, but Raven's had more of an ebony tint. She wore it loose around her shoulders, perfectly framing the roundness of her face and complimenting the rose undertone of her cool skin. Her hooded, angular eyes were now focused on the stranger standing on her doorstep, and Freyah faltered.

"I…umm," she stammered. "I'm sorry to disturb you. My name is Freyah. I was hoping you could help me with something."

"I know who you are," Raven said. She glanced down at the cat now weaving between her legs. "Zad told me you were hovering out here."

Freyah's racing thoughts sputtered to a stop. "The cat? It *spoke* to you?"

"He's not a cat," she said, as if the fact was perfectly obvious.

What did that even mean?

Freyah's brain could no longer decipher the information it was receiving. All at once, her thoughts came to a screeching halt, and she forgot why she was even there.

The cat seemed to register that Freyah was spiraling, because it crept out from between Raven's legs and came to sit by Freyah's foot in a comforting gesture. She looked down at the animal with a newfound sense of appreciation and confusion, and she swore she could see an almost human expression in his eyes.

"What is it that you need?" Raven questioned with urgency. "Sleeping draft? Birth control?"

Freyah shook her head and tried to rattle loose the ridiculous amount of chaotic thoughts that continued to flood her. "No," she stated firmly. "My, uh…*friend* told me that you've been giving him an elixir. Is it possible that you could do something similar for me?"

Raven's eyes widened and her brow furrowed with suspicion. "Your *friend*?" she repeated.

Freyah nodded and waited. She often found that in these types of awkward situations, she tended to let her words run rampant to fill the silence, but right now it was probably best to keep her mouth shut.

"Come in." Raven opened the door wider and Zad nudged his nose against Freyah's heel to urge her inside.

Freyah wasted no time questioning the invitation. She stepped into Raven's chambers and took in her surroundings with piqued curiosity.

The rooms were all connected by an open floor plan. Upon entering, Freyah was met with a large, sturdy work table laden with vials of flowers, stones, liquids, and what looked like hair. Also on the table was a well-used and grimy mortar and pestle made of granite, stained with a rich, earthy substance. A small fire pit sat smoldering in the center of the room with several cauldrons hanging above from copper racks. Dried bouquets of flowers hung from the ceiling, their muted colors casting a drab yet cozy backdrop within the space.

Freyah spotted a small cot separated by drapery that hung from the rafters in the ceiling. A large bath took up most of the area by the window, and to her left, Freyah found a room stacked with short bookcases that were filled with tattered tomes and journals. She spotted a leather arm chair by the fire pit and took a seat. Raven sat opposite her, and Zadimus crawled lazily into her lap and purred. The witch's gaze felt invasive, and Freyah had to look away.

"What do you need an elixir for?" Raven asked in that same straightforward manner. "I don't believe the one I gave *your friend* would be of much use to you."

Freyah was still taking in the room. It felt more chaotic and organic than the rest of the castle. The aesthetics throughout Larapuna were very simple and minimalistic—mostly cold and unwelcoming. But this room greeted her with a feeling of warmth. She felt comfortable here, despite being stared down by a stranger.

"So you know who I am," Freyah stated, ignoring the witch's snub. Did she think she'd been referring to Whit?

Raven eyes suddenly flashed with contempt. "Yes," she concurred. "You're quite the topic of conversation as of late."

"Why's that?"

Raven rolled her eyes and scoffed. "You're the queen's newest obsession. She's convinced that removing your father is the first phase of her brilliant plan. Bit of a stretch if you ask me. He's not important enough to make noise."

Freyah prodded further, excitement now coursing through her at the idea that Raven might be able to share something valuable. "So you know what she's planning?"

The witch studied her, her face contorting into something Freyah couldn't decipher. Then, without preamble, she asked, "Do you remember your mother?"

Freyah was completely caught off guard.

She rarely thought of her mother anymore—missing someone she'd never known was something she'd learned not to do a long time ago. It was pointless. But why was this witch asking about something she should have no business knowing?

"Why do you ask that?"

Raven smiled and cocked her head, seeming to want to say something else, but she thought better of it. "I can't help your father, if that's what you're really here for," she told her matter-of-factly. "But I can help *you*."

Freyah sat up straighter.

"Lema has no use for you now," Raven continued, "but she's never going to let you leave. If you want to go, I'll help you get out."

The offer felt too easy. Was she really that nice? Or did Raven have something to gain by getting Freyah out of the picture?

"Why?" Freyah asked. She forced her eyes to focus on the witch with at least some form of intimidation, just as Raven had done to her.

"Because you've caused nothing but trouble for Whit since you arrived," she said. "And I'd rather not have him distracted."

Whit?

So there *was* something between them.

There had been a small, nagging voice in the back of Freyah's mind ever since Whit told her about the witch that helped him disguise his demon features. The voice contained only an ounce of jealousy due to the developing connection between them, but this was different. Had he been with Raven the entire time? It wouldn't have been the first time he'd kept something from her.

"He's the friend you spoke of, correct?" Raven assumed. Her smile was now laced with a wicked superiority, like she knew she'd somehow won whatever game they were currently playing.

Freyah had actually been referring to Jessa, but she let the witch assume incorrectly. "You're together?" Freyah asked, needing to know the answer.

Raven smirked. "In a manner of speaking. He visited me the night before he left, to satiate some cravings in preparation for such a long journey."

Freyah's insides felt like molten lava. He'd been with Raven in this very room before leaving to arrest her father—probably in the bed that Freyah could no longer look at without wanting to vomit.

Had their own fleeting romance all been a farce?

Of course.

He was simply another lustful soldier playing his way into vulnerable girls' arms. All the effort he'd put into making her feel safe and taken care of was probably an act. All part of the plan.

Everything Freyah had learned over the last week was stacking on top of her like the stone bricks of the castle walls. One more layer and she'd be buried for good.

Her lungs tightened in her chest. It was hard to draw a deep breath, and whenever she tried, it felt like a sharp needle was sticking her in the sternum.

Raven ignored the panic now radiating off of Freyah. Without even the smallest hint of sympathy on her face, she stood, the cat leaping to the floor, and walked casually to her work table. She bent low and searched through the labels on the liquid bottles until she found what she was looking for—a gold vial filled with something thick and shimmering.

Freyah couldn't concentrate, so when the witch handed her the vial, she clasped her fingers around it a little too loosely. It slipped from her grasp and smashed at her feet, the thick, sparkly liquid oozing across the floor and soaking into the wood.

Freyah looked up to find Raven standing there actually looking amused.

"Well that's too bad. That was my only batch of Chrysanthemum

Glamor." Annoyance replaced the amusement on Raven's face as she continued. "If you want to get out of this castle, you'll need a disguise," she said. "That would have glamored you to look like anyone you wish. Now you'll simply have to camouflage yourself. It's much riskier, for if you aren't naturally stealthy, you'll give yourself away."

The explanation went soaring over Freyah's head. It hovered around like a gnat, and she absentmindedly swatted it away. Though she shouldn't be, she was more focused on the previous topic of conversation.

"He was here?" Freyah asked with trepidation, still focused on Raven's casual mention of Whit having been in her bed. "The night he left?"

Raven actually had the nerve to roll her eyes. As if Freyah's further inquiries were a nuisance, despite them being triggered by the witch's own bragging. She stepped closer so she could hover above her, like an animal taking the high ground to display its dominance.

"Listen, sweetheart," she patronized. "I didn't tell you to place some sort of claim on him. You need to know that his interests lie elsewhere. That way you don't get your hopes up. It's best to know what you're in for."

Freyah's shock was now morphing into repulsion and disgust at the mere sight of the witch's face so close to hers. Freyah forced herself to focus on the most pressing matter at hand—the real reason why she'd placed herself in this wretched woman's path in the first place.

"I'll take the camouflage," she said, her words clipped to precision. "Whatever it is."

Raven's mouth lifted into a sardonic smirk. "Very well."

This time, instead of searching the desk, Raven walked to a cabinet by her bed. Opening the top drawer, she pulled out a small leather pouch similar to the one Freyah had seen the man handing the cat.

Freyah's eyes fell on Zadimus, who was now curled into a ball on the floor beside the dying embers of the fire, tail hiding his face from view.

Raven dropped the pouch into Freyah's lap instead of risking a clumsy handoff. "Crushed tourmaline powder," she said. "Blow it into the air and step through it. You'll blend into your surroundings. But don't go running about making noise and being clumsy. If someone focuses hard enough, they'll see you."

Freyah stood and tucked the pouch filled with powder into the waistband of her leggings, then headed for the door. Before leaving, she chanced a glance back over her shoulder. "You're really giving this to me for nothing?"

Raven's expression stilled into seriousness. "If I decide I want something from you, I'll let you know."

LYRA

*L*yra sat alone in the darkness of her cell with an ache deep in her belly. It had nothing to do with the almost fully-formed baby inside her, constantly kicking in an attempt to birth itself into an unknown future, and everything to do with what her own future would hold.

Lyra had been cast aside. She'd spent two weeks hidden away, tucked beneath the castle's stone floor by Lema. The queen most likely hoped she could simply ignore the problem at hand, but time was running out, and soon she would have to face what was to come. Lyra was going to have a child, and that child would be third in line to the throne.

Regardless of its gender, Lyra meant to do whatever was in her power to protect the life of her baby. If it was a boy, she'd already put a plan in place to escape her prison with him and hope that Oram would be waiting for her on the other side. And if, by some miracle of Lillia, she birthed a girl, it still did not mean protection from Lema's hand. The queen had already threatened the life of the unborn child no matter the outcome, simply because of its parentage. But Lyra would not let that threat stand.

She'd been unable to communicate with Oram since her imprisonment, and so much time had passed that she feared her plea for him to protect her had been folly. He'd promised to be there for her and their child, but what if he'd already been seized by the crown?

Every day, Lyra waited with bated breath for Fatima to bring her news, and every day there was none. She needed a backup plan—something that would guarantee the safety and protection of the baby no matter if Oram was able to intervene or not.

Lyra anxiously waited for her supper to be delivered that night.

Fatima had been bringing her meals twice a day, along with a fresh wash basin to clean herself. Though she was a prisoner in her sister's eyes, she was still a royal and due a certain amount of respect. But as Lyra eyed the foul-smelling bucket in the corner of her cell, respect was the last thing she felt. She'd been forced to sleep not ten feet from her own excrement, and the slight felt entirely purposeful. The guards could easily let her out of the cell to relieve herself, but they'd been instructed to leave her be. It was clear to Lyra and everyone else that Lema was doing the absolute minimum when it came to paying respect to the princess.

Fatima eventually appeared with a wooden tray laden with several slices of fresh bread, an assortment of colorful vegetables, and a bowl of seared fish. At least she was being given a proper meal. She'd seen what the other prisoners in the dungeon were provided as sustenance, and the bowl of mashed beans appeared less and less appetizing the more she had to smell it.

Fatima raised a slat at the corner of the cell and handed Lyra the tray. She gave her a reassuring smile, retrieving a canteen of water from the pocket of her skirts and passing it through as well.

Lyra uncapped the bottle and drank desperately. She wasn't particularly parched, but the simple thought that she was dependent on others for water made her tongue dry. She then began taking bites of her food. Both she and Fatima waited patiently for the guards to take their positions at the other end of the dungeon. After several minutes, they determined that the handmaid's presence would be unproblematic and moved along.

Lyra looked to Fatima expectantly, but like all the visits before, this one bore no news.

Fatima shook her head and apologized faintly. "I'm sorry, my lady."

"Never mind that," Lyra said, harshly swallowing a bite of bread. It stuck in her throat, and she had to take a rather large gulp of water to wash it down. "I need you to do something for me."

Fatima shifted closer to the bars to hear Lyra's request more clearly. "What is it?"

"Gather these items and bring them to me tonight." She listed off a number of ingredients for Fatima to collect. She was going to perform a dream spell—one that would ensure a message got to Oram with instructions on exactly what needed to be done. "Insist that you be the one to bring me my nightly potion, hide the items so that you can slip them to me. This will only work if I have the exact amount of what I've told you. Do you understand?"

Fatima nodded, and Lyra hoped that her handmaid's memory could be relied on. Every night before bed, a witch brought Lyra a small cup of tea made from fig, geranium, and carrots. Drinking it was meant to promote the health of the baby and ensure a successful delivery. No matter what the queen intended to do with Lyra once the baby was born, there had to be a successful delivery. A newborn dying would be tragic, but it had to look natural. Lyra knew that once the baby was born, she and Fatima would have mere minutes to execute their plan before Lema stepped in.

From the moment that Lyra was captured, they'd decided that in order to pull off the escape, Fatima would have to take the baby. It would be tricky, given that the coven's full attention would be on the newborn, but if Fatima could somehow get herself alone with the baby, she could slip out of the castle with the newborn under her cloak.

Still, that effort would be pointless without Oram's help. They had to make sure someone was waiting for Fatima on the outside, and the only way to do that was to communicate directly with Oram.

Lyra knew she could get a message to him through his dreams, so later that night, when the moon was full and bright, Lyra would show Oram the plan. After that, all she could do was hope for the best.

When Lyra finished her meal, Fatima was instructed to leave by the guards. Lyra watched her friend walk away with that same ache in her belly that now seemed to reside there indefinitely. Yet again, she fought against it, knowing that she now had one opportunity, and she would not let fear dictate the outcome.

SEVERAL HOURS PASSED as Lyra paced back and forth in the tiny space of her cell. She watched the moon rise to its full height in the sky through a large crack in the stone wall—not big enough to squeeze through, but large enough that she had a clear view of the twinkling stars beyond. Soon, Fatima would come with what she needed to perform the dream spell, and their plan would be fully put in place.

The same guards that had been there during dinner sat casually by the door to the dungeon. They were playing a game of cards and boisterously keeping Lyra updated on who was winning. Their attempts at passing the time were the only things that kept Lyra entertained. Most nights, like this one, they played several hands until one of them got tired of losing and gave up. Other nights, it was chess. And only once, Lyra had seen them sneak a flask filled with liquor past their lieutenant and spent the night taking swigs back and forth.

If the guards were drunk, it would certainly make things a lot easier for Fatima. They'd be less likely to pay close enough attention to what she was carrying. But even in their current sober state, they didn't seem too interested in what Lyra's visitors brought with them. They checked for weapons of course, but humans didn't think about magic, nor the items required to wield it. It ought to have been the first thing on their minds when guarding a witch, but alas.

Lyra would take advantage of that thoughtlessness. And by the time they realized what had happened, the queen would already have their heads on spikes for such a foolish mistake.

The moon was wholly visible now from behind the clouds. It was full and luminous, the perfect setting for performing a spell. Especially one that required crossing a great distance to reach its target.

Lyra heard the heavy latch on the door to the dungeon slide open, and both guards got to their feet to receive whoever was entering. She held her breath and waited to see if it was her friend that appeared. At the sight of Fatima's small frame donning a heavy brown cloak, Lyra sighed with relief.

Fatima was carrying a tiny porcelain cup that Lyra knew contained the Ashwagandha tea. She walked carefully across the dungeon floor, taking small shuffling steps. Her small hands clasped the edges of the cup with precision, and she focused hard on trying not to spill the contents. When she finally approached, Lyra took the cup from her through the bars and downed the tea in one gulp. It was still extremely hot, and it burned her throat, but she paid the fiery sensation no mind. She was more interested in the bulk under Fatima's cloak, and she eyed the guards cautiously. After confirming their attention was fully diverted back to their card game, Fatima reached beneath her cloak and shifted a crossbody canvas bag over her chest.

Lyra knew the bag contained everything she needed for the dream spell: lapis lazuli and sodalite for psychic awareness and communication; a length of rope tied in a two half hitch knot to bind two souls; lavender and jasmine oil for deep sleep. She also needed an item belonging to the contact, and Lyra had nothing in her possession that belonged to Oram, but she'd already thought of a possible loophole to solve that problem. Technically speaking, the unborn child inside her womb was a piece of Oram, and she hoped that would be enough to connect her to him.

Fatima positioned herself in front of Lyra so the guard's view of her was blocked and handed each of the items through the bars. Lyra proceeded to place each crystal on the floor in front of her, making sure they fell directly under the light of the moon. She pulled at the knot in the rope to secure its tightness, then rested it atop the stones. Unstopping the vials of oil extract, she released two drops of lavender and three drops of jasmine onto the rope. It soaked into the hemp and turned the fibers a deep brown. With everything in place, Lyra hovered one hand over the display of items while the other rested on her protruding belly.

She focused on Oram. The roundness of his face and his wide brow. The calm, inviting look in his eyes whenever he saw her. The tenderness of his hands when he touched her. She could picture his demon features in her mind, but in her heart, they weren't there. It was only him, and the sense of comfort he made her feel.

The spell wasn't dissimilar from the one she'd used to communicate with him the day he'd delivered supplies to the castle, though at that time, she could see him. Lyra had used a lapis lazuli stone in her pocket, keeping a tight grip on it as she spoke to Oram in her mind. The premise was the same, but this spell required much more focus, and a different set of tools.

When she had a solid grasp on Oram's image, she shifted her focus to the message. She imagined the Saldanni Forest with its towering trees casting shadows over the forest floor. And she saw herself, being placed in her cell—the last time she saw her sister's face painted with rage.

"Wait for me in the wood," she whispered. The faintest breeze filtered through the crack in the stone and brushed tenderly across her cheek. It took her words, along with the aura from the spell items, and carried them across the wind, to where Oram lay his head to rest. As an extra precaution, she added a silent prayer to Lillia that it would reach him.

33

ORAM

Oram found himself wandering through a stretch of dense trees.

At first, he did not recognize his surroundings, but upon further inspection, it was clear he was under the looming canopy of the Saldanni Forest. He'd traveled through the woods many times on his way to deliver crop shares to Larapuna, but he'd never taken the time to truly appreciate the vastness of it. The Redwoods towered above him with a strength he couldn't quite comprehend, their thick trunks traveling up and up toward the boundless sky, never wavering from the spot their roots were planted. They stood firm and true, holding their position in the earth like it was their sole purpose—to mark a moment in time, or simply to be.

The wind rustled the quickly-turning leaves and circled him where he stood. It embraced him like a friend, or a long-lost lover aching for home. He savored the feeling of it on his cheeks as it blew through his clothes and caused gooseflesh to appear on his skin.

There was something he was meant to be doing, but he couldn't put his finger on what. The calmness of the forest embraced him like a comforting hug, and he wanted to remain with that feeling for as long as he could. But that sensation of responsibility gnawed persistently at the back of his mind. He tried to push it away, yet it remained. So, with great reluctance, he pressed onward through the stretch of trees, aiming for whatever was calling to him.

The wind howled as it whipped around the tree trunks, and for a split second, it sounded like a voice was speaking through it. He waited a moment and listened for the voice to speak again, but the only sound he heard was the rustling leaves. Then, as he took another step, he heard the words whisper on the wind again.

"Wait for me in the wood."

The voice felt familiar.

It held a soft, feminine lilt like someone he knew. Someone important to him. This time, the voice did not wait to speak again. The message resounded loudly around him, echoing off the trunks and bouncing around him, trying to find its target.

"Wait for me in the wood. Wait for me in the wood."

That voice. What was that voice?

Oram walked over to the nearest tree and hesitantly placed his palm against the bark. He wasn't sure what made him do it, but the second his hand made contact, he knew it had been the right thing to do.

His vision was suddenly hijacked by images of Lyra being tossed into a cell, a pale and furious woman with hair as black as night scowling across the room. Then he saw a woman slipping quietly out of the castle under the cover of darkness, a cloak over her head. He saw Lyra holding her own belly, swollen by pregnancy though it had only been two weeks since he'd last seen her. Then he heard the message again, as clear as if Lyra had been standing right next to him.

"Wait for me in the wood."

Oram's eyes flew open, and he was met with complete darkness. He blinked furiously, trying to adjust his vision, and began to see the outline of his bedroom. The trees were gone, and the only sound now was the subtle *tap-tap* from a lone branch knocking against the window.

Had it all been a dream?

He looked down to inspect the hand he thought had been touching the tree and flexed his fingers. The feeling of the rough bark touching his skin was still there. And that voice—the voice still rang in his ears, as if someone had been in the room with him.

He sat upright and looked around, but there was no one there. He slipped out of bed and collected his nightshirt that hung on the bedpost, slipping it over his head. He tiptoed across the room and down the hall to where his brother was still sleeping in his own bed. Perhaps Kirra had been the one calling.

Then it came to him.

Lyra…along with images he'd seen of her being locked in a cell and very near giving birth. Something in the back of his mind told him that it hadn't been a simple dream. It was a message, and he needed to act fast.

Lyra had warned him of the danger their child would face. It would seem that the queen had discovered their secret, and if that was true, it meant Lyra was in trouble. He knew he needed to go after her, but he had no idea how he was going to stand up against a coven of powerful witches and their queen.

Oram turned back to his room and hastened to get dressed. He gathered his riding boots and gloves from the chest at the foot of his bed without considering how much noise he was making. There was no time to waste, for he knew in his gut that Lyra was currently sitting alone and scared in a dark dungeon.

He couldn't explain how, but he knew that dream had been sent to him directly from her. It had been a clear message to come for her—to do whatever he could to rescue her and their unborn child from the punishing guile of Queen Lema.

But no.

Lyra had given him a specific message: *wait for me in the wood.*

Maybe the woman he'd seen escaping under the cloak had been Lyra, and she was already on her way. She would be expecting him to be there when she made it through the Saldanni Forest, so he had to leave now.

In his rush to get ready, Oram had forgotten about Kirra sleeping down the hall. The chest slamming shut had probably woken him, as soft, padding footsteps now headed his way.

He knew Kirra would try to stop him—his brother had been against Oram's relationship with a witch from the very start—but Kirra had heard the pleading tone in Lyra's voice when she'd come to him about the baby. Though Kirra had originally suggested Oram stay out of the situation, he surely wasn't going to stand by it. Not now that a woman and her unborn child were in danger.

The door to Oram's room creaked open, and Kirra's small, hunched form stood within the frame. His eyes were heavy with sleep, but a deep frown was already creasing the lines of his face with worry.

"What are you doing?" he asked.

Oram didn't bother to beat around the bush. "Lyra is in trouble. The queen knows about the baby. I have to go."

Kirra pushed the door open wider and stepped into the room. "The full moon must be playing tricks on me, because it sounded like you're going to Larapuna to save a witch."

Oram whirled on his brother and looked him square in the eye. "I have to help her!" At the sight of Oram's sudden anger, Kirra shrank back, and the action caused Oram immediate guilt.

"She sent a message," he explained in a calmer manner. "She's escaped, and I have to meet her in the Saldanni Forest."

Kirra shook his head in disappointment. "The moon must be fogging your senses as well."

"What do you suggest I do?" Oram demanded curtly. "Sit here and do nothing? She came to me and warned that this would happen. She asked for my help, and I promised her I would. I can't take that back now."

"Of course you can!" Kirra pleaded. "Think about what it is she's asking of you, brother. If you go after her, you'll be putting your entire family at risk. What do you think they'll do to you if you're caught? To me? To Galiana and Petra? You'd risk all of us to help the enemy?"

"She's not the enemy." Oram's tone of certainty had not wavered. "The queen is."

He knew the risk he was taking, and his family meant everything to him, but Lyra was now his family, too. Even more so, Oram was a man of his word.

"You're making a mistake," Kirra urged as he tailed Oram out of the bedroom.

Oram was headed straight for the front door, but Kirra was right there, nipping at his heels. With every step he took, he ignored the attempts being made to dissuade his decision. But when he got close enough to reach for the handle, he suddenly felt the absence of the body behind him.

Kirra had fallen silent.

Oram turned to see that he'd stopped in the middle of the living room. The fox-demon was staring at his brother with a desperate look in his eyes. The same look that Lyra had given him when she'd stood in this very room.

"Please," Kirra begged.

It was only one word, but it held the weight of their entire relationship in its grasp. If Oram walked out that door, Kirra would not come after him. He was placing an ultimatum in front of him, and Oram would have to choose—his brother, or the mother of his child.

Oram's face fell.

He couldn't face the hurt he was going to cause, so he opened the door and stepped out into the night.

Without looking back, Oram gave Kirra only two words in return.

"I'm sorry."

WHIT

Walking back into Castle Larapuna was like walking into the den of a lion.

Whit knew precisely what awaited him as his boots clunked across the ancient stone floor. The air smelled stale throughout the throne room, and it carried a certain reputation with it. A long history of violence and scheming.

As he marched obediently to the dais where Madam Lema sat, he was careful to note which soldiers surrounded her. There were those such as Ryker and Colonel Nyadahma that stood sentry on either side of the throne, and then there were the men that remained in the shadows, hugging the walls in fear. They were there for appearances, but they were not a part of this.

Whit shifted his gaze to Brennan as he was escorted into the Grand Hall, hands tied behind his back, with Fallon and Cleetus holding his arms on either side. Whit had tried to speak with Brennan multiple times on the journey back to Larapuna, but he'd insisted there was nothing Whit could do. Brennan didn't care about facing punishment for his crime; he only cared about seeing his daughter, and Whit couldn't argue with that.

The stale air in the room was suffocating. It felt like there was little room to breathe, and Whit could sense it was the queen that radiated that power.

She sat with one leg daintily crossed over the other, her head resting lazily in the palm of her hand and her elbow perched on the arm of her ivory throne. Those tainted fingers of hers were still stained with that putrid blood color. Whit hadn't known what it meant when he'd first laid eyes on them, but after the queen had admitted to using Blood Magic on Freyah, he understood. Raven had mentioned the magic before, and that the stain was the consequence of using something forbidden by the coven—a permanent mark to label her sins.

Madam Lema looked bored as she sat on her throne, but the closer Brennan got to the dais, the more she livened with interest. Her pale skin flushed with sinful anticipation, and she lifted her head to get a clear view of the present her guards were bringing her.

Whit moved to stand in front of the others, stopping short of the steps that led up to the throne. Up close, Madam Lema's delighted expression sent cold chills racing down his spine.

"Lieutenant Avlon," she greeted him in a cloying tone. "I didn't realize I had assigned you to this particular mission."

Though she'd previously looked delighted to see Brennan Kenpaw entering the throne room, there was a clear hint of confusion now sliding over her features. Whatever her plan had been, it failed. And she now knew Whit had been the one to steer it off course.

Whit gathered his nerve and addressed the queen. "Madam, Micah Wighthall was unable to make the trip, so I took the initiative and stepped up in his place." He paused, stealing a glance at Freyah's father as the man took in the sight of the witch-queen before him. "I present to you, Brennan Kenpaw: Last Cove's resident leader of The First Men."

One side of the queen's mouth raised with keen interest. She leaned forward and examined the man in front of her with knowing eyes. It seemed as if she was attempting to peer into his very soul, but what was she looking for?

An admission of guilt?

Some sort of underlying motive that fueled his desire to rebel?

Whit waited patiently with his hands folded in front of him while Madam Lema sat in stifling silence, the quiet making the air even thicker than before.

After a moment, she leaned back on her throne. "And what do you have to say for yourself, Mr. Kenpaw?"

Brennan peered up at the witch-queen with utter disdain, holding his ground. There wasn't an ounce of fear or cowardice in this man. With his shoulders wide and his chest puffed out in confidence, he said, "I am no longer a leader in this rebellion you speak of. If you wish to speak with him, he's still in Last Cove."

Whit couldn't help but react to the statement. His muscles stiffened, and he carefully turned his head to eye Cleetus, who stood between himself and Brennan. The soldier was still holding onto Brennan's left arm, unsure of whether or not to let go, but his grip had loosened. He, too, looked confused and apprehensive at the man's statement.

"What is this?" Madam Lema questioned brazenly. She addressed her question to the entire room, as if someone there could explain what Brennan's vague statement meant. When no one answered, she looked back to Brennan. "I have it on good authority that it was you who issued the destruction of your shipping port. I also have witnesses that have seen the secret meetings you hold in your council chambers. Pulling the wool over the eyes of your magistrate, no less."

Brennan barked a laugh, but everyone else remained eerily still. "That man has pulled the wool over your own eyes," Brennan said through a bout of scoffs and chuckles. "It's the magistrate that orchestrates the rebellion now." As an afterthought, he added, "Madam."

Madam Lema's eyes flew to Whit, and he adjusted his stance, trying to appear calm and collected.

"This is news to me," he stated, though it wasn't.

Whit had been right. He'd sensed the truth behind Matthias's schemes upon first sight. He'd suspected that Last Cove's magistrate had been the one to sell Brennan out to the queen, but what Whit hadn't understood was what the man was getting in return. Now he knew. Matthias wasn't simply spying for the queen. He was using his connections to hide his own involvement with the rebellion in plain sight. He'd probably nearly been caught, but with a simple mention of Brennan's name to the queen, he'd managed to pass the blame onto someone else.

Did Madam Lema know her spy was a double agent? Or was this also part of the illusion—her way of having a man on the inside?

The confusion on the queen's face seemed genuine enough. Her focus darted back to Brennan and, for a split second, it looked like she was unsure what to say. But then her features hardened again and she spoke clearly. "Pointing the finger elsewhere, I see. It's no matter. I have already spoken with your daughter, and she has confirmed every accusation against you."

Brennan's demeanor changed significantly at the mention of Freyah.

It was obvious he'd been sick with worry over her disappearance, but with his sudden arrest he'd probably been temporarily distracted. Now his face was full of remembrance—that his daughter was here, within the same castle walls where he now stood. Brennan glanced around frantically, as if he'd find her standing amongst the soldiers, watching from the shadows.

This sudden change in Brennan brought glee to Madam Lema's cold features. She welcomed his fear by smiling with triumph, knowing that her words had hit their intended mark.

"You will be permitted to see her, of course," she said, then added, "before you're sentenced to death."

Whit's stomach dropped to the floor. Secretly, he'd known where this was going to end, but hearing his suspicions confirmed felt like the final hammer of a bent nail being driven into a thick wooden beam. Brennan's fate was now cemented in place, and there was no way to pry it out.

Not without the wood splintering.

With a wave of her hand, Madam Lema signaled two soldiers to step forward from the shadows and grab Brennan by the shoulders.

Fallon and Cleetus were shoved out of the way, their duty now complete, their presence no longer necessary.

Whit watched as the soldiers guided Brennan behind the dais to a door that led to a meeting room. He knew that within that room, there was a set of stone steps—another entrance to the dungeons.

It was how he and his sisters had attempted to escape all those years ago.

Another figure caught Whit's eye, and he turned to see Ryker striding from the room. He did not address any of the other men, and as Whit watched the general silently exit through the front doors, he wondered what the witch-queen's next move would be.

35

FREYAH

Freyah was trying her best to focus on the text laid out in front of her, but no matter how hard she tried, the story wasn't sticking. It was a romance between a farmer and a princess, but the stakes weren't realistic enough to keep her interested. The idea of such a perfect and instant connection felt ridiculous to her, especially after her own personal experience. Such feelings couldn't be trusted, and she didn't want to read about mushy romance and happily-ever-afters. She wanted something that told the truth—something that didn't gloss over the many disappointments that love had to offer. For she knew all too well that when everything seemed to be going right, it would inevitably all go wrong.

She'd heard from the other guards at breakfast that Whit's team had arrived back at the castle early that morning. Freyah had expected him to come find her immediately, and she'd waited anxiously throughout the rest of the morning for the sound of a knock at her door.

But it never came.

For hours, she'd sat on her bed with a dusty book in her lap while silence pressed against her eardrums and made her feel sick. She'd had to get up and walk around on several occasions to create a disturbance in the pattern. The sound of her own footsteps was a small comfort, but the waiting was becoming too much.

After one final attempt at reading the same page, Freyah finally decided to get up and go find Whit herself. She was immediately reminded, however, that this was not possible, due to the new guard stationed outside her door where Whit should have been. It made his absence even more evident.

Freyah wasn't allowed to roam about the castle anymore, and with Whit gone, she'd been left with a soldier named Conrath as her personal escort. Conrath never left his post, which meant Freyah had no chance of sneaking out again.

But she still wanted to test her limitations. Perhaps she could ask him to escort her to the library to exchange the book. She approached the door, but before she could grip her fingers around the handle, the door creaked open, and Freyah was startled into backing up a step.

And just like that, Whit was there.

He was still in his riding leathers, which consisted of a worn vest caked in dirt, a pair of brown trousers that had a hole in the knee, tall boots, and protective forearm guards. He was as devastatingly hand-some as she remembered, but there were new lines in his face from exhaustion. His beard was fuller, and his shoulders hunched with an unknown heaviness.

Freyah took another step back. Then another.

"Where is he?" she asked, immediately thinking of her father.

It was the first thing that needed to be addressed.

Whit shook his head and looked back at Conrath, who still stood in the hall. There was no one around but the three of them, and he didn't appear comforted by that fact. "You're relieved of duty, soldier," he said to the man. "I'll take it from here."

Whit waited for the sound of the soldier's footsteps to disappear down the hallway, then Whit turned to face her again. He had one hand on the knob of her door and he gestured for her to follow. Whatever needed to be talked about, it would have to be done some-where else.

"Are you allowed to do that?" Freyah asked. Whit had been

removed as her personal guard by the queen, but she wasn't sure how many knew about it. Or why.

"Probably not. But let's not stick around to find out."

Whit led her from the castle and out onto the grounds. It was still magnificent the second time around, for this time she got to see the sweeping lawns that cut across the front gates and led to the stone steps of the entrance. She saw the barracks at ground level and realized how small the buildings were. From high up in her tower, looking down at the cluster of buildings made them appear like normal houses. But down here, they were nothing more than huts.

The soldiers were given an outdoor shower system, something Freyah had seen before because there was a bathhouse in the mountain with the same mechanics, and there was a small training yard with gear scattered about. Lining the stone pathways were statues like the ones outside the library. More witches and warlocks that Freyah guessed had lived in the castle at one point in time.

They made their way to another garden, different from the one where she'd been tricked by Madam Lema into taking the Eriocyper. A few of the flowers still glistened with leftover morning dew, but the sun was now high in the sky above them as they walked. They followed a path where a line of rose bushes created a barrier around a small pond. Lily pads floated gracefully across the surface, and small insects buzzed around the vegetation that crept up the edges of the water.

Whit stopped and crossed his arms over his chest. He didn't seem happy or upset, only a little melancholic, and that worried Freyah more than if he'd come running into her room screaming her name.

"He's here," he told her. "Your father. I brought him in first thing this morning." Whit took her in fully for the first time. There was a longing in his eyes, like he'd missed her, and Freyah had to fight the feeling in her gut that told her she'd missed him, too. "He's okay," he added. "She's keeping him in the dungeons, but he's unharmed. I made sure of it."

Audibly, Freyah sighed with relief. Her shoulders sagged with the weight of her fear being lifted from them. But there was still some-thing holding her down, because her father wasn't in the clear.

Her hands uselessly hung at her sides. She hadn't expected there to be this awkward tension between the two of them, but she found herself twirling her thumbs in apprehension. Whit watched her as she fidgeted, both of them waiting for the other to make the first move.

He tried to reach for her hand, but she pulled away. She couldn't touch him, or her resolve would shatter, and she'd forget why she was angry in the first place.

She noticed his right wrist was wrapped tightly with bandages.

Had he gotten hurt on the journey to Last Cove?

"It's nothing," he said when her eyes lingered on the injury.

He didn't try to reach out again. Instead, Whit crossed his arms again. "We had to search his apartment," he said. Then his head lowered in defeat. "We found evidence of explosives."

"So it's true."

"I'm sorry, Freyah," he said quietly.

She couldn't accept the apology. What good did it do? It wasn't on him that her father had killed innocent people. It wasn't her, either, yet somehow it felt like it was all her fault.

She couldn't think straight. She'd spent the past two weeks waiting anxiously for news about her father, yet now she found herself wanting to talk about anything else. So instead she blurted, "I met Raven while you were away."

She hadn't meant for it to sound so snarky. The conversation she'd had with the witch had been scratching away at her resolve the entire time Whit had been gone. Now she was able to drop it at his feet without concern for the collateral damage. She had nothing to lose when it came to Whit, for he'd already taken everything she had to give.

His expression said it all.

He closed his eyes and rubbed a calloused hand down his face. His hair fell over his scar, and he didn't push it back.

"It's not what you think, Freyah." He spun on his heel and walked further along the edge of the pond. "Whatever she said to you, it's just to get under your skin," he said, facing away from her. "She does that to people. She does that to me."

"You have a relationship with her." It wasn't a question.

To her disappointment, Whit let out an exasperated breath but didn't deny it. "We have an understanding," he corrected.

The clarification didn't make things any better.

"What was it that you expected from me exactly?" She let her tongue loose with the questions she'd needed answered. "Why did you even bother helping me? Was it just to get into my bed? Was that your play? Lure a girl in by making her feel like she owes you?"

"No!" he barked. He stomped back to her and didn't stop until they were face to face. "Do not think for one second that I did anything for you because I wanted something in return." He took her chin between his thumb and index fingers and lifted her face so that their noses nearly brushed. Her breath hitched at the tease of contact, and his hand shook slightly. "I am going to gain your trust back, Freyah. I swear it. I just hope all that's happened hasn't ruined my chances of kissing you again."

Her eyes fluttered closed, and her resolve slipped out of place like removing a mask. She'd wanted so badly to be angry with him, and she had every right to be. He'd lied to her, kept secrets, and played a part in one of the most traumatic things that ever happened to her. Yet, as she stood there in front of him, Freyah had to fight the urge to let it all go. She wanted to wash the indiscretions away like an ocean tide, but she feared the hurt his actions had caused would still remain, like imprints in the sand.

Her trust might have been broken, but not her desire for him.

Perhaps she didn't have to forgive, only…forget for a little while.

Whit slowly moved his lips closer to hers, and for a brief moment, she anticipated the soft taste of them. But then she was hit with the image of him standing before her in the library, ears and black eyes and talons on full display. The image made her shutter, and she quickly raised her hands to his chest to push him away.

"I need to know everything. And even then, we can't just pick up where we left off. We would be starting over." She clutched her chest as if she were holding her own heart in her hands. "You hurt me, and I don't know if I'll ever be okay with that. But I still need your help."

The glint in Whit's eyes was hopeful.

"If you are willing to give me that chance," he said, "then I will take it." He tucked both hands into his pockets and took a step back to create a safe distance between them. "What do you want to know?"

They began walking again, and Whit made sure to leave an appropriate amount of space in front of him as he trailed behind her.

Freyah thought again of her father and wondered what he was doing at that very moment. Was he cold? Hungry? Were there others down there in the dungeons to keep the silence at bay? There had been many prisoners behind rusted bars when Freyah had been led to that room. She remembered the quiet loneliness it stirred within her, despite only lasting a couple hours.

"Has she sentenced him?" she asked, keeping her back to Whit.

He hesitated, then said, his voice gliding to her over the breeze that wafted across the barely stirring water, "Yes. It's not good."

Freyah's heart lurched with a grief of something yet to come. She felt the anticipation of it, like a firework catching flame before shooting upward and igniting the sky.

She stopped to allow Whit to catch up, but remained facing the other way. "How long?"

She heard him come to a stop behind her, then he was there at her side. "They are going to execute him in one week."

"Good," she accepted. "That gives us time. Raven gave me something that will help us slip out more easily. We just need to find the right moment to use it."

"Wha—R-Raven?" he stuttered. "What did she give you?"

Freyah pulled the pouch from where she'd tucked it into her boot and flattened her palm for him to see. Whit peered down at it with panic in his eyes.

"What does it do?" he asked with trepidation.

"She told me it would camouflage me. You blow it into the air and step through the cloud."

Whit made to grab for the pouch but Freyah pulled her hand back before he could snatch it away. "What did she ask for in return?" he pried, not even registering her previous action.

"Nothing." It was the truth.

"Listen, Raven is not the type of witch to do favors for anyone without strings. I would know."

"*How* would you know? What do you do in exchange for your little potion every week?"

Shame washed over Whit's features. "She told you we were together the night before I left, didn't she?"

Freyah's eyes narrowed and she scrunched her nose at the memory. "And it's true?" She lured the confession out of him, hoping he'd give it willingly. And to her own detriment, he did.

"It's not what you think."

The excuse didn't matter. The simple fact that it was true made Freyah's skin crawl. She'd been so close to feeling Whit's body for herself, and now she was racked with the images of him and Raven together. Writhing naked and sweaty, their skin catching and clinging to one another.

"Freyah, please." She'd tried to walk away again, but he caught her by the elbow. The contact sizzled her skin like a white-hot branding iron, and that heat made her look at him fully—the scar on his face and the pain that was buried beneath it. "You have to let me explain," he begged.

"I don't have to let you do anything," she argued. "It's not like we had anything particularly special going on, right? I mean, let's face it: I'm going to be leaving this place the second I find the right opportunity, so what's the point? What is it you want from me, Whit?"

He appeared to be out of breath. His chest heaved like he'd sprinted after her, but she was still only a few steps away. It was as if the simple thought of having to say goodbye to her made him struggle for air.

When he didn't speak, she demanded, "Tell me what you do for her."

"It's me!" He made a gesture noting his own body, and Freyah immediately understood. "She wants me. So I let her have it."

"You pay her with sex?"

He closed his eyes and nodded once.

"And you've always done this?"

"Since the moment I arrived," he confirmed.

That was even more disturbing. "But you said you were seventeen. She's like, what? A hundred?"

He tilted his head and shrugged. "She's actually only forty."

Like that made a difference.

Freyah tried to picture a younger and more impressionable Whit, worried for the safety of his siblings and willing to do anything to protect them. The thought summoned an intense sadness in her chest, and she yearned to tell that boy not to listen, that he was strong enough to face the unknown.

"I wasn't the only one," he continued. "Apparently, there are others. I don't know if they pay her, or if they're like me. But I didn't know. I only just found out."

It was the exact type of thing Freyah expected from a witch. It matched everything she'd ever been told, and that made her sympathize with him, despite not wanting to.

"I understand," Freyah admitted, "and I feel for you—I do—but that doesn't change anything between us. How did you think something could happen between us while you were doing that with her?"

"I don't know, Freyah. But I wanted to try."

His words were desperate, and she wanted so badly to reach out and take his hand. "Do you really think the queen would kill you if she found out?"

He thought on it, scouring for the right answer, but nothing came.

"I'm not afraid of what she'll do to *me*," he finally said, and Freyah knew what that meant.

"Freyah, I know this is a big deal to you," he continued, "and I promise we will address it and work through it however you see fit, but you were right before—right now our biggest concern should be getting you and your father out of this castle."

It was the rational thing to do. They needn't be swept away by the currents of her scorned feelings, nor their desires to be together. Her father's life was on the line, and they needed to act.

"Okay," she agreed. "But just one more thing."

"Yes. Anything."

He really was willing to do whatever it took to win her trust back.

"Did you know what Madam Lema had planned when you came to get me from Last Cove?"

Whit's eyes glossed over with a thick sadness that stretched down to his mouth and formed a frown. "I knew she wanted to use you as leverage against your father, but I didn't know how far she was going to take it. If I'd known she was going to hurt you…" He reached for her but stopped short, his hand hovering over the spot on her chest that now had a scar to match his own.

Though he hadn't touched her, she still felt his fingers there.

"When can I see my father?"

"Not yet. But soon. I'll come for you when it's safe. The queen is going to be watching my every move now. But Freyah…I swear to you, I will get you out. And she *won't* touch you again. I swear it on my life."

Freyah allowed his reaffirmed promise to wash over her like a rainstorm.

She feared his inability to keep it like she feared being struck by lightning, but standing under the shower of his oath felt too good to seek shelter.

36

WHIT

hit lingered in the garden for another hour after taking Freyah back to her room. He needed to think without the distraction of other bodies and senseless chatter around him, and neither the barracks nor the dungeon was the setting for that. He only wanted the crisp autumn air and the early afternoon sun beating down on his skin.

Now that he'd securely brought Brennan to the castle without incident, it was his job to scout for the perfect opportunity for Freyah to make her escape. However, throughout his planning, Whit kept seeing flashbacks of his own attempt with Willow and Wendi—the plan that they'd thought was perfectly executed but had morphed into the worst day of his life.

It's not like before, he tried to remind himself. *She has help, and we didn't. It'll be different this time.*

Though he was craving the solitude and time to create a plan, he also needed to confide in someone. He needed someone outside the situation who would see the most practical solution. Of course, the first person who came to mind was Willow, but he was still angry with her about her involvement in Freyah's injury, and he'd yet to confront her about it.

As Whit gazed out at the still waters of the pond in front of him, he figured now was as good a time as any.

It was most likely that she'd be in the laundry room this time of day. Though Freyah had the weekends off from work duties, Willow never took time for herself. She spent every waking moment folding and ironing, and scrubbing stains from clothes. It was her way of keeping her demons at bay. She'd told him once that intrusive thoughts couldn't find you if you kept your mind occupied, and that notion seemed to work for her.

He needed to stop by his room in the barracks to change from his traveling clothes. He smelled of the road and desperately needed to bathe. Plus, it would give him time to prepare what he wanted to say to her.

It wasn't in his sister's nature to ever apologize for anything, but he prayed that this time she'd see the error of her ways. Ratting out Freyah like that had put her at serious risk, but surely Willow's intention hadn't been to cause her harm. His sister was pragmatic and planned for the worst, and she came off as cynical because of it, but she was not cruel.

The barracks were mostly empty when Whit arrived, but he spotted Cleetus and Paul changing their own musky clothes by their beds. As a lieutenant over a small team, Whit was granted the luxury of having his own room. Well, technically, he couldn't classify it as a room. He was separated from the others by one wall and a moth-eaten curtain, but it was better than having no more than five feet of space between his bed and the one beside him.

He pulled the curtain to close off the area and stripped out of his reeking clothes. He piled them in a discarded lump on the bed, knowing that he would have to remember to place them in the wash basket later. As he searched for a clean shirt and trousers, he couldn't help but overhear the conversation between Cleetus and Paul. It was one of the negative sides of not having an actual door, but sometimes it had its advantages. Especially now, considering what the two men were murmuring about.

"He said they're putting together a war council," Paul told his comrade in an excited whisper. "It's happening, man. I told you, now that she's got an actual member in custody, she's got all the proof she needs to get this thing started."

"But that's just one man," Cleetus interjected. "And one shitty, seaside town. That's not enough to take down an entire rebellion."

"I'm telling ya, it's starting. Just you wait. Pretty soon, they'll be splitting us up into platoons and sending us off. You better kiss that girlfriend of yours while you've got the time."

Whit heard the tell-tale squeak of springs being compressed under a mattress, then Cleetus asked, "So you don't believe him then? The guy we brought?"

"Of course I don't," Paul fussed. "He's just trying to save his own skin. Besides, whether he's got anything to do with The First Men or not, the queen's gonna use him as a scapegoat. She's gonna have her war. It's what she's wanted from the beginning—to finish what Ruella started."

Whit froze in place, one foot inside the leg of his clean pants while the other was still planted on the cold floor.

Madam Lema wasn't trying to stop a war.

She meant to start one.

Whit managed to dress himself the rest of the way and waited for Cleetus and Paul to leave before pulling back the curtain and exiting the barracks himself. He walked straight past the bathing stalls, neglecting his plan to clean up altogether, and hurried off to track down Willow.

He walked briskly across the lawn. The season was changing faster than he could keep up with, and the cool autumn breeze he'd felt before was already turning to a bone-chilling cold. The sky had become overcast, the sun hidden behind a wall of thick, dark clouds. He spotted a cluster of leaves caught in the wind and watched as they swirled around in a tight spiral while the others around them remained still, like a maiden twirling her dress while the crowd stood still around her. The sight felt like an omen somehow, but he forced himself to ignore it.

He spotted Willow as she was leaving the laundry room. She

carried a large woven basket propped against her hip, and she appeared irritated. At first, he thought she was muttering to herself, but as he approached, he saw General Ryker exiting the room behind her. He also seemed ruffled, but his menacing face held more frustration than annoyance. They were clearly in the middle of an important discussion, but Whit couldn't imagine what it was about. He'd never seen his sister give Ryker a second glance, much less hold a conversation with him.

Whit cleared his throat to alert them of his presence, and Willow blanched. She'd been startled, but after realizing who stood there, she sighed with relief.

"I've been looking for you," Whit said casually, attempting to mask the timorous note in his voice.

"And now you've found me." Her own tone was clipped, and it turned Whit's stomach. She turned to acknowledge Ryker again before continuing down the hall. "Your uniform will be pressed by tonight. Good day, General."

The wolf-demon momentarily scrutinized Whit's interruption with a narrowed gaze, but he brushed it off just as quickly. If he had said or done something to make Willow upset, Whit would have the general's throat—no matter his seniority.

"Are you alright?" Whit asked as he walked carefully next to his sister. She was making her way toward the barracks to collect whatever needed washing for the day. Whit immediately regretted having left his dirty clothes on the floor.

"Fine," she replied, though her tone still reflected otherwise. "Why did you need to see me?"

Whit waited until they reached the barracks before dropping such a heavy topic on her. When they entered, she immediately began wending her way around the maze of cots and collecting various items from the floor, depositing them in her basket one by one.

"I want to talk to you about Freyah," he began, moving to sit on one of the cleaner-looking cots. He'd chosen one that was freshly made versus the others around him that had rumpled sheets and smelled of sweat.

Willow didn't acknowledge his request. She only focused on her task, her face showing no sign of care or concern.

"You had to have known the queen would punish her," he tested, trying his best to claim her attention.

She moved to the other side of the room and sat her basket on the floor, balling up a set of sheets but remaining silent.

"Please, Low," he pleaded. "Just talk to me."

At that, she finally turned to face him. They were separated by six rows of beds and an ocean of unsettled tension, but when she focused her eyes on him, he felt instantly at home. They weren't happy eyes, but they were familiar. They were hers.

"I know you're mad about what I did, but she needed to understand," Willow finally said. "Can't you see? I helped her before she could make an even bigger mistake."

"You hurt her!"

Whit closed his eyes and let out a heavy sigh. He hadn't meant to raise his voice, but his need to protect Freyah had awoken a primal instinct in him.

At least he'd been right about Willow's intentions, though she had no clue what the implications were.

"You didn't help her," he said, this time more calmly. "You've only motivated her more. She's going to get out, Low. And I'm going to help her."

"That girl has completely distracted you. Why do you care so much about what happens to her?"

He didn't need to think about how to answer her question, because he'd known all along. "She's just like us. She didn't ask for this."

Willow scoffed. "Do you realize who her father is? What he's done? You can't get yourself mixed up with rebels!"

That was the lynchpin, wasn't it?

Once Whit aligned himself with Brennan, there would be no going back. His position in the guard would be jeopardized. The protection he'd placed over Willow would shatter. It was the problem he'd been fretting over the most. Whit was at war with himself over whether to be the hero or step aside.

One choice might gain Freyah's trust back, but the other would lose his sister's. It wasn't even about his feelings for Freyah anymore—at least, that was what he told himself. It was about wanting to do the right thing.

"I couldn't save Wendi," he spoke softly, raising his voice enough so his words reached her across the room. "But maybe I can save them."

Willow had stopped trying to collect the tangle of balled up sheets and bent low to retrieve her basket instead. She crossed the room in silence and didn't speak until she was standing directly in front of her brother. She placed one hand on his shoulder and squeezed, the most comforting form of affection he could hope to receive from her.

"No one holds that against you," she said. "Not even me."

He looked up into her sad eyes. He wanted to believe her, but there was still a hurt there that he could not fix. "Then why do you look at me like that whenever I bring it up?"

Willow's chin dipped to her chest, and her hand retreated from where it rested on Whit's shoulder. They both knew there was a part of her that resented Whit's decision to bring them here. Willow had been the most adamant about staying in The Mounds, but Whit had insisted on doing better. *Being* better…for them. If only he'd known what would happen, perhaps then he would have listened to his sister's pleas to stay.

Willow gathered herself and regained that determinedly languid demeanor she'd adopted since losing Wendi. Ignoring his question, she said, "I'm just trying to stop the same thing from happening again. I don't want anyone else to die." She paused, barely meeting her brother's eyes, then looked away. "I don't know what all has transpired between the two of you, but I can clearly see that you care about Freyah. She will die if she tries to escape. So if you care about her as much as I think you do, you won't let her leave."

Whit's eyebrows scrunched together. "No one is going to die. Not if we help her. That's the difference." He needed her to see that. "We didn't have help before, but she does. It will work this time. I will make it work."

She didn't respond. Instead, she gripped the edge of her laundry basket tighter, her knuckles turning white. "I won't stop her this time," she finally lamented. "But I won't help her either. You do what you think is best. And I'll do the same."

With that parting statement, she left the barracks, leaving Whit alone with an impossible decision to make. In one week, Brennan would face the gallows. That left them very little time to come up with a plan. But as Whit sat there staring at the dirt-caked floor beneath his boots, a realization popped into his head.

With everything that had happened, he hadn't realized what time of year it was—what event loomed. He'd never cared or celebrated before, but this year, it might be the perfect distraction. For, in one week, all of Larapuna would be gathering to celebrate Samhain.

At the end of the harvest season, the castle hosted a festival in which they invited important guests from all over Ghoma. Chancellors and magistrates from every district came to represent their constituents, important families showed their faces to reassert their status among the people, and most importantly, the common folk sang praises of gratitude to the earth for a bountiful harvest season. There would be dancing and bonfires and exquisite banquet tables full of every type of food custom to all corners of the country.

Whit hadn't once shown his face at the festival, having spent most of his time stationed in the dungeons. And even after being granted the position of lieutenant, he found the celebrations not worth his time.

But this year would be different.

This year, he would use the festival to his advantage. It hadn't occurred to him before, but the perfect opportunity had finally presented itself. On the night of Samhain, when the day's festivities came to a conclusion at an annual ball, that was when Freyah and Brennan would be able to slip out. There were a few minor details to sort out, of course, but he'd figure those out later.

Finally, it was time for Whit to make things right.

37

FREYAH

The preparations for the Samhain were well under way.

Freyah had celebrated every year with Corianne in Last Cove, but their meager caramel apples and bonfire on the beach was nothing compared to the extravagance that Larapuna had planned.

Along every corridor of the castle were strings of twine tied with cattails or garlands made from fallen leaves. The Grand Hall was no longer filled with the long tables used for dining, for they'd been pushed aside to allow room for giant wooden alters covered in orange and yellow flowers. Some were in the shape of stars, others looked more intricate with nods to the witch-mother Lillia and the four seasons. An arch constructed of hay lined the entrance to the Hall, and grouped on either side were stacks of fresh gourds in varying shades and sizes.

If Freyah wasn't so focused on trying to escape, she might have enjoyed the excitement. Everyone in the castle was buzzing with some sort of job to do. Even Willow had been tasked with making several dozen ornaments to hang from the now barren oak tree on the front lawn. Freyah had seen her carrying around boxes of bells, ribbon, and salvaged pine cones.

Freyah had no job. Other than carrying out her regular duties in the laundry rooms, she'd barely been let out of her room after her confrontation with Madam Lema. Even then, a guard escorted her to and from the west tower and remained outside her door.

Whit had been busy with preparations of his own. Last they'd spoken, he'd told her that luck had presented her with the perfect opportunity, better than the one he'd tried to take advantage of when escaping with his sisters.

Apparently, the Samhain festival was a nightmare for the guards due to how many people they had to keep track of. Every soldier would be on high alert, but it also meant that the witches would have their attention fixed elsewhere—including Madam Lema.

Being the lieutenant of the guard meant Whit was in charge of the schedule of every soldier on his team—where they would be stationed and when. This meant he'd ensured an "accidental" thirty minute window between Friday night's shift change. At least, that's what he would claim if his superior noticed.

Their window to escape would take place at midnight, right at the height of the ball. Until then, Freyah had to continue to play her part as the concerned daughter waiting for her father to be executed. As it so happened, the part wasn't hard to play. She was incredibly worried for her father, no matter how straightforward their plan seemed. If anything went wrong—if even one of them was caught—everything would fall apart. Instead of one person facing a noose, it would be three.

Freyah wasn't as concerned for her own life as she was for her father's, but she also didn't want Whit risking his life because of her, no matter how she felt about him or his sister at the moment. It seemed a perfect twist of fate that he would be the one to get her out of Larapuna when it had been him that brought her there in the first place.

Six days had passed since Whit explained his plan to her, and now they were a little more than twenty-four hours away from making it happen. Freyah wasn't sure what to expect when it came to the celebration. She knew that higher dignitaries traveled to Larapuna and made an appearance at the festival because the magistrate of Last

Cove had made a big deal about it every year, but she had no idea what sort of activities were planned. She hoped there would be a giant bonfire—it was her favorite part back home.

Samhain was celebrated on the last night of October to signal the official end of the summer harvest season and the beginning of winter. It meant that food would become scarce, and they'd have to depend more on their own goods, since traveling with imports would become near impossible after the first snow. For Last Cove, the winter season meant the seas were rougher and traveling across them more treacherous. The people living in Mount Mirela used that time to come together and prepare for a hard few months. The festival was the last chance for fun and relaxation until spring, so everyone drank and danced and enjoyed the companionship of one another.

Larapuna certainly wouldn't be faced with food or supply short-ages. Freyah didn't even truly understand what the witches were cele-brating, because *they* weren't the ones that harvested the food they were thanking the gods for—the common people of Ghoma did that.

Freyah had been thinking about all of this as she walked down to the front hall of the castle. She carefully stepped through a large expanse of candles that were melting to the stone floor, creating a pool of collected wax beneath them. Whether that was the intention or not, Freyah thought the display was beautiful. She moved to stand by the large oak front doors. Her current guard, Conrath, was hovering a few feet behind, slumped against the wall and looking incredibly tired. He most definitely did not want to be spending his time monitoring her.

She'd been eternally grateful for the reprieve from her room, but she wasn't sure why she'd been summoned. She'd already finished her laundry duties for the day, and she'd made sure to be a perfect little ward ever since the incident with the scissors.

Freyah looked out onto the front lawn to where Willow was hooking her ornaments onto the barren tree and caught sight of several soldiers hauling logs from the forest and stacking them for a bonfire. A large pit had been dug, and stones were purposefully placed around the edge. The soldiers piled the wood a few feet from the pit, and Freyah watched in awe as it grew taller, taking the shape of a pyramid. She could already feel the warmth the fire would bring once the sun went down.

Suddenly, she was startled by a hand clamping onto her shoulder. She turned to see Jessa beaming at her, and she relaxed.

Jessa frowned slightly. "I'm sorry. I didn't mean to startle you." Then, after assessing that Freyah was alright, she smiled and handed over a crate filled to the brim with pumpkins.

"I personally requested your help!" Jessa squealed. "I didn't want you to be cooped up in your room and miss out on all the excitement."

Freyah beamed and thanked Jessa profusely. She hadn't the faintest idea how the girl had managed to convince anyone to let Freyah out of her room, but she wasn't going to question it.

Freyah's nerves had been on edge since her father arrived, so she was happy to have something fun to occupy her time. She wouldn't truly be relaxed until she was able to see her father in person—to ensure he was okay—but she knew there would be no point in asking Madam Lema for a visit. She'd thought to ask Whit, but time with him was hard to come by these days.

Since he'd managed to talk with her in the gardens a week ago, Freyah hadn't had a moment alone with him. He'd been relieved of his duty as her personal guard now that all secrets were out, and it was best that they kept away from one another so as not to arouse suspicion.

In their one brief exchange since then, he'd hastily informed her of his plan for Samhain, and the conversation hadn't strayed past that. He didn't linger, and he didn't bring up any of the other things that had caused such a chasm between them. He was all business, and she'd listened to him in the same manner. Neither of them seemed to want to push things any farther than they already had. Freyah didn't think she could bear one more inch. There was too much to think about— too much for her heart to handle—and her father had to be the priority.

"You look like you've been visited by a spirit."

Jessa's voice reeled her in from her spiraling thoughts. Freyah shook her head and schooled her face into neutrality. She hadn't seen any spirits, but she certainly felt like she was being haunted. Haunted by an endless string of choices and devastating blows.

"I'm alright," she told Jessa. "Thank you for thinking of me." She lifted the box, showing the girl's gesture was appreciated.

Jessa smiled brightly and led her into the Grand Hall. "I thought you might want to help with some of the decorations?" Her statement came off as more of a question, and Freyah realized that she was waiting for her to confirm.

"Okay, yeah," she agreed. "What are we working on?"

Jessa's smile spread all the way to the creases around her eyes as they approached a small table on the left side of the Hall. It was already set up with a bucket, five medium sized gourds, and a cloth that was draped over the surface of the table. "We're carving pumpkins!" she exclaimed.

Freyah had never carved a pumpkin before. In Last Cove, pumpkins were set outside of shop windows as decorations, but they were left as they were. She wondered what sorts of pictures or symbols the witches used and how it was done.

Jessa answered her unspoken question by pulling out several carving knives from the pocket of her ragged brown apron. She handed one of them over. At first, Freyah was hesitant to take it. Were the witches really giving her access to another weapon? She seized it, a thrill of excitement running through her veins, but then she saw it had been dulled.

Of course.

Jessa dug in her pocket again and placed what looked like two oversized spoons on the table in front of them.

"There are certain designs we do every year, but I was given permission to create a couple of my own!" she said, as if it were a great honor that had been bestowed upon her.

Freyah gave her a soft smile and reached for the closest pumpkin. "What do we do?"

"We need to hollow these out for candles," Jessa instructed, pointing to the ones in front of them. "Then we'll carve some for the front hall."

They spent the next several hours doing just that. Every time the table emptied, a soldier came by with an armful of new pumpkins. Between the two of them, they'd halved and hollowed out twenty different gourds. According to Jessa, the unused tops would be used as compost for gardening, and the stems for potions. The insides were being scooped into an iron bowl, separating the seeds from the mush. Jessa told her that the seeds could be roasted and eaten, but Freyah didn't imagine they would taste very good.

After she'd finished scooping out her tenth pumpkin, Jessa picked up another carving knife with a hooked end and began stenciling an intricate pattern onto the skin of the next. It was a series of inter-secting lines that created a sort of woven design, like the weaves in a basket. In the center were two interloping oblong shapes and over top was a square with rounded corners.

Freyah didn't recognize the symbol. "What does it mean?"

Jessa didn't look up from what she was doing, only crooked her head slightly to indicate that she'd heard the question. "It's the True Lovers Knot," she explained. "It's supposed to represent infinity and protect against evil spirits."

Freyah had never seen anything like it, and the finished design looked beautiful. She had to admit, the witches had intriguing customs, but what sort of evil could they be warding off besides their own?

"Do you know the symbols for the elements?" Jessa asked offhandedly.

Freyah pulled her attention away from the knot and nodded. "I know runes. It's like the one the soldiers wear on their armor."

"That's right!" Jessa looked as if Freyah had answered a question correctly in school and was ready to give her passing marks.

"Why did they choose the earth symbol?" she asked, remembering the upside down triangle made from vines with a line through the bottom point that she'd seen on Whit the day they'd met.

"The witches get their powers from the earth. In order to wield magic, they use natural resources as conduits."

Freyah hadn't realized this before, but she'd never seen any of the witches display magic with raw power. It always came from flowers or stones, or elixirs that required skill to make. Even the camouflaging powder tucked away safely in her boot was made from crushed tourmaline—a gemstone Freyah had uncovered on many occasions on Mount Mirela. Thinking about it made her feign an itch on her ankle simply to check that the pouch was still there.

But what did that mean for someone like her? As a human, was she capable of using the powder like a witch? Would it even work for her?

"Do they have to have the magic already in them to wield the items?"

Jessa nodded. "That's right. Magic's in the blood. Not just anyone can pick up a crystal and wield it."

Freyah nearly dropped her carving blade. *That bitch.*

Raven had willingly handed over the camouflaging powder because she'd known it wouldn't work for Freyah.

Reigning in her anger, Freyah focused on whittling away a fresh pumpkin. The elemental runes weren't complicated to draw, so the task went by a lot faster than the previous one, mostly because they weren't scooping out the insides. While she worked, Freyah thought of Whit and the small figures he carved from wood, imagining he would be quite good at something like this. She wondered if he still carved, or if he'd been too busy to work on any new projects. She still had the small bird figurine sitting on the shelf in her room, and suddenly, for the first time, she realized what it symbolized.

Freyah hadn't paid enough attention to Whit's demon features when he'd turned, for she'd been too shocked to really process it, but thinking back on it now, they looked familiar.

She'd seen how the shape of his pupils had changed. His fingers had turned into talons. That leathery texture to his hands. Freyah had no doubt that if Whit had lingered even a second longer, she would have seen him sprout wings.

He was the bird he'd carved for her—a silent message meant only for her when she was ready to see it.

As Freyah attempted to focus back on her work, she was drawn to the sound of a familiar voice entering the Hall.

It was as if the gods had whispered to him that he'd been on her mind.

She turned to see Whit striding in, wearing a simple white tunic and brown pants. Her heart leapt at the sight of him, but her gut lurched in response.

Here she was again…letting her feelings get in the way.

Freyah wanted to ask Jessa another question, anything to make it look like she hadn't been completely thrown off by Whit's appearance, but the girl was now wrapped up in a conversation with a soldier while she loaded him up with her finished carvings and he replaced them with new ones. Freyah stood up to go over and help, simply to show she was doing something, but when she turned around, Whit was standing right in front of her.

She stumbled, nearly falling back against the table.

"Whoa there." He steadied her, putting a hand on each of her arms. "You alright?"

She forced a small laugh. "That's up for debate today, I think."

He cocked his head to show he didn't quite understand the joke, but he laughed anyway. After that, the awkward tension between them immediately filled the space, and Freyah longed for that one second of lighthearted reprieve to return.

"Are you helping with Samhain preparations?" she asked, wanting to fill the silence.

Whit gathered himself and straightened his shoulders back into a soldier's stance. "I was given the day off. We have a new recruit that's shadowing one of my guys in the dungeons today," he explained. "Actually, I came to get you. There's someone that wants to see you…"

His unfinished statement hovered in the air between them, but she knew what he was insinuating. He was finally taking her to see her father.

In that moment, Freyah didn't care what hostility she was

supposed to be feeling for him, because all she wanted to do was reach out and hug him.

She wanted to thank him, but he gave a subtle, knowing shake of his head.

She would have to act as if this were an unpleasant request.

Freyah stepped to where Jessa had sat back down at the table and leaned over her shoulder. "I have to go with Lieutenant Avlon," she told her, feigning annoyance. "I'll be back in a bit. Thank you...for getting me out of my room."

Jessa's eyes softened, and she gave Freyah another of her warm smiles. "Don't worry about it. You've helped enough. This is the last batch anyway."

Freyah nodded and followed Whit to the back of the Hall. They were walking straight toward the dais, but off to the left behind the ivory throne was a small door. Whit glanced around, waiting to see who had taken note of their movements, but everyone appeared to be engrossed with whatever task they'd been given. The entire castle was on a tight schedule, and everything had to be finished by tonight. Even the guards looked stressed, but thankfully, that meant they weren't watching as Whit opened the door and gestured for Freyah to step through.

Once the door was shut behind them, he placed a hand on the small of her back and guided her to a set of descending stairs.

"This is how you'll get out of the castle during the ball," he told her. "It's a faster way to the dungeons, and when the time comes, I'll make sure Brennan is ready. You'll just need to wait for my signal."

"How am I supposed to sneak into the Grand Hall and get to the door while a bunch of people are attending a ball?"

"That won't be a problem," Whit stated matter-of-factly. "You'll be disguised as guest."

Freyah was so stunned that she nearly missed a step. Whit had to grab her by the hip before she tumbled down the stairs, and his tea tree scent hit her like a strong gust of wind.

"Are you sure you're alright?" he asked. "You aren't typically this clumsy."

She waved off his concern and his touch by pushing his hand away. "I'm fine. But what do you mean I'm attending the ball? How? I doubt Madam Lema is going to let me celebrate Samhain while my father awaits his execution."

"She won't. But that doesn't matter."

"I don't understand."

"I'll explain once I've taken you back to your room. We need to hurry. I've only bought us a little bit of time."

It was extremely hard to stop herself from asking more questions, but she managed. Her stomach was in knots at the thought of finally seeing her father again, and it was enough to distract her from prying further.

When they entered the dungeon, there were no guards.

"My friend Perry is giving a new guard the full tour right now," Whit explained, reading the confused expression on her face. "That includes a very extensive walk-through of the grounds." Freyah nodded in understanding, then he added, "I imagine Perry can draw it out for quite a while, but still, we should be quick."

Whit hurried her through the dank space, and Freyah tried not to stare at the prisoners as they passed. She recognized a lot of the same men from when she'd been brought down here. They were still there, rotting away under the floor of the Grand Hall where no one could hear them.

Where no one cared.

At the opposite end of the dungeon sat the very same closed room that she'd been kept in herself. Whit knocked before opening the door, showing respect for the prisoner inside.

The door creaked open, and sitting slumped against the back wall and clutching a tin bowl of rations was Brennan. He was filthy and covered in bruises, almost unrecognizable, but the moment he met his daughter's eyes, the father she knew looked back at her.

FREYAH

Freyah rushed to her father. She fell to her knees and wrapped him in a fierce hug, causing him to drop his bowl of food. She breathed in the sour scent of sweat and dirt that clung to his skin, but it didn't matter, because underneath all that grime was the familiar blend of fire and smoke—the melting of iron from his workshop. She pulled back to look into his face and let out a strangled sob. The smallest hint of relief washed over her father's features at seeing his daughter alive.

It was the first time they'd laid eyes on one another in a month, but it felt like years.

"Are you alright?" she asked, pushing up the sleeves of his shirt to search for more bruising, then she whirled on Whit. "You said you would protect him," she accused.

"I did," Whit swore. "It must have happened after we got here." He looked to Brennan. "What happened?"

But her father wasn't interested in explaining. He was transfixed by the sight of his only daughter sitting in front of him.

"You're here," he muttered softly, as if he were in a dream. "I knew you were alive."

"Of course I'm alive," she reassured him. "And we're both going to stay that way, because I'm getting you out of here." She rested her palm against his sweaty cheek. "We have a plan."

At that, her father stole a glance at Whit. It must have looked odd, his daughter who had been stolen away by soldiers now coming to him with one that appeared to be helping her. Freyah registered the trepidation on his face and nudged his cheek to look at her.

"I'll explain everything, I swear. Just hang on one more night," she told him. "That's when I'll come back for you."

Her words didn't appear to comfort him as he pulled her into a tight embrace. "Don't leave me again, sweet girl."

Freyah didn't think there was anything left in her to break, but her father's plea managed to tear off another piece of her heart.

"I'm coming back," she promised him. "I swear it. We have a plan, but it has to be during the ball. While everyone is distracted. I *will* come back. I promise."

He seemed to finally accept it and released his hold on her. She moved to stand, but before she could he latched onto her arm. "Matthias," he hissed.

"What about him?" Freyah knew the name—he was the magistrate back in Last Cove. But why was he on her father's mind?

"He'll be coming to the ball," he warned, his words rushing out in a haste for her to hear them. "He's working for the witches. Do not trust him."

She understood the command, but she couldn't grasp the importance of it. "What do you mean?" she questioned. "Is he planning something?"

"Come on," Whit ordered. He pried her father's fingers from her arm and replaced them with his own. "We need to go."

"Wait!" Freyah tried to pull away from him, but Whit was too strong.

She reached for her father, but he was already slumping against the wall. That brief conversation had been enough to wear him down. She wanted to stay with him—she wanted to clean him up and make sure he was properly fed—but Whit continued to pull her from the room. He then closed the door and just like that, her father disappeared from sight. She could still feel his presence calling to her from the other side of the door, but she couldn't break through.

Freyah dug her boot into the divots of the stone beneath her and tried to slow Whit, but he wouldn't stop. He continued to yank her through the dungeon and all the way to another door that led outside. They breached the threshold just as the sound of footsteps came stomping down the stairs behind them.

Perry and Thomas were back.

And they'd barely missed being caught.

"Come on." Whit tried to grab her again, but she managed to step out of his reach.

"Tell me what that was about," she demanded. "What do you know?"

Whit dragged a hand through his hair and groaned. "Please let me take you back to your room. I promise we can talk there."

"No," she refuted. "Tell me how I'm going to be able to attend the Samhain Ball. And why did my father just warn me about the magistrate?"

Since she wasn't budging, Whit caved and gestured for her to follow him further across the grounds. They walked quietly within the shadow of the turrets until they reached a small alcove. He pulled her deep into a space where they were surrounded by stone on three sides.

Across from them, Freyah could see several groups of men hauling collapsed tents through the grass, no doubt preparing to set them up for tomorrow's festival. Behind them was the stretch of bushes that lined the small pond where she'd stood with Whit a week ago—where he'd confessed his final secret. Or so she hoped.

She still didn't know how to approach her feelings for him, and there was no denying their physical attraction to each other, yet he'd touched another woman. He'd allowed someone else's hands on him, and Freyah didn't think she could ignore that.

They were crammed into a tiny gap within the alcove that was no bigger than the size of a broom closet. Here they would not be able to dance around the things that needed talking about, for there was nowhere to hide. It was only the two of them, face to face with mere inches of space between them.

"Talk," she commanded, focusing fully on the point at hand. "Now."

"I think Matthias set your father up," Whit started. "I could feel that something was off about our meeting when I was in Last Cove. Your father kept saying he wasn't the one in charge anymore. Is that news to you?"

Freyah shook her head. "I didn't even know my father was involved with The First Men until Madam Lema showed me my memories."

"That's what I thought. I think Matthias is one of the queen's informers. It's how she knew where and when to find you. It was part of her plan from the beginning. And now with Brennan out of the way, his position is up for grabs. I think Matthias wanted it for himself, but what I can't figure out is if he wanted it for the rebellion, or for Madam Lema."

"So he's a filthy spy," Freyah deduced.

"He's more than that. I think he's playing double agent. I don't think the queen knows he's actually part of the rebellion. She's been using him for information, but I think he's been doing the same with her. I'm not sure what his endgame is, but he definitely wanted Brennan out of the way."

"If he's going to be coming here, we can try to find out more then," she suggested, "but what about the ball?"

Whit smirked and, within the shadows, it was easy to mistake the look for something sinister. "It's a masquerade ball," he said. "Everyone will be wearing masks."

Of course. Why hadn't she thought about that before? The traditions surrounding Samhain were quite different in her little village by the sea, but the children still dressed up in masks. Typically, they were representations of different animals. Freyah remembered a little boy that had donned a mask that made him look like a reptile, and he'd paraded it around in front of Jago, the lizard-demon. She'd thought nothing of it at the time, but now she understood how cruel it had been.

"Are you going?" she asked. They were standing incredibly close. Her arm had brushed his several times, and she relished the warmth he exuded. She wanted to bury her face into his neck and soak in every ounce of body heat he could spare. But still, she fought against it.

Whit nodded curtly but didn't meet her eyes.

She wanted to keep the easy nature of the conversation going, but without something important to talk about, their words became stagnant.

"I'll need a dress."

This seemed to spark some interest from him. "I've got something in mind, but it requires asking someone for help that doesn't want to get involved."

"Willow," Freyah finished the thought for him. "Have you spoken to her?"

It was another thing that had nagged at her since his return. She hadn't known how to talk to Willow after she'd thrown her under the cart with Madam Lema. Freyah was now physically marred because of her, and she found herself hating the girl even more than she hated what Whit had done.

Whit nodded again, but this time he followed it with an explanation. "She never meant for you to get hurt."

He was still defending his sister.

Freyah instantly pivoted away to leave the small space but he stepped in her path. There was little room to maneuver past him. With Whit crowding her, there was nowhere left to stand but between the inner wall of the castle and his hard chest. She remembered how it had felt beneath her fingers, the planes of his muscles firm and irresistibly smooth.

Her thoughts were cascading again, but with his mouth not a inch from hers, she could feel the hotness of his breath on her jaw. He was blocking her escape with his body, one hand placed beside her head against the stone.

"I don't want to talk about my sister," he whispered against her skin, and Freyah shuddered. "I don't want to talk about anything. I just want to stand here with you, in our own little pocket of the world."

Freyah closed her eyes at the thought—at how marvelous that would be.

If only it were that simple.

If only her father's life weren't in danger. If only she could forget all the things that Whit had lied to her about. She still hadn't processed how she felt about him being a demon, and though the sight of him in the library that day had scared her, right now, in the shadows of the castle where they were all alone and no one could see them, he didn't seem scary at all. He was warm and inviting.

"I haven't stopped thinking about that kiss," he said. His free hand crept to her waist and pulled her closer. Her torso was now flush against his, and a heat pooled in her core.

"It's too complicated," she murmured as her lips barely brushed his. They were seconds away from meeting, and the pull was so intense Freyah felt like her resolve was going to crack right down the middle.

One half for her to keep.

And one for him to hold.

"Can't we just forget about everything for a little while?" he asked.

She wanted to. Gods she wanted to, so badly.

His fingers played at the skin just above the waistband of her leggings. She'd opted for a thickly woven button-down that hung loosely on her slight figure. Her leggings were skin tight, and if he lifted the back of her shirt, he would be able to see the roundness of her ass on full display. He didn't need to see it though, because his hands were now gliding over her backside. His fingers squeezed, and he pressed himself further against her, his hard length bulging beneath his trousers.

"Please, Freyah," he begged her. "I want this."

His voice was like honey and silk washing over her. It warmed her from within and flushed her cheeks with heat, a bittersweet respite from the chilly autumn air that blew through their little hideaway. The stone wall was cold against her back, for there was no sunlight here. No prying eyes or spotlight to shine on what they were doing in the shadows.

With his body so close to hers, it only took the feeling of one last heavy breath against her throat before Freyah lost the will to resist.

She grabbed the back of his neck fiercely and pulled him to her.

His lips were as soft as she remembered, but this time they were slow to roam. Whit ran his tongue along her bottom lip and she quivered, biting him in return. A low growl released from the back of his throat, and the sound instantly sent a new wave of heat between her thighs. She clenched them together, desperate for friction, and when he felt what she was doing, he shoved a knee between hers and pressed firmly against her core. A whimper escaped her, and for a moment she felt embarrassed at her blatant display of excitement, but Whit was clearly enjoying it.

She felt the smirk that played at his lips as he continued to devour her mouth. His hands made their way up her back beneath the fabric of her shirt as he pressed his thigh into her center for her to ride. That delicious pressure made her want to grind harder against him, but it wasn't enough. Freyah began unbuttoning her shirt with shaky fingers, needing to feel him in more places. After the first two buttons were undone, Whit saw what she was doing and used his own nimble fingers to free the rest.

He slid the fabric from her shoulders and kissed her collarbone gently. Freyah arched her back and craned her neck to give him better access. Whit took full advantage, his tongue gliding along her skin to the hollow of her throat. He sucked and tasted every inch within his reach before making his way down to the center of her chest.

Freyah had opted out of wearing a bralette and instead chose a beige camisole. Whit circled one of her peaked nipples with his thumb through the thin fabric, the cool air and his touch creating goosebumps along her skin.

Freyah released an involuntary whimper, and Whit looked utterly pleased with himself. He bent to press his hips harder against her own, the hardened muscles of his thigh doing wonders to soothe the ache between her legs.

"I have no problem pleasing you like this, beautiful," he told her between heavy breaths, "but I think you'd enjoy it better if I used my hands."

Freyah nodded fervently, giving him permission to proceed with whatever plan he had in mind. The thought of his rough hands against her sensitive flesh sounded glorious, and she was overly wet for him already. Again, she felt slightly embarrassed, but when he dipped his hand down the front of her leggings, the look on his face was nothing less than unadulterated elation.

"Fuck, Freyah. Is that all for me?"

She couldn't answer him with words, because his index finger had slipped between her folds to tease that most sensitive bundle of nerves. Freyah bit her bottom lip and tossed her head back against the wall. She gazed awestruck at the sky above her, but the sight was meaningless. It didn't matter that it was still daylight, because she was seeing stars.

That deft finger of his slid inside her and crooked to find the perfect amount of pressure that would send her reeling. After a moment, Whit added another finger and began pumping slowly into her. Freyah moaned into his shoulder at the fullness he provided. She wanted more of it—all that he could give her—but it was too much.

It was too soon.

She couldn't let herself get carried away with a fleeting moment of euphoria. And that notion was all good and well until his thumb slid over that bundle of nerves again. She was already entranced by the feeling of him inside her, but with a few long and languid strokes of his thumb, Freyah could feel her insides start to tighten.

She needed the release.

"Faster," she muttered, dropping her forehead to his chest.

Whit tilted his head so that his lips were pressed to her temple, just above her ear. "What was that, beautiful?"

"Faster, please," she begged him. "I need you to move faster."

That time he must have heard her instructions loud and clear, because the next thing she knew Whit was yanking her leggings down her thighs along with her underwear.

"Since you asked so nicely," he purred.

Then, with the fingers of his right hand still buried within her, Whit began to use his left to massage her clit. His fingers slid over her at a steady pace, slick with her desire, and with every moan or whimper that escaped Freyah's mouth, he moved a little bit faster. He used one hand to rub small, quick circles while the other continued to pump into her.

It didn't take long after that.

Whit sent her careening toward her climax, and as she tumbled over the edge into that awaiting abyss, they held each other close and savored the last few precious seconds they had left.

Before reality came crashing back in.

Freyah threaded her fingers through his hair and accidentally brushed his ear. She lingered there, remembering the absence of it the last time they'd kissed. Whit felt her hesitation and retracted his fingers as he pulled back to look at her. She immediately hated the emptiness it created within her.

"Do you think of me differently now?" he asked, a resigned look on his face.

She should have considered the question longer—she should have taken her time and given him a thoughtful answer—but instead she found herself telling him, "No."

A wave of relief seemed to settle over him. He clearly thought she'd answer differently. Would he regret what they did if she had? He captured her face in his hands and gave her a long, meaningful kiss. Then he reached to tug at the waistband of her leggings and pulled them back into place.

Whit helped her fully redress and then proceeded to adjust himself. She reached to touch him, but he grabbed her hand gently. He kissed the inside of her wrist, traveling all the way up her arm, then he tucked a lock of hair behind her ear.

"Not yet," he told her. "If I let you touch me like that, I won't be able to stop myself from taking you completely."

Freyah shuddered at the thought. She wanted nothing more than for him to fulfill that threat. Even after being rocked by the most intense orgasm of her life, she was still aching for more. She'd tasted a very addictive drug, and now she didn't know if she'd ever be able to live without it.

She entwined her fingers with his. "What if that's what I want?"

His smile was like the warmest rays of sun in a world full of shadows. "I'm sure you do," he told her smugly. "But we still have a lot between us that needs sorting out. I don't want you to act on something out of impulse and later regret it."

It was irritatingly noble, and it made her respect him even more. But still, she couldn't help but be disappointed. What they'd just done was act on an impulse, and as far as Freyah could tell, the world wasn't falling apart because of it.

Not yet anyway.

After all, Whit had been the one to initiate it—he'd practically begged to touch her—but he'd probably just been responding to the look of desire in her eyes, egging him on.

"You did that on purpose, didn't you?" she goaded.

There was no way for him to hide his own pride.

"Now you've had a taste of what I can give you," he teased. Then, with a more serious tone he added, "When you're ready to trust me again, I'll be there."

He tugged her by the hand and led her out of the alcove and back across the sweeping lawn. Once they were in the open, however, he released his grip.

The act was necessary, but it created a new type of loneliness that hadn't been present inside Freyah before. It was a different sort of loneliness—not one that yearned for her family or her home. It was a new longing for someone to love her. Someone to complete the missing half of her heart and protect it. It wasn't likely that Whit would be that person for her, but in that moment, as they trekked back up the castle steps and into the front hall, she pretended he could be.

WHIT

Whit leaned casually against the entrance of the barracks and looked out upon the Samhain bonfire climbing higher and higher into the mahogany sky. He'd never wanted to participate in the celebration of the end of the harvest season before, but knowing Freyah was locked in her room, away from the food and the dancing and general merriment…he found himself changing his mind.

For her.

Everything about this year felt different.

He wanted to walk the grounds with her and try all the delectable treats from different districts of the country. He wanted to show her the tents with fortune tellers and laugh together about the one set aside for kinkier games. But more than that, he wanted to protect and cherish her. Her courage and determination amazed him, and he was envious of her for it. Whit had always been stubborn, but never in a way that counted for anything. He wanted to be the good guy, and Freyah was naturally good.

Especially after what they'd done in that alcove.

The sounds of her whimpers still echoed in his ears, and he had to constantly redirect his thoughts so he wouldn't get hard in front of other soldiers.

Their stolen moment hadn't made much of a difference, though, because despite her clearly wanting to share her body, she still didn't trust him with her heart.

If only he could take it all back—go back to the day he'd first laid eyes on her in Last Cove and warn her and Brennan.

If only he'd told them to leave the country and not look back. Whit wished more than anything that he could take it all back and stop things before they'd ever begun.

Then again, if that were the case, he never would have known her like he knew her now. And *gods*, he couldn't imagine a life not knowing Freyah Kenpaw.

Once she and Brennan were free and safe from the witch-queen's clutches, maybe then she would finally forgive him. Maybe then, they could truly start over. Because even though she'd let him past her walls the night before, she'd remained guarded.

Freyah may have opened the gates to her personal kingdom, but she hadn't lowered her weapons.

Throughout the entirety of their stolen moment together—while he'd had his hand between her thighs and her fingers tangled in his hair—Freyah had been aimed and ready to fire. She could have let an arrow of refusal shoot straight into his heart. But she hadn't fired. She'd let him pleasure her, and she'd allowed herself to enjoy it.

He'd felt like such a prick afterwards, teasing her about what she could look forward to. Whit knew better. He was only torturing himself. Knowing what she felt like—the way she'd clenched around his fingers as he'd slid into her slick heat—had driven his lustful thoughts to the brink for twenty-four hours straight. The thought had kept him awake the entire night, and now here he was again, thinking about how wet she'd been for him.

Fuck.

Whit's gaze lifted from the fire in the distance and was drawn to the turret of the western tower above him. From where he stood outside the barracks, he had a perfect view of her window. He squinted his eyes to better focus on the room beyond, and he could just make out the faint glow of the lantern beside her bed. She was probably reading one of those swoon-worthy romance books, or maybe she was gazing out the window, just out of sight, watching the festival below.

He hoped that she was looking for him, just as he was looking for her.

He hated that she'd been bound to her room, unable to visit the library that had become their small haven for such a short time.

But tonight, he would make up for all of it. Every regret that haunted his dreams at night. All the pain he'd caused Freyah and her father. His lack of courage to stand up to Madam Lema. More than any of that, he wanted to make up for failing his sisters. Whit still felt the sting of Wendi's death with every breath he drew into his lungs, and though it might not seem like it from the outside, he held that pain close.

It reminded him to always do better.

Be better.

For Willow, and now for Freyah.

As he continued to stare longingly at Freyah's window, Whit let his chaotic thoughts drift, so much that when a hand slapped against his shoulder blade, he instinctively jumped.

"Steady now," Oliver coaxed him with a wide smile. "You day-dreaming about that girl of yours?"

"Sorry. I've got a lot on my mind right now."

"Yeah, about that." Oliver handed Whit a tin mug that was less than half full. "Why don't you offload some of those thoughts with a pint?"

Whit scowled at the offer, but Oliver insisted, so he took the mug. The swelling in his wrist had gone down enough that he no longer needed to keep it wrapped, but the strength in his grip hadn't fully recovered. As his fingers held the mug, a sharp pain shot through his wrist and up to his elbow, but he ignored it.

"Go on and down the rest of that," Oliver said. "I'll get us some fresh ones."

Whit didn't feel like drinking, but the thought of alcohol numbing his maelstrom of emotions was somewhat enticing.

He swallowed what was left in the mug in two gulps and grimaced at the taste. It was beer. Whit hated beer—he much preferred the taste of ale or wine. Beer fell flat on his tongue and left a bad aftertaste. It also wasn't nearly strong enough to drown out all of his thoughts and feelings.

Nonetheless, Oliver returned a minute later holding a large pitcher and another tin mug. He'd already poured a helping for himself, and the idiot was now attempting to fill Whit's before he stopped walking. The beer splashed over the top of the pitcher and sloshed onto the grass.

"Watch it!" Whit exclaimed. "How many of these have you had already?"

"M'ot enough."

That was definitely a lie. The man's words were already slurring.

Whit couldn't help but laugh. He wanted his friend to have a good time. The energy in their group had been tense as of late, and he knew the responsibility for it had fallen mostly on his own shoulders. He didn't like the idea of Oliver and Perry helping to hold his baggage. They had enough of their own to worry about.

As far as Whit knew, Perry had not told Oliver about his part in burying the Spyder, and that knowledge added an extra layer of guilt onto Whit's ever-growing pile of sins. Perry and Oliver were honest with one another to a fault—they were one of the healthiest couples Whit had ever known—so Whit understood how significant it was that Perry had chosen to keep such a massive secret from his partner. All to protect *him*.

Not thirty feet from where Oliver stood, Micah's body lay rotting beneath a pile of shit. Whit envied his friend's ignorance. He wished he could enjoy a cold drink without the murder of a fellow demon looming over him.

Whit hadn't fully accepted the fact that he'd killed another person. It hung there in the recesses of his conscience, but he refused to acknowledge it. This was only the second life he'd ever taken, but neither were just *lives*. They'd been demon lives—one of his own—and yet he'd killed them. Both for Freyah.

Whit was beginning to think he would be willing to do just about anything for her.

But had Micah been an actual demon? He still didn't understand how the Spyder had changed his form at will. The ability reeked of dark magic, and it only made him all the more fearful for Freyah. If Madam Lema was using such magic to somehow create her own demons, the war ahead of them was looking even more grim.

The constant threat of what could happen next had caused a consistent tightness in Whit's chest. He felt as though his heart was beating at triple the speed, and he couldn't force it to slow down, no matter how many deep breaths he took or relaxing thoughts he tried to conjure.

He needed to relax and enjoy himself for one night, probably more than anyone. But he had so many secrets to keep, and the pressure of his impending plan to help Brennan and Freyah escape weighed him down like a stone, causing his shoulders to visibly slump with the reminder. He wanted to set that weight aside for a few hours and take a break—to fully let himself go and succumb to his diluted inhibitions—but he couldn't do that. He needed to keep his mind clear for what was ahead of him. Not to mention he definitely didn't want another embarrassing incident like the talking fish in Last Cove.

Whit and Oliver wandered the outskirts of the festival with their beers in hand. Whit had yet to take another sip, but Oliver had poured the remainder of the pitcher straight down his own throat and caught the eyes of several others around them—some having been impressed and some downright disturbed.

Oliver had informed him that they would be meeting up with Perry by the fire. His partner was one of many soldiers that had been instructed to stoke the fire in shifts throughout the duration of the festival, and it was actually an impressive feat. Whit had always thought the massive bonfire was kept alight by witch magic, but knowing how it was actually done added to the allure. The fire was kept alive by the hands of those that served the earth—the perfect way of showing respect to Mother Nature.

When they spotted Perry offloading the last of his logs onto the burning pile, Oliver rushed to his partner's side with a yelp of excitement.

Perry was nearly knocked over by Oliver's overly enthusiastic embrace, but he righted himself with a massive grin and pulled him into a tight hug. Perry placed a kiss on Oliver's temple, and Whit's heart tightened in response.

Though he was happy to see it, watching his friends embracing in front of him sent a rush of jealousy flooding over him. He ached for that sort of connection with someone—the physical and the emotional kind—and for just a brief moment, he thought he'd found it.

But of course, he'd gone and screwed it up.

Royally.

There were so many things he could have been doing at that moment. There were more drinks to be shared, games and dances to participate in, but he wanted none of it. What was the point of enjoying himself when he couldn't share it with someone?

Whit tried to imagine a world in which he didn't have to hide his demon identity. One where Willow hadn't been hurt and was standing beside him by the fire with a smile on her face.

One where Wendi was alive and well.

He imagined Freyah being there, too, walking the castle grounds hand in hand with him and perfectly safe.

He thought about going to her rooms right then and sneaking her out under the guise of a cloaking spell or anything else he could convince Raven to give him. But that was just it...no matter what solution he came up with, it always involved dragging someone else into the mess. And out of everyone, Whit especially didn't want to add any more to his debt with Raven.

After their less-than-consensual time together before his trip to Last Cove, approaching Raven for anything was the last thing Whit wanted to do. He dreaded having to ask for his next elixir refill, but at least he had a few more days before that would be necessary. She'd provided him with enough to get him through three weeks, allowing for any unexpected complications on his journey to Last Cove. Whit didn't want to wait until the last minute and risk missing a dose again, but he couldn't settle the unrest in his gut at the thought of seeing Raven again.

He had three more days.

He would be fine for three days.

Perry approached with Oliver hanging on his shoulder. "Looks like the two of you got a head start," he teased. "You couldn't wait for me?"

"I didn't have a say in that," Whit protested, tapping his now empty mug playfully against Oliver's chest.

But Oliver wasn't listening. He was too preoccupied with gazing lovingly at Perry's right ear. He raised a hand to stroke it, but Perry swatted it away.

"You get awfully touchy when you drink," Perry teased.

Oliver nudged his nose into the crook of Perry's neck. "I thought you liked that."

Perry looked at Whit and rolled his eyes. "Looks like we'll be calling it an early night."

"Whaaat?" Oliver protested. "But the sun's still out!" He squinted his eyes to peer at the ball of fire hovering low in the sky and scowled. "Is that the sun? I can't see it. Too bright."

"I think you're right," Whit told Perry.

He glanced around and noticed there were a handful of other soldiers eyeing Oliver's public display of affection. Everyone knew about their relationship, but that didn't mean they liked seeing it. Their judgment made Whit's blood boil, but there was no use shouting at a brick wall. He knew no matter how hard he tried, there was nothing he could say to change any of their minds.

No one could cure ignorance.

"Nooo!" Oliver cried, fisting a handful of Perry's shirt. "You haven't had a drink yet."

He looked around wildly in search of another beer, as if it would appear out of thin air on command, but Perry caught his jaw and swung Oliver's attention back to him. "You've had enough for the both of us, darling. Time for bed."

Whit lifted his eyes to the changing sky. The sun slipped closer and closer to the distant horizon, now merely a sliver of light in the impending darkness. It would be time for shift changes soon, and he would have to check in with the men guarding the dungeon for the rest of night.

There were four guards on Whit's team that he was responsible for, and two of them had just sauntered off to bed. That left Thomas and William to handle the evening shift, and they were both good men. William had been in line to make lieutenant before Whit, but he'd given up the position because he didn't want the responsibility. Thomas was new—he'd been recommended by his older brother, who was a member of the tactical team—and his lack of experience meant the prisoners might try to get one over on him. He would have to grow a bigger set of balls if he wanted to keep being a guard.

Whit drained what little beer remained at the bottom of his mug and added it to a stack of empty tankards that were piling up on a table nearby. Perry gave him a knowing nod, then escorted his partner back to the barracks as Whit headed in the opposite direction.

He reached the outer entrance of the dungeons by the time the sun had completely tucked itself beneath the horizon for the night. The previous mahogany hue was now a deep purple, and Whit could see the shadows of everyone congregating by the fire as they cast themselves against the outline of the forest beyond. The wind was beginning to pick up, and before continuing down the dirt slope that led into the dungeons, he glanced back up at the night sky. The shift had been sudden, but the clouds were now dark and full of rage.

It was going to rain.

40

FREYAH

The hours trickled by like the raindrops now slowly dripping down Freyah's window. She'd known she wouldn't be allowed to participate in the Samhain festivities, but she had thought that Whit at least might visit her.

But he never came.

Instead she'd been confined to her room, the only entertainment being what she was able to glimpse on the castle lawns below her.

Her room was located in the smallest turret of the western tower, so the view below was mostly covered by the Saldanni Forest. Other than the area around the barracks, there was a short stretch of the grounds that led around to the back of the castle. It appeared to go directly to the gardens, and within that small area were several looming tents that had been erected the night before. She'd seen them when Whit had pulled her into that alcove.

Gods. The things that man had done with his hands.

That *demon.*

When Whit had touched her, she'd forgotten what he was. Forgotten everything he'd done, and everything he hadn't. None of it mattered as long as he was touching her. Stirring that desperate pull deep in her core that made her want to scream his name.

She could separate her attraction to him from her guarded heart.

She could keep her feelings at bay until this was all over.

At least, that's what she'd told herself after he'd led her back to her room and she'd been forced to sit there for hours reliving the orgasm he'd given her.

There was no use getting caught up in her lust when she would soon be running for her life. And her father's. They were escaping tonight, and she would most likely never see Whit again.

What did it matter if they'd momentarily given in to their lustful desires?

It was like a goodbye of sorts. A final farewell.

Freyah had told the truth when he'd asked her whether or not she looked at him differently now—Whit being a demon had been an incredible shock, but it wasn't a dealbreaker. It didn't bother her, but for some reason that felt wrong.

Was her prejudice so deeply ingrained? It was as if her brain was telling her to see him as a creature, while her heart saw nothing but a man.

Yet his greatest offense had not been his demon nature.

No, Freyah still hadn't grappled with the fact that Whit was the one responsible for kidnapping her. If it weren't for him, she and her father would be safe at home in Last Cove. It felt impossible to forgive Whit for something that had forever changed the course of her life, but her desire for him had won out. In that one moment, alone in the alcove, it felt okay to let all her grievances go. She wanted more times like that with him. She wanted more opportunities to turn off her brain and let her heart take the wheel. Being in the shadows had felt safe. It had felt like a secret she could keep even from herself. So she told herself that as long as she kept it there, within the shadows and tucked away from the light, it was okay.

Freyah had to shake her head to stop herself from tumbling back into the memory of last night. Just thinking about it made her clench her thighs together. Instead, she moved to the window.

One of the corner panes was loose, so she'd tilted it to let in the fresh air. The smoke of the large bonfire wafted into her room. The orange haze of it climbed high along the side of the castle, and she imagined its warmth, even though she was too far away to actually feel it. The raucous conversations and laughter had echoed throughout the grounds, but as it got later, the voices morphed into music, and she was lulled to sleep by the sound of a string instrument playing a soothing tune.

When she woke, Freyah was glad to have caught at least a short nap while she could, because there would be no sleep for her tonight. She felt rested enough in her mind, but her body protested as she shifted out of the stiff position she'd landed in while sitting in the loft. This time when she looked out the window, she'd found rain droplets smudging the glass.

Still, the bonfire remained alight.

The sweet and somber string music from earlier had given way to intense drum beats and chanting from those below. Their looming shadows danced across her walls.

Tonight was the Samhain Ball, and Whit had yet to provide her with a dress like he'd promised. Still, Freyah couldn't help but perk up from the excitement of attending an actual ball, at a castle no less. It would be the most extravagant party she'd ever attended, but she had to remind herself that she wasn't making an appearance as herself, and she wouldn't be there to have a good time. It was merely a cover— a way to get her past the soldiers and into the dungeons so she could escape with her father before his execution tomorrow.

The days leading up to her father's execution had passed in record time. It felt like Freyah had only just heard the news. They'd had one week to prepare, and now that week was gone.

Tonight was their one shot.

It was all or nothing.

As the deep purple of the night sky bled across the clouds, a sudden knock came at her door.

Her heart leapt at the thought of it being Whit standing on the other side, and she was across the room in seconds to open it, only to find that it wasn't Whit.

In fact, there was no one there at all.

Only a long rectangular box tied with twine sat on the threshold. When Freyah bent to pick it up, a small note fell out from where it had been tucked beneath the string. There were only two words.

For tonight.
- W

Freyah closed the door quickly. Whit must have delivered the package discreetly, dropping it at her door quietly and then darting away as quickly as a cat before anyone else could see him.

Her excitement took over, and she eagerly pulled at the twine so she could remove the lid. She unfolded the wrappings inside to find the most gorgeous gown she'd ever seen, along with a pair of strappy gold heels.

This was from Whit—a present in its own right, and the first he'd ever given her. Well, that wasn't entirely true. He'd given her the hawk carving, and that was certainly more meaningful than a dress. But there was a part of her that hoped he'd picked this out with the thought of seeing her in it. He had only ever seen her in drab clothing. Dirt-worn and torn from travel or hand-me-downs given to her as a courtesy. She'd never worn dresses at home in the mountains, for they were impractical and not her style. But she wanted to dress up for him. She wanted to style her hair and wear a fancy gown and cherish his reaction to seeing her like that for the first time.

With all of that in mind, Freyah eagerly prepared for the ball.

She brushed her fingers through her hair and managed to get rid of most of the tangles. She braided it against her scalp on either side and pulled it together into a low bun at the back of her head. Then she slipped into the dress. It hugged her in all the right places and showed off her curves even more than her leggings did. She didn't realize until the dress was already on that there was something else inside the package.

Fit snugly into the bottom of the box, staring back at her with an invitation of bravery and power, was a mask.

FREYAH STOOD before the entrance to the Grand Hall in her new, shimmering gold gown. The straps criss-crossed down her back and knotted into an elegant bow at the base of her spine, exposing her shoulder blades and a swath of skin. The front showed off a high neckline embroidered with delicate lace and sequins, and the skirt cascaded down her legs in multiple layers of smooth silk.

She felt elegant, even regal, as she walked across the Grand Hall in a pair of heels for the first time in her life. Her steps were unsteady, but her newfound confidence kept her upright.

She took in the grandeur all around her, noticing the tiniest of details in the decor that she and Jessa had helped to create. Small trees with bare branches had been erected along the dais at the front of the hall, adorned with handmade ornaments that would bring luck for an easy winter. There were hundreds of candles dangling from string along the ceiling, illuminating everything with a golden hue. There were pumpkins on every table, as well as elaborate bouquets of orange and yellow flowers. The result was magnificent, and Freyah felt like she was walking into a fairy tale, instead of the endless nightmare she'd been living.

Her eyes sought out the only person in the room she wanted to see, but she knew she would have difficulty finding him in a mask. Her own disguise consisted of a gold-flecked deer mask that covered her face from forehead to nose. It had elegant white antlers protruding from the temples, and while was heavy to bear, it empowered her. She felt like a weapon ready to be wielded, while still maintaining a sense of anonymity.

It appeared that everyone else was donning animal masks as well. There were bears and lions, birds with long beaks, and even a few others with horns. The ones on Freyah's mask were long and elegant, but she spotted one similar to the ox-demon she'd come across in the Saldanni Forest—the one Whit had killed.

The fact that witches wore masks to look like the creatures they deemed to be lesser...They were clearly mocking the demons, openly and under the guise of being festive.

The act made Freyah sick, and she wanted to rip off her own mask in protest, but she knew she couldn't.

She had to stay hidden, or the entire plan would fall apart.

Freyah wound her way through the throngs of people who sipped wine from thin goblets and murmured fanatically about each others' attire and elaborate headpieces. She overheard a witch going on about not having the right shoes to match her dress, and Freyah had to suppress an eye-roll beneath her mask. She wanted to swap the dreaded heels she wore for her leather boots, but it was imperative that she blend in and look the part. Whit had made that the utmost priority, for if there was even the slightest hint of suspicion, they'd lose the element of surprise.

Her father's life now hung on Freyah's ability to keep her self-control and not interfere. And it was proving to be more and more difficult, because on more than one occasion, she'd overheard something dreadful that made her want to smack the wine glasses from those awful witches' hands.

She needed to get a grip on that, or slapping things might very well end up becoming her signature move.

She'd purposefully arrived late to give herself as little time to mess things up as possible. The clock wasn't far from striking midnight—only half an hour to spare—so she didn't have to worry about dallying too long. Freyah would sip her wine, appear to be having a good time, then casually slip out unnoticed. Except as soon as she took a glass from beside the fountain of wine, a tall stranger began walking toward her with purpose.

When he approached, he stretched out his hand and bowed low, nearly kissing his own kneecaps in the process. He had a head full of curly black hair, and he wore a simple white mask just large enough to hide the space around his eyes. Several black tattoos creeped down the neck of his lightly bronzed skin and underneath his collar.

"Would you like to dance, my lady?" he inquired. He rose to his full height, his arm still outstretched and waiting for her to take his hand.

"I couldn't help but notice you've been wandering alone for several minutes, and I couldn't bear the thought of not offering my company."

His voice was lathered in a thick accent that Freyah couldn't quite place. It was unique and clipped, unlike anything she'd ever heard before. Almost like he hadn't spent much time among the people of Ghoma to pick up on their dialect. Growing up in the seclusion of the mountain had made Freyah extremely curious about those that were not like her, and she was definitely *curious* about this stranger.

Where was he from?

Perhaps Pykard?

It was probably best to shrug it off and bid him a good day, but her intrigue was too strong to let such an opportunity pass by.

"And you are?" she drawled, keeping her head tilted low in order to cast shadows onto her face.

"Koa, my lady. Pleased to make your acquaintance, Miss…?"

He left the sentence hanging in the air, waiting for her to provide him with a name of her own.

"Corianne," she said without thinking.

It was the first name that came to mind, and the mention of her best friend made her heart race, knowing they would soon be reunited.

The man's brows drew together above his thin mask, and his mouth tightened in a skeptical expression.

Did he not believe her?

"Interesting," Koa finally said. "Not what I expected."

"Excuse me?"

"I'm sorry, my lady," Koa apologized dramatically, sweeping himself into another low bow. "I meant no offense. It's just that, for a moment, I thought I had finally found the person I've been looking for."

Now Freyah was even more curious.

They'd drawn the attention of several others, who watched their interaction with keen interest, waiting for something amusing to happen. No doubt listening in for gossip.

Freyah dismissed the man's gesture and shook her head. "No offense taken. But you must excuse me. I have somewhere to be."

She hoped he would take the hint and leave her alone, but Koa merely lifted his head and eyed her, his longing clear through his mask. He clearly wanted something from her—*needed* it almost. Did he know her somehow?

That was Freyah's cue to leave. She couldn't risk being identified, so she didn't wait for Koa to respond. Instead, she ducked past the gaggle of women that still watched the exchange and made a beeline for the front of the hall. She had to squeeze between couples as they glided in step across the floor to the beats of the shawm as it continued to play a jaunty tune. It was a fast song, so Freyah was continuously knocked about by elbows and colliding with backs. Eventually, she made it to a fairly vacant area right in front of the dais.

There were a handful of witches speaking in serious tones with various men of nobility as they stood beneath the barren branches of a decorative tree. Freyah knew that there would be representatives of each district attending the Samhain Ball on behalf of their people, but she had no way of recognizing them, with or without masks.

Freyah hovered close to the ivory throne that had been moved into the Grand Hall and scanned the crowd once more for Whit. He should have shown up by now, but he hadn't told her what his mask would look like, so she didn't know what to look for. Her gaze landed on several guards of the same height and build, but he was not among them.

She was near giving up and planned to move back through the crowd to the other side of the Hall when a sudden pull in her gut made her turn her head.

She knew it was him by the immediate way his presence filled the room. He was walking straight toward her, head held high and face covered with a stunning blue velvet mask. The edges of it fanned out into delicate wings that spread around his cheeks and looked as if they would catch the wind and take flight at any moment. The center of the mask stretched down the length of his long nose and tapered to a point resembling a beak, the bridge covered with shimmering glitter that reflected the light from the candles above and stood out starkly against the rest of the matte material.

His hair was swept away from his face and tucked behind his ears. She'd never seen it styled so nicely—for as long as she'd known him, there had always been at least one stray hair out of place. He gave her a welcoming smile, and she could see through the slits in his mask that it reached his eyes. They were creased with genuine happiness to see her.

Whit stopped in front of her, and she took in his outfit. He wore a light blue tunic beneath a vest of navy crushed velvet. The vest was adorned with gold buttons that matched her dress and a swirling fleur de lis that began at his shoulders and curled down his chest. He wore dark trousers and a sash around his waist to match. Seeing him so freshly dressed and put together was odd. It made him even more handsome. Despite the juxtaposition of his clothes and the permanent scar that peeked out beneath the mask, he actually fit in with the gaudy crowd around them. The scarred skin still stood out, but that mark was simply a part of him now, and Freyah could no longer think of Whit without it.

"You look beautiful," he complimented her.

He reached for her hand, and she gladly offered it. The hesitance she'd previously felt around him had somehow disappeared, so she let him kiss the top of her hand, his lips brushing lightly against her skin.

He then grabbed her waist with his other hand and pulled her against him. They began to move rhythmically to the music and, all the while, Whit kept his head on a swivel, taking in his surroundings. He'd told her previously that demons were not invited to the ball, for the celebration was meant for the queen and her coven to host the human representatives of Ghoma. The soldiers and their families were invited to attend, but no demon was to set foot in the Great Hall during the ball. Despite the absurd command, Freyah still felt their presence all around her. They were in every animal mask the people wore as a mockery of their kind.

She wondered what Whit must think of it all. At least his mask reflected his own demon-nature. It was beautiful, and for a moment, he could proudly display who he was to the world.

"Where did you get the dress?" Freyah asked him skeptically. She'd been curious ever since opening the parcel.

"Willow found it in storage," he said. "It fits you perfectly."

Her breath hitched, and despite the loud music and the constant chatter of the crowd, she knew he'd heard it.

His grip tightened on her lower back, and his fingers dug into her flesh, bunching the material. Her mind wandered to what it would feel like for those fingers to slide beneath the fabric. She remembered the rough calluses at his fingertips and how they'd grazed the sensitive flesh between her thighs. She instinctively clenched her core in response, and heat rushed to her cheeks.

His head cocked with curiosity, and he smirked. "Thinking about anything in particular?"

Freyah tried to rein in the blush she knew was spreading down her neck. That was one of the negatives of having such pale skin: she couldn't hide her embarrassment.

Whit's hand trailed lower until it rested on the curve of her backside. With his other hand, he began tracing small circles with his thumb along the inside of her wrist. He leaned his head down, and she felt the brush of his stubbled chin against her throat.

"I've been thinking about it, too," he said, his voice lowering to a deep and seductive whisper.

His words sent a shiver down her spine, the deep thrall of them sliding over her like honey, and she wanted to taste it on her tongue. She missed the way his body had felt so close to hers. She needed to feel him inside her again.

All of him this time.

To feel his mouth on hers, their breaths mingling.

"I wish we could go somewhere alone," he whispered against her ear.

The shivers he elicited traveled from her earlobe to her ankles, and he tensed as he held her tighter, knowing the reaction he was causing. She could tell he reveled in it. She clearly hadn't been the only one to enjoy herself that night, and by the way he still gripped the small of her back, he wanted a repeat occurrence just as much as she did.

Freyah parted her lips to say something, but she held onto her words when she realized that the conversations around them were quieting. The constant chatter from those nearby had dulled into low murmurs. Something had enraptured everyone's attention, but Freyah couldn't determine what.

It was Whit that caught on first, and he spun her around to face the dais. His body remained pressed close to her back, his warmth keeping her calm in the face of her new greatest enemy.

Madam Lema had entered the Grand Hall along with every one of her personal guards. They flanked her as she walked up the steps to her throne of ivory, one of them even extending his hand to help her along the way.

She wore a long, black gossamer gown that resembled pure starlight. The top was made of a sheer tulle emblazoned with golden stars bursting across the fabric, and the skirt hugged past her narrow hips and down to her knees before fanning out in a circle of night sky that hit the floor. She wore a pair of black lace gloves—to hide her stained fingers, no doubt—and on her left hand was a large gold ring. Her collar was cut low to her navel, and around her neck hung the same ornate black gem Freyah had seen her wear every day. Tonight, Madam Lema had matched it with several thin gold chains that hung above and below the stone, one settling deep in the low neck of the dress. To top it all off, a crown of purest gold sat atop her head. Freyah could imagine the weight of the elaborate piece as it balanced atop the witch-queen's head.

This was the first time Freyah had ever seen Madam Lema wear a crown, and it made her look even more intimidating than she already did. She hated to admit it, but Freyah thought it made the witch look stunningly regal.

Freyah glanced around and noticed that the majority of those in attendance were wearing items of gold as well, whether it be in the color of their fancy attire or the jewelry they bore. Apparently, gold was on theme, and Freyah wondered if Whit had known that and planned accordingly with the dress he'd gotten from Willow.

Madam Lema sat down on her ivory throne and gazed out at the crowd with haughty importance. Freyah had never stood close enough to the chair to note its detail, and a gasp caught in her throat when she realized what it was crafted from. Each leg was a complete columned spine, and an odd-looking skull rested on the end of both arms. She could see Madam Lema's long, sharp nails clutching the pates, her index finger sinking into empty eye sockets. The back of the throne was made of mismatched bones of all shapes and sizes. They'd been shaved to fit into one another like a macabre puzzle.

Freyah's gut clenched.

"Demon bones," Whit told her with quiet restraint, noticing where her attention had turned.

And he was right.

At closer inspection, Freyah saw the skulls resembled animals she'd seen before: birds and bears, a wolf and a large cat. Those bones once belonged to demons, but because of their faction, they'd been killed. The bones were old, each one yellowed and brittle with age. It was surprising that the throne still stood to hold Madam Lema's weight, but it had been constructed soundly.

Madam Lema waited until everyone in the Hall fell into a reverent silence and the musicians had ceased playing. She basked in their undivided attention.

"Welcome," the queen bellowed, her voice carrying over the crowd.

Whit's hand remained on Freyah's hip protectively, and they both froze in anticipation of what Madam Lema had to say.

"On this night," she began, "the last of the harvest season, we show gratitude to the Mother for her blessings upon the land. We give thanks to Her nature for providing us with nutrients and the tools we need to sustain a healthy and purposeful life. As the full moon shines high in the sky tonight, allow it to guide you into the next season with intention. This winter will be hard, and we will need to remain strong. But know that as long as you are loyal to the crown, you will be protected and provided for. There is a storm coming. When it does, I suggest you know where your loyalties lie."

Whit's grip tightened on Freyah's hip, and she heard him release a low growl. Freyah turned to face him just as the queen gestured to the musicians to start up again.

Whit's face was contorted into hateful resentment.

"What is it?" Freyah asked. She attempted to release herself from his grip, but he only held her more firmly.

"Those fuckers were right."

He'd muttered it mostly to himself, but Freyah had heard enough to ask a follow-up question. "Who?"

Whit finally released her and ran a hand over his face. Even his facial hair had been trimmed into submission. The look suited him, but Freyah had to admit she preferred the rougher version of him.

"Two of the men that went with me to retrieve your father—I heard them talking, and they seemed to be under the impression that he is the catalyst for something much bigger." Whit paused and took a breath. "They think the queen is going to start another war."

Freyah had tried to understand Madam Lema's motivations from the moment she'd met her, but nothing the witch-queen asked of her had been clear. At first, Freyah had thought the queen was offering her temporary asylum in exchange for a bit of advice on how to keep the peace, but that had turned into the witch-queen prying into her memories and learning that her father was involved with The First Men.

Throughout all of it, there had been a clear question hanging in the air ever since: why Freyah?

Had it been mere coincidence that Madam Lema had chosen the one girl in the furthest village from Larapuna who happened to be the daughter of a rebellion leader? Or had she always known?

It was almost like she'd needed an excuse to go after them—proof to validate an impending war. The First Men were faceless, and their acts of protest had all remained anonymous. Part of their mystery was the idea that no one knew who was behind it all. Freyah had walked past hundreds of men and women in the Hub every day, and any one of them could have been a member.

Freyah's brow furrowed. "How?"

"The rebels are organized. Loyal," he explained. "If anything happened to one of their own…"

"She's going to make him a martyr."

Whit nodded.

With her father clearly outed, Madam Lema now had the perfect scapegoat. He was a smaller target, one that had been easiest to catch, and now that she had him, she would publicly shame him and execute his punishment for Ghoma's most important leaders to see.

The queen would wait with weapons drawn for The First Men to make their move. And if they struck first, the responsibility of starting a war wouldn't fall on her shoulders.

If the entire thing hadn't uprooted her life and threatened everything she cherished most, Freyah would have to admit that the plan was genius. It was just the type of passive-aggressive, manipulative bullshit that Madam Lema would pull.

Whit's face was now determined, no longer creased with worry. "We can't fail tonight."

Gathering as much calm and focus as she could muster, she took Whit's hand in hers, and together they made their way to the dungeon entrance right as the clock struck twelve.

41

LYRA

In the early hours of the morning, before the sun's rays were able to spread their warmth across the stone floor where she rested, the pain woke Lyra. It greeted her with a sharp stab to her lower abdomen, then a tug in her core. She could feel her muscles stretching and contracting as they started working to dispatch the new life that had developed inside her.

The month had flown by, and throughout that final week, Lyra watched with fear and fascination as her stomach grew to bursting. She had no way of knowing whether or not Oram had received her message, but she hoped for his sake that he trusted her enough to follow her request.

Wait for me in the wood.

She was due any day, so when the first bouts of pain began to cascade from her lower back all the way down to her knees, she knew the time had come.

Her cry had startled the young guard keeping watch, and he rushed to her cell to see what was wrong. When he spotted Lyra writhing on the floor, hands clutching her belly, his face grew pale and he rushed off to alert the others.

A bell chimed from somewhere on the upper level, and the echo of it reverberated through the cracks in the stone wall. The elders were being alerted that a new life was coming. There were candles to light and prayers to be muttered to the Mother, all to usher in a new generation of witches that might be born. Lyra did not want the fuss or the pomp and circumstance. She wanted to give birth in peace and then quietly slip away to be reunited with Oram. But that was only going to happen if her and Fatima's scheme went according to plan.

When the baby was ready, the eldest healer, Astrid, and a few other witches would need to be there to help with the delivery, and Lyra should be granted the presence of her handmaid to assist. Any more than that, and Fatima wouldn't be able to swap places with her. There would be too many witnesses—too many prying, watchful eyes to foil their plan.

She wondered whether or not they'd take her to a private room. Someplace with a comfortable bed and a pillow to prop her head up with. It was more likely that they'd leave her in the dungeon to give birth like a cat in a barn.

Lema didn't care how comfortable Lyra was. She only needed to know what came out of her when it was all said and done.

The waves of pain crested closer together.

She was definitely in labor.

Lyra had barely been able to enjoy her pregnancy, for most of that time had been spent in a cage. It wasn't supposed to be like this. Witches having babies was supposed to be celebrated. Instead, she was being treated like a criminal.

She let out another cry of agony and moved into a crouched position. Her knees dug into the stone floor painfully, but the pain in her core was much worse. She tried to take deep breaths, remembering the only time she'd witnessed a member of her coven give birth. It had been sixteen years prior, and the thing that stood out most vividly to Lyra was the cries of pain that clawed out of the female's throat like a banshee. She'd never witnessed nor felt pain such as that before, but now she was living it. The elders had instructed the mother to breathe, slow and deep and, at the time, Lyra had thought it to be a simple task. But she'd been terribly wrong. Lyra tried to gasp for air, but the contractions stole the breath from her lungs, and instead, she found herself gaping open mouthed in a silent scream to Lillia to make it stop.

The door to the dungeons burst open and several witches filed in carrying wet rags. One held a full bottle of what looked like kratom powder for pain, and another was already prepared with a set of sharp knives still glowing red from being freshly sterilized in a fire. Lyra prayed that they would not have to cut the baby out of her. She'd never seen it done, but it had been written about in their history—one of the elders, Ada LeBlanc, had been delivered by blade, her mother then bleeding out in her bed.

Lyra was determined to remain in this world to personally see to the protection of her child, but based on the amount of pain she was experiencing, she worried that her chances were growing slimmer.

Astrid's face appeared in front of her. She was still on her knees, her head bowed low to the floor. Astrid crouched beside her and tried to lift her into a sitting position, but Lyra could not move. She wanted to stay like this forever, clutching her belly with her cheek pressed against the cool stone.

"We must get you into position, my lady." The voice had come from another witch in the room. A hand pressed to the small of her back. "Let us help you stand."

The most recent contraction had finally subsided, so Lyra was able to raise herself to sit back on her heels. Her skin was clammy, and she could feel a dozen loose strands of hair clinging to her forehead from sweat. Immediately there was a damp rag pressed to her temple.

Astrid wiped the hair from Lyra's face and dampened her cheeks. "Can you walk?"

Lyra nodded. If she was going to move it needed to be now, before another landslide of pain overtook her. She managed to steady her feet beneath her with the help of two other witches, but her mind was so foggy she couldn't recognize who they were—they were just bodies on either side of her, guiding her out of the cell and through the dungeon.

She took one small step at a time, hardly aware of the men in the other cells watching the commotion. When she came to the stairs, she found that she barely had the strength to lift herself to the top of the landing. When she finally got there, she had to stop and take a breath. She didn't know how long it had taken to finally reach the outer door of the dungeon, but by the time they did, she felt the pull of another contraction.

This one was stronger than the last, and she immediately collapsed into the arms of the witch on her right, her weight nearly toppling them both. She heard Astrid giving commands to the others, but the words sounded far away. Lyra was stuck in her own body and unable to concentrate on anything other than the tidal wave of pain that washed over her. She felt like her legs were going to completely give out from under her, and they probably would have if not for the witches propping her up.

After the second contraction subsided, she made it as far as the front entrance outside the Grand Hall before another one rocked her. She didn't know where she was being taken, but she knew she wasn't going to make it. This spot was as good as any. They would have to leave her here, or else carry her up several flights of stairs to her chambers.

Astrid appeared to be thinking over that very possibility. "We have to keep moving," she told them all, not a hint of sympathy in her voice.

It was true. Lyra couldn't birth a child in the front entrance of the castle, so they continued through the corridors as she protested the entire way.

It took what felt like hours, but finally they reached her personal chamber.

"We'll need extra blankets and pillows. Sanitized with cleansing mist, of course." Astrid commanded the attention of every other witch around them, and per her instructions, two younger females scurried away to retrieve the items.

Lyra noticed that the witch holding the knives had stayed by the door. Her name was Samira, and she looked frightfully eager to be there. The way in which she clutched the utensils in her knobby little hands made Lyra's gut clench with a deep fear, for the witch looked far too willing and happy to slice into her.

Lyra prayed silently as she was lowered carefully into her bed. *Please, Lillia. Keep us safe.*

The next contraction was now rearing its ugly head, so Lyra braced herself on her elbows and held on to Astrid's forearm with a viselike grip. Her knuckles turned white with the force, but the tighter she squeezed, the more Astrid seemed to encourage her.

"I need to inspect the cervix, my lady," Astrid told her once the pain had ebbed. "You musn't push until it's time."

Lyra nodded like she understood, though she had no clue what that meant. All she knew was that she needed to get this child out of her before it ripped her in two. She flattened her back into the mattress once more and waited for the healer to do what she needed to. Lyra felt the witch's cool fingers touch her fiery flesh right where the ripping and stinging sensation felt the strongest. The witch felt the opening within her and seemed satisfied with whatever she'd discovered.

"It's wide enough," she confirmed to the others. "On the next contraction, you need to push. I felt a head, so the child is close."

Lyra's eyes went wide.

There was a head inside her, and it was trying to get out.

The realization sent a wave of nausea over her, and she had to fight the urge to pass out. Astrid stayed between her legs, so Lyra no longer had anyone to hold on to. She reached out her hand and grasped at thin air, hoping to catch hold of someone. Anyone that could help her through this agony.

Her fingers met flesh, and she looked over to find Fatima's kind caramel-colored eyes peering down into hers. Her handmaid clasped both hands over Lyra's and squeezed. "You can do this," she encouraged. "I'm right here."

Fatima's newfound confidence filled Lyra with a burst of determination so raw she swore she could feel the ground below her start to quake. Or maybe it was her own body that was shaking violently from nerves? She couldn't tell. All she knew was she had to let the untapped energy out. So when the next contraction hit, Lyra pushed with all her might. She clenched her muscles and shoved her entire will toward bringing her baby into the world. There were cheers of encouragement all around her, but she kept her focus on the only one that mattered—the only one still holding her hand.

Finally, after a long stretch of what felt like a fruitless effort, Lyra felt the most intense release she'd ever experienced. She felt weightless and drained. Her head immediately fell back, Fatima's hand right there to break her fall.

There was a brief moment of silence, and then a cry broke into the void. The words were spoken by Astrid. "We have a new witch in the coven!"

The relief was palpable. Lyra not only felt it fill her own chest, but she could see it in the beam that spread across Fatima's face as she leaned over her. There was a chorus of cheers and several prayers of thanks to Lillia.

"Get her cleaned and checked," Astrid told the others.

No one had given Lyra a chance to look at her own daughter, or hold her in her arms, for the two females that had gone to retrieve blankets were back just in time to whisk the child away. Lyra reached for them, but she was too weak to speak. She saw a small body being tucked into a fresh blanket, and then she was gone.

Fatima patted Lyra's head and wiped the sweat from her brow. "They're just going to make sure she's healthy and perform the proper spells," she reassured her.

Lyra nodded in vague understanding. Fatigue had settled over her like a fog so thick it clouded her vision. She now felt very close to succumbing to sleep.

Her eyes closed for half a second, and when she opened them, everyone had left save for Fatima, who was humming a soft tune and stripping Lyra of her soiled clothing.

"It's only been a few minutes." The girl had clearly noticed the look of fear and confusion on Lyra's face.

"When can I see her?"

"They'll be back soon. You need to rest so you can heal."

But something was wrong.

Lyra could feel the tightness in her stomach again, like another contraction was ready to form.

But that couldn't be right. Could it?

She sat up and grunted in pain, clutching her abdomen in horror.

"What's wrong?" Fatima asked, lines of concern etched into the creases of her eyes.

"I don't know. It feels like I'm about to give birth all over again."

Fatima stiffened. Her eyes darted around the room as if searching for answers. "It might be the placenta," she guessed. "I read about what happens in Astrid's medicinal journal. It's the home the baby lived in while you carried her. It has to come out."

"No, this is different," Lyra said. "This feels…the same."

Fatima's brow furrowed. "What do you mean?"

It seemed impossible, but everything in Lyra's gut told her that this was not over. She groaned as a new wave of contractions began and clenched her teeth.

"I think I'm having another baby."

FATIMA

Fatima had never delivered a baby before.

She was merely supposed to be a hand to hold when her lady gave birth to a beautiful and healthy baby girl. But as she stood in front of Lyra and watched as her entire body convulsed with pain, she knew that something else was coming.

Her lady was having another baby, but how was that possible?

Then she remembered what Astrid had said.

'I sense two heartbeats.'

The elder witch hadn't been referring to the baby and its mother—she'd sensed two separate heartbeats in Lyra's womb.

Fatima had only ever seen twins once in her lifetime, and that had been in the early years of her childhood back in the capital city, before being sold to the crown. There was a set of twin girls that bullied her in school, constantly dishing out hateful remarks with twice the grit, and Fatima had endured their wrath for years until one day, her mother confessed that she could no longer afford her younger brother's medicine. He'd been sickly as a baby, and that sickness had followed him throughout the seven years of his young life. He needed special tonics to stop the shakes that racked his small body.

Fatima had understood the sacrifice her mother had to make, and she had been willing to do it without fuss. For her brother. For the one person in the world that understood her like no other. So, she'd been sold to the castle in exchange for a handsome pay to her family, and she'd never looked back.

Fatima would never have let her brother die, so there'd been no real choice in the matter, but no matter her fate, she'd been willing to do whatever it took to ensure her family a small sense of security. And somehow, by the luck of the gods, the princess had taken a particular notice of her before she'd been handed over as a warm body for Madam Lema's soldiers. Fatima still wasn't sure if it had been pity or potential, but either way, Lyra had saved her from what could have been a terrible life.

As she stood several feet from the edge of the bed, staring down at her lady in shock, Fatima realized it was now her responsibility to save Lyra in return.

The other witches were long gone, busy fussing over the newborn of the coven. No one had stayed behind to clean Lyra or stitch the tear in her core, showing that they couldn't care less what happened to the princess. Lyra could very well die of infection before ever setting eyes on her baby girl.

Fatima could run after them and get help, but she couldn't bear the thought of leaving Lyra all alone in agony. What if something went wrong and there was no one there to help her?

Instead, Fatima climbed onto the bed and crouched over Lyra's writhing body. "Can I have a look, my lady?" she asked, trying to keep her voice calm.

Lyra's only answer was another cry of pain, so Fatima took it upon herself to assess the situation. There was blood and fluid now spilling freely from between Lyra's legs. It soaked into the sheets and coated Fatima's hand as she tried to feel for another baby's head, but fingers brushed something foreign instead. She realized in horror that it was the baby's foot.

"Miss Lyra," Fatima spoke hesitantly. "I don't think you should push."

"What's wrong?" she demanded. A fresh sheen of sweat coated the princess's brow with her effort to deny the urge to push.

Fatima held onto the answer greedily, not wanting to set it free. She knew it would only cause her lady more distress, and she wanted desperately to save her from that future torment. Lyra had plans to hold both of her babies in her arms, but once Fatima let slip those next dreadful words, those plans would shatter and never come to fruition.

"I'm sorry, my lady. The baby is breech."

Fatima watched as the realization that she would have to be cut open settled over Lyra's face, and the princess's body immediately relaxed. "You must do it."

Fatima's heart lurched with terror and trepidation. "No! I can't! It will kill you!"

"I'm dead no matter what, Fatima. You have to make sure this baby is delivered safely." Lyra placed a clammy hand on her abdomen and closed her eyes. "I know it's a boy. I can feel it. And it's up to you to take him to his father."

The immensity of that job sent a shiver down Fatima's spine.

Lyra reached for Fatima's hand and squeezed. It wasn't unlike the gesture Fatima had offered Lyra earlier. "You can do this," Lyra told her, her words steady. There wasn't a single ounce of hesitation or fear. Then she added a single plea. "Please."

Fatima rolled up her sleeves and sucked in a deep breath to steady herself. She needed a knife to cut into Lyra's abdomen and yarrow root to staunch the bleeding. They needed more blankets and sanitizing spray. There was so much to do and not enough time to prepare.

Lyra clearly saw the panic welling in Fatima's eyes and tried to reach to calm her once more, but Fatima was already scurrying across the room searching for something…anything that could help her.

"We need the others," she said apprehensively. "You need a steady hand, or you could risk bleeding out."

"I'm not concerned about that," Lyra said.

Fatima couldn't believe the pure, blind faith in her lady's words.

She shook her head to try and clear the panic growing stronger in her chest. Her heart felt like it was being squeezed by taloned fingers, holding her hostage.

Lyra was a mother now. She had a perfectly healthy baby girl, and a boy on the way. She needed to survive this—to make it through to hold her children—but it looked like Lyra already knew she wouldn't.

Her utmost priority was now the life of her children.

Fatima stiffened her upper lip and shoved down the anxiety clawing its way up her throat. It screamed to be released, but she would not let it have a voice. Not when her best friend needed her.

She found one of the knives that had been left behind by the other witches and took it to the fire that burned quietly in the hearth across the room. The flame had nearly been snuffed out, but the coals were still hot enough to disinfect the tool. She did not wish to use such a gruesome technique to open Lyra, but there were no other options. By the time Fatima ran to find the yarrow root that would staunch the bleeding, the baby's life might be compromised.

She'd read about all the possible complications that could happen in order to prepare herself, but now she was wishing that she hadn't. Worrying about the worst was only going to cloud her judgment, and all that mattered now was getting the baby out. So, once the edge of the blade glowed bright orange, Fatima walked back to Lyra's bedside with as much conviction she could muster.

With one last smile of encouragement and understanding from the princess, Fatima gathered all of her strength and began to slice.

ORAM

*L*yra's instructions carried Oram forward with each step he took.

He'd hardly packed anything in his rucksack after leaving in such a frenzy, and now he regretted not bringing any food. Kirra would have been the one to remind him to do that, but Oram could no longer rely on his brother for such things. He'd disappointed him for the last time, and it might have very well been the last they saw of one another.

A sharp pang of guilt stitched in his side at the thought. He hated that he'd upset Kirra so badly, but his intentions had been pure. He'd promised to be there for Lyra and their child, no matter the consequences, and he would not go back on that promise, even if it meant letting his brother down.

Oram trekked through the Saldanni Forest with nothing but the light of the moon in the midnight sky to guide him. At this rate, it would take him several days to make it through.

Given the canopy above, the air was colder here than back in Caster Valley, but at least he'd managed to bring a warm coat. In a cart, it took a day and a half to get to Castle Larapuna, but without a horse, he feared he wouldn't reach Lyra in time. He wasn't even sure where to stop and make camp. She'd instructed him to wait for her in the wood, but she hadn't specified how far to go.

He told himself to push at least halfway before taking a break, and by the time he reached the middle of the dense forest, his legs were throbbing from overuse and lack of sleep. His thighs ached, and he was grateful to find a fallen log to sit on and massage his muscles.

The meager supplies he'd packed into his bag would give him plenty of warmth and quench his thirst but would do nothing to satiate his appetite.

TWENTY-FOUR HOURS PASSED in the blink of an eye, and the sun was beginning its descent in the sky, casting orange tendrils of light streaming through the blanket of trees.

What would he do if he keeled over from lack of nutrients? He had to stay strong, conserve his energy for when it would be absolutely necessary. He would take a break to sleep and gather his strength.

Only a few hours, then he would be on his way.

Just a short rest, he told himself.

Oram slid to the ground and rested his head against the log behind him.

Seconds later, he was asleep.

KIRRA

Kirra Foster was no fool.

No, that would be his brother.

He'd warned Oram of this—he'd told him point blank that nothing good could come from fraternizing with witches. But the idiot had gone and followed his heart instead of his brain. Actually, he'd led with what was in his pants, but that was beside the point.

Kirra was the rationalist of the family, and Oram was the dreamer. It had been that way since they were young demons in the care of their adoptive parents. Kirra loved Galiana and Petra for the sacrifices they'd made, and he was grateful for them. But he also saw their ceaseless love and kindness for what it was. Weakness. A weakness they'd passed on to Oram, and one that Kirra fought against every damn day.

It wasn't that he wasn't kind—Kirra tried to be a thoughtful and compassionate male—but he never let those feelings overtake his common sense. He knew how the world worked. He'd witnessed the cruelty of men even in the rural farming town of Knox Hill. While most demons felt safe enough to walk freely so far from the witches, that did not mean prejudice did not exist there. So Kirra guarded his heart and let his head take the lead.

Unfortunately, he hadn't been able to convince Oram to do the same.

Right now, his brother was trekking through the Saldanni Forest after a witch he'd known for less than two months. Sure, she was having his baby, but that didn't mean he owed her anything. Men abandoned their children all the time—hell, Oram had been a child of abandonment himself—so why couldn't he follow the example that had been set for him?

Because Oram was a good male, that was why.

And though it pained him to see his brother chasing after trouble, Kirra couldn't very well leave him to flounder in the dark.

Of course he was going to go after him. He had to.

That's what the fox-demon reminded himself as he packed a small messenger bag with a handful of homemade protein bars with pomegranates and almonds, two canteens filled with water, and a spare cloak. At the bottom of the bag was a canvas pouch already stuffed with camping supplies, but on the way out the door, Kirra made sure to grab his trusty compass. It had been handed down to him from Petra as a housewarming present, and he'd cherished it with care, but he'd yet to find the need to use it. It was as if they'd been preparing for this moment—for when the brothers needed to find their way back to one another.

Kirra swung the strap of the messenger bag across his chest and donned a heavy jacket. The winter season was upon them now, and he knew the winds that whipped through the forest trees would be brutal.

As he walked down the path away from his front door, Kirra looked back one last time and prayed to Ghidorah to help guide him.

And that he would see that front door again.

FREYAH

Masked in their disguises, Whit and Freyah hurried through the crowd. The closest entrance to the dungeon was located within the council chambers behind the dais, and that meant they would have to blend in meticulously with the crowd in order to slip past Madam Lema and all of her guards.

All night, the queen's attention had bounced fixedly from one guest to another. She scanned every face in the crowd, as if she were looking for someone in particular. Did she know that they'd planned something tonight? If so, they now had to be twice as careful.

They lingered behind a throng of councilmen talking boisterously about local business and regulating current laws. Based on how he had been addressed, Freyah deduced that the tallest of the men was the Chancellor of Balandra, the capital city of Ghoma.

The chancellor wore a sleek green tailcoat with gold trim and a broach on each lapel, one being the witches' symbol for earth, and the other a bright sun cresting over two waving lines.

Freyah had dreamed of visiting such a bustling city one day, with its variety of people and culture. It had once been a dream entirely out of reach, but now she'd actually seen a world outside her bubble, witnessing actual magic and being forced to confront her own prejudices against demons, realizing that underneath they were no different than humans.

She wanted to listen in further on the councilors' discussions with the chancellor; perhaps they knew the Last Cove's magistrate, and she'd find out more about what Matthias had planned, but Whit called her focus back to the task at hand. Madam Lema still eyed every person in front of her with rapt attention, but she'd yet to spot her or Whit within the crowd.

"We need a distraction," Whit said. "Something that will keep her attention away from the door."

Freyah tried to think of something that would cause a scene. Perhaps she could "accidentally" bump into someone and spill their drink. That would certainly cause enough commotion to get the queen's eyes to stray. But something that trivial wouldn't draw out the guards.

Then a gentleman stepped up to the dais and bowed in front of the witch-queen. Freyah recognized him as Koa, the strange man that had introduced himself earlier. He began talking very animatedly to Madam Lema, his hands flailing about dramatically as he appeared to be telling an enthralling story. Madam Lema's focus was pulled taut with great agitation, but it was entirely on him. He then stepped up onto the dais, and her guards drew their swords.

For a brief second, Koa's eyes met hers, and she could have sworn he winked.

"Now's our chance," Freyah hissed, not daring to take the time to analyze the man's motives.

She grabbed Whit's arm and dragged him past the group of councilmen with deft speed. They slipped into the meeting room like shadows and hurriedly raced to the other side, where Whit pulled back a curtain hiding the secret door leading down to the dungeons. Freyah pulled on the latch to open the door, and together they descended the stairs into darkness.

It was hard to see at first, but as they walked further, light from the sconces along the wall illuminated their way. It was the same path Whit had used when he'd taken her to see her father, and she tried to follow the route by memory, but when they approached the first turn, she stuttered to a stop. She couldn't remember which way to go.

"It's this way," Whit said, stepping in front of her to take the lead.

Freyah blushed. Despite her embarrassment, she was grateful to have Whit with her, because she didn't think she'd be able to get to her father on her own.

They continued zigzagging through the shadowed tunnels until they reached the first row of cells. All of the prisoners were asleep, some snoring loudly from their makeshift cots, the sound saturating the damp space. It didn't get any easier for Freyah to pass the men without notice, for she still couldn't resist the urge to stare. She felt badly for the poor conditions they were forced to live in, but she had no way of knowing what they'd done to deserve such a sentence. These men could be murderers for all she knew. Or they could be simple pickpockets trying to get by.

Once again, Whit led her to the door at the end of the furthest hall, and Freyah's heart began pumping wildly in her chest. She'd been anticipating this moment for a week, but now that it was finally here, she couldn't stifle the nerves that wracked her body.

Her limbs began to shake with bottled anxiety.

She was about to openly defy the queen of Ghoma, and if she messed this up, it wouldn't just be her life on the line. Whit was putting his career at risk, not to mention his own life.

But it was a risk he'd clearly been willing to take.

For her, and for the possibility of *them*.

There was a small part of Freyah that felt guilty for not being able to give him that guarantee, but she'd tried not to let it sway her from accepting his help. If Whit needed motivation, then she could give it to him. She just hoped that he wouldn't be too disappointed when they never saw each other again.

Whit pulled the keys from the inside of his vest and unlocked the door of her father's room. He hid it well, but she was able to see a slight shake in his hands. He was nervous, too, and knowing that made her relax a little.

At least she wasn't alone in her fear.

Her father wasn't slumped on the floor like they'd seen him last. This time, he stood against the opposite wall, his posture stiff and his face reflecting the same nervous anticipation that Freyah felt.

"It's time," Whit told him as they entered the small room. "Are you ready?"

Her father nodded curtly, and Freyah took his hand. She'd been waiting for this moment for weeks, and now she was finally going home.

They both were.

They were leaving this gods-forsaken place and getting back to their lives. And yet, though she craved the safety and familiarity of home, she couldn't help but feel that she was leaving something important behind.

Whit removed his mask as he stood by the door and waited for Freyah and her father to collect themselves. She saw the stiff way he held himself, the subtle hesitancy to go through with their plan, and his face had become ashen, as if it had finally hit him that this was their goodbye.

There was something large left unsaid between them. But Freyah couldn't allow herself to be swept away with fleeting feelings for a stranger. She needed to ground herself with the priority of going home. The ocean was calling her name, and for the first time in her life, she found herself never wanting to leave the mountain again.

"We need to hurry," Whit said in a hushed tone. He kept looking over his shoulder, keeping an eye out for any unwanted visitors.

He was right. The next guard would be arriving for his shift soon, and Whit's purposeful scheduling blunder had allowed them only a few minutes to get her father out unseen.

Freyah removed her mask and dropped it to the floor. She grabbed her father's hand and held it tightly as they followed Whit from the tiny room. They moved carefully through the deepest section of the dungeon, aiming to reach the outer tunnels quickly and quietly.

"You don't have to hold on so tight, little bloom," her father murmured as they walked. "You're cutting off my circulation."

Freyah pursed her lips in annoyance and shushed him, but she knew her face was probably as white as a sheet. She tried to pass off the response as playful and lighten the mood, but the truth was her heart hammered violently against her ribs. So much so that she was afraid the sound of her heartbeats were too loud.

They turned into the next tunnel, past another handful of prisoners in their cells who would be the only witnesses to their grand escape. But that wouldn't matter as long as they made it far enough away before any of them could talk. Once they hit the end of this particular tunnel, they would be more than halfway to the outside entrance. More than halfway to freedom. However, before reaching the final few yards, Whit halted suddenly in front of her, causing her father to accidentally step on her heel.

"Sorry, little bloom," he winced.

Whit turned to face them, appearing incredibly serious in the shadows of the tunnel. The light from the sconces along the wall highlighted his scar.

"This is as far as I go," he told her.

"What?" Freyah exclaimed, a bit too loudly.

Her father's hand tightened around hers. A subtle encouragement. Then he took a step back, giving them space to talk. Somehow, her father always knew the right thing to do. And in that moment, he knew to allow Freyah and Whit a proper goodbye.

Whit pulled out a small pack that had been hidden behind a boulder and handed it to her.

"What's this?"

"You can't go traipsing through the forest in that," he said, as if this were something obvious. Frankly, Freyah hadn't even thought about the fact that she was wearing a fancy gown. "You need to change," he instructed her. "There's also some food and water in there for you both. It should get you far enough until you come to the next town."

He'd prepared supplies for her.

For her and her father.

It was that small gesture that made it that much harder for the next words to come out of her mouth.

"Thank you, Whit," she said quietly. "For everything."

Though the space was small enough that her father could no doubt hear everything she said, Freyah still tried to speak in a whisper. The relationship she'd formed with Whit felt sacred somehow—a special thing to hold close and protect. She didn't want anyone else's opinions about what might or might not have happened between them. Not even her father's.

Whit brushed a hand across her cheek and tilted her head up to look at him fully. He forced her eyes to meet his, and in them she saw his heart breaking in two. "Stay safe, beautiful," he said softly, his words caressing her skin. "I'm sorry."

He didn't need to specify what for, because they both knew those two words were strong enough to cover the weight of everything he'd done. He'd apologized before, but this time felt different. It felt bigger. And as she stared into his warm brown eyes for what would be the last time, Freyah felt all of her resentment washing away. She didn't blame him anymore.

So she gave him the one thing that would mean the most.

More than a simple goodbye.

"I forgive you, Whit."

She saw the moment her words struck true. At first, his eyes scrunched in pain, but then they softened, the edges lining with silver. He'd needed that forgiveness from her probably more than she would ever know, and she was glad to have given it to him.

Whit leaned in to brush a kiss to her forehead as his hand trailed to the back of her head. His touch still felt hot on her skin, and as he slid his hand down to her arm and squeezed, Freyah tried to memorize the feeling one final time.

He slipped something into her hand. The wooden carving of a hawk.

"You forgot this," he said quietly.

She hadn't forgotten, she'd just been too much of a coward to take it with her.

"Did you hear that?"

She'd nearly forgotten her father was there, but at the sound of his voice, Freyah's senses went back on high alert.

Whit stiffened in front of her. "What did you hear?"

Her father shook his head. "I'm not sure. Like dirt shifting. I've heard that sound before. Just like in the mountains."

"Someone else is down here." Whit nudged Freyah to get moving. "Hurry and change. I'll stall whoever it is."

"Whit…"

His name fell from her lips naturally—it felt like breathing air—but she didn't know what to say. Only that she'd needed to speak his name one more time.

"It's okay," he told her. He smiled tightly, trying to show as much confidence as possible, but she knew he was just as scared as her. "Once you make it to the outside, make sure the grounds are clear, then make a run for the forest. Stick close to the eastern tree line and follow that all the way along the cliffs. You'll avoid most of the Clans that way. Don't stop until you see the sun. You must put as much distance between yourself and the castle as you can before they notice you're gone."

Freyah waited for something else, one last word of encouragement, but nothing came. She stripped off her dress around the nearest bend in the tunnel and listened to the sound of her father taking Whit's hand in his and the exchange of thanks between men. By the time Freyah had stuffed the wooden carving into her boot after donning leggings and a thick wool sweater, Whit was gone.

She stepped out from behind the rock to find only her father waiting.

He smiled and reached for her hand. "Let's go home, little bloom."

Freyah opened her palm and showed him the tiny pouch with crushed tourmaline powder she'd kept hidden within the lining of her dress. It was flat enough that it hadn't shown beneath the fabric, but she'd known Whit had felt it when his hands were on her waist.

For some reason, despite knowing that the powder would not work for them, she'd chosen to hang onto it. Maybe Jessa had been wrong about natural conduits only working for those with magic in their blood. And if there was even the smallest chance that that were true, Freyah had to try.

She gestured for him to take the pouch. "It will camouflage us. Blow it into the air, and then we walk through it."

He followed her instructions, and after stepping through the opaque cloud of black, Freyah pulled her father along as fast as her feet would carry them.

Her boots pushed off hard against the flattened rocks of the stone floor and propelled her forward. She followed the path as it turned into dirt. Closer and closer to the outside.

A dozen more yards, and finally they were on the other side.

Earth surrounded her from every angle, and Freyah could smell the deep layers of mud and trees and living things. It felt so euphoric to stand under the night sky again, without a guard or a witch looking over her shoulder, even in the pouring rain. But there was no time to stop and appreciate it.

Freyah spun to face the tunnel entrance. The front gate to the castle was on her right, and the long cobbled road that led through the forest. That must have been the path she'd been brought in on, but she couldn't go that way again. Whit had instructed her to stay to the eastern tree line.

She made sure the coast was clear, and then with the midnight sky looming high above them, Freyah and her father ran.

Together they burst across the grass with inhuman speed. She'd never run so fast in her life, and she feared that her father wouldn't be able to keep up, but somehow he matched her pace. Maybe it was the fear of getting caught that lit a fire under their feet, or maybe it was the sheer excitement of knowing they were finally going home. Either way, the adrenaline pumping through Freyah's veins continued to push her forward with lightning speed.

She was going to make it.

They were both going to make it.

But then Freyah's boot slid out from under her.

She stumbled forward and tumbled roughly to the ground, her knees giving out beneath her and slamming into the muddied earth. She swore as she felt her skin tearing against rock and tried to catch herself, but as she reached out her hands, her wrist twisted violently beneath her weight.

Her eyes welled with tears as she tried to stifle the pain now scorching her knees and wrist. All around her, roots were breaking free from the earth, reaching for her like wicked hands. They wound around her legs and pulled her down, preventing her from rising and looking for her father. She tried to scan the grounds for any sight of him in the rainy, darkness, but he was nowhere to be found.

Did that mean the camouflage was actually working?

To Freyah's horror, when she peered back over her shoulder, she was greeted with her worst nightmare. Her father had fallen as well, but the terrible part was not the sight of her father lying helpless on the ground with roots tangled around his ankles.

It was the witch-queen that stood behind him.

LYRA

The pain was excruciating.

Like lightning striking through her abdomen.

Lyra tried not to think about the details of being sliced open. It wasn't that bad. Not really. Only a simple cut to release the baby and all would be fine.

She knew it wouldn't be, but she tried not to dwell on that fact.

While the searing hot pain cut deep into her core, Lyra pictured the stars. She conjured an image of the night sky to the front of her mind and focused with all her heart. She imagined that she was gazing upon the same stars as Oram where he waited for her in the Saldanni Forest.

That image of twinkling silver shining against a velvety blackness would be the last they shared. And it would have to be enough.

As the edges of that blackness crept closer, she told herself that this was meant to be. Lillia would guide Oram through the night and protect their baby boy. Because yes, she knew as the cloud of velvet slipped over her eyes that this child was a boy.

It would be up to Fatima to get him to safety.

To unite him with his father.

Lillia, she prayed. *Watch over my son. Provide him with a protector that will never abandon him. Build him a shelter, impregnable and hidden from those that wish to harm him. Bless him with both patience and strength so that he shall one day fulfill his purpose and be reunited with his sister.*

The last thing Lyra saw before the darkness swallowed her whole was the image of a white tiger, a crown of thorns atop his head.

47

FATIMA

atima held the silent infant in her arms and waited desperately for its first cry as Lyra's blood seeped into the bed sheets beneath her.

Her friend was gone—she'd watched as the light in the princess's eyes was snuffed out like a candle, and yet there'd been a smile on her face.

Fatima had struggled to finish the job, the tears streaming from her eyes making it near impossible to see as she'd cut into Lyra's flesh. The baby had indeed been breech, and it had taken all of her upper body strength to wrestle the child carefully from its mother's body. The amount of blood that had gushed from Lyra's abdomen made Fatima nearly gag from sickness and heartbreak.

That blood—the death of the princess—was on her hands now.

What did that mean for her? Once she left the castle, she'd never be able to return. She'd be a criminal on the run for the rest of her life. And even if she somehow found the courage to explain what had happened, no one would believe her.

She waited to hear the first cry that would draw breath into the baby's lungs, and for almost a minute nothing came. But then she heard it, that beautiful first intake of air, and Fatima sobbed in relief.

She had no idea when the witches would be back to take care of Lyra. They clearly weren't concerned about the princess's current state and were more focused on the new life that had been brought into the coven, but the cries of this newborn baby boy would no doubt summon their return. Fatima hurriedly cleaned the baby's face and small body as best she could with the skirts of her dress and, though she thought it would be harder, sliced through the umbilical cord with surprising efficiency.

This was not how things were supposed to go. They'd planned for this, sure, but Fatima had hoped for Lyra to at least be able to say goodbye to her precious baby boy before she whisked him off into the woods. Her eyes continued to sting with fresh tears as she gazed down upon the now lifeless body of Lyra, her protector and friend. The princess's eyes remained open but unseeing, and though her death had been brutal, she looked at peace. There was no sign of terror or pain etched onto her delicate features. Just acceptance, and a willingness to make the ultimate sacrifice.

"I will protect him with my life," Fatima whispered into the void, despite knowing that Lyra would never hear it.

In the weeks leading up to the anticipated delivery, Fatima had prepared a bag with all the essentials needed for her travel. The leather satchel consisted of spare cloth and blankets, goat's milk that had been purified and enhanced by Lyra to feed the baby, medicines and tonics for emergencies, and enough food and water to make it to Oram.

She'd been told that a subconscious nudging in his gut would guide him to the exact halfway point in the Saldanni Forest—far enough out of the Spyders' reach, but close enough that it would mean the least amount of exposure for the baby. It would take Fatima half a day to reach that spot, and she prayed to Lillia that Oram was already there waiting.

Sneaking out of the castle was the easy part.

The witches were so focused on their new prize that they never noticed the petite handmaid slinking past them down the hall carrying a lump in her arms. Almost every witch in the castle had awoken and gathered to see the beautiful bundle of joy that the princess had given them. There were praises to Lillia for such a blessing, and they all wanted to place a hand on the divine child.

No one remembered the mother that was left alone in the next room, now having given the ultimate sacrifice. No one spoke her name. No one shed a tear. Only the lonely handmaid had given a moment of silence in that mother's honor, and now she was going to finally repay her debt.

For everything Lyra had done to protect her all those years—for giving her a home and a family, no matter how small—Fatima would do this. She would ensure that Lyra's baby boy grew up safe and loved.

So Fatima ran.

She made it to the front entrance outside the Grand Hall, where soldiers and their families had also been stirred awake to talk about the news. She ignored their slurs about having '*another witch*' to deal with and focused solely on the little life taking small breaths against her chest. She held the boy close, keeping his face covered and his body warm with hers. Blessedly, he'd stopped crying with a drop of lavender oil on his tongue and was now dozing peacefully without any awareness of what was happening.

Yes, getting out of the castle was the easy part. Now, however, Fatima faced the open expanse of the sweeping grounds. And after that, the gaping mouth of the dark forest beyond. She'd only ventured through it once, as a girl on her way to be sold, and she remembered very little of the experience after blocking out most of it.

No, this part would not be easy.

But she would persevere.

For her friend, she could make it.

So with a heavy pack on her back and courage in her heart, Fatima sprinted for the trees.

48

FREYAH

Madam Lema smacked Freyah hard against the cheek. She'd chosen to use the back of her gloved left hand—the one that bore that golden ring.

Freyah could feel the sting of the newly-formed cut just under her eye and the warmth of blood bubbling in her mouth. Though this pain was nothing compared to the intense ache in her wrist, somehow it felt worse.

It was the pain of failure that stung the most.

The pain of knowing she had failed her father.

She spit blood onto the floor, disgusted with herself.

She could see her father's hunched form shackled to the floor in front of her. She had also been locked in chains—a long one attached to her left ankle—but she wasn't nearly as restricted as him. Both of her father's ankles and wrists had been bound, and they were latched to a large hook in the floor in front of him. He was balancing most of his weight on one leg, forced to hunch due to the length of the chain. His injured leg was dripping blood, and Freyah thought she saw a small shard of bone piercing his skin.

Freyah tested the length of her own chain, but when she stood to try and walk toward her father, someone was there to yank her back.

She looked over her shoulder to find Evanora, the curly, gray-haired witch she'd met the same day as Madam Lema. It would seem that the witch was more than a sentinel advisor meant to stand by the witch-queen's side. Freyah wondered why the queen's general wasn't here to do the job, but it was clear that Evanora was a glutton for punishment. She could see it in the gleam of the witch's eyes as she yanked on the chain, causing Freyah to stumble.

Freyah fell to the floor once more, avoiding landing on her injured wrist. This time she stayed put.

Instead of trying to move, she took the chance to scan her surroundings. She was in a meeting room of sorts, one that held a massive amount of seating in the style of an amphitheater. She recognized it as the room where she'd eavesdropped on Madam Lema and one of the elder witches. Though at the time, the seats had been empty.

Now, they were completely filled.

Freyah peered around to find dozens of hate-filled eyes staring back at her. All of the witches and dignitaries that had been at the ball now sat before her, and though she doubted any of them knew her by name, they judged her anyway. Because of her father, and what he'd been accused of.

Madam Lema had surely woven a story of utter treachery about Freyah and Brennan, telling anyone that would listen about their masterful plan to end the witches' rule over Ghoma. When in reality, it was the queen's plan that had been carefully crafted to fruition in front of their own unseeing eyes. Freyah doubted that a single person in this room cared whether or not the two of them were actually guilty. They only wanted someone to blame. Someone to pin their problems on.

Whether her father had been behind any of the rebel attacks or not, at this point, Freyah no longer cared. He didn't deserve this. Not this level of shaming in front of a crowd of strangers. Nonetheless, this was how things had ended up. No matter how hard Freyah had tried to stop it.

So close.

They had been so fucking close.

And yet, they hadn't been close at all.

Freyah had known the tourmaline powder wouldn't work, but she'd been so desperate that she'd been willing to try anything. For a brief moment, she'd thought it actually had worked. Madam Lema's focus had been solely drawn to her father as he lay writhing in the mud beneath her, tangled in roots that seemed to move by the witch-queen's hand. It wasn't until Freyah screamed for her father that the witch-queen looked up and saw her, as if she hadn't noticed Freyah there before.

It was probably a coincidence, but if not, why had the powder worked for Freyah, and not for her father?

Regardless, their plan had failed.

Madam Lema had no doubt noticed Whit and Freyah at the ball, and when they'd disappeared, the witch-queen would have gone straight to the dungeons. Their plan had been foolish, and Freyah hated that Willow had been right. The girl had tried to warn her—she'd tried to stop her, knowing how it would end—but Freyah had persisted. She hadn't listened, and neither had Whit.

Freyah's heart then clenched with panic.

Where was Whit?

She didn't see him anywhere in the room, so she would have to pray to the gods that he hadn't been caught. She then lowered her gaze back to her father and murmured his name, trying to get his attention on her, but he wouldn't meet her eyes.

"Too ashamed, I suspect," Madam Lema sneered.

Freyah's lip curled with disgust, wishing she could rip out the witch-queen's tongue for every lie and hateful word she'd ever spoken.

"I was planning to spare you this spectacle," she continued with mock sympathy, "but after this stunt, I have no choice but to make you watch."

Freyah could feel the promise of that statement—the power behind the threat—but she didn't believe for one second that Madam

Lema hadn't planned for Freyah to watch as her father died in front of her. The witch-queen meant for everyone to see.

At the sound of Madam Lema's voice, Freyah's father stirred from his hunched position. He seemed to want to defend himself, but he couldn't manage the necessary words. Freyah saw the pain in his face as he lifted his head to face the queen. His lower leg had snapped from the fall, and she could clearly see a shard of white bone protruding from the nasty split in his pant leg. It looked like he was trying his best not to put any weight on it, but balancing was hard in such an awkward position. Though he couldn't straighten his back, and agony was written all over his features, he still remained defiant in front of the queen.

He released a raspy breath, but his upper lip was stiff and his brow firm. For the first time, she actually saw a leader in her father's eyes. His stare was unwavering as he gazed upon the witch that had caused his family nothing but pain and said, "You are making an insurmountable mistake. And it will cost you."

For a brief second, Freyah could have sworn Madam Lema faltered. Her throat had constricted in fear, but before anyone else could see, the queen quickly lifted her chin and replaced the look with stern conviction.

Was she actually questioning her decision to do this?

No. Madam Lema wouldn't back down from her threats now.

Not with so many here to witness.

"I'm pleased to see that I have not killed your spirit, Brennan Kenpaw," she mused.

The witch-queen then motioned to Evanora over her shoulder. The sentinel obeyed the silent command by hoisting Freyah onto her knees and wrenching her head back to fully face the scene ahead. Freyah was going to see every second of her father's death; Madam Lema had made sure of it. Even as the witch-queen paced tauntingly in front of her father and Freyah tried to close her eyes, Evanora squeezed her nails an inch deeper into the skin at her neck to keep her in place and force them open again.

How would the queen do it?

Surely she meant to draw the execution out as long as possible—to make the spectacle worth such an audience—but anything too violent would send the wrong message. Brennan's death needed to be swift, but effective. Just enough to see the light of agony leave his eyes and then vanish into the ether.

Madam Lema stopped her pacing and looked down at Freyah's father as he crumpled into a hunched position. His foot slipped against the floor, either from blood or sweat Freyah couldn't tell, and he landed hard on his injured leg. His cry of pain echoed around the room, and though the defiance had faded and given way to exhaustion, Freyah did not fault him for it. She knew that courage still beat triumphantly in his heart.

"For your crimes against the crown," Madam Lema began, her voice like a smothering blanket of velvet, "I hereby sentence you, Brennan Kenpaw, leader of the Last Cove chapter of The First Men, to death by fire."

It was then that Freyah realized what her father had slipped in. Something else coated the stone floor, not quite mixing with the blood that seeped from his broken leg. The liquid was thin, and it surrounded the place where her father now sat.

Oil.

They'd poured oil from the lanterns on the floor. The same oil they used and produced in Last Cove. A resource from his own home was going to turn against him. Madam Lema meant to burn him alive.

Before Freyah could protest, the chamber doors swung open and another figure stepped hesitantly into the room. There was a shuffling of feet and the clanking of more chains, and then a large body holding a crossbow stood beside Freyah.

The scent of pine and tea tree filled her nostrils, and her entire body went limp. Even Evanora couldn't hold Freyah's weight at the sight of Whit with his finger against the trigger that would take her father's life.

She'd thought his execution would be the worst of it. But yet again, she'd been wrong. And Willow had been right.

'It can always get worse. It's best to remember that.'

Whit's right hand shook as he aimed the crossbow at her father's feet, where the majority of the rendered oil had been spilled. The tip of the bolt was carved from an orange stone, glowing like an ember clinging to life in a dying fire. There was no visible flame, but Freyah knew somehow that as soon as the trigger was pulled, a magical spark would ignite.

She wondered what horrible threats Madam Lema had made to ensure Whit had no choice in this. It no doubt involved Willow, and Freyah hated that, once again, he was having to choose between her and his sister.

She silently begged for him to look at her.

Please, she pleaded in the back of her mind. *Make it quick. Make it painless.*

And there it was. The smallest of nods as his chin dipped in confirmation. Perhaps he'd seen her look of desperation from the corner of his eye. Or perhaps he simply knew this was what she wanted.

"Any day now, Lieutenant," Madam Lema drawled.

Whit straightened his posture, pretending to secure the line of his target. He breathed in once. Twice. And the watching crowd seemed to collectively inhale with him. Then his index finger tightened around the trigger.

At the last second, his aim shot upward—straight for her father's heart.

It was over faster than Freyah could scream.

One second, her father was gazing at her with peace and understanding in his sorrowful eyes. And in the next, he'd collapsed to the floor.

No more pain. Only the sweet embrace of death.

It happened so quickly, yet the pain Freyah now felt only strengthened. It started in the pit of her stomach and crawled up her spine. Then, with monstrous claws, it gripped her heart and squeezed like the magical roots in the soil that had brought her down.

A single tear fell down Freyah's cheek as her heart constricted then shattered onto the stone floor. She could actually hear the sound of it as the pieces splintered and echoed inside her chest, but it was not as loud as Madam Lema's cry of outrage at what Whit had done.

To Freyah's surprise, the witch-queen advanced on her. Madam Lema wore her rage like a stormcloud, and she meant to drown Freyah with it.

"Don't fucking touch her!" Whit bellowed.

Madam Lema halted her approach. Freyah was convinced she was seconds away from another hard slap to the face, or worse…

But the witch-queen changed course and advanced on Whit instead, snatching the crossbow from his grip. She furiously ripped the gloves from both her hands and grabbed his throat. Her fingers were now even blacker than they'd been before, and she used one sharp nail to outline the contours of Whit's face from forehead to ear to chin, then back around again on the opposite side. Whit stood there, looking quizzical and afraid, waiting for something to happen.

They all did.

Then the invisible outline Madam Lema had traced around his face suddenly began to glow—burn, more like—and Whit screamed. White hot pain erupted from his throat in a bellow so deep and so raw it made Freyah feel sick.

It was as if Madam Lema had taken a thin wire and was digging it deep into the outline of Whit's face. Any deeper and his skin would be removed altogether.

"No!" Freyah screamed, her voice hoarse. "Please! Stop it!"

Madam Lema lingered in her vengeance for a few seconds longer, then she swiped her hand across Whit's forehead and the agony ceased.

Whit clawed at his face with desperate hands, feeling for whatever flesh was still left, but his skin was intact. There were no new burn marks or raw skin. Outwardly, no damage had been done, but there was now a faint white line highlighting the path where Madam Lema had traced her finger.

"Take him back to the dungeons," the queen commanded. "Our business is done here."

The crowd murmured with fervor at what had been done. They'd come to watch a man get burned alive, and their promise of entertainment had been spoiled. But Madam Lema didn't bother addressing her audience. She swept from the chamber, her gossamer dress billowing behind her in a phantom wind.

Whit was dragged from the room, and Freyah had no doubt that she would soon be headed to the dungeons along with him. For now, the guards left her to stare at her father's lifeless body. Everyone moved with palpable disappointment from their seats as Freyah knelt on the stone floor across from him and wept.

She wept for every moment she'd been forced to remain strong. She wept for what Whit had been forced to do. She wept for Willow and everything she'd endured living in this castle. She wept for the families of the soldiers that lived blindly under the witch-queen's thumb. She wept for the country of Ghoma, which would now undoubtedly wake the next morning to the first acts of war.

And above all, she wept for her father. For starting something he could not finish—for trying to make a difference in a terrible world.

49

ORAM

Oram awoke to the sound of twittering birds.

He hadn't planned to sleep so long, but the sun was now high in the cloud-covered sky, an alabaster hue peeking through the canopy above. He'd struggled to keep warm as he slept, but now his clothes soaked in the sun's rays, making him sweat, so he ditched his jacket and gathered his things.

Now that he'd made it to the halfway point of the forest, Oram didn't know what he was supposed to do. He trudged onward across the uneven forest floor, trying his best not to trip over protruding rocks or fallen branches. Some were bigger than his torso, and he'd been forced to wend his way around them rather than climbing over. Sweat continued to trickle from his brow, but the cool breeze dried it almost immediately.

He tried to look for a decent place to set up camp. He'd been comfortably tucked away behind that giant log, but staying someplace similar would make it harder for Lyra to find him. He also didn't want to remain in the open for predators to spot. Climbing a tree would grant him the best vantage point, so he searched for one with the best footholds and found one a dozen or so yards away, split into a vee and deformed by several knots protruding from the trunk.

Grabbing onto the lowest branch, Oram placed one boot on the first knot and hoisted himself up, climbing higher and higher until he reached the split in. He was only about ten feet in the air, but from here he could clearly see the path that cut through the trees and led north. It was the direct route to Larapuna, one he'd driven many times, but he knew that Lyra would not want to take such an obvious route from the castle if she was leaving in secret. More than likely she would stick within the trees, but Oram also knew that it was easy to get turned around with no distinguishable landmarks as a guide.

It would make the most sense for Lyra to follow the eastern edge of the forest that ran along the cliff face. With the ocean on her left, she could easily keep herself moving in the right direction.

So, Oram climbed down from his perch and headed that way.

As he descended, however, a harsh wind tore through the trees. It raced across his dewy skin like a warning, and Oram's senses immediately went on high alert. He scanned the ground below for threats and found nothing but dirt overgrown with moss and weeds. Perhaps his mind was playing tricks on him after being alone in the woods for so long.

That hesitancy cost him, however, because the moment his guard was down, Oram felt the sting of an arrow pierce his shoulder.

The grip he'd held on the branch above him instantly went slack. He tried to grapple for purchase on the knots at his feet, but he only slipped further. His face skidded along the bark of the tree, and his flesh felt as if it had caught fire. After falling the last few feet, Oram landed hard on the mossy earth with a thud, his back taking the brunt of the fall.

The air had been knocked from his lungs, and he lay there wheezing as the face of his attacker appeared above him.

The skin around the demon's eyes was covered with war paint, making his pupils look like endless pits in a midnight sky. His head was shaved and covered in the same war paint, and from his mouth protruded two giant tusks that curled over a snarling upper lip.

Oram's chest contracted and burned as he tried to draw fresh air into his lungs, but a sharp pain bit at his insides with each inhale. He couldn't focus, and as the image of the demon blurred above him, he struggled to formulate a plan.

He'd been so stupid. He hadn't even thought about the wild demon clans as being an obstacle.

Stupid. Stupid. Stupid.

He tried to push himself up off the ground as his breathing finally returned to normal, but the arrow protruding from his shoulder pinned his muscles in place. They contracted around the foreign object, silently screaming to get it out. Oram flexed his fingers, and the pain almost made him faint.

He glanced around quickly to assess the situation.

Three demons surrounded where he'd fallen, each with a different weapon drawn. The closest one with the absurd canines jerked his head to one of the others, and before Oram had time to hold up his hands in protest, the butt of a machete was slammed into his temple.

The last thing he saw was the blackness of the demon's eyes as he fell into the embrace of night.

50

FATIMA

Fatima made it far enough into the Saldanni Forest that she could finally stop to catch her breath. No witches or soldiers followed as she'd run through the night. She'd run and run until her lungs burned and her legs gave out. All the while, the baby boy dozed without a sound in her arms. Not even the jostling of her body as she sprinted for safety had been enough to rouse him from his lavender-induced slumber.

But it hadn't been the exhaustion that made her finally stop. It was the small creature now standing directly in her path. As it approached, Fatima realized that it wasn't a creature, but a man.

A demon.

He had a bushy tail the color of cinnamon that rose almost to the full height of his small frame, and what little amount of skin that showed beneath his clothes was covered in a thin layer of brown fur. A fox-demon, with the most clearly defined animal characteristics Fatima had ever seen. He was more animal than man—even more so than Ryker, who was almost entirely a beast with his snarling mouth and wolfish claws and tail.

The fox-demon stood completely still, like a deer caught at the end of a hunter's bow. So still that Fatima couldn't even see his chest moving to draw in air.

This was not the demon that Lyra had described. Oram was a tiger-demon. He was tall and manly and covered with black markings. This demon was minuscule in comparison and clearly fearful of Fatima's presence.

It could be a coincidence that they'd crossed paths, and it was possible that this encounter meant nothing. He was but a stranger taking a hike through the forest, and they would pass one another with a simple nod and a bid good day.

But Fatima did not believe in coincidences. She believed that the Mother would guide her and Lyra's baby to exactly where they needed to be. And right now, her path had led them straight to this demon.

"Do you know Oram Foster?" she questioned bravely, hoping to Lillia that it was the right thing to ask.

The fox-demon's scared features relaxed, and recognition registered on his face. But there was also confusion.

"You're not Lyra," he stated matter of factly.

"No," she said. "Lyra is dead."

It was the first time she'd had to say it out loud, and it hurt as much as when she'd seen it happen.

The fox-demon's eyes misted with tears, and Fatima somehow knew that this news was somehow as crushing to him as it was to her.

"Who are you?" Fatima asked.

They could not linger here in the open. The wild demon clans were not far off, and though Madam Lema's Spyders did not venture this far from their posts, she did not want to risk them discovering her current whereabouts.

As if the baby knew this, too, he stirred in her arms. He cooed and stretched, emerging from that deep sleep, and finally cracked open his eyes. They were the most beautiful shade of hazel—the perfect mixture of brown and green.

The fox-demon fidgeted with the strap of his bag, visibly nervous.

He looked unsure of how to answer her question—whether to tell the truth or to lie.

"Oram is my brother," he confessed. "He left to go after Lyra, but something didn't feel right, so I followed him. I'm only a few hours behind. Have you seen him?"

Fatima frowned. "I came straight from Larapuna. I haven't passed anyone."

This was not good.

What if something had happened to Oram? He could be hurt or lost. Or worse, what if he'd already been captured on his way to the castle?

She'd made it all this way for nothing.

Now what was she going to do?

The demon looked as if he were going to speak again, but the sound of twigs snapping cut him off. They both whirled around but found nothing. Fatima listened quietly with bated breath for the sound of footsteps. A warning on the wind. Anything.

The sound came again, and Fatima realized it had come from below. She peered down to find thin roots climbing out from under the earth. They reached for the open air, grasping for purchase and finding one another amongst the mossy earth.

Both Fatima and the fox-demon skittered back as the trees around them began to tilt and sway. They bent backward over one another, forming a sort of shelter. Branches became walls. Leaves stitched together to create a roof. The forest floor was lifted into a foundation, and soon, erected in front of them was a complete and fully functional cottage.

"Mangana," Fatima whispered.

The wind kissed her cheek in response.

"What?" the fox-demon asked, gazing in shock at the building in front of them.

One minute there had been nothing but forest, and then, out of the earth itself, an entire house had grown. Fatima had never seen magic like this, but she knew in her heart exactly what it was.

Lyra had made the ultimate sacrifice when she'd died. And in doing so, had cast an unbreakable spell of protection.

Mangana: the act of giving up one's life to seal a spell. Once done, no curse could break it. No loopholes could change it. Fatima had heard it spoken of like a legend, a myth that witches only whispered about. It was something that had always been possible, but no witch had ever been willing to try.

This cottage in the woods—this tiny fortress that had been created by Lillia herself—had been Lyra's final request. A final prayer to the Mother to protect her son.

"What is this?" the fox-demon asked again, this time with less hesitancy. "Magic?"

"Yes," Fatima confirmed. The baby in her arms was now fussing. They had to get him inside. "Come on."

She took a confident step toward the cottage, but the demon yelped as if she were about to get caught in a snare. "We don't know what this thing is!" he hissed.

Fatima scowled. "I do."

"Are you a witch? Did you do this?"

She shook her head. "No. But I trust the one that did."

Ignoring the fox-demon's continued protest, Fatima approached the front of the cottage and reached for the handle. It turned easily, and then the door opened with a soft *click*. As she passed over the threshold, the magic washed over her like she'd stepped through a gentle waterfall.

The fox-demon still debated with himself outside as she placed the baby down in a crib already laden with soft blankets. She pulled out a fresh bottle of milk and held it to his lips. He did not suckle immediately, but she would have time to figure that out. They both had time.

At last, Fatima relaxed.

To her surprise, the fox-demon appeared in the doorway a moment later.

"My name is Kirra," he said as he took in the sight before him, and the instant both of his feet were past the threshold, the door slammed shut.

51

WHIT

As Whit stared down at the shackles pinning his ankles together, he did not feel one ounce of regret for what he'd done.

Whit had felt Freyah's silent plea without having to look her in the eye. There had been no way out of the mess they'd made. Brennan was going to die one way or another, and at least by Whit's own hand, it had been a swift and painless end. There was no way he would have let Freyah watch as her father's skin melted off his bones. And though he did not regret shooting that bolt through Brennan's heart, Whit was now going to spend the rest of his days in a dank dungeon cell because of it. One of the very cells he used to guard.

He'd been hauled below by two strike team soldiers, and he had no doubt that they'd enjoyed every second as they tossed him behind the bars. Word had finally spread about Whit's involvement with Freyah and her father, the traitor.

There was still a dull burning sensation around the edges of his face where Madam Lema had used her magic. He'd never witnessed the witch-queen do anything like that before, but the pain had been excruciating. Whit wondered if there would be a mark. He felt under his chin and around his jaw, but no welts remained. Madam Lema's magic had clearly changed. She was no longer playing by the rules of nature and was now in a game of her own making.

He sighed heavily as he leaned against the cold stone wall. Their plan had failed so spectacularly that he'd had no time to reflect on it. Madam Lema had been one step ahead of them the entire time.

He should have listened to Willow.

No one ever escaped Larapuna, except through death. It had been the only way to free Wendi. He realized that now. Her death, no matter how violent it was, had been the price to pay for her one true escape from a nightmarish life. He'd been so tangled in the loss that he hadn't seen how thankful he should have been that Wendi did not suffer as Willow did. She'd escaped to a place with no pain and no suffering. He'd wanted a different sort of escape for Freyah, but now he feared that death truly was the only way out. It had worked for Brennan, after all.

No. He couldn't think like that. He couldn't give up just because he was now shackled and locked away. He needed to stay sharp and prepare for what came next.

Whit forced himself to stand. He was better than this. He would not wallow or throw up his hands in defeat. He'd made a promise to Freyah, and though he'd failed to protect Brennan, he would not fail her.

He looked around the cell for anything that might help him break the shackles around his ankles. The cuffs were too tight to slip out of, but he might be able to break the chain with something heavy. If he found the right tool, he could try to pick the lock.

His switchblade.

Whit cursed when he realized he wasn't wearing his uniform. To his dismay, he was still in the formal dress attire from the ball. Why hadn't he thought to slip the knife into the pocket of his vest? They'd been planning an escape for Ghidorah's sake—he should have been armed.

Before he could spiral completely, the door to the lower dungeon unlatched, and Whit saw the queen's general descending the stairs.

Ryker had not dressed for the Samhain Ball. Instead, he'd opted to stay in his army uniform—a full set of fighting leathers adorned with embroidered vines and the rune symbol for earth stitched into the center of his vest.

The general walked unhurriedly down the path between the cells until he reached the one holding Whit. Up close, the wolf-demon was ferocious. Whit hadn't spent much time fully taking in the threatening features of the general, but as Ryker stood on the other side of the bars with claw-tipped hands flexing menacingly at his sides, he noted every detail.

Ryker's jaw was elongated to resemble the maw of a wolf, his hair cascaded in silver waves over his thick shoulders, and he was covered in gray fur to match. His ears remained perked to attention, constantly shifting to listen for threats, and the tuft of his tail held steady behind him like a weapon on high alert.

Whit waited for whatever punishment Ryker had been instructed to dole out on Madam Lema's behalf. Given that the queen had sent her general in her stead, it would no doubt be severe.

To Whit's surprise, however, Ryker did not open the cell. Instead, he tossed a set of keys through the bars. They landed with a *clang* at Whit's feet, and he openly stared at them, not knowing what to do.

Was this a trap? A test?

"Your sister is waiting for you in the tunnels." The wolf-demon's deep voice had never sounded so soft.

"Willow?" Whit rasped, trying to understand.

Ryker nodded once. "You've got half an hour to make it to the forest. Good luck." With that, the wolf-demon strode off, whistling as though it were any other day.

Whit grabbed the bars in front of him forcefully. "What about Freyah? Where is she?" he yelled.

But the wolf-demon gave no reply.

Whit only allowed himself another half a second to question his sudden opportunity, then he was snatching the keys from the ground and unlocking the shackles. His hands shook with the effort to keep them steady and find the right key, but the second the metal clanged to the floor he was aiming for the door. He tested the bars, pulling to slide the door open, and found it unlocked.

No one had locked the cell?

Again, he didn't stop long enough to truly question it. Whit hurried for the tunnels that would lead him outside. Only hours before, he'd been escorting Freyah the same way and telling her goodbye.

The thought caused him to stutter to a stop.

He couldn't leave without Freyah.

But he could already see the faint profile of a small figure illuminated at the end of the tunnel ahead. Willow was waiting for him just as Ryker had said.

He continued down the path until his sister was a stone's throw away from him. She wore a thick wool cloak and carried two leather satchels stuffed to the brim with supplies.

When he approached, she handed one to him without explanation.

Whit took the bag and slung it across his back, but when she began to walk ahead, he did not follow. "Freyah," was all he said.

He spoke her name like the flash of a lighthouse in the dark, as if saying it would summon her.

Willow did not stop walking. She continued briskly toward the tunnel's exit as she peered back over her shoulder and said, "She's already gone. We can catch up with her."

Freyah was gone? But how?

"Come on," Willow hissed with urgency. "Didn't Ryker tell you? We have to hurry."

Whit's head was spinning. None of this made any sense. Was Willow working with Ryker? Had they already helped Freyah escape?

He jogged to catch up to his sister, the pack of supplies bouncing heavily against his lower back. "Why would the general help us?" he asked.

"There's no time to explain," she said, fully focused on their destination. "We need to catch up to Freyah. I promise I'll tell you everything later." She grabbed the crook of his elbow and pulled him along, urging him to move faster. "Hurry up."

By the time they made it to the outer grounds of the castle, there were dozens of soldiers swarming the front entrance, but their attention was on the hundreds of attendees that flooded past the gate that led away from the property. Everyone was leaving the ball, so Whit and Willow were able to dart across the lawn without notice. They slipped behind the barracks and the bathing stalls, waiting for the right time to sprint across the last open stretch of grass before they reached the tree line.

They burst forward into the trees, but they didn't make it far before someone stepped into their path. For the second time that night, Whit was surprised to find Ryker standing in front of him.

"She's not far ahead of us," the general said. "We should catch her by morning."

Willow nodded in understanding at Ryker's words, but Whit was even more confused than he'd been before. "Someone needs to tell me what the hell is going on."

"If you want to reach your girlfriend before the Wild Demons do, I suggest you move along," Ryker jeered. "You're welcome, by the way."

Willow tugged her brother again by the elbow and frowned when he dug in his heels. He wasn't going anywhere until someone explained.

Finally, she caved. "We've been planning this since the day Madam Lema scarred your face," she confessed with an exasperated sigh. "He's coming with us."

Whit dragged his eyes from his sister to look squarely at the wolf-demon standing impatiently a few yards ahead of them.

Ryker grumbled and gritted his sharp teeth, daring Whit to challenge him. "There are things about the queen that even you don't understand, boy."

Ever the menacing general he had come to know.

Whit cleared his throat and stood his ground. "I know she's using Blood Magic. And I've seen things—things that would make every man in her army question their allegiance."

"And what sort of things would that be? Did you find some *buried* secrets?"

Ryker's choice of words struck Whit right in the chest, hitting a little too close for comfort. There was no way the general knew about Micah. Was there?

He opened his mouth but Willow interjected. "We don't have time for this!"

Whether Ryker was truly on their side or not, Willow was right. Freyah was out there waiting for them, and Whit had no intention of letting her down again.

He decided to ignore the gnawing in his gut—for now. Whit tightened the strap on his shoulder and looked his sister in the eye, choosing to trust her implicitly.

"Fine," he said. "Let's go."

FREYAH

Freyah pushed further into the forest at full speed, ducking beneath branches and sliding over the slick surface of dried fallen leaves. It was cold. She didn't have a jacket, and the tear in her leggings exposed most of her left calf. Her wrist was not broken but badly sprained, and Raven had wrapped it.

Freyah had been sprawled across the floor, tears still trailing down her face and staining the stones beneath her when Raven had entered the meeting chamber where Freyah had been left alone with her father's body—forced to share the silence with a corpse and her own grieving thoughts.

The witch had not said anything as she'd begun tending to Freyah's injuries. She'd patched the cut on her cheek and set her wrist with several layers of bandages. Freyah had not pushed her away or told her to fuck off like she'd wanted to. Instead, she'd allowed Raven to help her, and when the witch was done, she'd listened to every word of her instructions.

"Madam Lema is addressing everyone at the ball to tell them her version of what happened. I suspect they'll have a lot of questions, so she'll be a while. There is another exit just below the western tower, hidden behind a statue of Lillia and Ghidorah outside the library.

Follow the route, and it will lead you back around the side of the castle. There won't be anyone standing guard at that entrance. Get to the trees and don't look back. The others will be close behind you."

Freyah had looked into Raven's eyes, searching for where this unexpected kindness stemmed from, but she'd only found cold indifference.

"Your powder didn't work," Freyah had said bitterly.

Raven had risen to her feet and smiled cunningly down at Freyah as she struggled to stand. "For you? Or for your father?"

Freyah had not dared to voice the question that spiraled through her head. Instead, she'd asked, "Why are you helping me again?"

She'd needed to know if there would be a cost this time.

The witch had backed away, staring placidly at her when she'd finally managed to stand. "There will come a day when I call in the debt you owe me," she'd said, "and you will not refuse."

Freyah had nothing but the clothes on her back, but she'd done as she'd been told. Miraculously, she'd made it to the tree line without a hitch, and though she could have sworn the queen's general had almost spotted her as she moved swiftly across the lawn, no one came after her.

It felt like hours, but eventually she cleared the perimeter of the grounds. She was too far from the castle to go back now—not that she'd want to—so she had no choice but to move forward, away from it all. Leave it behind.

She came to a halt and clutched the stitch in her side, bending over and gasping for air. The forest seemed endless. A maze of trees surrounded her on every side, and the canopy was too thick to see the sky. She could barely make out the glint of moonlight bouncing from the highest leaves, but she couldn't tell which direction the light was cast from. If only she knew which way was north, then she could gather her bearings. She forced herself to remember what Whit had told her about sticking to the eastern edge and following the cliffs.

It had taken two days to ride through the Saldanni Forest in that supply cart, but she wasn't sure she could muster the strength to walk that far. Perhaps she could hitch a ride with a market vendor traveling along the main road.

No. That would be too dangerous.

The queen would no doubt dispatch her soldiers the moment she realized Freyah was gone. Not to mention the wild demon clans lurking in the forest. How the hell was she going to make it out alive?

A sudden breeze blew from the bay, meaning she must have been closer to the cliffs than she realized. Up ahead, there was a clear break in the trees she hadn't noticed before, so she walked toward it and was rewarded with the sight of a rocky cliff. She took in the waves below, the world in front of her open, and after everything—after feeling so small and worthless—Freyah breathed in the fresh, open air with a newfound sense of strength.

But soon, that strength was pushed aside by a fresh wave of grief.

Her father was gone. She would never see him again.

That realization crested over her like a relentless wave, and it just kept coming. Never ceasing. Only growing in strength.

Her father had been her biggest supporter, and one of the few people she could always lean on. Without him, who would guide her through the darkness? Who would hold her hand when she could not find her way?

She thought of Whit, and another surge of guilt hit her with the realization that she'd left him behind, but then she remembered what Raven had said.

Don't look back.

Freyah knew if she did, she would see the outline of Castle Larapuna behind her. But on the opposite side of the cliff face, something much bigger than her desire to go back for Whit called to her blood. Freyah followed the line of the horizon all the way across the bay until she found it: her mountain.

Home.

Mount Mirela loomed in the distance like a beacon calling her back to where she belonged, and she suddenly felt the urge to cry. Freyah had to return to Last Cove—to the community that raised her, and her best friend. They were all she had left in the world. And she needed to warn them about the witch-queen's plans.

They needed to know what had happened to her father.

Freyah wouldn't be able to withstand her grief on her own for much longer. She needed to lay that burden on someone else's shoulders. She needed the community that had raised her. She needed her best friend.

They were all she had left in this world.

She tried to calm herself by breathing in the salted air that blew across the bay from the Outer Ocean. It was cold enough to burn her lungs, and she realized that the season had changed since her arrival. When she'd left the mountain, the leaves had just been on the verge of turning crimson and orange, and the edge of the cliff had had a thin layer of knotted vines and moss adorning the surface. Everything had still been alive, but now it was as if the earth around her reflected the death she'd witnessed. Brown and rotted leaves disintegrated beneath her boots, and it was like stepping on her own soul, watching them crumble beneath her.

She remembered Raven's warning, *"Don't look back. The others will be close behind you."*

Though her loss ate away at her every second, Freyah knew she had to keep running or eventually Madam Lema's soldiers would find her. She could only hope that Raven's words meant Whit had escaped, too.

It was time to move.

She turned back and continued east. Now that she'd found the cliffs, she had a clear sense of direction that would lead her along the treeline and back to the Northern Sky Mountains. She knew she wouldn't make it more than halfway before morning, but she pushed herself to travel as fast and as far as possible.

Freyah didn't like the idea of camping out in the woods overnight, knowing there would be wild demons lurking in the shadows. It was imperative that she find some sort of shelter to wait out the night. But Freyah didn't have the faintest clue where to start.

Continuing to run through the trees, she came across another clearing. But instead of leading to another lookout point, this time the forest opened up to reveal a small cottage.

Freyah didn't think it was common for people to live so far from the villages, yet there was a house right in front of her, placed randomly within the thickness of neighboring green. It was as if it were there just for her, waiting patiently for her arrival.

Freyah approached the structure with caution. It was quaint. Tattered eyelet curtains dressed the windows, intricate spiral carvings covered the wooden shutters, and the front door sunk into the entrance, as if the house was holding its breath. The structure itself was made from the trees, like the forest had carved out its own little hideaway.

Freyah saw no movement or light from inside. All was still, save for the light breeze still whistling through the trees. She knew this was her best bet at finding shelter for the night, and as she approached, she silently prayed that the owners wouldn't come home to find a stranger welcoming themselves into their humble abode. But something else occurred to her. It was possible that Madam Lema had personal acquaintances in these woods, meaning the house could be a trap.

Freyah took a step back and examined the property with careful scrutiny. She couldn't tell if it had been touched by magic—her eye was not trained for such things—but it was possible that some sort of entrapment spell had been placed on the house. The moment Freyah stepped over the threshold, the door might disappear, locking her inside until Madam Lema's soldiers came to retrieve her.

Yet something about the house called to her. With great reluctance, Freyah reached out and placed a shaking hand around the oval shaped doorknob. It turned, and the door released from the lock.

She stood sentient on the threshold, waiting for something—some sort of sign that would tell her to turn back and run in the opposite direction—but nothing happened. The cottage remained still.

Freyah stepped forward into the entryway, taking in the elaborate fireplace ahead of her. Everything was painted with blue or mint pastels and trimmed with hand-stenciled vines or other floral designs. It felt comfortable and safe, so she settled on staying. By the time whoever lived here made their way back, Freyah would be long gone. She could rest her legs for the night, long enough to restore her energy, then she'd disappear into the early morning hours before dawn. Even if there were wild demons lurking in the woods, maybe she could borrow some sort of weapon to defend herself.

A sudden rustling from another room made Freyah's blood run cold. There was a light coming from the den that she hadn't noticed before. She followed it and found candles illuminating the center table against the darkness.

Was someone home?

Then a high pitched, raspy voice sounded from the shadows. "Announce yourself at once!"

Freyah spun on her heels and found herself face to face with a small, middle-aged looking demon. He was holding an unopened umbrella like a club, his beady little eyeballs staring menacingly right into Freyah's soul. He had a thin layer of fur that coated his arms and neck instead of skin. Swishing back and forth behind him like the steady hand of a clock was a bushy, cinnamon-colored tail.

"I'm sorry," Freyah begged, throwing up her hands in defense. "Please, I'm not a threat."

"How did you get into this house?" he demanded.

Freyah stammered. "I-I just walked in."

The demon lowered his makeshift weapon and stared at her in awe. "By, Ghidorah's name," he gasped.

She lowered her hands and took a tentative step back. "I'm sorry," she apologized again. "I was merely seeking shelter. I can go."

Freyah made a move for the door, but the demon waved a furry hand to stop her. "You've been allowed entry, so you're obviously trustworthy. There's no reason for you to leave. Make yourself at home."

She wasn't sure how the demon could make such an assessment

with such little information, but at least he was no longer brandishing the umbrella at her.

He then straightened the collar of his jacket and held himself a little taller. "My name is Kirra," he stated grandly. "It would seem that Lillia has brought Lyra's daughter home at last."

EPILOGUE

20 YEARS EARLIER

Madam Lema stared blankly at the body of her younger sister. Lyra's white-blond hair was matted to her head where the strands had dried in sweaty clumps, her face no longer porcelain but ghostly white with a slight sheen of gray. Her eyes were closed, the expression on her face peaceful.

The princess had gone into labor hours earlier and given birth to a healthy, beautiful baby girl. Yet, somehow, no one had thought to inform the queen. As Lema took in the sight of Lyra's stiff body, still and void of warmth atop the stained bedsheets, she felt an unfamiliar pain, a deep ache that spread from the center of her chest to the rest of her body in a wave so powerful it nearly brought her to her knees. She'd never felt such emotion before. It was as strange as it was overwhelming, and Lema clutched at her heart as she took in the sight of her sister's lifeless form in front of her.

No one had told her.

No one had come to report the news that a new witch had been born. Lema had only heard because of the commotion outside the meeting chamber where she'd been holed up with Evanora and forced to listen as her advisor shared yet another message of discontent from the rebels. There were dozens of witches and soldiers gathering in the halls and discussing the excitement of the birth for all to hear. Even the queen.

Madam Lema had run straight for Lyra's bedchamber, hoping to set eyes on the newborn witch herself. But the moment she entered the room, Lema's heart had stopped. The princess was dead, yet no one seemed to care.

Lema had never claimed to have the best relationship with her sister, but she also hadn't expected to feel her loss so strongly. It wasn't meant to happen this way. Lema had wanted to control and punish Lyra for the treasonous acts she'd committed by mating with a demon, but Lema hadn't wanted this.

As the queen of Ghoma stood silently in shock, the rest of the castle bustled around her, loud and chaotic. No sense of respect to mourn the princess's passing. Lema understood their excitement—having the first of a new generation of witches in the castle meant magic would live on—but they were so swept up in their joy that they'd missed the tragedy less than a few feet away.

Suddenly Lema's insurmountable sadness shifted to something more sinister. An untapped anger began to grow within her—a rage so raw and powerful the pulse of it threatened to burst through her skin.

Before she could control it, the feeling exploded from her in a literal wave of magic. It swept across the room in the form of a pulsing wind. Madam Lema held on tightly to the physical manifestation of her anger as it wracked her body, the only sense of control she had. The magic escaped her without direction, casting its claws out into the land like a fist clutching its prey—its enemy. The people were her enemy. She was surrounded by those that did not understand her, did not know what it was to grieve. Because Lema was certain she was the first and the last to ever experience such heartbreak. No one had ever felt a loss such as this.

THE NEXT DAY, as the queen sat atop her ivory throne and listened to the official briefing concerning the princess's death, she learned that the town of Stuarts Draft had succumbed to a flood. The entire village was underwater due to a tidal wave that witnesses say formed from a great pulse of energy from the west. Villagers could not explain the phenomenon, but when asked directly by her advisor how she wished to address the matter, the queen replied with a simple statement.

"Tell them it was me."

ACKNOWLEDGMENTS

The concept behind this story was born from a Walking Dead fanfic I wrote called *My Girl is a Switchblade*. To this day, it's one of my favorite things I've ever written, but I couldn't publish it because of the copyrighted material, obviously. So, I took the bones of that story and started from scratch. I filled it in with fantastical elements of magic with witches and demons and completely new characters, and after A LOT of revising, Of Magic and Men was born.

I will always remember the beginning stages of writing this story, because a lot of brainstorming happened with my best friend, Yohannah. We sat in the Barnes and Noble Cafe at a corner table for hours talking about dozens of great ideas for what could be my first fantasy project.

"Wouldn't it be cool if this happened?"

"Oh, that character definitely has to do this thing."

We even sat in my car for another hour after the store closed, because we weren't ready to stop talking about it! I still have all the voice recordings from that night, and perhaps one day I'll share them so we can all compare the rough beginning to the finished end.

I want to thank my incredible alpha readers Eva, Ashlynn, Sam, and Vanessa. Each of you helped shape the bare bones of this story when it was in its first draft. Especially, Vanessa. I am so thankful to have met you through the Sisterhood Bookclub. Without you, no one would be holding this book in their hands. I'm grateful that we were able to help each other through the trials and tribulations of self-publishing. You are my ultimate teammate.

Thank you to Maria Spada for creating a jaw-dropping cover

design. Because of you, potential readers can judge my book with a positive first impression! You captured the essence of the story perfectly!

Thank you to each of my beta readers! You guys were the first to give "reader" feedback, and some of your initial reactions (especially to the ending, lol) were priceless! At the time, I was beginning to doubt my ability to write a good fantasy novel, but your comments and praise really allowed me to channel that inner confidence again. Each of your feedback is more appreciated than you probably know.

Thank you Beth Crowley, for being my accidental developmental editor. I cannot even begin to express how much you helped me during the editing process. Your critiques and early editing skills were what truly helped OMAM be the best it could be. You are the absolute best!

Thank you Amanda Chaperon for being such a boss-bitch editor! Girl, not only am I thankful for your eyes and brain, but I'm thankful for your friendship. Your reaction to the book gave me a massive boost of confidence, and I'm so grateful for the time and expertise you lended me!

Thank you to every Instagram friend I've made since re-starting my Bookstagram account in February of 2022. So many of you cheered me on throughout the drafting process and showed up to support me during publishing. I love every single one of you dearly!

Thanks to YOU. The ones that took the time to read my book! By reviews and word of mouth, you are the ones that can help get OMAM in more readers' hands!

Thanks to my husband, Trent. Thank you for believing in me and supporting my dream. You always believe I can do anything, and you're the reason I always try. I love you super, rawr! Marriage.

And finally, most of you holding this book know the struggles I've faced when it comes to the future of this series. I don't know when book 2 will finally see the light of day, but it WILL come. I promise.

Though it was originally supposed to be a trilogy, I have decided to end the story with Of Demons and Dreams. Of Magic and Men will now be a duology, and I hope to have it in your hands in the near future. While my imagination and mental health might be pulling me toward other projects at the moment, you can rest assured I have not forgotten about that crazy cliffhanger I left you with at the end of OMAM. It will have its conclusion, I just can't give you an exact date just yet.

In the meantime, please enjoy this beautiful new hardback!

I appreciate every reader who has chosen to stick with me through my ups and downs, and I can't wait to see what the future holds for us!

ABOUT THE AUTHOR

Meg Alivien was born and raised in Nashville, TN. She currently resides outside of the city with her husband and five cats. You can find Meg either listening to audiobooks, binging television shows, following her favorite Youtubers, eating Japanese food, or fangirling over her favorite fictional characters.

Meg is the author of cozy and spicy paranormal romance. Her small town *Monster Boyfriends* series, described as Halloweentown meets Gilmore Girls, has over 3 million pages read on Amazon and can be found in indie bookstores nationwide!

Of Magic and Men is her debut novel in the fantasy romance genre. Represented by Brittney Brunelle at the Seymour Agency.

www.authormegalivien.com
@authormegalivien on all socials!

* 9 7 9 8 9 8 7 8 1 3 4 1 6 *